OTHERS, INCLUDING
MORSTIVE
STERNBUMP

OTHERS, INCLUDING MORSTIVE STERNBUMP

A novel by MARVIN COHEN

The Bobbs-Merrill Company, Inc.

Indianapolis ○ New York

The author acknowledges support from the Creative Artists Public Service Program (CAPS) for aid toward the completion of this work.

Designed by Viki Webb
Manufactured in the United States of America

First printing

Library of Congress Cataloging in Publication Data

Cohen, Marvin.
    Others, including Morstive Sternbump.
    I. Title.
PZ4.C67720t   [PS3553.0425]   813'.5'4   76–11615
ISBN 0–672–52145–8

*To Tom Gervasi,
who helped this book see daylight*

PREWORD∘∘∘∘∘∘

The events take place around 1960, which may explain occasional seeming social anachronisms. It's hoped that now the souls of these people drift on a more enduring plane.

PART 1

ꝏꝏꝏꝏꝏꝏꝏꝏꝏꝏꝏꝏ

ꝏ1ꝏꝏꝏꝏ

To control his appetite, Morstive vowed he would eat more, since a full stomach kept hunger at bay and reduced the temptation to eat and curbed his tendency to be a hog by nature, during the duration of his inclination, which was semi-always, so indulgently did he enjoy himself and make pleasure refine his sensuality, for he was crude and was every inch a beast, not the least of which was a man, which also he was. Morstive Sternbump, a creature after his own heart. Nor did he quite neglect himself.

Not that he was selfish—he would be first to deny it. No, he was merely being right.

He ate all he could, and then stopped. Which reminded him to worry about money—a primary material consideration. It was Sunday, and New Year's Day. The night before had been a party. He'd been drinking himself sober, and now he was paying for it.

He promised to make resolutions, for he didn't want to be behind in planning ahead. Soon his future would occur—and where would he be?

He promised that he ought to have a girl friend, so that people would respect him for not being lonely. His reputation was entirely devoted to people, without caring what he really was. Not that he would boast: his reputation could do it for him, if only he could improve the appearance of his image, and be respectably admirable, loved if not liked, but quite approved. For part of him was social, and only the personal part was not. And even that privately tried to be conspicuous, for what would people think of him otherwise? If only a mirror were there, he would have seen himself, not as others saw him, but as others would be *made* to see him. Not that he cared. Of course not: he was too independent.

He was sitting at a table in his apartment, and his mind was working. He was subject to all kinds of feelings, for, if only people knew it, he was sensitive. But people knew it. And they knew it to his disadvantage, and blamed him for it.

It was one o'clock in the afternoon, a normal time for *any* time, so that he felt just simply average. Average to *him*, that is.

However, it wasn't long before two o'clock came. He hadn't exactly planned it, but unconsciously had expected it. And, in due course, he was proven to be right.

And so he adjusted to it, and felt appropriately two o'clock. A man of parts, he was.

But he was unprepared for three o'clock, being then asleep. It overtook him, passed him by, and he lived anyway, dreaming (or thinking he dreamt, after waking) of Hulda Stock, who at that time certainly wasn't aware of him. She had no reason to be. He wasn't there.

Feeling uneasy, he consulted himself. Something told him he was wrong. But he went ahead anyway.

It was just like him. That's the way he was. Why not, after all?

But this was special. It was New Year, which meant that the past was all over, and couldn't be brought back. So this was it. At last, today had moved out of the past, and become right now. It inspired him, because he was afraid. He felt very proud to not be running away, and considered himself courageous. So much to be

2

afraid of, and yet he wasn't all *that* afraid. A real man!

He looked out of the window, and realized it was cold. Then he shivered. Imagine him not being seasonal! A scandal, for calendars were cheap, and even free if you didn't care what year it was. Morstive was modern, because as every day approached he was pulled along with it, no matter what his past had been. For example, now that it was the New Year, his life had charged up-to-date, even to the very second. Which was perhaps why the telephone began to ring.

There would be no test of will-power, so he answered it. By doing so he had stood up, and received the communication. It wasn't long, but he had acquitted himself well, and made the right impression, though just a bit too casual, to make sure he wasn't pretending. No one could call him a phony, his behavior was so natural.

Morgan Popoff, a friend barely not an acquaintance, had told him something relating to last night's party, in a mild reproof of friendly gossip. Morstive was too sophisticated to be surprised, but had allowed himself to show an interest, which was courteous as well. How many things he could handle! The number went untold.

But of Morgan Popoff, here's a new consistency's character. A being by himself.

For him the day was New Year's as well, to establish him as a contemporary. Of whom? Of anyone, that's who. Morgan hardly bothered when, just where. For example, he was in a pay booth, hearing himself tell Morstive what was what. The weather was edging around six o'clock, but to what purpose not even the most brilliant magician could surmise, with the cards falling out of his sleeves and the rabbits reproducing. Living was in the wind, these days. For a price, the stores had things to sell. Security was all within.

Outside the booth, waiting for him, the desirable Hulda Stock, object of Morstive's recent dream, or rather midday nap's imagery, felt cold in her overcoat, and thought thoughts very personal to herself. She had an angry snap in her look, and attacked Morgan when he rejoined her. They had been arguing, until pride was stubbornly dividing them, and dignity stood insulted. "You lethal weapon," she said. Morgan, a very tall and heavy man, forgot how attractive Hulda was, for his manhood was at stake. He wouldn't take it.

Walking a few blocks at odds, while evening pierced them, dim with holiday lights, they regulated their disagreement to allot for reconciliation, each fearing permanent alienation. If only one would just begin to give in, the other would be struck by this kindness and guiltily relent, affording such concessions as mercy and atonement demanded, and applying a sentimental sponge to rub away recent harshness: dreams following blood. This was not what happened. The bitterness grew vicious, and, while a bus was pulling by, they abruptly separated. Hulda was not even in tears, so indignant was she. She knew her rights. As for Morgan, he blew up. Madness, insanity, assailed him. If only for something to crush, a hated act of destruction to enjoy, an object smashable. Vibrant with power, the force weakened him, for he couldn't employ it. As he gave way to frustration, he felt okay again.

And Morstive, still home, wondered why Morgan's voice was so strange on the phone. Why the call at all? Maybe Morgan was stalling, for what he said was unimportant. What had been going on? And without knowing it, Morstive gave his thought over to Hulda Stock, and in his mind her existence lacked the hard will of her pride, lacked herself even, for now her wool-like flexibility softened and consoled his daydream. Until he expelled a sigh, to pop the bubble through.

"I'll get a new boyfriend," Hulda decided, entering her apartment. As though the thought would be answered, her telephone rang immediately. Morstive's appeal was timely. Fast-working, he surprised himself with the ease by which she consented for a date tomorrow night. As if she even wanted it. *Her* desire! But what about his? And he wondered why he called her, at all. He was doing everybody a favor. Don't they realize his needs? Then let him be the eager one. For his judgment of himself was low. And he valued people according to the way they dismissed him, approving their sound taste in giving him the go-bye. Which he deserved. When people recognized his inferiority, they were superior. He himself was superior, for he knew of it better than they. So he prepared to be nervous, against tomorrow night's disaster.

Nearing midnight on the first bad day of this foul New Year, Morgan was at home too. He had contrived to lose a girlfriend, with the maximum of difficulty. His rage snarled again, and he plunged his big body into sleeplessness. Hulda would feel good now. But she also had a mind, which was proof against his. He'd retaliate, and how: the best way to punish Hulda, he figured, was to get married.

4

Now who were the candidates? Emma Lavalla? Not bad. Tessa Wheaton? How could he think of it? Out of the question. But there were lots of girls floating around. Who would be ideal? Hulda Stock, of course. And he shut his eyes, to open them again. Life was awfully funny, he concluded, by way of philosophy. It was pleasant to be so deep. Did he know any more ideas? No, but suffering, torment, misery, would produce them. And with cunning, he smiled. And with guile. The day would come. A plot of perfect revenge. And after marriage, perhaps Hulda would become his mistress. To be contrite, begging his big pardon. And he would be benevolent. He would refuse her!

 oo2oooooo

On the morning of January second, Morstive Sternbump, the introvert, was filling out forms at the State Employment Office, applying for a placement. A private agency would be costly, so here he could get his job and keep his first week's salary, at least. He was already in his twenties, living away from home, and possessed of a college degree. Why was he so untalented? So commercially unfeasible? Because he was a poet? Such a soft soul he had, it was probably brimming with creativity. Once he had taken an aptitude test, and when the score was in he was warned against a pronounced bohemian tendency. This would alarm his mother. So he kept it secret.

Waiting to be called by a placement assistant to an interview, and attired in his best business suit, he allowed Hulda Stock to take considerable precedence among his Monday contemplations, and hoped he was handsome. But his body sagged in the waistline, bulging at the wrong place. Morgan Popoff was another story. A big bold guy like that, a hero type. What was between him and Hulda? Plenty, probably. Morstive received jealousy, to complicate his emotions. To relieve him, his turn was announced. On unsteady feet, he approached the interview table, thinking how he could get out of taking Hulda to dinner that night. He hadn't invited her. Would she expect it? Their appointment was for eight o'clock. Time enough for her to have eaten. And to justify his parsimony, enforce his stingy poverty, and pad out his self-pity, Morstive Sternbump was told that he wasn't qualified for the jobs open, and all other jobs were closed. So at present he would have no position. Go home.

Morgan Popoff was at work, and doing very well. Within weeks, another promotion. The ability, the application—he had everything. He knew the game. Hulda had been hot to marry him. Was it for his promise, his future? Why not be a tramp, and find out? At this, he was forced to smile. The smile was of dubious business value, at the time, so he canceled it and scribbled something to be typed. He had powers. What he needed now was another good affair, and perhaps some substantial prosperous marriage. Help his career, too. To be known for his seriousness. A man who didn't fool around. Mr. Popoff, the Vice President. Would he ever be that? He dared his limits to be defined. And pompously borrowed a secretary. A solid man. Good, too.

"Yes, I *am* hungry," said Hulda, in a surprised tone. Unemployed, insecure, and already half in love, unfortunate Morstive would have to go down to the bottom of his wallet and negotiate his wits about him, unless he could risk being cheap and suggest going to his place where he could cook it. But that wouldn't do, for why then call for her? And the refrigerator didn't have enough. It's amazing how far his appetite went—the poorer his financial state, the more he needed to eat.

"I know a good Italian restaurant," he said. Hulda was comparing him with Morgan, when they took the bus. Morgan's estimate grew, and Morstive, though slightly unique in his way, was really and truly nothing. Thus settled, Hulda's attitude acquired a positive boredom, leaving Morstive groping. Caught in a silly posture of futility.

Over their wine (she had suggested it) she put a casual emphasis into asking, "What did Morgan call you up for, early last evening?" Morstive didn't deserve any tact, for they were through after tonight. She could say anything she pleased, exploit him to gratify her curiosity, and be free. After the handling, the ordeal, Morgan had messed her up with, let another male pay mere penance: Time to act the bitch, with impunity.

"Oh, he just said how a mutual friend, who had introduced us a little while ago, tried to act like a martyr in front of Tessa Wheaton New Year's Eve at the party—it's nothing important, I guess."

"What's his name?"

6

"Oh, maybe you know him—Jessup Clubb."

"Oh, him," and she smirked. She wasn't in a good mood lately. The absurd and the petty ruled and underlined all things, and she felt a glow of hatred, and the license to turn it on. She had been abused. Here was a fool in front of her. A doting prey, a squash named Morstive—she would make him squirm. To assure this, she looked sexy. (A subtle twist to her shoulders, a soft sparkle, a subdued negligence, the evidence of a pout, the suggestion of a moist underlip—these little things helped.) She was beautiful. He controlled himself, for he wanted to kiss her. He was much more sensitive than her vulgar lover, couldn't she tell? Or was she too blunt to care? Too much in that lover's own vein?

Their meal was over, so she withdrew her chair slightly, and crossed her legs. Morstive wished they were married. Gaping was so obvious, he contrived to look sleepy. No use advertising his captivity. Maybe he couldn't win, but he could manage to lose proudly, with a show of indifference. Why was he always paying?

Leaning back, she inadvertently displayed a couple of uppening legs. They crowned her desirability complete. Morstive eyed this specimen of harmony, this lump of heaven, come down to tease proportion where the world bargains with reality, and heap perspective into disorder, and run chaos loose to upset values on scales of sanity, overthrow reason as it is known today, disturb gods, resist law, and substitute pagan authority, hoisting beauty's flag, chastity submitting to lust, and love grown violent: He'd unregulate the usual, doff his self, topple away from his past, and step into virile possession, rather than visual yearning based on pathetic shy voyeurism. . . .

"And how, may I ask?" she slurred, eyeing him with a twinkle.

"I'm sorry—what do you mean?"

"That," she pronounced, "in what manner, according to Morgan, was Jessup being a martyr?" And the smile was white and cruel, with cunning deliberation, for he was hooked. And she didn't want him. She despised him. It was fun.

Morstive knew that all dignity was gone, and now in the awkward display of ease, pressured by embarrassment, he affected a miserable play on nonchalance, ludicrous for its transparency. This was not his night.

"Jessup? Well maybe what Morgan said was confidential. He wouldn't want me to repeat it." There, that did it. An assertive

7

manliness, the fortitude of the undaunted. It was just the thing to say. Now, he wanted respect.

"But you *said* it wasn't important," explained Hulda, disguising her concern. Her curiosity sharpened with anger. Morgan and she had been arguing; then he'd phoned this fellow he didn't even know well—to tell him something that had no consequence? To be a gossip wasn't in Morgan's character; and anyway, what was between Jessup Clubb and Tessa Wheaton? He was known to be psychopathic, and grossly inhibited at that, and with Tessa only the platonic was possible. Something screwy was up. Hulda herself had not noticed what incident there was, for she was obscured in a conversation, near the crowded glitter of the drinks, and the whole party was just a noisy burst of confusion anyway, especially since the midnight charm had been broken and all rowdy hell sounded out as the dreary hours became drunker. And personalities, personalities! All this social keeping-up! Morgan himself had been flirting, to instigate strife and downfall. And now she was stuck with this boob—who wouldn't even talk! "If you don't tell me, I'm going home," she said.

Morstive kept control. "Then let me accompany you," he said.

"Suave, aren't you?" she said. It was a bitter clash. She kept her controlled temper, with the ironic ascendancy in hand. She won, though still chafing.

oo3ooooo

Another coffee break had ended, and now, this third day of January, a Tuesday, saw everyone's definition of a prude, Tessa Wheaton, start hitting the typewriter again—for which she was paid—in her organization's main office. It was three-fifteen, a clear time of day, and her neat mind exulted in precision, supremely steering order along. However, who would marry her? This was listed among her prime worries. She was not for the best types: Morgan Popoff, a superior young executive with his own office, was attractively much too high for her. Her virtues were but homely, and her charm, not being glamorous, had to aim for gentlemen of minor looks and capabilities, whom the Huldas of the world would invariably reject and scorn. Well, one must accommodate to level. And Tessa, prim, was honest without vainglory, an asset to some fortunate young man some future favored day—or old man? Time was in haste. But she was proud to be Morgan's select friend and confidante, the repository of his private troubles acquired after-hours in the large mystery of his masculine life. The other typists envied her. Morgan had told her that she was "sweet." A compliment unforgettable, because it was meant. What a sincere young man. She would help attend to the momentous importance of his affairs, expecting no reward. This thought was costly to her. Visioning her sainthood, that abominable Jessup Clubb was revealed to unwilling memory, and the distasteful although well-intentioned insult at that miserable party New Year's Eve, so stunning to the strict complacency of serenity aspired to by her prissily trained mind. She almost stopped typing. How jolted from a good mood—but by persevering, she would recapture her peace, and be purged of Jessup's taint. How waylaying were startling events. It was all too fascinating. One day she'd explore the psychology of life.

That night, her violator, disliked for his oddness, was speaking with the conventional Morgan. Their strange differences had melted into friendship, and Jessup displayed the latest results in his growth of a beard. (At that time beards shocked social custom.) Jessup had tawny skin and wore loose clothing, more like a robe than a suit. He looked spiritually anemic, and implied a wealth of suffering within, the source of a kind of unreal strength, more fitted to the soul than the body.

His good-natured friend was expected to kid him, with a hearty roar of disapproval, mingled with affection. Morgan, relaxed after his business day, frankly obliged his prey, and the latter was suitably chastised. How well they got along! "You sure floored Tessa Wheaton, with your antics at the party, you brute," smiled Morgan affably.

Jessup brought out his ecstatically special agony of hysterics. "It pains me," he said, and abounded in mirth.

"Don't you love it!" Morgan agreed, commanding astute understanding.

This gave Jessup an opportunity to display his awe: "You're wonderful!" he said. They were so harmless. Could they be faulted? Fun was always welcome, at times. Life had a place for it. They were good boys, both of them. Above all, they were not strangers to pleasure. Pleasure made things worthwhile. Time enough to repent. "Let's introduce Tessa to Morstive Sternbump," Jessup slyly suggested.

Morgan was enthusiastic over this idea. He had just phoned Emma Lavalla, and arranged a date—even though she had a boyfriend. He enjoyed a little complication, now and then. As for Hulda Stock, her jealousy would soon be aroused: being, after all, Emma's roommate. Morstive had gone out with Hulda, he knew. But nothing in it, that also he knew. His confidence could toy at revenge, and still get her back.

"You're so naughty to go around and pal up with that hideous Jessup," said Tessa Wheaton, admonishing her admirable Mr. Popoff, who occasionally dabbled in flaws. The more heroic was he for them, and she beamed. Such a stubborn young man, with such grave ambition, and surely he would accomplish his goal. She was so privileged to even be his friend. Thick-hided that he was. Secretly, she adored him. But in a very distant way.

Their lunch hour (though he could take his any time), and they were hidden in a corner of a cafeteria, sharing a small table, convenient for their exclusive freedom from neighbors. Their plates were about empty of food, and conversation was intimate. It was her glory. Such a big man one day, too.

"Tessa, I have an idea for you," he said. "I have a nice young man in store for you, because I want to see you happy. I've told him all about you. The meeting is set up."

"I should be indignant," said Tessa. "For what do *you* know what makes me happy? But if you suggest it, my dear, I don't see how I can avoid heeding you, my sweet master. However, I'm not the least bit interested, I must warn you. I'm quite cozy by myself, thank you. What do I need a young man for?" She wore glasses, which twinkled and sparkled as she talked her face in motion: the reflected sun was bouncing off something shining somewhere. Tessa concealed her joy. It would really be wonderful.

"Well, I generally get my way," Morgan admitted, in candid expansion. His plan had turned out. Morstive had been notified, and, smarting from Hulda's rejection, was game, even for such a spinstery candidate as this. His prestige would diminish, too, for she was somewhat homely. And undoubtedly, there would be no love involved. But Morgan had assured him that the evening wouldn't be expensive—so why not, after all? It was to be a double date, Emma Lavalla as Morgan's partner (a daring move for Emma to spite her roommate Hulda, and invoke her antagonism); and refined, quiet, considerate Morstive as willing dupe to Tessa Wheaton's chilling defensive femininity, on guard always against men's impudent threat and propensity to reject her. Morgan would pay, from his affording funds, and be the generous proprietor of the evening, and call the quarterbacking to the plays, dictate uneven terms, and set the table clear. Jessup was avid, but couldn't participate. He'd get a first-hand report later on; surely, some of the principals involved were likely to be singed, and emerge from the affair slightly staggering for the worst, limping crippled off their wounds with their characters shot to pieces and blood drenching the ego, paying an ordeal's-worth for the vanity of their presumption on fun. This delighted Jessup Clubb; it was the bread and cake of his living. They were all suffering—for Him!

$\infty 4 \infty\infty\infty\infty$

"Where're you going?" Hulda tossed off—too casually.

"Oh, anywhere—who knows?" answered Emma Lavalla, dolled up for the kill, with female social presentability evident all up and down her appearance, and sideways too.

"Why isn't it Merton?" Hulda quizzed her. (Merton Newberg having lately been traditional as Emma's fixed boyfriend, and Hulda knowing it wasn't he for whom Emma's handsome toilet had been prepared, just now.) "Are you quits with him?"

"No, not yet," the answer came. "But I have a better one in store."

"Who, do I know him?"

"Yes."

"Well don't keep me entertained—I won't guess—who is he?"

"I'd better go now," Emma said, and left. That was how Hulda knew.

This big special date, the heroic occasion, dramatic with overtones of romance, bargaining with fate to alter lives and leave a wake of depraved consequences torn from previous paths and contributing to the welfare of misery—causing Jessup inhuman joy and influencing those spiteful non-participants, that angry plotter Hulda Stock and that suddenly abandoned Merton Newberg—occurred on a Saturday night. By habit, Merton called on Emma, only to be informed by Hulda that he stood jilted—so would he like a drink? Merton collapsed, the contortions of his torture caught and held snugly in an armchair, whose embroidered designs were upholstered in a pattern of pure vulgarity, in keeping with the ugliness of Hulda's information, simple and sordid at once. "Without telling me!" he cried, receiving the news with his composure down and his dismay up, staggering to hold the rhythm together.

"And with Morgan, no less," Hulda concluded, allying her despair to the alarmed Merton's, equally were they the victims of love's stunning reversal, the downfall of darkened luck, love swooning from hope and converted to revenge, in the grime necessity of plot. "Let's put our heads together," she said, "and do them in."

"But I'm inclined to pity myself," Merton answered.

"Save that for later, and be terrible now," she advised. "I have a plan," continued Hulda; "and we can salvage them, yet."

Merton Newberg was reformed to be a Catholic, but he had also lapsed from that Church, and was, by now, a professional atheist: which did not jeopardize his amateur agnosticism, another of his organizational roles, for he believed in being a Member, but was intimidated by the Communist scare, so he joined literally anything, whatever party or persuasion, turning renegade to the last, and apostating his new one to go on to the next. He had no stability within, so was flying from marginal institutions to fashionable devices, to outlying sects, raging parties, and fickle regions of belief, betraying them all. He had been a vegetarian, a homosexual, a passive resister, a pseudo liberal, a progressive, a pink, a militant black, a Zionist, a Zen Buddhist—and, at one time, even a girl herself. (But his mother had threatened to expose him, so reconverting to the masculine persuasion, he took on Emma Lavalla as a girlfriend. It had worked well, and he affaired her, thrusting his latest fad between the latent hesitancy of her legs, and there pulled out all the stops, until finally he found love: an illusive object, a mangling intangibility of idealism, penetrating the psychological block of his heart, melting his traumatic repressions, and curing his tendency to be a neurotic. This was

Merton Newberg, quite an up-to-date person.)

"I'm so bitter," he said. "Pardon me, I must weep." He took out his handkerchief, and waited while his face contorted, transforming its trembling rage into a magnificent semblance of grief, superbly rendered: it was very affecting. Even Hulda, hardened as she was, broke up, and produced a handkerchief on her own account. They vied, as one tear after another cruised down, and wet ones following, until not a duct was dry in all their whole faces, between the both of them. To form a united picture, the weather rained outside; and nature added in: a complete January dirge, despite the Savior's birth, celebrated or mourned but two weeks past.

The doorbell rang through the deluge. Hulda, putting back on her realism for this outside mystery, steadied up, and without asking who was it, released the inside lock, and saw, in the threshold, that grinning scavenger, Jessup Clubb. Sensing their emotional corpses, he had swooped down; and as the odor of decay spread, he landed. "Through me," he declared, "your sufferings are redeemed. I'll bear your cross." And he laughed. Merton flew at him, and the assault was a wonderment to behold. Soaked by the elements, Jessup twisted, and tore away. Merton dove, barely averting the intruder's escape with a clutch tackle at the ankle, at the half-open doorway. Hauling him inside, he mutilated the captive, tormented by his own cruelty. Hulda, too strong to faint, merely watched. Elsewhere, the double date was proceeding: Morgan presiding, Morstive attentive, Tessa sweetened, Emma throbbing: four into one.

Nerves ran through all these, and linked them to the absent trio, Hulda and Merton and Jessup, whose knocked-outness lifted so that he could see the two victims, in a murderous clinch of hatred, plotting the double downfall of Emma Lavalla and Morgan Popoff.

Tessa Wheaton was thinking, "Isn't this Morstive nice," while Morstive was envious of Morgan's conquest, for Emma was transparent in her fascination, and exerting all her powers of appeal. In relation to Hulda, Emma was less endowed, her qualities sagging into the ordinary. But Morgan's might stood high. His success made him feel beautiful, good, and clever. Tessa, as always, adored him, and Hulda was stuck, so in the eyes of three women he summoned a gorgeous triumph, a multiple mockery of others' feeble efforts to withstand. Morstive was no problem, Merton was little challenge; and Jessup stood by him, adding a diabolical note in this concerted and total harmony that attested to his own humble duplication of

13

God's supremacy—Morgan, God's daily self. No mystery about him: he simply, by existing, drew in benefits to himself from the charitable air of others' nature, as the scheme worked out. And wholly innocent: it came; he hadn't asked. No contriving, but fully made.

Tessa Wheaton was nervously angled into proposing an invitation for a cup of coffee up in her apartment, for Morstive was stalling, delaying the good-night, down at the building entrance. All right, so she let him in. All evening she had been gay, riding high into a tide of entertainment, splashed and giggly. Here the serious moment had arrived, and she had to front herself with a false face, to escape in a new beat. Morstive relaxed in a sofa, while his "date" spilled some coffee over her clean, stiff habit. "Can I put the radio on?" Mr. Sternbump asked, but was told how late it was, a reply graphic as the very clock, that prattles of time overtangibly.

She sat the whole length of the room away, sipping the indifferent coffee, hoping the distance would tell the story, and suggest he should leave. "I don't want to say it, but I'm tired," she added, just in case.

Morstive was very unwilling to hear that. The evening had aroused him, and he wanted to "put her away." It would be a delightful gain for his ego, to make a successful pass and be consoled with a conquest for being "stuck" with a ripe undergraduate in the University of the Old Maid. He knew failure awaited. This was precisely what he wanted: to have safely tried, and achieved a rejection, and posted an "end" on this quiet little adventure. He didn't want it hanging over, because to avoid another "date" with this demon was a primary solution to his immediate problems of survival. "So I'll be repulsed," he said, and made his pass.

Morgan Popoff guided Emma by her elbow, and sometimes by her waist, up the stairs to her apartment. To keep him for the future, she had refused going to his place, and maintained minimum decorum. It was safe this way: Excite his interest, sustain his suspense, and be assured of his call. Postpone surrender now, to ward off doubt later. But they both feared encountering Hulda Stock, who might still be up. They didn't expect Merton Newberg to be with her, but he was waiting too. From the street they hadn't seen a light, but perhaps some interior room, by the entrance, was lit for accusation. Within, Merton was preparing confrontation. He knew Morgan but slightly, and now he was about to apprehend the villain,

14

expose his cheat, claim back Emma Lavalla, dress them down with a lecture, perhaps enlist them in a new "party" of his, and recriminate Morgan for immoral confiscation of his property Emma: also to make straight her who had strayed. The impact was readied. Hulda was in terror, afraid of her desire: Morgan was more dear than ever, and now the confidence of his footsteps was heard, and the door-knock. It knocked louder; and the mixed-up couples found oxygen scarce, and breathing an abandoned liberty.

"How dare you!" Merton immediately said. Emma suddenly slapped him. Morgan didn't restrain her, but centered his proud smile on Hulda, hypnotized into focus. Hulda turned around. Merton retreated, squaring his passive resistance upon the dread Morgan. The girls were frozen. They avoided looking at each other, each in petrified hope for Morgan. Merton was the lesser male animal of the two. The pecking rank had come out.

Jessup was home, and in bed. He slept the sleep of the just. He had fled the girl roommates' apartment upon recovery from Merton's harsh dealing, unnoticed, when Merton and Hulda were planning some just revenge on their betrayers. Jessup just up and went. With the scene brooding trouble, he had become redundant.

"No!" shouted Tessa, with Morstive pulling down her dress. The drinking earlier, pouring off Morgan's generosity, was still not appeased, and drink could be cited as an excuse. By squirming, Tessa trapped herself more fully, and the rape was dangerously enfolding. Morstive panted with fear, to add renewed daring to his assault. The old regime was coming down. Tessa's hot moment. And all but completed, except for one thing: the telephone rang. And when she had finished with it, the moment had averted itself, and her coldness frigidly spilled over. Morstive was useless, and he left. Morgan had chosen that moment to call! Of all the absurdities!

Merton was on the floor. No blood, but not aware either. Here was a sight to behold: The estranged roommates, kissed in a clench of tears by each other's embrace: sobbing Hulda Stock, and hysterical Emma Lavalla. Morgan Popoff had rung Tessa, appealing for advice. Discarding her prudence, she said she'd be over right away! The skies had to give off some sign, and so, as Morstive walked his faded walk home (no use waiting for a bus) dawn came alive. A bright golden wonder, a superb fate. It was Sunday, and all was well.

5

Dampness from recent rain, and a cool harsh wind, and the waste of exhaustion to remove passion, as Morstive crossed street after street. Monday positively, he must get a job. Tomorrow, that would be. Sponging was all right on a temporary basis, but dignity cried "Desist!" when his friends demonstrated impatient disapproval and people confirmed the wild timidity of his fears with popular indications of disdain. Withdrawing their respect, they removed his self-respect. He had played a fool, and Tessa Wheaton would report it to Morgan: then Jessup would hear. Why not forget this, and be an artist, Morstive thought safely within, free from nosy business and the affairs of others. "Why do I have a poetic temperament," Morstive wondered aloud, stepping on top of a curb and splashing the pavement near the sleeping form of a parked car, "and not have industry, or craft, or a vehicle to express myself? I'm dormant, that's why. I have to get going, but don't have habit to boost me, or confidence to assist. I just like to eat, and try to scrape by. A break should come my way. Commercial success looks bleak. It bores me, I count the hours. Yet there's nothing *in* me, either, to be active to, and count rhythms at. And without money, I can be alert and still be dead. Where is *me?* When I can find him, then it's goodbye to Morgan Popoff, and that phony Jessup Clubb, and girls I can't even have, poking fun at the desire to want them. It's nice to believe that my failure is complete. So I can be just sad, and nothing else." Having consumed his interior monologue, he felt very drowsy, and walked the remaining mechanical distance to his familiar home: a bleak bed, and a telephone he couldn't afford. When he'd wake up, maybe he'd be someone else: a nice thought.

He thought he had a dream, but only dreamed that thought. That was how marginal he was.

He was soon awakened by a desire to eat. He moved through a fog of dreary frustrations, accumulated from all parts of his "nothing" life, and now swarming to compound his atmosphere of particles of defeat, generalized despair, and particularized gloom—the

16

climate of his "life." The depression clouded up so dark, he laughed, with gaiety and mirth. What's left, after all, to him? The refrigerator proved to be empty, except for morbid leftovers, which he confounded into a sandwiched excuse. A dead cockroach completed his plate. "Death is the end," he concluded, wry.

He contemplated Tessa Wheaton's recent essence. "Almost had her," he remembered, and was somewhat glad to have missed. The complications would have encumbered his already messed-up simplicity, as though life's purpose was to be difficult, resisting order by reason, insanity, or any other scruple of the mind. An unprofitable cogitation. It allowed Morstive to sigh, and he took a deep one. Yes, his chest was still there. The rest of him was worn out. And what wasn't, was anyway. Justice is always thorough, interested in perfection. At the word "perfection" he smiled. His meditations passed many ideals, traveling from thought to thought, along introspective air. "I'm a born philosopher," he announced, but responded with silence, to arrest the flattering image of this thought. "And I'll be one after I'm dead," he replied, believing in balance. How adroit. His mind was a pain-killer. But a killer of the rest of him, too. He let his eyes close, and watched sleep overcome him. Flat on his back, in bed. But by being aware, he soon discovered he was awake. The window blinds were open, and a clearer day never appeared. The sun, that's what did it.

"No more of *her*," he concluded, grimacing and turning a wry face when he remembered—just the night before, a few hours ago —Tessa struggling with reluctance against his almost sincere efforts to deprive her chastity of technicality. "It was close, for both," he admitted, and while the idea returned, he was aroused to passion. Ah, why was he forever alone?

And then he was through, as soon as Morgan called up. She answered it with guilt; offered her merciful talent of compassion to assist a fourfold emergency of squared-off people caught at bending angles. It had no doubt pleased Tessa to see her active "rivals" tormented in coils of jealousy for that one beautiful man's heart, a heart manly and poignant, revealed to her frequently during lunch hours, its contents open for her perusal, tended by soft blandishments, mended by her exquisite sensibility. Truly, their hearts were locked.

Morstive knew Tessa's mind, and projected it excellently. Why didn't he write a play about it? Because he wasn't detached. The

17

drama included him, as foil to Morgan's greatness. Great why? Because he was liked. Can alchemy conjure up that formula; can magic and science, and applied psychology, induce people to conceive immense worth in Morstive himself, despite his modest protests to the contrary? Why weren't his kisses in great demand, and his body held dear? Were people blind to his soul? He had a good one. Why didn't they ask him to show it? He'd gladly oblige, and remain humble. He was unique. Universality hovered over him, conferring deep and basic qualities on his God-infested personality, which the world should swoon over, and grant him rituals of celebration. Instead, he found himself starving, to be poetic about it. He got up, and dressed. He should see someone. His identity should be asserted, not mulled inert.

Sunday morning, with empty blank sunshine. Cold, and the streets deserted. A few church-goers preparing. Commercial silence, the industrial day of idleness, the tremendous pause of this city's gigantic business. Too early to visit anyone, but the coat was sufficient to hold out, and a sparkling walk wouldn't be bad. As far as the river? Let's see. And Morstive set out, saying inwardly, "This will be inspiring. All I need is a magic thought. The right insight." He went on. But the thoughts didn't flow. Frozen by the killing weather, they merely poked sympathy at him. He received no answer. And after several blocks, soon even the question eluded him. "Next time!" he said. Sure, next time. Plenty of *that*, in reserve.

He glanced at the river, saw it was there, and admired himself for accomplishing his mission. Guardian, he was. Supervising the maintenance of things, he made sure to provide for their future reappearance, by checking up now. That way, trees remained, buildings stayed, the river didn't move: unless it had to, and only within itself. Morstive felt in touch, connected with objects of intimate duration which a city trained him to notice, so he could keep a level hand on a persisting sanity, inside and out. But this pressure didn't last, for it led him to loneliness. "How are they doing?" he wondered, thinking of that magnet of admiration and envy, his well-adjusted friend Morgan; and of Hulda, his recent tormentor, now herself tormented, in indirect reciprocity; Emma, whom he didn't know too well; Merton, whom he knew even less; Jessup, quite known, yet undecipherable, a mysterious character, carrying a morbid threat; and Tessa, whom he shut from his mind. Where were his other friends, the older and safer ones, that he knew be-

18

fore? This present batch was too recent, too thick, and closer than comfort would permit, if it chose. And tomorrow, he needed a job.

Morstive kept walking. So he wouldn't notice the cold. Poor strategy, for the cold enforced itself on him, simply jolting his awareness. He felt like freezing. But that would be extreme, and increase his discomfort. Against tomorrow, with its reminder of security, the pursuit thereof, he replaced his mind with frustrations already forgotten, endeavors heaped up in the past with harmless failures tame in distance, softly devoid of emotion, memory purged of fright. "Let's review the past, digested and put to bed. It's quiet, there." So he pondered back. Meanwhile, he visited no one. Thought was his solitary company, that day.

A few snow flakes came. Yet he saw a twinkle. An airplane. "Well, I guess I'm alive," he said. And plunged into doubt.

The airplane scattered its roar, but land vehicles were louder. Morstive drew in fresh air, but so deeply that he coughed. "No money, no health," he said. His poor smile was left, with no one to see it.

He extinguished that feeble asset, and slept poorly. He put a sweater under his suit next morning, followed up a want ad, and was accepted for a position. The personnel hirer, riding through a hangover, gave the applicant little trouble, barely bothering over qualifications and neglecting to compute the nuances of "background" and "over-all desirability," "fitness for the position." Morstive Sternbump was hired: to work immediately: in the firm where Morgan was executive, and Tessa Wheaton a typist. He intruded on coincidence, and it wasn't until five o'clock, seeing Tessa pass through his room with finished copy, and Morgan in his own office burdened behind a desk, that Morstive diligently realized where he was, breathing less strenuously now, the fear of being fired having diminished, since he had put in a day's work, and was found acceptable, with only minor errors compiled against a beginner's record, normal for the first day. "May I see Mr. Popoff?" he asked an official.

"He's busy," the latter said. The clerks and everyone were going home, and Tessa, without noticing him, left too.

"I'll wait," Morstive decided, self-satisfied. "I'm getting to know the firm's ways," he praised, "and soon I'll be breathing on Morgan's very heels, and pass him. Then I won't need his friendship."

Morgan kept him waiting. Morgan was in no mood for talking

19

to Morstive. There was a back exit in Morgan's office, which he used. Fretting, Morstive finally got the message. The sweeping woman was sweeping. Left passively to himself, Morstive then actively left. He had been "stood up," by his indirect boss and dubious acquaintance. His self-rating fell.

∞6∞∞∞∞

Next day, at work, Tessa was typing, and Morgan had an idea. "Show the new man, Morstive Sternbump, into my office," he said, to some non-Tessa employee, of which the firm abounded, with one exception.

"Hasn't arrived today," he was told.

"Any explanation?"

"No, he didn't phone."

"Bad, very bad," Morgan sighed, and did his work.

"Was it because of me?" he thought: "I wasn't nice to him lately. He could be afraid. I'll ring him."

No answer, so guilt assailed Morgan Popoff. He concluded that Tessa's account of the absentee's bad manners was perhaps hysterically exaggerated, in keeping with her prudish nature, her easy shockability. "He probably didn't even touch her," Morgan wisely smiled, and was glad he understood things. He felt kind again.

How could he express that kindness? With this benevolent attitude, he waited till lunchtime, then asked Tessa out: "Miss Wheaton, won't you join me?" When Tessa swooned, the office whispered, stopping work. Morgan was about to lecture them, when the hour struck, and they shoved his reprimand aside, wolfing to the door of temporary escape. Hunger was on fire, and Morgan treated his friend, at a private little place, to something he could really call a meal. He couldn't resist a burp: nor did he.

"So you still hate Morstive?" he asked, and carefully calculated the answer by the pre-comment, "Did he rape you?"

"The very idea!" She was so indignant, her glasses almost dropped, but her ears gathered together and held them up, with unity from opposite sides. Tessa forgot how grateful she was, stunned by so crude an interrogative blow, an insinuation cruel as it was undiplomatic, issuing as it did from her most favorite gentleman, the unimpeachable glory and the fond brilliance that painted colored light on her quiet soul. "I wouldn't let him," she confirmed, recovering herself.

"Then are you angry at me for introducing him?"

"My dear"—and she even pressed his hand, a very generous outburst on her part—"to be angry with you isn't in my nature; you know that."

Her paragon barely obliged this compliment with the courtesy of recognition, his haughtiness now dictating terms to the conditional rest of him, and to his pet loyal annex, her. "We won't discuss it then," he said, with an impressive intonation, on a flat note: "The issue is closed."

"I thank you," she said. And he acknowledged it, grandly, with grace and power. An executive type, his least word and seemingly inconsequential act augmented his firm dignity, obedient to his central theme. He was all himself, every inch.

"But just incidentally, he happens to be working here now."

"With us!"

"Yes. Absent today. On account of you, no doubt." And his smile soured her pastry, which she had chosen for sweetness. She cared more for the speaker than for the spoken-of. Even his mockery was welcome in any blunt form. Directness was his mode, and what *he* believed in, *her* philosophy included, during the marvelous moments ornamented with the flattery of his attention, when his convenience was relaxed, and his manner was assured, over these fine lunches. It snowed. So they commented on it.

They passed on to trifling subjects. But a white descending spectacle kept visual predominance. They refrained from alluding to it. But it got whiter, more flowing.

Then they spoke of the snow, that was so snowing. They had a window view of it, as coffee brought their little lunch to its dark brown end.

Jessup Clubb feared snow, for everyone requested it on his birthday, distracting attention from *him*. "My money is giving out," he said, concealed behind the window, and darting a quick look out, when the thick snow obscured him. He imagined deeds of evil of harm to people. Chuckling, he acquired a malicious air. "So naughty," he said, "that I must punish myself. Perhaps mental cruelty will do. It doesn't leave a scar." And he twirled his beard, feeling foul and loathsome, therefore perfect. To no one in particular, but to the air at large, he pronounced himself "Good." "And I ought to know," he said, examining so many credentials that he fell apart, his moral self detached from his physical, his brain soul divorced from any signs of emotion, despite his enthusiasm. "I feel so young again," he declared, while his happy insanity danced wildly about him, gloating and pouring bliss all over him, from every conceivable direction, in this mortal sphere. "Ah, I'm so cosmic," he asserted, "so definite. Is there anyone like me? No. Let me remedy that, and get children." Therefore, though being unwashed, he dated Hulda Stock, and seduced her without rubber. (This was before women swallowed birth control pills.) To make sure, he repeated this act with Emma Lavalla, ignoring her protestations of her avowed love for Morgan Popoff. Compassion shouldn't spoil evil, nor sentimentality delay it. Hulda was still in love, but Morgan wouldn't call her. Jessup merely stepped in, and substituted. "Sin is no crime," he said, "because everyone does it. There aren't enough jails. So we just lock up virtue, when detected. The world deserves a good deal of justice, having been around for so long." These ethical principles sustained his every moral fiber. His credo was deeply sacred with solemn conviction. What credo, what conviction? Sufficient unto evil is action. Belief is windy, but action does. And doing enters into being. "Bad being is well done," he thought. So many people. *Act* on them: don't let them be.

∞ 7 ∞∞∞∞

Neither Hulda nor Emma aided Jessup's immoral intention by fertilizing the instinct in his seed, so no new Clubb was born, however unholy and illegitimate. The roommates were good friends now, and shrugged off life as just another of those tireless impediments to a good time. They both lost grip, shared their thorough love for Morgan, and their fascinated repugnance for this insinuating Jessup, with his creepy power. Merton was gone forever, for a while. February had come upon the scene. With it, a new month.

The girls kept their jobs, and between them supported Jessup as well, who now openly lived with them, the sponger honored and welcome. Merton was involved with a new club, named "The Newbergs," after him. He was its sole member, but was backward in his dues. He had a sense of belonging, until he lost himself. His mother had to find him, and then he was institutionalized: and was incurably pronounced insane in official terms psychologically binding.

Jessup was riding high, and March came out of the world, giving vent to spring, soon. Hulda and Emma remained unpregnant, so Jessup's future was still dry. He kept trying. Where was his old friend Morgan? Married to Tessa Wheaton, thus touching on miracle to spring the unlikely to scare the improbable, although the impossible was unmoved, and serene as ever. Tessa supported Morgan by typing in the same firm by which he, though vice president, was fired; for graft was corrupted, or discovered, nicking him with a frameup, he shouldering the responsibility, as executives must. While Morgan fled disgraced to the Unemployment Insurance Compensation Bureau, Morstive Sternbump was inserted in his former stead, with the added bonus of sharing the company's profits. Unlikely? Unbelievable and incredible. Just like the very truth. In fact, plain.

Two women didn't conceive to Jessup. But one did to Morgan. Smoothly treacherous, Jessup renounced his currently misfortuned friend, whose fall from favor in the world's jaundiced eye was symbolized by a child, due next year, in Tessa's enlarging stomach. She was a prude no longer, spreading at length to treat Morgan fairly. But soon she must give up being a typist, if pregnancy got too stout. And Morgan, formerly generous, was now poor, as Morstive used to be. How would the wedded couple survive?

Morstive became a success, and ate and ate. This caused him to grow fat: even nature succumbed; and now June had given in to summer, sweet July. The weather was marvelous. The sun appeared daily, and shone. The clouds didn't block it up, for harmony was essential, to teach mortals below the wisdom of order and freshness, the grand vigor of something usual. Construction jobs demolished buildings, replacing them with taller ones. The big city so matured, it could afford a lazy mayor. He arrived at City Hall every day, and took a bath. The filthy sloppy slob owned a festering odor. How did he become mayor? Pure politics, of the dirty variety. Ira Huntworth his name was, entitled to "Mayor Huntworth." He reigned in City Hall. So much for the city.

Thus the world changed, and got newer every day. Too new, in fact.

The extremely new requires the old to tame it down. This has long been known.

Morstive was doing very well in his business, and even had a private secretary now. Soon his vacation would come. He was too fat to move, but he would go away. Perhaps to find romance. His love life needed an uplift in his new executive position. He would finally now be deemed eligible.

He had become corporate. Thus when the typist Tessa Wheaton, or rather Mrs. Tessa Popoff as of present, begged the adept Morstive to give her husband a job, he smiled sardonically, as far as his stomach could stretch. "No," he said; which she took for refusal, and reminded him how he had once attempted to seduce her. "Past, merely past," he pompously put.

"But where's your humanity?" she pleaded.

"Here it is," he indicated, pointing prominently below his stomach. A gesture of superior and contemptuous obscenity.

Tessa wept, and pleaded poverty. Lunch hour struck, but her husband couldn't take her out. He was struggling somewhere now, searching, with his future hiding behind him in his past, where he didn't dare to look. Morgan Popoff, a comedown. He had fallen. And this was his very office, the desk where Morstive was sitting. The window showed July sunshine, and though the puny typist in front of him was miserable, Morstive himself exulted, with triumphant elation. "Here have a cigar," he said, proffering one. She snapped it to the floor, and screamed. He fired her on the spot. She had to be removed, while Morstive glowed. He felt perfect, and displayed for the world a warm smile, causing his staff of clerks to cringe and exhibit symptoms of dismay. "Ah, I feel fine," he said. And went out to lunch. Truly, he did eat.

At home that night, Tessa admitted her failure, and told Morgan that now they both were out of a job. This doubled their unemployment, which for a single family could become ruinous. Help would have to be turned to. The Unemployment Bureau had refused compensation, on some inhumane technicality. And this was before liberal welfare code.

Morgan phoned Jessup Clubb, appealing for some intervention or charity. This appeal was denied with mocking glee.

Jessup had turned crucifier. Morgan was suffering. He became cranky. He was an expectant father. But not to outlive the birth, the way events were falling and in small doses destroying him, committing mechanical murder with such impersonal complacency that Morgan couldn't but accuse God of being deliberately indifferent, and not alert enough. God and Jessup and man were all to no avail. Even Tessa was losing faith. She became a shrill scold, and excelled in the role of a shrew, despite her loss of weight. Her due child was embryonic to lean times. But birth was far off as yet, and Tessa stood scrawny, abject. She was unbearable. And she bandied in hysterics. Fortitude was too much for Morgan, so he decided to call the mayor. He needed official help, and not municipal bungling. So he went right to the top. He bypassed the deputies.

"The mayor himself," he asked.

"He's taking a bath now, can I help you?"

"No, it's a matter for him alone. Drag him dripping out. He's all wet anyway, even when his wit turns dry."

"Look, I'm merely his secretary. What do you want?" The phone literally stung, and the wire was snappish.

Morgan said, "I'll wait." That's how time passed. The line went dead. Morgan was cut off. He joined his plain life, that fell below political intervention.

∞8∞∞∞∞∞

Before Morstive had risen as Morgan fell, he had known somebody named Page Slickman. This somebody had been resorted to in hunger duress by Morstive, who phoned the somebody after years of no contact. But instead a girl had answered, and told Morstive that Page Slickman had moved years ago, to anywhere out of the town, and that now she was renting the apartment that had been formerly his. Would *she* feed the phoner, Page being gone? No, not a stranger. End of call.

Anyway, back to the present. Morgan had failed in the phone call to City Hall he had put through. It was true that Ira Huntworth, the mayor, was taking a bath, just as his secretary had rudely informed Morgan. Now the scene is up to date.

What was happening in the mayor's bathtub? The mayor, that's who. He was busy removing a freckle. Just then, a visitor. Page Slickman entered, looking shy: he had never seen a man in a bathtub before. "I have a business proposition," he said. The freckle went ignored, while the mayor listened with compound interest.

September was about to arrive. No one could prevent it. It came about, and business perked up. After Labor Day, most of the working force was unemployed. But in November only a President would be elected. So the mayor was free to act according to his convictions, and not totally regard the public. Thus, the big deal: He bought, at taxpayers' expense, a bathtub big enough to swim in, known as a swimming pool. Another trump card by Page Slickman, a clever dealer. The shady transaction was strictly hushed up.

Morgan Popoff was still workless. His wife Tessa had learned to hate him, and wore him out daily with invective outlandish and brutal. Hulda and Emma, her two ex-rivals for someone she scorned now with conjugal insult, were Jessup Clubb's degraded mistresses. And now Tessa herself was having an affair with Jessup Clubb despite being big in an interesting condition or, as some would have it, the family way. Yes, Tessa Wheaton, who had been insulted at the New Year's party by that same cunning Jessup, and tried to persuade Morgan to dismiss his friendship and sever connection, was embroiled in big deep heat in flaming embrace. And not only that, her lover knew the mayor, to defend him against evil. Evil? What sort? The swimming pool swindle came out in the open, as the newspapers unleashed sordid articles, in a mud campaign, and the fair mayor was much maligned. The mayor would have to get out of this stench. But how?

Piper Cole was a someone who had once not paid back a long ago favor by Morstive. Anyway, now he was the attorney to Ira Huntworth, the only official mayor the city had at the time. The mayor was splashing in his new illicit bathtub (a swimming pool, courtesy of Page Slickman). Expert attention was given by the mayor to his own freckle. All this, in the basement of City Hall. The mayor was residing there, rent free. (During business hours, anyway. The city being liberal to its Highest Servant, he also had another house to sleep in. Mayors get privileges, see?)

Piper Cole, his attorney, came in. "Here's a wooden boat for your bathtub—see?—it works."

"But it has a motor on it," His Excellency said.

"That's to make it go," explained Piper.

"You're not my right hand man for nothing," praised the mayor, in deeply sonorous tones. It was a moving declaration.

But now the mayor remembered that he was in trouble. He must extricate himself from it—not from the tub or pool, but the public scandal brewing. Dirt was being detected, and it just won't blow over. Publicity media were hounding him mercilessly. It was an ooze partly of his own making. But the mayor knew Jessup Clubb, and knew how to reach him. The stink was afoot. How to wipe it away?

By placing a strategic phone call? A desperation maneuver, at any rate. But the one he called was rung up in the middle of a certain "act." This inconvenience was untimely, to the hilt.

The mayor called up Jessup Clubb, as he was inside Tessa, and requested, "Stop this newspaper rot, will you? They want to clean me up. I can do it myself."

Still inside Tessa, without stopping, Jessup breathed into the bedside phone in a dissonance of pants and orgiastic shivers, "I'm your man, boss."

"Your beard is tickling me," Tessa cried up.

"Who was that?" the mayor asked.

Then Jessup came, Jessup Clubb came, the second coming. "Only a woman," he said.

"Sounds like it," the mayor came back splashing in his tub-pool, and capsizing the vessel Piper Cole had gifted him with, with the motor humming. The pool filled with scandalous dirt, the more the mayor bathed. He was "in it"—up "to here."

And Jessup couldn't help him. Jessup wanted a baby. He had just screwed Tessa, who was big with Morgan's child. Will justice never be served? Is there no fairness, here below?

∞9∘∘∘∘∘∘

What an era all that was happening in! "The error era," it was called.

The world was in wide alarm; evil wrestled with itself, and was all knotted up, twisted and ascrew. Morstive Sternbump was living then. His innocence outlasted everything, the most constant factor. He was changed, as was every other character. To revert back was foolish, so well was he sped ahead. His soul hardened, and sentimentality was weeded out, and the pretense to poetry. He was solid. But it was time for a wife. His salary, plus a share in the business, boomed a steady uplift, and let him be eligible. His stomach to the contrary, he was popular, and his favors sought. So he saw people now (not needing to impress) as they were, and sniffed their game. This occupied him, until Christmas. Christmas is traditional for a change of pace. Something was bound to take place. He could feel it. His bones bruised it about, and his soft skin. What was to be? What, oh what?

Here he was, tied to a season. Frost and snow, weather real because cold, warned him. All his life, he had been living. Even so, so he was to be. But his self died along the way, and the self replacing it was respectable as any other, to his satisfactory and essential gain. Time confronted him, and with strong fortitude he was adequate to the occasion. Somebody was singing a Christmas carol, in a bar.

The voice was mellow, and down cruised a tear. Morstive bubbled up his beer, and wished a deal of cheer to the old poor fellow he used to be, now living a pauper's life with free room and board in heaven's slum, where all his daily needs were washed away by a celestial staff of social workers, distributing wings among the Welfare State for flights of fancy into dreams of better escape, far from the hardihood of responsibility and the obligated attendance on deed. "To get where I am today," Morstive mumbled to himself, "I had to be where I was yesterday. So all is forgotten, if not forgiven." He went to the telephone booth, and waited outside. Its occupant, however, was drunkenly asleep. Christmas Eve, and he had refused a parents' invitation. They were feeble, now. Those obsolete Sternbumps, a past refuted.

It was natural, poised outside an occupied booth in the noisy celebration of a bar crowded with artificial merrymaking on the eve of that single birthday most vital to the self-deception of Western Civilization, and loaded with enough drinks to be high on, to indulge that cerebral activity, thinking. This was why Morstive thought, all things being otherwise equal when not accounted for, in realms of contemplation. Soon, he would be required to go to the bathroom. "Get into a liquid flow," he ordered his ideas. A few woke up, while the rest lounged in comfortable armchairs of repression, nursing traumas in slumbering disarray, bitter experiences sweetened by oblivion and jerked to frantic forgetfulness by the anxious concern with tension-reduction, safety in the moment. "My mind is unevenly sprawled," Morstive observed, hiding his head. "It discovers outrageous preoccupations, and dawdles into dim danger-areas of regret, the fitful playground of remorse, where slender conscience submits to torture and is bullied by the brutes of memory, for in all things I did what I wanted. Now I'm well off. And yet I still hate myself. People are watching me, but I'll fool them, and become happy. But the technique, that's what puzzles me. It's obvious I need a girl. Stroke the right formula, and behold me married. But isn't this what Morgan wanted? Let him be my lesson, to avoid."

A brawl ensued. Somebody swung, missed his object, but instead struck Morstive at the side of his head, dislodging a loose thought from its precarious perch. Down went Morstive, bang. He was briefly out. But when revived, he discovered the idea burning with further intensity, so much so that he laughed. "He's crazy," someone said.

"Or drunk," the bartender observed.

Morstive was placed on a stool, which swirled around. "Dizzier," he said.

"Leave him alone," the general consensus was.

"Who's going to Midnight Mass?" asked someone. This began a discussion. Was Christmas just a holiday, or was it actually religious? Secular theology, slightly luked over, was doled out as the likely topical topic.

"I'm born today," said Jessup Clubb.

"And I'm unfaithful," Tessa Wheaton whispered.

At home, Morgan Popoff wondered where his wife was, while loneliness was dementing him solo. His head wandered off into fitful intermittences.

"Some day I'll be a success," he said. Then stared.

It was after midnight, and he became scared. "Tomorrow I'll apply to Morstive for a job," he said. "No, it's a holiday, then the next day. I only have time to wait. What else can I wait with?" Then his belly was pinched, but the refrigerator offered no consolation. "I was better off then," he said, recalling an identity so immensely real once that it shook his self of old forlorn tonight. "Does Hulda Stock still love me?" he asked, and the black silence answered it. "Is Emma infatuated? But where's my Tessa? I married her. Has she recovered?"

Tessa was being confessed to by Jessup, no less: "Emma Lavalla and Hulda Stock alternate for breeding purposes, and still no result." They were both away for the night over Christmas, so Jessup had their apartment to himself, and was gladly entertaining Tessa, knowing that Morgan would be missing her. Sufficient unto that night, was the evil thereof.

Tessa listened drowsily, but with obedience readied. "I'm disappointed," continued her bearded lover. "But take off your glasses." She did. "You say you give birth when—next month? Good. I want it to be mine."

"But darling, Morgan was the one who created it."

"Your objection is merely technical. Consider, now. I've needed a Son for a long time. I'm divinely inspired. Someone must take my place. Redemption is a sacred matter. I'm not fooling around."

"Did God tell you?" asked Tessa.

"Pay attention to earthly things," he said: "Theology is no place for women." His own voice aroused him, commanding as it was. She was a month away from motherhood, yet they fell to it, toiling and plunging where the legs start. The embryo or little fetus might be jolted that way. Jessup would want him alive. But he wanted the end of his tool to come up close to where his little future son was. It was Christmas, his own day.

But everybody shared in it, no matter who. Christmas devotees went to church, and morning rang true. New York was not Jerusalem, nor were they exactly in a stable twinkled at by a Bethlehem star. It was modern times. All evidence, every indication, each hint truly detected, verified an unheroic age, displaying sacreligiosity with an unholy deficit of reverence; though old customs like church thronged with empty survival.

Tessa before, Tessa now: where's the consistency? Jessup had just used her. He covets her soon-to-be kid, that's Morgan's, whom she's just betrayed. Time once was when he was too above her spinstery hope. Now, he's beneath her respect. Is she one character, or several?

"Her career had taken an unexpected turn," as a nineteenth-century novelist would put it. But a twentieth-century one would say, "Ain't she different, now!"; and the reader would recognize she was modern, and with reflex spin the television dial for the latest magic of communication, to assure himself that really today has no match, as far as reality goes: being newer than anything before.

But still not as new as what's to be. Bypassed, in its very, novel, aging.

∞10∘∘∘∘∘∘

Previously, Morstive was a sensitive bum. He mooched off others, and did favors only for a better return, registering an account bulging with receipt and diminutive in his calculated giving, for which he exploited ample generosity and withheld his own: goods and assets piling up on his side. Those petty, tight deceits had been employed by a sufficient reason: starvation. Now things stood differently. Power and an improved station in life obviated thievery and abject scroungy sponging and hypocritical service designed to suck the donating blood of substance from unwarned suckers that fell to his wiles. They had, though, seen through him, mostly, but let him milk them because his knack of flattering their pride and his subservient cajolement and fawning lowliness had given boost to their supremacy illusions, the dear images of a wish-fulfilling ego determined on grandeur and now assisted by cooperation from an outside source, as though reality confirmed the inflated extravagance within, encouraging vanity to assume superior proportions beyond notions of dim pretense; for here was Morstive actually saying so, feeding hopes with words of creative magic, so that identity was founded on one's own ideal, sponsored and given recognition by Morstive's willing compliance, fostering absurd myth where myth was needed, spinning out one's self-legend to the audacity of presumption verified and rendered authentic by this outside source, Morstive, objectivity's impartial agent. He was the dupe and clown to anyone's dream. Thus was Morstive a former lackey to one and all, while now revenge ranged within opportunity; vindictive atonement for debasement of self to lift others came attractively to his reach, the more his influence increased with his moneyed assumption on power; and his disinterested treatment of others quickened his cruel impulse to serve a fair balance and tip the scale on his own victorious greatness, privileged to call people's puny bluff and trump them, wipe them out, clean the ground with them, annihilate their call to personal dignity and sweep them off their moral base, really do them dirt. "My day has come," Morstive said, in his clean executive office.

"Mr. Popoff here to see you Sir. No appointment, but he insisted. Shall I send him in?"

"Do so," Morstive grinned, and revenge seemed sweetly perfect. Morgan like a lamb was led in for the sacrifice. He was crunched out, pumped through, and caustically examined, and deliberately wrung, dealt with without mercy and with dubious justice administered by a rough and ready code of rules of whim, barred of all standard. Ethics blushed, and decency hid its fair face in trembling hands, for by this trial Morgan met ordeal and agony, and submitted to this gentle crucifixion. "Let Jessup help you," Morstive said, as Morgan barely staggered away. Morstive's total past was rectified now, in this arbitrary doling out. Morgan had only taken. His current condition admitted of no giving resources.

For controlled receiving, a controlled giving is required. Tessa had given herself for money, prompted by poverty. The family Popoff was seeing hard times, bitten by the hand of death, and a miscarriage killed away their offspring, a life dipped out and unused, falling away. Morgan asked for a divorce. "Not on your alimony," Tessa taunted, pale and gaunt with exhausted suffering.

So their ideal marriage continued, in the scarcity of bread, and no longer did Jessup solicit her favors. Strangers shared her bed, at a cost. Morgan slept under. Concealed, he derived a perverted satisfaction from the erotic doings above. His wife was unusual, and he fell in love with her. She struck him dead, and he revived gently. "A little more, please," he asked.

"Go out and beg," she said.

Doing so, he met Hulda. She walked alone, but wouldn't recognize him. "Do you remember?" he asked.

"Go away," she said. Scorn tinkled in her voice, the last week of a fatal year.

"My wife had an abortion—I mean a miscarriage—and repaired quickly," said Morgan, hounding her.

"Go away, you ugly man," she said.

"I think Jessup caused it, but now she's with other men, still spry."

"Don't talk at me. There's no more dignity in you."

"I used to like you," he said.

"You've lost what you were, I once loved a self who isn't you any more, he was in my heart, but you're only a mockery that shadows that sweet person and I hate you with any power God gave me," she bitchily arose, practically snarling at him, out in open public exposed to daylight. It roused the flurry of a scene, as people stared. "I don't respect you, but I'll love you out of memory," Hulda sadly conceded.

"But my wife doesn't," he dutifully reported, aberrated so far that he felt compulsive about the truth, even inventing it if necessary, dispensing with literal fact and letting fiction poetically triumph to convey the spirit of essence, down to the letter of the core.

"I feel sorry for you," Hulda Stock said, going away.

"So do I," he said, and then, sure she was out of earshot, added something inaudible, heard by the vague ears that gather about, searching the skies for information. Morgan felt very tired. He opened his mouth to yawn, but nothing came out except a flat scream. So he was arrested.

"Jail is good for you," said the warden, feeding him cereal out of a spoon.

"Am I crazy?" the prisoner asked.

"Not yet."

"Why not?"

"It must be legally verified."

"Oh how so conventional," said Morgan, a former businessman.

33

Was he *ever* a businessman? Or is his memory a pretentious strut, the glorious peacock within living fantasy?

∞11∞∞∞∞

The last day of the year was a working day, and business offices let the work go slack, emotion was moving toward a blowup, a crescendo, for parties would be traditional that night, time to whoopee and let loose. Bottles were produced in offices, and drained. Merriment punctured the air, as for example in the firm where Morstive helped to reign, with here an impromptu speech, helpful to the high morale. He was amiably surrounded, he smiled and laughed, his inferiors wished him well, and an atmosphere of good cheer prevailed. "We'll all get drunk tonight," the Big Man said, and that brought down the house, the applause rang solid. "Get worked up," he said, "but be civilized people, at least. We'll collect your bits and pieces next year, when you report on time—and that's a warning. You have a full day to work out your hangovers, so let's see you sharp when the firm greets you for another good sober business year. So my friends—and I speak personally now—happy New Year, and prosperity to you and yours." The weeping was copious, and the day's early drinks were downed, an annual expense the company was pleased to absorb, in the interests of morale. By noon, everyone was scattered. Morstive's speech was a great executive stroke. He felt democratically happy, all around.

The political situation was a little disturbing. Mayor Huntworth had shown conflict of interest, and a gullibility to bribe disturbing to moral leaders. Piper Cole, his party's number one hack, was in trouble, for his bar license to practice law was forged, and condemned to be counterfeit. A slick character, Page Slickman, was involved, and held for contempt. It was an outsized scandal, with implications farfetching, and city government was at stake. Morstive, as a businessman, and as the former "friend" of all the principals accused in this misalliance, kept up a vulgar interest, for personal gain. What would happen?

Jessup Clubb was at low ebb. Morgan's child through Tessa,

34

their legitimate fruit, was miscarriaged out of existence, whom Jessup was to adopt and, by training, form forever, according to the sacred mysteries of religion. He broke openly with Tessa, although their liaison had been secret, known only to thousands of spooks and some dead people pretending to be alive to please relatives who loved them and friends who didn't.

Mayor Huntworth was politically in jail, but on the literal level was only behind bars, the concrete penal ones, while his term of office went officially through a sentence of public time, leaving the city ungoverned. In an adjacent cell loyally stank Piper Cole, whose humanity contributed to weigh over two hundred pounds, mostly flesh and illegal legality. Prison sullies all honor. "Jessup Clubb can help me," the mayor continually said, until, hearing his own words, he believed it. His tongue respected him, and where it wagged he followed, like a dog searching for a missing tail. Piper Cole snored accompaniment, buzzing along to the mayor's tune. Following his boss got him just where he was. Politics breeds bedfellows, ranking a cell apart.

December thirty-first, the calendar said, through lip-reading silence. A year was up, the jig was up. The mayor had been dishonest. "Well, at least I took a stand," he said. Moral fortitude upset him. "I'm determined to serve justice," he said, looking grim, like in his campaign poster, when, defeated by the primaries, he nevertheless hitched his bandwagon to his candidacy, threw his ring into a hat, and swept over opposition, with ruthless cunning, a machine boss if ever there was one, backed by sly business interests sneaking in a dollar here and there to drum up a little profit and make things hot for the outsiders, if you know what I mean. An invested lobby, bullies in business suits, politely persuading you to listen. So crookedly on the up-and-up, even priests had trouble rectifying this matter, with their Catholic majority, and Jewish hangers-on. It was a minority triumph, pledged to democracy, corrupting the whole idea of a vote-supported election, because the muscle racket hung on to a nice payoff and swept civic municipality off its collective cold-pigeon's-feet, and sat in the hot-seat cooling its well-padded fanny, while reformers wrote indignant letters to newspapers and influenced editorial setup, promoting chief columnists to the Washington bureau, where at least the dirt and filth had a national character, and thus international repercussions, threatening the very rotundity of the globe, for the world was out flat, taking the count

35

of ten, kayoed. "You're some lawyer!" the mayor said, addressing Piper.

"Prove it," the latter answered, naked without official identity, of which the District Attorney had stripped him, teasing the reporters.

"Wait till next election!" the mayor said, firmly clenched. Determination flared from his eyes, and drool leaked out of his mouth, slobbering. He was the picture of conviction, a rat pretending to be a mouse. And within the mouse, the caricature of the man stood. Or crawled. He was imperfect, but what mortals aren't? But even his mortality was dubious. He was a set type.

Morstive, in days beyond, had known this former thin man, Ira Huntworth, to be supple beneath an orderly stench corpsed up with rotten perfume. Filth was his purifying element. This he lived up to, by raising a huge stink, which ruled the atmosphere by refusing to subside, despite violations attributed to the Sanitation Department, a bureaucratic organization that neglected to clean itself up, although the mayor had washed his hands of it, the own hands of the very mayor momentarily embarrassed, who, in jail, was now bemusing his garbage, picking himself like his own scavenger, whom he admitted in privacy, sharing one odor that was too much for two, aligned by equality to his very self, whom, in envy, he hated, as was his nature. "Don't get too close to me!" he told himself, but now that his power was waned, this advice was easily discarded, for he was a deposed elected official of suspect scent. Thus disobedient, the self smelled him, and responded with a nasty frown, in the limbo of his exiled decline from the vow of this highest civic office. That's why the mayor needed followers, and had to lead: spurned by his own snubbing self, he turned to others; and the puddle of his influence, the mud of his cult, were stained with increase and a loyal body of his perennial faithful, with their noses bandaged up and their fingers outstretched for a profit, their lips gently pressed to buttocks from which issued violent sounds that preceded falling matter, behind the scenes or wherever it was. Piper Cole smelled moonly, to the mayor's offal sun.

Underhand deceit, shady outlawed shenanigans, duplicity cut and dry, deals dealt by stealth, royal cutthroat competition, and low demeaning tactics, were Page Slickman's stock in trade, but he was hauled in by the law, and examined for proof of marriage. A wife was found out of town, but neglected and sick. This wouldn't do.

A detective went to his old apartment, in the city, discovering there someone called a person, if so served by such a euphemism. Questions were flung, for what they could detect. That person promptly shut up about Page Slickman, and the detective resorted to torture, self-inflicted, to request her mercy. She didn't have any to give. Weak with loss of blood, the detective fainted, and was dismissed. Criminology had failed.

On his upper lip, or thereabouts, Page owned a mustache, his own south-of-head hair, formed along a neat black strip. He dressed sharply, almost to the point of obscenity, but was a ladies' man, if he so chose. An unfulfilled bride was weeping for him. He loved, however, money. He was in a cell next to Piper Cole, while the city administration fell. No clean lawyer was available, and the dirty ones were being investigated. The clean lawyers were trying to defend the latter. Page Slickman clamored for more liberal laws tolerant of injustice and all crimes that compassion may justify and mercy bless forgivingly. He needed a "hands-off" clause, to indemnify his susceptibility to the bribe of human temptation, to which, in sensitivity, he was not immune. So he sinned! Who doesn't?

Those jailbirds sulked. However, a visitor arrived. The warden looked them over, a trusty notebook handy, as Jessup Clubb, with an overflowing beard and in unconventional robes, approached the mayor's temporary living quarters, with a scheming look in his eye. The year had all but run out of surprises. The mayor was awakened, and a whispering conversation began, while Piper Cole and Page Slickman, ignored, exchanged gambling sheets, thrilled to risk nonexistent cash on the famous horses of the day, running down South, where racetrack weather handicapped no odds and bookies were concealing fortunes in advance, waiting to open bottles that night. Celebration was in the air. Too bad they weren't free.

Into the mayor's honorable ear, Jessup complained about things. Suffering was too intense to be ignored. "If I get you back into office, with a clean slate," offered Jessup, "then I want, out of your stud stable, a likely son to call my own, no matter who bred it. I need a youngster to carry on my—er—business. As a mayor, you got power."

"But how will you acquit me?"

"I have influence unseen by man," Jessup hinted, broadly, darkly, wickedly. "And all *I* want is a son."

"And a son you shall have," it was promised, from the highest municipal authority, whose discredited esteem then put in, "You can trust on me."

Jessup stipulated further, from his sub-priority catalogue: "And I want a coupla babes, Emma Lavalla and Hulda Stock, to lose their irregular license for whatever they didn't do, or did, anyway. They haven't produced a son for me. Not one son! So treat them in kind."

"Depend on me!" the mayor obliged, rosy with hope—his own, not Jessup's. This was really a special multiple deal, transacted in jail. It had complicated edges to it. And an inlaid veneer of magic, with its protective glow.

"And I want a legal divorce to transpire, between Tessa and Morgan Popoff, though *he*'s in the nut house."

"Most likely," agreed the mayor.

"And Merton Newberg I want pronounced sane."

"That I'll do," the mayor testified. "Anything else?"

"I want Page Slickman's friend cleared up, and the mystery doped out: She lives where that swindler used to in the sunrise days of his American career in crime."

"Of course," the mayor answered. "While you're at it, anything else? I'm giving you wholesale rates, if you clear my fair name of all alleged and impugned against the merit of my record. Restore my credibility, and you win a permanent patron!"

"One more soul, Morstive Sternbump," Jessup said.

"Yes, doing very well, I hear," said the mayor. "What should his fate be?"

"I haven't tampered with it yet, but I'll let you know my decision later. And someone else, now."

"Who?"

"A black man, Keegan Dexterparks. I want him to *be* black, if he is."

"I don't know him. But while a skin can decay, it retains its essential coloration. Isn't he his own blackness? Or does he have to stand in the night with the lights out, for help?"

"Just keep his blackness intact. Do what I darkly say."

"As you please," the mayor obeyed. "But how will you free me?"

"By proving you innocent."

"And Page Slickman—is he guilty?" Jessup smiled, and left this unanswered. "And what of Piper Cole?" the mayor asked, opening his mouth and fouling the air with his breath, while his body exuded a similar fragrance.

"I'll take care of him," Jessup whispered slyly, shading his eye on covert slant to the next cell, where their subject was in a sulk rot. The warden signaled to Jessup, visiting time was up. All business had been dispatched, and the dealers heaved a sigh of hopeful trust for mutual assistance that would unstifle their respective circumstances. The year was wiltering down its last day. "Happy New Year, I must leave," said Jessup Clubb.

"Get me out of here," was the mayor's parting word. Piper and Page, facing each other from stiff necks poked out of bars, sighed for the wishful bottle. The jail drinking list was too bland. Ah for a bird's freedom. (The uncaged one's, that is.)

The inside wants out. The warden reported drunk, and the free crooks outside prison were all going to party, ready to liberate the wild instincts untamed by bargains of primitive conscience that compromise civilization to the internal hotbeds of sneaky guilt from deeds yet undone and thoughts that outdo the undone deeds in action unenacted, violently prohibited, forbidden under dire code of criminal punishment, as drawn up by desperate law to safeguard the legal peace as yet unravished, and stop a flood of chaos from overtaking the defenseless principles of harmonious good conduct by which cowardly survival is contrived, enforced, and arbitrarily condoned, making even suicide suspect, and outlawing violations of life's careful obligation to itself, letting quiet obedient citizens live to satisfy health and other material needs, and sacrificing offensive individualism that proposes greedy mayhem and oversteps clear rules without respect to property, person, and other conventions.

Jessup stepped out of the pseudo-Greek building with classical colonnades and false facades, and was ready to cut loose. Unburdened, he desired fun. Preserved by uneasy sleep, let each official captive of the law murder his contemplation and be condemned by dreams, to torture his private offense and his public act of culpability, already broadcast and committed, filed in record. Worse crimes go unpunished. Gaily, Jessup Clubb set his strides toward a great party, where open personality will be published, ugliness observed. He crossed the gutter. Morstive Sternbump bumped into him, coming from where he had previously been. They hailed an open cab, and the "friends" sat together, imprisoned in a moving vehicle,

39

having joined ranks on the wayward chance of accident. They'd finish the year together, along with swarms of similar party guests, promiscuously linked to anonymous festivity. The weather had about run out; it too would go celebrating. Rain gathered out of the sky, blown down. The last few drops, of a good-bye year.

"Where to, Mack?" the driver had asked, and received the puzzling reply, the surprising answer, "To the party, and go fast." "Inebriated," he thought, but obeyed, hoping to make a buck. However, an address was soon given, on the way. Correct, with all the glittering guests, and a host or hostess, and bottles with powerful liquid incentive to dismiss ordinary circulation and substitute the joy of flame, the abandonment of pagan ritual.

∞12∞∞∞∞

Without speaking, they arrived early. The apartment was on the first floor. Morstive paid for the cab. Jessup led the way in. A few guests were observing uneasy silence, and nervously avoiding any introduction. Timidity seemed the scheme, and the usual extroverts were shy. "Who's the hostess?" Morstive felt obliged to ask.

"Or host?" answered Jessup; "I don't know." It was self-consciously early. Even the drinks, those beautiful symbols of release, were slurped with slow strangeness, and no glass was refilled. The pace would alter, after this awkwardness.

Jessup's saintly gown and monkish aspect, his otherworldly worldiness, and his "protest" beard, received no sensation; bohemianism being a normal occupation with those in the know of fashion, so the style ran those days. Each guest was studying his own toes, through the opaque customariness of shoes. A record played classical jazz. The rooms were large, but no one dared dance. The drinks were at a "bar" table, self-served. When glasses ran out, cups were in reserve. The year was holding on, delaying its death by a few hours. But the inevitable would arrive. There was a brisk tension. Every now and then, a scared young unmarried girl donated a giggle, which the sparse crowd immediately dismissed. It wasn't the time for it. Later, the giggle would be buried by crowd noise. Now, it was out of place, like any nervous twitter that betrays prematurity's embarrassed impulse.

Morstive was a free agent, and all but wandered standing still. He held in his stomach, to look slim. But no one caught that affectation, since each was embroiled in the toils of his own absurd fetish or deliberate compensation for the assumed paranoia of inferiority, although unheeded, unglanced at, unguessed at, by the mythical "others," whose interest was but fabricated by the sensitive vanity of egocentric preoccupation. "I have money now," Morstive proudly told himself, "so I won't leave here till I find a wife. First, to uninhibit myself, I'll compulsively drink, and then the free life will ooze out, and gallant energy will tide me with conquest. Yes, for I'm in a sexy mood." After this self-confession, he boldly studied his opportunity, and decided to wait. The really desirable girls won't arrive till late, for their conceited pride permits them to conceal their eagerness, disguise their interest, hide their desire to get married, and pretend infinite boredom, the French version of ennui, with cool nonchalance and offhand dignity, stunningly casual, establishing their value all quickly at once, for they were beautiful, too, in bed or in soul or in person, as every gentleman would like to know, impressing them with market sales pitch, like a country State Fair, with prizes and gifts, accomplishment and renown, boastful promise, and romance lurking. Love was in ambush.

Now, discouragingly, only couples were arriving, married or "dates," and steadies, and lovers of illicit status, but not just single women alone, the prey for Morstive's artful approach when fortified by talkative whiskey and a stubborn declaration of confidence, a denial of fear. Morstive wore a gray suit, of elegant mold, and was quite a prince. He snatched edible goodies and tiny sandwiches from a cordial tray, to stay the pangs of his hunger, the products of symptomatic nervousness, for he was "on show." Let him present immaculate behavior, and win a refined reputation. Then, love was sure to follow, and he'd be adored. As Morgan used to be. As who was now?

Then, the appearance of Hulda startled him. Gorgeous!, and memory leapt back. She wore a white dress, and her hair said, "Touch me." "I will," Morstive vowed, so he most certainly hid. Ah, the coward came out!

41

Hulda and Emma had arrived together, as the party was filling out: taking shape and form, helped by those of women. Enough non-couples were there. The mating market was underway. All wares were being presented.

"There's Morstive," Emma said, pointing, laden with a gown of temptation, as her sharp friendly rival followed her arched finger and saw, in a new light, an eligible knight, concealed behind shy armor. "He's making a name for himself," Emma said, "in Morgan's old job, but improved with promotion, and a salary that's remarkably handsome." Hulda perked up, and sniffed a kill. Here was her complete marriage.

Though attracted to him, the girls stopped, when Jessup Clubb's readily recognizable identity openly flew into focus, for they craved back their old apartment. He cordially declined to move, and jutted an unflinching smile to oppose their angry threat. "Go find a hotel," he said, to his former mistresses whom he had tested on a racy mission to propagate eternity, so that calculated humanity may survive, and find favor with Almighty help. "Don't make a scene," he warned, as their volume rose, in a combined sputter of outrage. They had cooled off on this creep who exploited a divine pretension. Ten-thirty, and noise clashed with drinks, while excitement gained a head, and intensity became the prevailing emotion.

Morstive was pacing his drinks, rising to a calm powerful confidence, ready to cock assaults in any direction, to protect the ivory tower of his virility from false downgrading and whispering insinuations. He overflowed with man-of-the-world talent, and needed but the merest challenge, to arouse all his mettle. Then, he saw Tessa Wheaton, testing his impatience. She wept on his shoulder, and complained that her husband was insane. "Help me divorce him," she begged.

He had slighted her, and later Morgan also, when that couple had fallen to the necessity of imploring him for a job. So his conscience reared up, and he became her protector. "Here, drink this," he said, offering his.

"The last time, you offered me a cigar," she said.

"Won't we forget that now?" he asked.

And Hulda Stock had his arm: "Darling, you look wonderful," she interrupted, with a cozy voice, and naked desire. So they danced, while Tessa raged, and vowed revenge.

The party was scattering its elements, amid confusion. But the hostess hadn't showed. This added intriguing mystery, as the gathering kept building up time's speed, held fast in common to the clock, approaching midnight, just an hour and ten minutes away. Some balloons clouded the air, with indistinct color, and an outbreak of brittle drunkenness occurred, encouraging the rest to emulate. So no one stopped. More bottles were found, and the gay libido romped. As further guests arrived, the packed assemblage obscured evident view of anyone in particular, while collective humanity conferred an immunity privilege on any individual's guilty responsibility. The moral vacation was here: morality had vacated.

Whispering into Hulda's ear, though he didn't have to, Morstive asked if she still loved Morgan. She shivered down her spine, and let go his grip. She needed another drink. Emma was still bargaining with Jessup, while now some spectacular people arrived, dressed like a carnival. While haranguing with Emma, Jessup was installed in the loquacity business to barter for some promiscuous souls on the loose, to boost his acquisitive collection of lost gullibles for a future kingdom. His sermon had already converted several people, whose lives they placed in his hands, in return for a comfortable death, and a divine afterlife. The old quack was at work. But his victims would slip away, untenacious, but tentative, of slipperily instilled faith. Religion was getting jittery. Drunken nerves went grimly pagan.

Things were really thumping now. The beat was to a drum, frantically being banged. Oh boy! And midnight still an hour away!

The lights went out, for the electricity failed. Women gasped, being kissed. Then all was light again, but the gasping women were still being kissed: and even kissed back, when their lips could gain the offensive.

Unknown to the others, some paroled convicts entered, out on informal bail: or else, escaped jailbirds, turning a loophole trick on a keylocked warden drunk with stupor. They had civilian outfits though: the oft-photographed mayor, unrecognized (for his odor got lost in the hazy fumes of alcoholic mergers); Piper Cole, in his shadow; and Page Slickman, grinding his teeth, thoroughly at home here, observing the risks and detecting the odds, willing to molest a few suckers and milk them of their honesty, bilk them of a fair exchange of goods, leaving them a little the worst for wear, but not much better off. The party was now a hunting ground, and open season was declared: under no rules, with "Everything goes" the keynote. Some unsavory characters were present.

On holiday from a mental institution, Merton Newberg joined in, a great mixer. And, under conceal of false identity, that once-proud monument of greatness and personal appeal for anyone's integrity, the immense Morgan Popoff, discarding his lowliness and donning a resurrected triumph for heaven-hell, came clandestinely under cover, and grabbed his faithless wife by the wrist, almost yanking it off, as Tessa Wheaton repressed a sharp wail, and saw the apparition of her husband in effective costume, until her feet failed, and a faint-spell hit her. But overhead, above all, came Jessup's insidious sermon, calling for sinners to enlist in private sacrifice, and yell screaming at God to come down; and a lucky couple would win a priceless indulgence, if they gave a new baby boy to Jessup outright, who would in turn confer immortality on their lost child, to mankind's generous advantage, prospering earth: for stocks were on the upswing, now that Mayor Huntworth was in jail. Tessa recovered from her faint, pleased to remember that exactly a year ago, to the minute, she had been a foil, a tool, in this clown's phony hands, and had endured an insult, whose deep scar had led to vagaries of immorality; for Jessup had preached at her, and termed her "a strumpet," in old language: in new language, a modern whore. And now, everything was as he said. What an unholy year! The ominous incarnate. And she wept with mercy, asking for forgiveness; she prayed in silent adoration, for the Virgin, and swooned into a fit of womb-bitten hysteria, as though a bitch had bitten her, and she had inherited a spirit beneath her belly, between her legs, of hot ferocious intent, craving any madman. "Take me in the bedroom," she asked her husband: and Morgan, upright, was shocked to his very skin, and beyond. What a pathetic sight! She was cringing. Morgan was not mad: he was cured, the victim of psycho-analysis, of swift duration: for he realized himself. He had been on the wrong track. Perhaps a pimp's career was best. He went in for occupational therapy, and kissed his wife, selling her to the nearest bidder, on close hand. Then he felt good; about to earn a living, and invest his sincerity in a trade.

Merton Newberg, pawing at Emma, asked, "Do you remember me?" while slapping her. She sobbed, with a hysterical fit.

Elsewhere, in another corner, Morstive necked hot on Hulda's ear, but she said, "I must go to the bathroom." It was eleven-fifteen, for the clock's honesty was only mechanical. It was really the newest old time of the whole world.

More and more drinks were consumed. This had effect.

The mayor thought of taking a bath, but the bathroom was always being occupied for other purposes, so His Honor reneged on that plan. The jail bathtub was pretty scrappy. Piper Cole's saliva had to reinforce the depleted water. That's hardly in the comfort bracket.

Jessup was conducting community singing, and had converted Merton to the rage of the age: Christianity. Merton loved to be religious, for it gave him hope. So nice to belong. He regained all his lost sanity, as he sang along.

Morgan wanted revenge, so he attacked Morstive from behind, who, in exclusive self-defense, stepped on and inadvertently squashed someone too near-by. There was a confusion stage, in the mix. The interpenetration of people scattered some identities. The rooms were bulging. Yet, the hostess hadn't shown up. The mystery even deepened. What about Page Slickman? He was outside sight, gambling with dice, rolling in the dark. Also on two knees was a skeleton. They were closed up, in a grim wager.

The floors thundered, the ceilings screamed back. A crescendo was rumbling. The momentum grew louder.

Page, gambling with the skeleton in the closet, made no bones about winning the loser's shirt, as the dice rolled, for they were loaded. The skeleton was obviously rattled, and losing his sense: but not his nerve: "Double or nothing," he thrust, for he figured, what had he to lose? Page was fighting scared, but couldn't back out now: besides, the door was locked. "Snake-eyes," he declared. But his luck was bad. He was reduced to his skin and bones, and the skeleton was a man again. In sheer modesty, Page put a barrel around his precious blushing genitals. The skeleton wore a bow tie, and a zoot suit, and admitted to an ambition of growing up into a bad boy. Praised for having a goal, he flashed a winning smile, and fell apart. Therefore the loser gathered up the spoils, felt for a lost skull, and thanked whatever lucky stars there be above, as the cold sky closed into midnight with but fifteen minutes to spare, and God's chill was felt, in the frost-tumbling heavens, wide open, to allow the penitent sinner to enter. Page had his wad back, kicked the closet door down, and a fracas was on. The noise was densening: a screech of Protestant hymns, low sexual moaning, stomach roars, deep belly groans, trumpets imprisoned in drums, a Bach organ blast, nondescript wooing, courtship covertly pursued under penalty of Indian-giving, coarse sounds of muffled scraping, animal tidings of release, rumbles of toilet plumbing, empty bottles clinked, sparkling glasses rewatered in the bubbling merriment of spirits, the chaotic choreography of thudding feet, throat static, hideous tramples, copious weepings, a harsh miscellany of sobbing, tinkle tonks, brick bocks, ug oomps, urghes, lpp ppp, and grrr. And that wasn't all. There were others.

Sensation was very active now, and midnight was peeping eight minutes away, the climax to be drawn down, the glands shooting out of the skin, secretions devouring their organs, human chemistry at work. Molecules of explosive dynamism swirled through the crackle. An agitated hostility reared, with snide jokes; and tempers swung up, lungs stretched, hearts heaved up an extra pump of blood, and brains were confused with ideas. Morstive was fighting Morgan. Morstive wanted to be the former Morgan. The present Morgan tried to regain himself up to the present Morstive. They grappled at past and future power.

The party is a flurry of mankind massively stacked in random panics of mobility. The born are living it up, in a selectively socialized fury. They're living down their own mortality, in the ritualized frenzy of living it up; while children still wait to be born, and a mating union is chosen between men and women, for the selfish sake of pleasure, against the barrier of death imposed by time on those who take their watches seriously and burden the clock with all the hazards of attention, ticking out the old year, kicking the past out of existence, and abstracting the consciousness, to universal consent, erecting midnight to intervene between the last month's final minute and the first weak second of January first, setting free joyful ghosts from stuffy tombs and resolving some improvement, even minor at that, in the personal happiness quota, a successful change of emotion to gratify the lonely greed of self, plus stakes of security, stalked by hungry wolves advancing from next year to now, as we, with our guard down, embrace the smothering distinction between two crucial armies of time whose warfare, along lines of alternate retreat and advance, must never slacken, or the heart would dwindle forever and dismiss future from past, sinking through now into never.

"It's midnight!" someone said, and each distinctive identity lost

46

ground and gave way; while noise, to the loudest tempo and pitched high to the violent range of volume, invaded those party rooms, from those temporary joined inhabitants, dressed down to the very shoes below, guests of an unknown hostess the sex of whom was even indeterminate, she being out of town, located at the heart of ambiguity, an address honored by any post office. Page Slickman took over. "It's my house," he said.

Some clothes were put on the mayor, some shreds of common decency. He had dared to bathe in the bathroom, sponged by his trusty Piper Cole, and left a stench there upon his retiring from that private room. Hulda had next entered, but the noxious fumes left in there neutralized her man-killing perfume. Separate riotings flared out on spaced intervals. Morstive's and Morgan's feud had dissolved; for distractions were disrupting other distractions. What was *not* a distraction, any more?

Disorder was the order of the early year, now. Morgan kissed Hulda, recently returned from the bathroom with cotton sticking out of her nose, so the engagement was off: and Morstive had no bride.

Emma, in tears, pulled herself away from Merton and asked Morgan to marry her. He dismissed the notion, with cold tones of haughty resentment for imaginary damages, as a figment of sentiment, an arbitrary wish. He was in business, pimping his lawful wedded wife Tessa, who now, hot fright, was undergoing a trauma, having been rented out in an enclosed bedroom, under a pile of coats, by a sadist-tenant, who was now lodging in her, and paying her rent in painful installments, uncorrected by the housing administration, despite the landlady's flagrant violations in the rat-infested premises, and a leaking staircase. The house was out of order. Order was out of the house. Order was no boarder, in *anyone*'s house. It was outside all borders.

Even inanimate things were acting like people. That's how predominant the people were. The people were the order of the day. But this was disarray, in the night's disorder.

A window was sighing, as though human. Its pleasure was paneful to behold. It was transparently glassy-eyed. Blackness was outside.

Jessup Clubb was given exclusive rights to everyone's children, and the childless even donated theirs, being the least they could do. Thus, his Divine Rights dynasty would be guaranteed.

The brawny party kept its hectic brain going, while music poured freshly from the record player, in pulsations of melodic throb. Dancing steps were being shoved along. It was gaining full sway, this horde of animate parts, replenished by late arrivals all the time, in undrained sheer quantity. Individuals were debased currency, for the collective ruled. No one was leaving. A new supply of drinks, an endless round, gave incentive. A revolting animation occurred; and anyone who was human at all had a change of heart, alcohol-induced, and now emerged superhuman, characteristically consistent with the altered tale of personality, as reputations went flying off, and timidity hibernated deep within, burrowing underground, and uprooting the silliest inhibitions as well as the gravest taboos.

No disguise was left. Bare down to every quivering motive, these weird guests were transformed to beasts of honesty, having exhausted every affectation and affected every exhaustion; and came alive, in a brittle supercharge, like cannibals on a vegetarian holiday from their rigid codes of meat, set free from the conventionally carnivorous, to frolic with the carrot and the lettuce.

In a twixture of orthodox rules, impulse stroked a short circuit and orgy burst a fuse, letting instinct devour itself with an almost criminal exhibition (despite the mayor's presence), and all mild moderate restraint proved inadequate, and demoted to unfashionable, under this haphazard majority regime. Fury there was, and behavior oddly at variance with the assorted convivial amenities and niceties of our religion-administered society. Anarchy couldn't describe the occasion, and words were impoverished by feelings; passion, ungovernable, ruled all other forces and currents and dominated the multitude. Humanity was sumptuously arrayed, in its full regalia of all myriad aspects. Not a facet was lacking, in all that affair. Nor one trait, embossed to the stamp of our species.

Nor was horror absent, and other accompanying sensations, joining in the fray. Memory was being created, right there, in the power of Now. Things were stirred, and jarred loose. Nothing ordinary was happening, but only contrary phenomena, serving no link of identification to the similarity of the usual. It was a "good time," for all. Later, some were to rue it, others protest a complete denial, and the leftovers were absentmindedly devoid of memory, reduced to psychotic mumblings and great lacerating repressions, suffering disintegrated splits of personality and torn to pieces by overwhelming gaps in the mind's honest record, having no recourse but to apply to insanity for a final resolution, meaning economic prosperity for the Union of Journeyman Psychiatry, those rare skulls thrown out of medical school and turning off brains to legally transact a living, their patients on couches, going into dreary relapse the moment a cure is possible, since these are crazy times and absurdity is respected, aberrations are normal, flying off the handle is a way to keep your feet on the ground, and black makes white, under democracy's unflagging banner. These principles were served allegory by the party's universal application. The guests were emblematic, to the world's transcendence. There it was, here, now.

∘∘13∘∘∘∘∘∘

The party was still the scene in the newest hours of the year after the party started, though the two years were bond to the same night. Last year's characters went through the antics of survival, heirs to a circumstantial flux of alterations. Their *names* were consistent, against bouncing fortune.

Morstive was looking for a wife, now that his Hulda Stock was reconciled (though adultery was committed) to the fascinating Morgan Popoff, whose old self was regained, shining like a candle against a neon jungle. Tessa, his wife, was being devoured by a sado-masochist, to unsag the family's sunken finance.

The mayor was making a big stink. "You oughta be in politics!" a heckler taunted, whom then Piper Cole assaulted, in his legitimate role as the mayor's popular bodyguard, an ex pug (heavyweight, at that). He was a defrocked attorney now, and a refugee from the law's sanctuary. The mayor was now being roundly recognized, and was no stranger. He was the coup-de-disgrace for a party already dirtly down degraded.

Page had a few deals cooking, including attempted blackmail, and a few other stunts. The hostess was never going to show up. Doubt of her existence was voiced, by a few skeptics.

Rumor went around that Page used to live here. He had known the absent hostess. Was that why she was absent?

Thus the new year inherited a transitional mystery, or a mysterious tradition. So many unasked questions!

Jessup Clubb was asking to be crucified. The Jews among the audience said yes, but asked to be compensated with usury (their tribe was in their bones). No, Jessup wanted a free lynching. He had many children to succeed him. Put life in abeyance, and death was beautiful, by contrast.

Merton Newberg joined a new club: the Emma Club. It included Emma Lavalla, as a non-paying member. She took him on the rebound, fast from Morgan's rejection. At last, a bride to be.

However, they disputed on religion. Merton was willing to join anything, for a purpose. His identity was embarrassing, and, undetected in a group, melted in a joint united cause, it spread itself away, diverted by aims of multiple action, smattered into worthy scatterings, where he lost himself. For face to face with himself (it once happened) the truth sharply insulted him, and he never recovered. Therefore he turned himself out, and converted to reality, to avoid the real: "Objective" now, he safely was hidden in his loss, and gained the superficial world. This depleted his soul, betrayed any core of integrity, and he found himself abandoned by the true God: for he had found many idols, and worshipped at graven images: all, all, distractions.

A black man, Keegan Dexterparks, had some annoyed score to equal versus Morstive, for some anciently forgotten reason. A more than physical revenge, he carved: assaulting Morstive at that vulnerable level, job security, though without foreknowledge of the really maligning consequences.

It so happened, perchance, Morstive's boss, his executive superior, the company's controlling interest, was in attendance, along with his pluffy wife. He was Turkel Masongordy, and she was his Missus, in the order of their precedence. Then, something bad happened. Worse for the latter, than for the former.

Keegan took the wife aside, seduced her way up the bladder, damaged an internal tissue of intestinal plasm near a ligament at the flex of a capillary where cells had a duct to secrete spasmodic waste for physical exercise at the turn of health near the morale, where safeconduct was assured, and well being was welled-up, like too much gas inside a bottleneck, for an emotional crisis. Thus, she was harmed. After this neat little operation, Keegan shoved the blame on to Morstive, conspicuously. "I'm offended," Turkel Masongordy addressed the innocent accused, "for you've made a cuckold of me. That's an act of insubordination, by firm-hierarchy. There's only one solution: To fire you."

"But," Morstive gasped, "Sir, isn't that logical—I mean it's not."

"We're in business," said the flaired-up boss, dangling over his wounded wife in a genuflection of belated respect for her whose money he had betrothed, as a capital investment, assuring his life of a worthwhile success from the commercial angle, an angle of segment total to his whole goal, making him cold about diversionary scruples; "and you haven't cooperated. So, as of Monday, you're fired, and your back salary confiscated, as a clause of justice, to do me good."

"But it wasn't my fault concerning your wife," Morstive explained, his rational faculty intact, and patience crawling all over him. "That black crook did it, that guy, Keegan Dexterparks."

"You're a biased bigot!" the boss proclaimed, with indignant amazement, stuttering all at once, aghast at any commercial industrial prejudice with personal private individual undertones here humanly applied in sexual misunderstanding.

Morstive recoiled, and said, "It's a simple fact: Keegan, not I, molested your wife; it doesn't matter that he's black."

"Don't dare use that word, *black*," the righteous boss demanded, for this was in the era preceding "black" with "Negro."

There was a "lynch" atmosphere, with Morstive in the middle, as the crowd sensed the kill and claimed a victim stripped of his life-blood job. Collective guilt claimed Morstive for the spectacular scapegoat, by the circumstantial bloodthirst of opportunity. The mob had Morstive for a scent.

"He didn't do it," said the wife, creating surprise.

"You shut up, what do *you* know," her irritated husband responded, in a mood to eat Morstive's blood and be a local hero, at least for the moment.

The mayor had *his* voice (but still substantial?). "I move we try the case," he said.

"You're nuts!" everyone said, and he apologized for his insensitivity in assessing the ignited tone of an aroused, vociferous majority—a fatal flaw for any statesman, however currently defunct. Public opinion was essential. What is democracy without it?

51

Jessup Clubb, with his religiosity, intruded. "Why not punish *me*, instead?" he offered.

"A *splendid* idea!" Morstive put forth, thus confessing his subjective guilt for which his was no objective fault in the case under "discussion."

Jessup had volunteered to substitute for the falsely accused Morstive as the party-crowning martyr. His appeal was briefly considered, but the chieftains decided against it, for Jessup had been too eager, which would have rung a wrong climactic note for a party already memorable. What other culminating grace could be sought?

The crowd was disappointed. Its spirit was broken. All it had had was a good time.

The mood for a victim had dissipated, the tension released. A wave of tiredness took over.

Morstive was happy again, carefree, and spontaneous. He flirted outrageously, and was rejected. Funny: wasn't he handsome? And he always made an intelligent sound, when he opened his voice. It just wasn't right.

Tessa was trampled down, her genitals outnumbered, and simply crushed. Oh, for her former prudery! She had been so correct then. Now, it was too late.

"I love you," Hulda told Morgan.

"So do I," he confirmed, knowing it unwise to contradict a lady, on a gallant principle he was loath to compromise.

Other people said and did other things, too numerable to account for. People were getting lost by their own abundance. They had been "together" too long, or apart in the same company. So much solitude would need regaining! It had been diverted, loudly serenaded away, but never totally strung loose.

"It's my apartment!" Page Slickman shouted, but no one heard him. Or if they did, it wasn't apparent. A silence was gripping the evening. And dawn approached.

Ultimately, the window introduced it. This was honest of the window, but furtive and mistimed of the dawn, whose traditional fresh purity found a supreme misplacement here.

Some sleepers were still sleeping. Other people snored awake. Morstive, observing the sprawled heap of decadent and worn-out humanity, admitted to himself a pang of hunger, experienced privately in the stomach cavern, and asked, out loud, "Doesn't anyone like me? If I get a job, and a girlfriend, can't I be popular, if I please?

But I'm independent of it. That's because I'm a true realist." Then, to back up his words, he fell down, and didn't get up. Not for a long time.

New Year's Day! But where was everybody?

No more party? No more job too. The party's fee was costly. Keegan Dexterparks had smudged him on a grudge, but was gone. A year ago there'd been a New Year's party that set tongues to wagging. But it was no party next to *this* one! This one would set off endless repercussions, waves of more magnitude than the ripples before. What a dreary end, to what a living event! He wouldn't be long through, with what he'd just been through. (Exhaustion was here, offering a brief punctuation.) A party to end parties, and begin a new one.

PART 2

ooooooooooooooooooooc

oo 1 ooooooc

Physically as well as emotionally alone, in the familiar privacy of his apartment, recuperating from complicated aftermaths in reacting to his own recovery from symptoms of the party hangover on which his useless nerves were drying out, Morstive, a few days remote from the event, still shook occasionally, and shuddered down a sympathetic chill, glancing away from shocks rawly recent, into disengaged agony, from which the forces of his involvement were in major retreat, wildly fleeing. "Enough of that," he said, and took another aspirin. "There. Be still." The swallow would divide worse from better: a good, symbolic physical act. "I want to be alone," he said, seeing how he *was*, and desiring only what could be attained, thus maturing his ideals into dull moderation and curbing the riots of expectation. "This is sufficient. Now can be enough. Let me be. All I am is only Morstive," he said, and confirmed this by the mirror, which reflected, without deviating, his self-enclosed image, direct as the sun's warmth. Thus Morstive shrunk, to gain out his fullest stature.

His window recognized a winter sun, and kept out the all-night frost. His muscles were gluttons for nonactivity, that most quiescent of all sports. His easy-to-gratify tiredness produced so comfortable a relaxation that the dynamics of tension evaporated almost visibly; and only a soft indolent glow, diffused all over warmly, sagged him to splendid ease, floating on a rich cloud of laziness that glided into graceful serenity and loafed into the vacant breeze, a tranquil calm of well-being. "What's next?" he asked, instantly on the alert, when regrets piled on to recent disasters to disturb past traumas and renew the alarm of fear to ruin the knitted harmony that worried the beads of his brow and wrinkled the flabby deposits of his brain, folded in a box of thoughts with the lid operated by a close emotional currency rigging dangerous wires to the soul's emergency valve, automatic to an explosive breakdown, deep back in the utmost layer of the repression-clad unconscious, where impulses are chained down and kept under constant torture, and sanity hangs on to life by a whisker of death, pulled on the leash by a veil of the tear on the verge, rescued by God's question of existence, for which "Nothing" has approximated the modern version of an answer, and despair faces nihilism while happiness fades, increasing the social significance of psychology as a major science, with mental health a patriotic "must," if this country is to remain strong. Reassured, he became inert. The telephone mustn't ring. The door is locked. Security is safely at hand. The refrigerator is near, with loyal handle. Ease outthrusts worry; will it stay?

His bank was swollen with savings, and his unemployment was compensated by insurance, so no need need go begging, as he withdraws from worldly friends and enemies and their savage confrontations, to sink inward and bask in scars nursed by mother soul, the wounds of experienced innocence. "And I have a few shares in the company," he said, intending to hold on. Be lulled, there's no pinch. Just don't shift, avoid contact with outward conflict of people, and sit cool to be still, negate the efforts to accomplish desire by hauling down desire's banner from its own pole, divorce frustration from its unattainable objects, renounce the cure of loneliness (a girl friend), accept deprivation of glory and approval in others' eyes, scorn the frantic popular fear of rejection, and simply settle in. Be based sweetly deep, balance out a sufficiency of self, the freedom to give oneself a gift of independence and to receive the use of that gift, unhampered by vain regrets, pinings, longings, for the luxury of the unnecessary, fluff of empty frill. Strip bare, shun temptations toward an illusory extravagance of pleasure and values of possessed commodities dear to a mean instinct, an acquired acquisitiveness defiant of the soul's delight, contrary to joy's sweetest modesty, life enhanced by its own beauty, not padded out to a faithless fascination with things or drugged out bloated by a pouring on, a piling up, of thin excitements in delirious sense, rewarded by agony and remorse. No, he decided to be genuine and not look for too much. "I'll be creative," he said, and explored himself for evidence of a writing talent, a literary bent. How great, to define life by refining groups of words into related significance, and restore order to a remodeled universe, seeing people as they are. "Now I'm not afraid," he said, feeling powers of God drift into him from dimensions in time and motions of space, granting him an insight into cosmic unity. So he began writing, but unfortunately, he wasn't talented.

"I'll make a play," his inspiration declared, "using as my central character the rise and fall and rise again of that tragic nonentity, the heroic Morgan Popoff. There, that's a subject of magnitudes, and a fiery test of style. Hulda Stock, unless I change her name, will love or even adore him, though she lives with a roommate, patterned after Emma Lavalla, who has her own affair going, with the confused and lost Merton Newberg, whom I shall portray, however, as one deserving of the reader's sympathy—an outcast in an outcast age. Already, I can see my play taking shape. As a genius, my fame is assured, and majestic royalties will accumulate. I'll tour Europe, and donate to charity, philanthropically. Constantly photographed, I'll be known to every newspaper reader. And yet, I'll be sublime, and ideal, indifferent to glory. Simple at heart, despite my complicated art, over which the critics will wage unending disputes, debating my immortality and my other literary merits before my works are even half completed, so swift are laurels impatient to decorate my brow and perform other fancy conceits that I never labored for: I'll be a natural primitive, like Burns and Blake, despite the sheer Pope-like sophistication of my polished craft and exquisite chiseling. I'll be technique's wizard, yet modest about the world's awe that gilds me in fame. For I'm devoted, utterly devoted, to art, as a substitute for love. No woman, no wife. Only art, the Spartan mate."

Pinching himself for unbelief, he sketched out a creation of characters, and outlined the play. He wanted to reserve space in the newspaper to advertise it, but it wasn't finished yet, and needed casting. Only the best actors would do, and a world-renowned director. Better, maybe he should make a movie? That would guarantee a larger audience, though albeit less discerning. But in his magnanimity, none would be turned away. No snob was he, for he even welcomed philistines, and other semi-illiterates, to appreciate his vast art, his moving drama. Surely, he was universal to the point of all-inclusiveness, of any human description. Even people from other countries should kiss his broad beam. Why confine luck to the mere American?

Then, he must think of translations, into foreign tongues. He would commission Dante to do an Italian version, Goethe to transcribe it into German, Cervantes to give it a Spanish flavor, Homer to impart Greek nobility to it, Rabelais to carve it into a typical French gem, and Shakespeare to translate it for the English. Indeed, what a masterpiece it would be! Something to outlast the ages, even with thermohydronuclear warfare destroying libraries, theaters, and other institutions for the dissemination of culture: for the printed word is sacred, and shall endure, like the black-bound Bible, rock of religion. Let culture admit Morstive Sternbump, to be an equal Maker with the former Gods. Gods aren't obsolete: isn't he the latest version?

oo2oooooo

Such thinking made him hungry, so he tore himself away from his play, with acute reluctance, and saw what the refrigerator had stored up for him—for he did all his shopping on a spree. He cooked out a tidy fare, and ate it dwindling down to the last crumb, which he also ate too. No waste. Spacious largess, and no haste. According to the clock, it was afternoon. Cozy to be home, at the typewriter. No one to interfere. And as yet, the telephone was still.

He went back to work, but mainly dreamed. "But this fantasy is fertile," he said, to encourage himself. Keegan Dexterparks had given him this serenity by costing him his job in the frameup at the party. He'll be depicted in the play in a bad light. Page Slickman, Mayor Huntworth, and Piper Cole will serve the art, too. Throw in Tessa Wheaton, for character study. And naturally, pathetic Jessup Clubb, to add mystique. This play had everything, and was completely symbolic, a metaphoric analogy symptomatic of modern times. How the age would know itself! For it would fully live in this satire-to-be, its own literal reflection and definitive testament. The author will release the man; the man, the author. Free of being persecuted, he'd persecute everybody he'd known, and smart with revenge, having cast them into outlasting form, for immortality to ponder. Then, if he should die, Morstive Sternbump would submit his name to fate, and let the years learn it.

Speaking of himself, shouldn't he be in it—as a character? Yes, an autobiographical portrayal as the author, competing with Morgan for prominence, and perhaps outdoing him—winning Hulda away, and exciting envy? What name should he give himself? Something subtle, not too obvious: for a hero he would be, and conquer, in love, and war: all is fair. "It's *my* creation. Life, as seen through me: the world itself. A dream made concrete. A mental actual, acknowledged to be true. Mine!" he gloated; and fondly fingered his typewriter, from whose explosive channels the truest fiction alive would emerge intact, to alter the real world, and guide the changed destinies of men forever.

"I want to instruct, and entertain, both," he said: "and convey emotion, showing human nature beyond its own extent, and border fantastically on the believable, distort the actual so far into abstraction that life is smacked in the face with its own image, and must swallow. I'll admit only what happens, adhering to the modest proportions in scope of the everyday, events shaped by their usual commonplaces, and behold the miraculous incredible, transforming all things to their supernatural ideal, however grotesque, however absurd, or ridiculous. What remains? Only simple truth, and lasting art.

"But life is so swift," he said, "I must hurry. But yet not be careless. Ah, balance is truly the artist's mistress." Let the brain thoughts be passed to fingers. And the typewriter rambled. He bit down on the keys, and poured out characters by the hour, living and smoking. True fire was in him, and naked muses inspired him, sexy but severe. He didn't neglect tradition, however modern he was. Finally, he was forced to stop, all written out. But when he looked to survey what he had done, to his dismay, and indignation, expressed by an annoyed grimace featured together in his compressed face, he discovered with fury yet with an appropriate dash of humility that, after creating until the middle of the night with intensity and devout application and painstaking detail of trivia and herculean fortitude of restraint, he had neglected to insert paper into his typewriter, on which it fed, and so all efforts fell to no avail. Yet it was good practice, and trained his discipline, and taught him a lesson of patience. And no critic would blast it! He had tasted the marvelous, and now there was no proof. But he would be his own witness, in the jury box, testifying that no more perfect work of art had ever, in annals of recorded history, been born by miscarriage into abortion, for all the world to praise, and mourn this stupendous loss. Never would he write this effectively again. For he had reached his prime, and now was sunk dismally past, imitating his better efforts. The swift career into decay. And still, Morstive had acquired no honor! How to undo this undoing? By his own just act. He would come back, and write another play tomorrow, restoring something of his old heat and never-failing taste, the promise that was his, ambition realized, youth crowned with mature triumph. So he went to sleep, and dreamed that he was inserted into a typewriter, and rolled flat. When released, he walked out. "Your story is written all over you," his friends said, and it was true. How revealed he felt, secrets exposed, published gossip and a walking version of enduring art, life in the flesh. Next time, he would be more objective, and leave himself out. As an author, stand detached. Merely produce, and marvel.

He slept. But his ambition was awake, his project of life's work. Sleep couldn't still it: only death had that power.

He woke up into cold morning, with the radiator hissing. His near-waking dreams had been fitful and mundane; morbid, gloomy, pessimistic, denying his magnificent literary resolve: Banal memories were now scourging. They were his insolent familiars. Normality looked ugly, and he yearned to retreat into art.

And he did, with will and motivation. He courted inspiration, with ardent caress.

"The words are buzzing at me like bees. I hear them stinging my ears, pouring each death into a sting: for vitality destroys itself. How can I harness them? By characters. The people I've been knowing, through the contact of my own vitals, or through observation's safer remove. People, I really knew. Who were they, for one?" And his mind flashed, as experience came back, exposing recent pain, suffering graced by a past. He couldn't bear it, but for art's sake he stooped to remember, and climbed to see. The leftover puzzles were prodding.

"Why did Morgan Popoff, early last year, argue with his girl friend, Hulda? What broke up so ideal a romance? My conjecture must be biting, and force the issue: I'll shoot through the curtain, and read hidden meanings into everything. He was big, handsome. An executive shooting up. Hulda was perfect for him, pretty and social. And love was a fact.

"He fixed me up with Tessa, later to be his wife, while himself dating Hulda's roommate, Emma. How did Tessa win him? Was it simultaneous with his decline, the loss of his business position? She had been his confidante, a lunch-hour friend. Prudish, she worshipped him at a distance. Myself was the first one to excite her, almost. How was he inveigled into marrying her? This mystery floats off the earth, and is not supported. I need God's vision: mine is too personal.

"I took over his job, and went ahead. There had been conflict between us, and I fired Tessa and rejected him, when he applied for desperate employment. I was in power, and wielded it ungraciously. Was I its corruptive victim? My personality changed. I was Morstive, but deprived of that certain crucial essence, that stamps my identity. When Morgan fell, it was big. He became a pauper; his wife miscarried, conducted an affair with Jessup Clubb inherently degrading (for that God is a monster), descended to a life of prostitution, reversing her original trend; and now Morgan, in his reascension, earns their keep with pimping of her, and thinks lightly of it: and Hulda Stock, whom he had lost forever, is his again (stolen from my arms, just at my crucial, loneliness-killing hour). His sanity is regained, but is it official?—he escaped from confinement for the party. What's his future, given that past?

"Now, I can't get Morgan out of my mind. What did he stand for? Was he only a mask, and blank beneath? What color, and texture, qualified his soul; of what density was it; where was its center of gravity? He must have been real, or I wouldn't think about him. If only I could be sure!

"I only knew him, in and out, and some of his behavior I can't explain. Why did he phone Tessa, when I was just seducing her? He had a big effect on my life, last year. I desired his Hulda, but she was always his. Who can explain this? And why was he such a friend to Jessup?—someone so unworldly, and he matter-of-fact. And we fought at the party. Here's a whole background to explore.

"And then, what of Tessa herself? How could a person change so much? Where is design; or can some formula tie this up neatly in a bundle, in a Christmas package, to be opened at will, and the truth sparkles out in concrete, tangible as a toy a child can handle? There she was, a thin typist. She wore glasses, and was going to be an old maid. Why didn't she, what held up that progress, the advanced evolution of her virginity? Now, she's nothing but an opposite, volatile like a jumping rubber hot coal.

"Jessup wanted to confiscate her child by Morgan, but she defied him by miscarrying, though unintentional. She began dominating Morgan, and shrewed him to bits. They were hard up, so she had to go to the gutter, after my dignified firing of her—how can I live it down, myself so harsh? Yes, she became a whore. And now that Morgan is himself again, he doesn't discourage her, but becomes her actual pimp. Shameful, at the party. They really wore her out. All this is so decadent! Such will my play be. Or will a novel better bear the material?

"And those other people I knew, now only as legends to me—

what fantastic realms they lived in, how they stood out, doomed by what they were! Who next would I tackle? A whole psychology book, by an expert, would revolve around Jessup Clubb, a complex cross between the land of idea and the earth of our sanity, in whom mingle all conflicts known to man, the worst deceits and ugly ruinings of self, that I manage only in horror to see, but clench my eyes. His mere existence staggers very credibility.

"Jessup is too much to go into. He dressed like an ancient savior, with fitting beard, and manners to match. He was always deferring, yet on top. The most accomplished hypocrite, and still a martyr. Viciously destructive, yet professing a holiness, which condoned everything. I simply can't understand. It all seems like it should be in a book, but not in the world itself, where only reality happens. Why do I doubt what I believe? Am I hardened against miracles, has experience excluded the impossible? I must take count, and go down to basics. A B C. The fundamentals. Or even what they're reducible to. I must strip every layer, to the irreducible core.

"But what would be there? Would I even understand it? It would be *too* basic.

"Maybe we can only recognize the *least* basic things. All the overlay, all the extraneous—but never the essential. The essential is exactly what we're blind to. We have superficial eyes, only.

"But back to Jessup—ugh! Is that necessary? For such an inhibited saint, unworldly, he did all right by the flesh, and got his. Hulda and Emma served simultaneously as his mistresses, and he moved in with them, being but essentially poor, as well as a golden opportunist. But neither conceived his all-wanted boy-child, to flesh forth a dynastic immortality of spirit. And Tessa Wheaton, he took, as her lover, when Morgan was removed by his decline. Formerly Morgan's good friend, he had now deserted him. Is *that* being religious? Some son of God!

"And Merton once beat him up. Good work. Complicated sex and violence in the life of a man of peace. And the disgraced mayor is his friend, imploring his help. And over a year ago, he had insulted Tessa, New Year's party before last. And at the last one, he begged to be crucified, despite the popular election of me for martyr. And he had so many conversions to his credit, with that sermon. Merton was one of them. Conversion to what, it's hard to tell. And all the children donated to him, in return for divine indulgences Hereafter. What wiles! Who will succeed him? It's all beyond me.

"Yes I met him going to the party, and we went in the taxi. Boy, what a party, for us both! And me, *I*'m a case! Boy, if you want material, how about me?

"But I don't dare to write about myself, since detachment is the artist's craft, and my content must bulge with these others. I must keep out of this. I'll narrate. I'll be the omniscient observer. How's that for a point of view? But everyone else will get it; they'll get it, but good.

"Keegan Dexterparks avenged me for some old offense at the party, getting me fired, by raping my boss's wife and claiming I did it. I owe my being at liberty to him. What had been our bygones? I've forgotten it, by some distortion. I remember his being very black-conscious. That's his own skin-coloring, over his entire surface. With certain exceptions, like for example teeth. What's his sperm-coloring? I'll ask Mrs. Turkel Masongordy. If she's conscious. People do collide lives in instants, don't they?

"People! All in my life. I'm a central meeting place, for their convergences. My contemporaries, in this city in time. I *am* the city. It's all in me."

 oo4ooooo

"Oh, I'm so hungry! But back to my thoughts. Oh yes, the people. And what I'll make of them. I'll make them all, in me.

"Just thinking of these people is already an act of arranging. Why, my novel is writing itself! The composition will be detailed out, in a generous pattern. I must find connections, between these separate sorts. Sorts? Individuals, that defy becoming simple types, or abstract concepts. Yet who can withstand the mind's grouping?

"Then how can I leave out Merton Newberg, and I'll treat him with sympathy, a lost soul. He finds himself everywhere, but it's not *him*. Now, he's joined Emma again, but only as on leave from his insane asylum, where he's a regular inmate. Morgan beat him up good, when he protested the abduction of Emma, after that notable and weird double date. This is a whole history! I can get carried away. I'll embroider whatever happened.

"This Merton, while he was waiting for his Emma to come back on the arm of Morgan, who was, as said, to beat him up, with Hulda in the girls' apartment, where now still Jessup holds fort, was visited by Jessup and really slammed him good, as only asked for and deserved, within the strange setting of the circumstance. Merton is easily convertible, like some kind of car. He never had the chance to do me dirt, but there I go with me again: I must stop. I must be invisible, and act behind scenes like God does, without taking the credit; except as the work becomes art, and I'm accused of being the author, the creator in the prime person. The hunger is increasing, and the limit it will withstand is a sandwich, breaded thick and separated by huge hunks inside. Showing me plainly human, despite my recent elevation to a cloudy artist's status, copying out fate with iron words as the Muse dictates. Well, Merton has taxed my imagination, sufficed it, and by association Emma must act upon the stage, assigned to my next interview. From this plateau, I view those mortals below, and infuse them with all the appearance latent in their spirit, by which they accomplish essence. But as I'm salivating, there's no choice. Let me refuel my mental arrangements, so that my stomach can't complain.

"Delicious. And the telephone, it's behaving beautifully, with all its peopled silence. Now who was Emma? She was plainer than Hulda, yet on planes of equality with her, except for Morgan. Refuted by him, she's taken on her Merton, for better or worse. Between reconciliation, Jessup tried her (with Hulda) for size, apparently fit, yet not one baby betrayed that wicked affair; leaving her ministerially clean, for the clergyman to ally her, in a church of all peace, to her just claim on Merton's remains; for halted things are often resumed, blind to intervals between, and take on the old way to usually continue, though on a more tired slant, following the road downhill beyond to the point from which return returns, embarking back on the same uneven course, and arriving where the start has fled, and the finish has barely begun. Motion moves life forward, but life stalls motion to move backward, so then where were we? Going somewhere; but the somewhere does all our going, and changes on route. Which is where we only were, to be. What I become. Hulda now is within threshold. But what can I reminisce? For I've put away vanity, while the register of past perceptions tunes the string of my instrument, with heard-already music. All tunes are by recollection. And yet, the notes must seem new.

"Hulda was superior rival to Emma, shared some same disgraces, but rejected me twice; and now her pre-original destiny, her truthful source Morgan on whom she waged dispute, has become reconciled, and I fear it's the altar this time. But first, poor Tessa must have her divorce, to avoid complicated enstranglements society will alertly prohibit. People overlap, and interlap. New sinnings keep old beginnings.

"And again, the telephone observes its usual silence. As a writer, I need an agent. Now who is crookeder than Page Slickman? Therefore, he will do.

"Ah, I'm all alone. I have freedom at home. Going to the daily work office had all that business stuff. But *here*, alone at home, I'm free to make my own business, out of all these people; to give them the business. To 'work' them in, somehow.

"As the raw material of people, they go through a conversion process, and come out as characters. That makes them truly mine. I've lifted them out, do them down, and now own their little effigies. But I won't *un*make them. They'll be let be—but on *my* terms, now. I'm boss. I run this business. They work, for me.

"*Me? That*'s a problem, in itself.

"Will I change the names of my characters, suitable as fiction requires, and to avoid infamy of sued libel, when coincidence occurs with life—no matter how living or dead? Maybe perhaps of course inevitably—if at all necessary. There must be a line, and in front of it life ends, while back of it art creates, departing to meet. I understand little of what happened, so by writing beautiful words I'll pretend I knew. I may not have talent, but I fancy myself a genius. My stomach tells me. Loving to be fed, it rewards me with grand illusions, and stout jolly thoughts. I'm hearty, and robust. I can even grip a fist, and squeeze the blood white: all on the same hand. On the *other* hand—but no, I hate to contradict myself. For I was born contradicted, so it's a cinch. The rest is easy. I *find* it hard; to accentuate the easiness. Being my own fool, I'm the first one to be fooled. Then I wait, and also become the last. The fun is what happens between. Self-deception is my code of truth, my unfledging principle of honor, a duty first and all. It teaches me all I know.

"Other than that, I guess. While Hulda and Merton, both betrayed, waited for Emma to return with Morgan, they planned and plotted. Though it failed then, now they both have their lovers back. The four met in the apartment, clashed their emotion against the rocks of dissipation, and now all is smooth harmony again, and love is distributed in regular allotments, like in the fabled romances of old. Are modern times so negative then? We want *when* we want, but later we get it—or we don't, and it becomes the same thing. But this is an idle philosophy, the gossip of fate, chattering destiny. I'm only one person. Who are the others? *Are* there others? Or are they just me, in variations?

"Then I'm all of them, as so many characters. I bulge and crack, with this pressure. Let it all come out."

∞5∞∞∞∞

"There, I have characters now, by having been alone. Being inside has 'turned out.' But it feels stale in here. I'm restless. A city apartment has good and bad sides, for isolation. Solitude creates characters, but leaves the people.

"I open the door, and someone has left a paper in the hall. I can catch up on world news. Keeping by myself tends toward ingrowth. Here is this fling outward, running through the headlines, and snatching at what's past.

"This paper is certainly no tabloid. Now, where is there not an advertisement? Perhaps on the first page. I see the world's in trouble, and diplomats are getting political, restraining ideologies to keep a warm peace while international differences divide harmony out, and costly ammunition is manufactured underground, capable somewhat of destruction. So nothing's new. But as I peruse the city news, those local headlines of minor disaster and less earthshaking character of consequence, I read here of three old friends: the honorable mayor, whom I knew to be Ira Huntworth; and Piper Cole, as always; and there's Page Slickman, trying to deny what he so outrageously did, with the goods pinned on him; and their photographs, showing detectives too. This is more than quaintly interesting. It's real human-interest, to spike up my story, with political overtones: demonstrating corruption rampant, and the higher circles folding horns with the lower, fascinating to behold. Innocently safe, smugly comfortably virtuous, I self-righteously view their public-scandaled guilt, with open culpability that improves my passive rectitude.

"All these tell-tale photos! Here's one of the mayor and Piper taken right outside the New Year's party I saw them at, for I recognize the house. They had just left the party, and they're shown as handicuffed together. I don't recall their being thus bound at the party. The crowd was swirling, to blur out detail. Thank God for historical retrospect, to iron out fuzziness by giving a belated focus. An event can only be seen clearly afterward, when the molecules have stopped tumbling about. Or do they *still* tumble about, later, but by our own direction?—since what's happening is over and stops dictating to us? Then *we*'re in control, for selective seeing. For the *having-seen*. For the conception.

"Back to the paper. Mingled text and pictures. Ah, look, here's Page himself, to the life. Or to his lives, for who is he?

"The photograph shows a mustache on Page, a semblance of his non-photographed self, when he twirls through his many dimensions, like a scape-rope artist, leaving tricky clues on a false mirror and following his own footstraps to print his criminality behind, outlasting a sordid record, a career blueprinted in crime. The paper says that after a New Year party a common-clothes policeman, on off beat, felt something in his nose, and on closer examination it proved to be an odor. Bent on this scent, he lit upon no less than the mayor himself, handicuffed to a non-lawyer, Piper Cole. They had been dumped in an ash can, which could barely contain them both. When revived, they displayed arrogant emotions, and snarling countenances. 'Go back in the apartment, and pull Page along,' authorized the mayor to this defender of the law.

"But the apartment was vacant, and an at-rent sign had been put up, presumably by a delayed superintendent. It was late at afternoon, on New Year's day. The ash can was in front of the building, down a few steps from the first floor entrance for where this party had been committed, against city regulations for concealing the minimum decency from the public maximum offense, which is shock and horror. But sprawled on the floor, there was Page. 'I confess to being drunk,' he said. It was the least he could be, considering the most he had already done.

" 'Dunk him into the swimming pool,' ordered a most benevolent judge, when the court was tried. (For when it had gotten out of order, the judge sternly shook his gavel and demanded 'Odor in the court,' which by then was superfluously redundant, as the wit-

68

nesses could testify.) Therefore the scandalous swimming pool sold at profit to a cheap city mayor was produced in the courtroom, and promptly filled with water.

"But the mayor intervened: 'Ask him to identify the whoever hostess of the assumed apartment, and to trace wherever her whereabouts may have been, for public consumption,' this high official suggested. Page was stripped, leaving only his torso, where hair still clung; then, demonstrating a breast stroke, he swam. Thus, he made a clean sweep of anything alleged, and was dried off the record, with a municipal towel off which moths had dined in better days, when prices were by far cheaper.

" 'Acquit them, Your Honor,' said the head of the jury, one Jessup Clubb, attired with no concession to the conventions as observed by these tumultuous times. Piper was set free, and told to do his dirty business. The mayor was washed all over, and then some. It was all ordered repeated again, as TV cameras snapped, focusing on private view. Thus the scandal was aired, and a prominent laundry called in (the courtroom was capacious). Crimes were reviewed, repented of, and the mayor was thrown out of office, for better service. Politically, he was snapped up by a State boss, and considered for Governor. For his slate had been wiped clean, and his public morality was high. The evil he had done had run out of consequences.

"As an upshot, the city is mayorless, and run by deputies. Page is at large, and the dirt that filled the swimming pool has since evaporated, returned to gaseous elements, and will descend with rain again. Nothing destroyed, nothing created. Matter, essential.

"Piper Cole, unhandcuffed, has bought a prizefighter, and become his manager. He's gathered his bookies together, for a major conference. The odds are expected to soar, with the championship in stake. 'Boxing is no racket,' Piper said, 'but a legitimate sport.' Offered a lie-detector test, he refused, it being beneath his dignity to be accused of a lie he didn't make before he even got around to invent it when necessity proposed, timing it to do the most good when truth is covered by suspicion and looking the other way. 'I'm not a fraud, I'm not a cheat,' he maintained, and his weight supported him: for the rumor was verified, as his heaviness was evident right there.

"Page, when questioned whether married, said yes but out of town. 'I'm a model of a husband's paragon,' he reported, and pursued an empire of makeshift enterprises that improvised some casual ways of coming by money, inventing unique techniques to force an unprecedented set of circumstances.

"I enjoyed these articles very much. I'll locate Page, and commission him my agent, so that his crookedness can be cashed in by me honestly. Even now, the book is being born."

He laid down his newspaper. Now, to put memory to hand. A miscellany of blended informations, to come out as what? Make the people make sense. Give them their own characters.

∞6∞∞∞∞

Morstive wrote, on penalty of pain, and swallowed down many an oath, ripping out page after page, burning the inferior passages and misplacing the even more inferior passages, due to author's-absent-mindedness. He wrote with a pen, intending to transfer its glittering contents to the hacking style of a typewriter, already well papered. He was endowed with immaculate technique, as proved by every word he didn't write. The plot was bad to begin with, and got worse later. Why spend himself all at once? Save something to be left over, to assure a steady jump of progress. He wrote with honest reserve, saying what he had to say, though of course failing to say it. His characters were Morgan, Jessup, Merton, Ira, Piper, Page, and little-known black Keegan, for a male cast; and for women, he used Tessa, Hulda, and Emma. But wasn't there something centrally essential missing? Too close to even notice? The more hideously blatant, then. He left himself out, yet was everywhere to be seen, as that absent obtruder, standing between the reader and his light. The typewriter clangled, sucked, and brutalized the message. It was a short story, in novel form; and too lengthy. "Now I must cut it," he said, and began editing. This he did deftly, with harsh imprecision, and left nothing standing. Then, it was ready for publication.

He asked the telephone operator to locate Page Slickman for an agent. "Oh, I know him by heart," she answered, for it was the mysterious non-hostess: and went on, "He's out of town."

70

"I want him back, as a subscriber to your company's service," Morstive requested, and waited, while the line was busy. "I'm not going to be an author for nothing," he said.

"Go ahead, here's your party now," said the operator.

"Hello Page, be my agent," offered Morstive.

"You strike a hard bargain," said Mr. Slickman, who at that time was involved in shady dealings.

"I wrote a non-book, so publish it," Morstive demanded, and struck a literary pose (for telephones will soon be televised).

"You're impressive," Page said, "but I want my money now."

"How much?"

"A lot."

"Fair; it's a deal." That concluded their transactions.

Loaded with the terrific urge of incentive, Morstive kindled a blaze of his frantic idleness. He struck with a shot of heat. "Now I'll write my autobiography," he said, and proceeded to do so. For he was a man of action. And the ink didn't run dry.

He wrote all about himself, under terrific pressure. He was thoroughly at home with the subject, and used notes from previous interviews, granted for lack of time. He wrote until his hand had squeezed the pen into invisibility, so intense and concentrated was his passion, at self-confession. "I want it sold to the movies," he said, and just then a knock was heard. That sleek opportunist had arrived.

"I'm here to deal with you," leered Page Slickman. "I have a swimming pool, dirt-cheap."

"But I don't need it."

"Of course you do: for writing underwater."

This argument was irrefutable. Morstive was in the swim, again. "Here are my memoirs," he pointed out.

"I know a publisher tomorrow," Page promised.

"And then an *objective* book, with all my characters, that I wrote beforehand," Morstive submitting it.

"Is it censored?"

"No."

"Then do it now, to win a clean bill of approval."

"Why?"

"Public morality is precious. We must safeguard it from all angles."

"But will I be famous?"

"Yes; you don't call yourself an author if you're not, do you?"

"No."

"Then pay me, and you'll be a rich man."

"Is that a promise?"

"Why not?—everything else is," said Page, beginning to cheat him. "You need a pen-name, a pseudonym," said the evil sharpster; "for 'Morstive Sternbump' sounds too true to be good, and so loses the color of its dignity."

"What name would you suggest?"

" 'Page Slickman,' at a shot."

"But won't we be confused?"

"That's the purpose."

(A pause while that was sunk in. The last speaker had won some ascendancy.)

"I won't buy that," reneged Morstive, turning puny again.

"Buy! Who said buy? Don't you want to sell it?"

"Yes."

"Then be me, under my name."

"Why?"

"Because I'm famous already, and you don't have a chance till you've already made your name."

"Made it?"

"Or changed it. Do like I told you. Why argue?"

"Give me a little time," asked Morstive.

"What for? If I give you enough time you'll die, from a natural old age."

"Then let my old age be artificial," said Morstive, "and nature create my fame."

"You're an idealist," said Page, who knew about these things.

They clashed. And Morstive rejected him. Page was about to play his trump card, and falsely sue, or threaten infamy by court. His strident voice was cut short. "If you don't stop, I'll write about you," threatened Morstive, already overheated. Soon, it would be February. That's how time goes.

They still argued. "I hate you," said Morstive.

"Now you're belligerent," said Page, who was sensitive along these lines, made delicate by adverse experience.

"But I do," Morstive insisted, with sincerity that would make art blush.

"I believe you," relented Page, and harmony was restored, on its only basis, considering the antagonists. "I'll have you published," Page offered.

And Morstive was shy: "But I don't want that," he said; "I'd be too popular." A compromise was in store. Page used every trick he could, and Morstive, by sheer luck, resisted. But what had been their dispute? Was argumentation, only, at issue? Or was money at the very point, in a personal tussle? Page was a confusing obstacle. But to what? Morstive was trailing in this contest. Time for more words. "You," he accused Page, "are reality in the cold world."

"Am I?" asked Page.

"I only think so, but perhaps you know."

"Where's your manuscript?"

"It's burned."

"Where's your other?"

"The same fate."

"Then it's not practical for you to become an author, and I resign as your agent."

"But our contract?"

"We have none—now goodbye."

"Well, I guess I'm not artistic," said Morstive, and abandoned his ambition, in Page's departing wake, the door fast shut. "So I'll give up my literary pretensions, and accept the world again. Its damage can only be neutral this time, for I'm immune, and surgery has numbed me. I'll leave my nerves home, open the door, and discover whatever befalls me. Thus, I'll force my fate." This he did, but tripped. He was weak from hunger.

So he ate. And attempted again, like a legless swimmer approaching the vast ocean, where even fishes drown, when lungs suction for the right liquid air but no swelling breath takes place in wetness everywhere unfriendly. So Morstive dove out. And sure enough, it was raining. Sob. Drop teardrops. Make from eyes what comes from skies. Let no place be left dry.

He plowed right through, cleansing himself. It was between evening and morning, yet not night, and still offered some dusk. Morstive wildly bellowed. He had allowed himself a month to write, both
about others in a rigid and selective style of scientific exactitude,
and about himself, speaking for the first person, of which he was
singular. His words were chosen, but in a hapless fashion, and as
the pages compiled, were dismissed out into the flaming window or
trampled underfoot, for all verbs and nouns failed him; and adjec-
tives, like sauce to cover up inferior meat, were appropriate to
nothing, dwindled into adverbs, flirted with pronouns, dated con-
junctives, and gambled away punctuation marks: until sentence
structure appealed to paragraph formation, and remained unaccept-
able to chapters, whose blank pregnancy of structure was an exercise in vacancy; and pages rambled off stuttering by themselves,
dismissing organization. The book had nothing to lean on, and the
characters merely quit, lending their ashes to the nearest fire, and
throwing their phoenix pins away. Morstive had failed, fame eluded
him; and even his self-confessions, in the worst autobiography ever
attempted, took their cue from no sense, and gave off none either.
So he dampened into the rain, raved steam into his boiling freeze,
and mourned his mad loss of ambition and career: Not even of a
preposition was he the master, and grammar was a wrinkled blur.
"It's the world for me!" he shouted, rejecting what he thought was
art, and had never created: scorning what he was beneath, and
hardening into a Page Slickman, whose values had to be materially
proven, or hid no consequence. "I'm all alone," he said, walking as
far as the post office. There was a grocery supermarket, there a toy
store, here a bakery, there an outlet for stationary gadgets, and
nowhere was paradise. The street was closed, and he soaked in the
rain. Here was a loan shop. And even a bookstore. Thus, his neighborhood had culture.

The night drizzled out, and bleak morning stretched grayly.

Symbolic outdoor weather Morstivated the universal inward of mood in a sludge life.

Morstive was drunk with power unpossessed, and crushed the crippled world to his slovenly chest, where the rib cage pressed at the skin, tiding away the minutes toward death. "I hate my own birth," Morstive said, and thought how heavenly romance would be. Abandoning the literary enterprise, what would he do instead? The firm glamor of action was required. "My being is made and remade by all my doings." Muttering thus to himself, he cruised his footsteps home, and went in on his own neurosis. Deep dissatisfactions craved for change. He grumbled mutinous broodings. Morstive gave up on ideals, and went to bed looking for a substitute.

He slept clenched in steel black, a fortress admitting no dreams. As usual, he slept alone.

Which might have been well, for his waking mouth was as foul as his mood, as sour as his hopelessness. His visions were dead.

There were no prospects. His project had been to write. He had holed himself up, and isolatedly did so. He had written in a cocoon retreat. He had sought inward, for the gushing fountain. It was dry, a mirage. Within—no yield. "Even writing troubles me into the world," he thought, as his ivory tower came crashing down. Among the splinters, he gasped. All hope was strewn in ruins. The private world failed. Let's exploit the *out*side, now. Let's invade.

Disillusionment. He'd lash out, at will. The relief had a nasty tang. Then so be it.

"Anything goes," he said, feeling bitterly arbitrary. Despair felt fleetingly free. He reached for his phone, anonymously called a friend, sank in an insult, and hung up with quiet complacency. It was pleasing to wound; destruction was best, when creation was withheld. Malice was the right tone now.

Irked by his incompetence, irritated by his insufficient support of spoiled and demoralized pride, he longed to do damage. Had he a friend left, to trust? He was out of contact. He phoned Hulda's and Emma's apartment, for now it was evening again, the hour for supper time. Jessup did not answer. The voice was familiar: Morgan's.

"As the mayor's last act before his removal from office, he cut me off from Tessa, and though I miss the pimping revenue I'm free to do what I damned only want. Here's what will be. Sunday, at an antidenominational church of open liberal tolerance granting any persuasion, I'll be hooked on to Hulda for life. Thus, I've made a bold circle to clasp my beginning. Here's where we all came in, before discord began whirling out its tricks. We're your friend again. Bring us a gift, and come to the wedding."

Fearing for a rising telephone bill, Morstive was fascinated to continue, remembering his tidy bank account. "A divorce, huh? And what will Tessa do?"

"The same, but she's out of my hands."

"I imagine other hands are soiling her," Morstive said.

"I'm through with it," said Morgan.

"And what has Jessup done? Your bride had some time shaking him out."

"He left swiftly, with a kidnapped child."

"But didn't everyone donate him one at the party?"

"Yeah, but they changed their collective minds, and left him fatherless. So he swiped a kid from a carriage."

"When?"

"The first week of this year. Didn't you read the papers?"

"No, I was writing a book."

"Has it been accepted for publication?"

"Yes, on tissue paper. It's rolling off the press."

"That's good. So you're a genius?"

"Sometimes."

"And in your *spare* time, what are you?"

"A general failure, all around."

"Isn't a compromise possible?"

"When I work one out, I'll let you know."

"I wish you would."

"Listen, we've been talking a long time," worked in Morstive, "and I'm tired of my own rotten food, as a male cook, keeping bachelor quarters in a stale miscast role, rather than being a rolling husband. So as a sign of good will, please do me the generosity of inviting me to dinner tonight."

"But it's already cooking—do you realize what hour it is?"

"Then let it cook a little more, and turn the fire down—I have claims on you and Hulda, and mean to assert them."

"You're welcome, of course—"

"I should think so."

"But aren't you intruding?"

"Not at all—don't you mind a bit."

"Then come over—but don't impose."

"Why should I? You're not put out?"

"Not the least. I'll just eat less, that's all."

"I'll be there in a few minutes."

"Won't the bus be slow?"

"But I'll tell the driver to hurry up."

"I think you've changed."

"So do I."

Morstive arrived, and table was set. He demanded huge gossip, and got it. He, Hulda, and Morgan chewed food, spewed words. Morstive felt at home—theirs. He carefully didn't look at Hulda, to whom his dangerous attraction was ill-fated on past occasion, met with that ultimate of replies, unrequition. And a history of ups and downs had stormed his relations with Morgan, requiring an arrogant tact. Demons snarled from the past. Dodge their forked venom. Act like nothing happened. It's now, isn't it? However past-plagued, now would put on a new face. Let trembling features dissemble. Make the look do the being.

"And are you completely sane?" the guest asked the host.

"In my opinion, yes. But I'm an escaped lunatic, you know. They're tracking me down, thus objectifying paranoia. When they catch hold of me, Hulda will sign a release, vouching for my sound behavior, and no visible mental quirks. Won't you, dear?"

"Darling, of course," Hulda smiled, just like in the movies.

Morstive was impressed. This warm demonstration of premarital fidelity consigned him to his usual envy, which, by taking pains to conceal, he suffered to increase, until, almost intolerable, it had to be discarded and other subjects promoted in its stead. For example, now that he and Morgan were both out of the same job, they discussed it from cynical, but pained, detachment; and avoided blows. "And where's Merton?" Morstive felicitously switched, swerving at a distance: "And he brings to rise Emma; so where is she at the same time? Is he cured of his affliction? Is betrothal their remedy? Where, along the progress of destiny, have they been committed? Ah, life, love, and trouble. What a trio!"

Morgan shifted his napkin, and pinched himself into manners. His benevolence shone forth.

Hulda went on being hungry, picking at the food. Nor could she be faulted, since her deportment was dainty, and feminine to a fault.

"He carried her away, took her right out of this apartment, and we haven't heard from them. We assume they're all right," Morgan spoke.

"And was Merton incurably pronounced sane?" Morstive politely asked. As a guest, it was his responsibility to keep interest active, and stray attention from slackening. For his were civilized times, when men eat with forks, and decorum is considered an excellent social skill, implying graceful manners, and an easy air, casual and nonchalant, yet stiffly formal. Of such extremes does civilization weave its complexity, allying instinct with poised denial, compromising the forbidden with the forbidding. Morgan was a beast underneath him, but he had his clothes on. And Hulda, of course, never went to the bathroom, having been born completely clean, and possessed of this habit ever since. She was so refined, that not the slightest fart gave loud outrise to necessity, shoving the gates wide open.

"This is a night I'll remember," Morstive complimented them.

"So glad you came," and they both shook his hand. And smiles were exhibited all around, darting from hand to mouth, and missing not a single cue. Oh, the evening had been successful!

ꝏ8ꝏꝏꝏ

As Morstive walked home, he was unsatisfied. Curiosity pricked him. Was it true about Jessup? Had he at last violated society, and subjected himself to a live crime, not his subtle sado-masochism, but one actually punishable, a deed for whose definite sake the whole science of criminology had been invented, police forces hired and trained to violence, and prisons built, as end products of an enforced penal code, to protect innocent citizens? If so, good. He deserved what he would get. Kidnapping is not a light misdemeanor, nor a felony on reflex, but an offense notoriously federal—despite the excuse Jessup would whip up from his occult cosmic theology, in his disguise as a holy man. The goods were on him. Fine; justice wasn't asleep anymore, for crime had prodded it awake, concretely and tangibly kicking it, in open daylight, or the stark spotlight of

78

guilt-ridden night, confessed as soon as done, and run hideously away. It was so clear. And Jessup Clubb was undone.

People to be written about. It was a soft night now, and on one corner of the sky a moon was visible to all who cared; though not in perfect roundness yet, it was, as a critic would put it, substantial. Yet critics ignore the moon, and concentrate on literature, to poke mockery into sacred words, tear poems apart, analyze novels out of existence, and occasionally praise: for a fee, or for kicks. So don't write. People not to be written about, are these people Morstive reflected on. They all reflected him. He was but reflected by these people he knew. The world was too peopled. It had a stupid low average level. To hell with people of all classifications, especially the "minorities," who are democracy's darlings. Minorities should be trodden on.

These were Morstive's thoughts, walking home. Feeling inferior to anyone but himself (whom he privately scorned), he wanted to trounce on the underdog, to borrow a limited glory, and feel safe. An artificial political confidence, rather than his own, born of integration and integrity within. In this sense, he was a Merton: but in reverse. For Merton lauded the minorities, and joined them handsomely, out of voluntary membership: Whereas Morstive found his security by being above, lifted out of pettiness, and beyond the sordid. For this excusable reason, he had neglected to vote. He was his own ego's candidate, on a split ballot: and praised himself into office, elected to an autocracy, being an indomitable king. And as every king has a fool, he was his own. The jester in him would crack jokes, and the king would refrain from laughter. Thus haughty dignity, imperial majesty, warred in lofty circles with cheap human reason and tawdry humor, the poverty of the soul. It was an internal conflict, and Morstive won, as Morstive lost.

He thought of Tessa, the mayor, Piper, Page, and the latter's out-of-town wife who never showed up except by a telephone accident—or was that the party's non-hostess, not the out-of-sight wife? "My cogitations yield negatives. There's a negative core at my life. What is my life, to me?

"I want always what I don't have. Wants always go wanting. My past is bankrupt. I have the future to fall ahead on. Have I learned enough lessons to control what will be? No. So I need a new regime. It will redirect old elements. I've tried art, and failed; kept up with my friends: seen their enmity; endured all. I must yield to the primitive, slough off the layers, and rock-bottom to the basic: What is at the core of my destiny? Am I a bestial scoundrel? An idiot intellectual imbecile? An ineffectual never-was? Earlier today, I made an anonymous phone call—and spit out an insult. And did my pride recoil? Never! Why do I have principles? What is honesty? How can this life deserve me—why do I live? Is there one worthwhile redeeming feature, some golden consolation overlooked? I wrote, and it was wretched. Nor am I a man in the world. And deplored universally by women everywhere, despite my adequate looks. I'm only of medium height. And I crave to eat. Given these, then, please explain, oh God, why I—especially I—suffer more genuinely, in all my passionate moments, than Jessup feigns to. Being barely above mortal, my vision penetrates each frustration, and strikes anxiously on the gateless residence of knowledge, opened by no door. Not one sublime entrance, while I stand beating with hope! Heart and pulse, blood, heat me through a ghost, and I radiate with spasms, and palpitate to eternity—and am not convinced! My happiest faculty is doubt—it's my only staggering capacity, the prodigious dowry for which I was born. Let me then harness it. But for what? Existence isn't enough—being born guarantees that. Let me do more—like soar. Or am I cut out for that?— For something to outlive life, during life's simultaneous duration. When?"

∞ 9 ∞∞∞∞∞∞

Arriving home, Morstive couldn't sleep. Visions moved him furiously, as he tossed on the rumbled bed, a bachelor out of sorts. Stimulations drove at him, whose temperamentally achieved outlets he could but impotently assist, so alone. Drives engaged him with images, and he saw Hulda and Morgan being married Sunday, in the smooth course of schedule. A total social event; having outlived its incertitude. A dauntless wedding, undotted by doubt. It was so natural, and shall become an easy fact to remember—intended, deviously averted, and now fulfilled. These assurances of the inevitable removed his faith in any miracle, while age without surprise would soon instruct him to expect the moderately possible, apprehend nothing further than the probable, anticipate on a percentage basis at a reasonable degree of hopelessness, and believe only in what destiny habitually provides through the merciful mechanics of wayward patronage, rewarding loyalty and dispensing a pattern of inferior compensations as tribute to years of strife and thousands of eternities spent stretching out suffering to the length of turmoil, beaten in the poor heart, lacerated through the cringing mind, creating an indestructible monument to the unquenchable pessimism of doubt, destroying the substance of hope, retarding quick promise, crushing faith, and burying the removable parts of youth in a grave forever out of reach from romantic aspiration, sentimental yearning, a nostalgic stab in the dark, and other illusions yielded by our low warm terror, begging for compassion. We implore the gods, but Morstive goes continually ignored, snubbed by Lady Fortune, whose harassed favors stray to random breasts where less deserving hearts are confined to knock, knock louder, always asking, occasionally receiving, and remembering with gratitude. "I'm tired of being myself," Morstive remarked, as casual dawn scattered the blinds and doomed him to another day. "In my solitude, I'm rarely content. There's so much to be thankless for; and if February replaces January, that's only as per schedule, and right on the mark. My future is unprepared for me, yet I'll withdraw it from the bank and use it, within the precincts of its economy. My self-pity is indefensible, since no one supports me, or passes a longing thought for my welfare and drops the consideration of a tear on my barren soul's cracked old soil, too dry to grow anything, and the sun's perennial stranger. A change is in order, dictated by futility, by the weed-crop that goes to hay on my sameness, a dismal farm of bones, where death is the most reliable product, the lonely surplus from year to year. I'll forbid myself the mirage of a self-perpetuated tear, the spring glistening with grief, breaking up the moon's shining into episodes of glimmer, sparks of fragment, moist as fresh semen from which the forbidden calculation of no child shall ensue, pleasure without progeny. Enough of too little or much. Change prays for itself. It's bought Now expensively. The tempered Now, riddled with past.

"Therefore I shall be governed differently, and the idle function of my selfishness shall be strictly useful, employed for gainful dividends, and fruits sour with delay. Spring bypassed me, and now

I return, claiming what I own. It's mine, I believe? Or is this presumptuous, to assume that somewhere in my life buried joy is mine to harvest, selected with frozen choice by fate to swing me into such eager happiness, all my bones shall sing, and my blood dances to the tide. Ah, I'm ready to reap bliss. Had I not sown remorse? Or am I moralizing, in a tone that God dislikes? I'm ready to improve. I'm sure, that in this Indian-summer of my hope, actual spring won't interfere, but be an external flower for the soul's symbol. An all-day sun-rose, red petals sweetly moist. Ah, I feel like leaping. But not right now: it's too drowsy for that. I'm already crunched in sleep. In one minute, I shall dream."

Which actually happened, except that he forgot it, being too busy asleep to watch for an extra thought with attached image, a secret code probing into his obvious unconscious, where self-preservation groped for a solution to survival, perpetuating the race. Yet, he was shy of women.

He dreamed of a Hulda-like woman, and as he was about to pull her down, she opened her chemise, and out popped Morgan, smiling his all-preserving smile of conquest, saying with true assurance, "Mine, look, she's mine," and pointing at his possession with a two-fisted finger, shaved down the middle for a wedding band, to tie a perpetual bond, for him and his heirs forever.

Hulda said, "Darling!" and kissed Morgan to the quick, igniting him to Popoff. As he fertilized her (Morstive a helpless captive to this observance), the infant was born precociously, jumping right out of conception and shunning the slow embryo stage, until ripe and male, for Jessup to quickly kidnap: "My apologies," he said, whisking the infant away, while Morgan pondered, "Why does he always act like a martyr?" and Hulda only answered, "Let's conceive another, dear," pulling him down to her.

Morgan fell in a twisting scoop: now busily invading white-shocked Hulda with a dizzy thrust of sensation, dipping in, for heaven, and even an extra heaven, even heaven's heaven.

"How jealous I am!" Morstive heard himself thinking, a witness to all this. Sad eyes, deprived of act. Sad eyes, when their owner is poorer than what they sadly only see.

Then he saw Merton Newberg, naked, frisking Emma Lavalla for any excess clothes she might be wearing under her skin, as an extra precaution, in this trapped age: "Join me," he asked, and they were united: both members of the same thing.

Still dreaming, Morstive saw Keegan Dexterparks pulling the tail of every lion in Africa, until the jungle was aroar. "We're going to be the master race," he said, to pigmy-blacks as well as to seven-footers, all war-like. He led them, and said, "Let's go, men," with an American accent. They whooped in their jungle chant, and danced in a ring.

One of them, an obvious heavyweight, boasted, "Piper Cole is managing me to de championship," with accents of a West Indian.

A swamp was uncovered, full of tears shedding crocodiles. In the stench, which included the dead corpses of monkeys, arose Ira Huntworth, saying, "Now I'm running for Governor: which way is Albany?" He was completely clean, except for freckles.

Then Page Slickman advanced, waving two unpublished manuscripts (which Morstive recognized as his, preserved some-how): "I'll sell you this for trinklets," he told the natives, "and for gewgaws: all sorts of colored tinsel, direct from a neon factory. And I'll sell you Manhattan Isle for the twenty-four-dollar Brooklyn Bridge, if you don't watch out. For my name is Morstive Stern-bump, in case punished. He's my agent, you know. This is a fair deal. Have I any buyers?" The Africans didn't understand, and called for a medicine man. It was hot, baked midday. Parakeets were whispering overhead, making dense noise, in the swinging vines. Apes were listening, closely.

A human female was being sniffed up, her presence scented by all the species afoot or on wing, in that dense creature-zoo. "Who's the campfollower?" one of the blacks asked, and Tessa Wheaton was produced, hidden in a knapsack. Between her legs, a deep red scar, powdered with aphrodisiac and other love potions, attested as to her profession.

"Take me, anyone," she asked, and the whole tribe had a whack.

"We want nationalism," Keegan insisted, and a mighty "amen" was heard, then a church-store "hallelujah."

"Let's riot," said a Negro intellectual, with a Harvard accent.

Everyone was worked into a frenzy; when lo, on the horizon, appeared Jessup, and in his hand, a Son. "They're divine," Keegan warned, and so all got down on their knees, as though the jungle were a church pew. Baboons shrieked.

"Worship me, but crucify him," demanded Jessup, pointing

alternately to himself and "Son." This was no sooner done, than said.

"There's Morstive!" someone said, spotting him.

"I ain't done nothin'," the latter admitted.

"That's tantamount to a confession," a judge decreed, and a conference was in session, plotting his elaborate fate.

Two handsome newlyweds, Morgan with Hulda at his side, heeded Morstive's prayer for instant mercy, and proceeded to rescue him, with little or no effort. "How did you do it?" Morstive asked, still breathing heavily.

"I have the knack," Morgan somehow said, in his proud business suit: for he had won his job back.

"My son is a little savior," Hulda boasted, and blushed, for she was no immaculate virgin.

Instead of sunset, the sky was rich with rainbow. "Heaven intervenes," said a religious mystic, from an unseen distance. For the place was smelling with hermits.

"Let's go swimming," Page offered, a pool proving handy. To avoid drowning, they didn't jump in. Piper was there, shadow-boxing his heavyweight potential from Jamaica. It was a colorful scene.

Then, behold: a phoenix. Rising from an urn where someone's buried ashes had been stored were two mangled manuscripts: Morstive's tale of all his friends, and his hasty autobiography, both distinctly non-typed, from a typewriter that was allergic to paper, but had genius written all over it. "They're mine!" Morstive claimed.

But Page knew better: "You're not Morstive, I am," he said, legally documented.

The mayor went over to Jessup: "You promised to restore my mayorhood, as a platform condition, to close the party ranks, and acquit me guiltfully innocent. Instead, must I kick myself upstairs into the governorship? All because you reneged on a magic vow?"

"I'm not God," Jessup informed him; "and I can only do *any*thing: but not *some* things."

"I like that!" the mayor said, indignant.

"I wonder what the United States must be like, if this is not it," pondered Morstive, for a brief political interlude. "How did these people get here? By hook, these crooks, the unsavory bunch. Did I know them? Then let me undo that knowing."

Now Turkel Masongordy was among them, the latest jungle tourist. Out of that tropical nowhere, Morstive's ex-boss had suddenly appeared. "You didn't confiscate all my back salary," Morstive reminded him.

"No, an oversight on my part," said that higher executive, who, because of shorter height, stepped on his mutilated wife, to make an effect.

"It was Keegan who raped me," she moaned, still dying, in her unearthly way. She was doomed soon to be a shade.

"But I have stocks and bonds out of your place," said Morstive, taunting the head of the firm.

"For marrying Hulda, I've given Morgan Popoff back his job," said the powerful industrial businessman, with his hand in his sleeve, from which he could teach Page Slickman a trick.

"You see, it was my wedding present, which you were too stingy to give," Morgan roared at Morstive, while wedding bells were heard, and euphoria predominated. It was an idyllic scene.

"Are we still in Africa?" Morstive asked.

"No, Albany," said the unemployed mayor, consumed by a political obsession, and wearing a bathtub for a hat.

Jessup asked, "Where's my son?" and was told, "Dead," by a native informing spy. "That's a damned shame," Jessup commented, and self-righteously shook his head, so contagiously, that when the mayor imitated, the bathtub fell off, and stubbed Morstive's toe, knocking a nail out: He yelled with delayed pain, until no one could hear him; and then complained about circumstance.

"Can you approve of my feminine charms?" Mrs. Hulda Popoff teased him, and wriggled into a belly dance, which so captivated the astounded Morstive that he offered her, for wedding present, his own head on a silver platter. "Don't be a fool, I wouldn't think of it," she replied, rejecting his offer.

"I need love," he said.

"You won't get it from me," Hulda told him.

"Nor me," added a chorus of other inaccessible temptresses, in stages of seductive undress. Voyeurs stared stiffly.

"I love to be religious, it's so divine," Merton said, now a veteran husband, after all these years, to *Mrs.* Newberg, formerly Emma Lavalla.

"How happy we all are," the mayor officially decreed.

And Jessup, in self-mortification, shaved his beard. "I'm free to descend," he proclaimed. His meaning was enigmatic.

Page tried to sell everybody to themselves, but it was no deal. His hidden ally had taken over his apartment, in the assumed identity of a woman.

Keegan glowered at Morstive, but mutely. Morstive was turned elsewhere, aiming for a decision to the affirmative. "But *what* to affirm?" he wondered. There he was, caught in one of time's moments. Which one? The one there.

There, happened to be. Such a given can be only accepted. On that base, progress may proceed. The jungle was crowded with neon lights, and lantern poles, mothflies, lightbugs, and a generous array of spooks. "Am I happy or not?" Morstive asked himself. This matter was held up to vote, and a majority presided. "Yes," it was decided. But Morstive wasn't sure.

He kept hedging. "No sense in being, for if I *am* happy, what will I have to search for? No I'd better be discontent. Then, my state can only improve." This was but selfish logic, but he stuck to it. Yet he cheated himself, and finally became happy.

∞10∞∞∞∞

He woke up from a sleepful dream, into golden sunlight. "I feel great!" he said.

"But do I? Is it true? Or was it?" Reflection, and passing time, alter what's reflected on. The next now is new.

"Yes, or at least I felt *good,*" he said, toning it down. He wanted to keep happiness at a distance, where it wouldn't scare him or catch him by sudden surprise: as it were, napping. "Well, I *am* happy," he said. It was a welcome thought, and a thankful confession. It had cost him much pain, but here it was: torn out of him.

"What to do with it?" he asked, closely guarded. It was like a pet insect: should you kill it, or let it live? At least he had a *choice,* now.

So he let it live. It multiplied, and bore children. All of them, however, illegitimate.

"Now that I have parented bastard brats," he said, "what on earth next?—or does heaven follow?" He felt at one. "I have a definite harmony," he said: "rooted deep in the heart of my conflict. I must overcome it, and be normal again. And seek my own level." He tried to, but the water was over his head. Was his body stale? He exercised for a little while, with arms and legs. They so perspired, a bath was next. That cleaned him off. Enough for self-examination to be spotless. "Now let me look in a full-length mirror. Is this me? Or I? I suppose it could be either, since their similarity smacks of real twins, I to myself. What is this ego of mine? Why does it hide its pubic hair? Now as I vigorously towel myself, and briskly the hair stands out, my throat is songed upon. Those notes that flew out—were they mine? Then where can my boundaries be?

"Is life only me? Or does it end somewhere else? There are my teeth, as they go smiling: How truthful the mirror can duplicate, too honest to lie. Here's my image. Are my thoughts separate, or included in the bargain? Life is everlasting with its mystery: If only it could reveal my dream, by which it could be revealed, which, in turn, would reveal more about my dream. Did the dream dream me, or I do the dreaming? Well, I feel good, anyhow."

He put on his clothes. The clock was stopped. According to his window, it was dark. Night was beginning. Indeed, he could celebrate with a big supper. An outstanding feast, huge; and plentiful.

He went out, and chose a restaurant. He sat near the window, and saw stars reflected on automobile fenders: cosmic mundanity. Heaven needed lower support.

Because it was a cheap restaurant, the waiter was actually the cook, on short order, his apron greased through, a sign of his trade. Morstive was approached, and handed a multiple-choice menu for taste to deliberate upon. "Food," he ordered, creating a general surprise.

"Yes, but what kind?" he was asked.

"The best, but the cheapest, and the most filling, but all my nutritive requirements, with vitamins and things. Hot food, but varied also, balanced between the salt and the sweet side, to delay the appetite being cloyed, but fetch it to linger in contrasting tastes, dividing pleasure into its sensations, and melting the variety in a harmony. That's what I want."

"We're all out of it," the cook said, looking stouter every minute, with the stomach protruding to a small ungainly bulge, staggering far out, its flabby folds hanging like dewlaps, rushing the air aside.

"Oh," said Morstive, and was subdued. Another disappointment. He saw the windowed moon, the fendered reflections, then turned to his server with a gut plea. He trembled with sincerity's ache. "Please feed me, I'm hungry," he said. For a while, he felt faint.

"We're all out of it."

"Out of what?"

"Food."

"Then what *do* you have?"

"Men's wear, assorted lines of haberdashery, dry goods, hardware, stationery supplies, cosmetics, furniture, rugs, toys, air conditioners, sports equipment, automotive parts, wigs, compasses, costume kits, sinks, lumber, light bulbs, cooking utensils, textbooks, slippers, camping tents, birth control devices, spare women, potted plants, pets, coffins, wedding gowns, cigarettes, baby carriages, original sculpture, musical scores, and a miscellaneous assortment of other odds and ends."

"But I'm hungry."

"Then what you need is food."

"You're right." Morstive ran out, and located a luncheonette, where he rushed in, ordering a cold plate for speed, and a hunk of hot soup first. He exhausted himself slopping it in. His rapid eating upset his metabolism, outbalanced his assimilatory ingestion of capillary absorption. His system burst into mismatched segments of time process. In protest, it coiled a guard over all exits, and put emergency regulations into effect, shutting an oblivion shade over the flustered mind. Thus ideas went unattended. He was just a corporeal block.

Thus Morstive slumped over, and slept the sleep of the just, his mouth hanging modestly open to receive an extra germ or two from the restaurant atmosphere, a dive of disarray, only dimly lit, with all his courses finished before him. So in comes the waiter bouncing a check, and spies the slumbering swoon, droopy dip stupor of this customer, his smoldering absence of an intellect. The breathing pants at ferociously spaced intervals, with shockingly increasing loudness, from that heavy glutton, as his new pounds shake fat hands with the usual rest of him, the solid core of his regulars.

Coarseness, a proneness to vice, are apparent, in and out. The waiter asks, upon his deaf ears, "I have a little lady in the back room if you'd like?" and gives way, for the victim to awake.

"How much extra charge?"

"By the hour less, and the night more, depending on you."

Morstive staggered up, and paid for the hour, keeping his wallet closely with him. He was led into a room without ventilation, just unrelieved wall, and thus procured the favors, scrawny and lacking in delight, of Tessa Wheaton, the former faithless wife and helpmeet workhorse of versatile Morgan Popoff, now about to celebrate his second wedding. Tessa did not notice who it was. Her eyes seemed flimsy, or filmed into obscurity. Morstive did what he could, and felt much lighter afterward. He was careful not to exchange a word. Because of delicacy, or the artist's guile. Perhaps he could write about this, such an interesting transformation, the progress of one backward year. He made his mental note, on a portable cerebral typewriter which required no definite paper, only an honest memory. Yet he corrupted his memory, inserting fiction in place of fact, to lie more creatively. The truth is often too modest, and has to be encouraged, coerced, or extorted. So he fabricated a myth, went home, and attempted a comeback as a writer of invaluable promise, with all his burden of failure behind him, and only success to come, plus the glittering royalty. But he must hide it from Page Slickman, who was now masquerading as him. Credit belongs in deserved merit to the deed, which he meant to promulgate. He couldn't calculate his genius, but its obvious scope went out of sight, and hid far on the high sides of the unknown outposts withdrawn from the globe's center. He was inspired, so well fed, and deeply blessed with rest. And so from his mind he plucked, to create.

He wrote with an aching pen, and drew a complete picture of Tessa, most recently physically encountered; featuring also Morgan, in the role of co-star. It was a fabulous hit, of immediate popular appeal—to himself. It couldn't miss. Such fantasy guided his hand, that he misspelled almost every word, to demonstrate his independence of convention, and begin a school of his own style, his own unique grasp of labored distortion in the sentence, to better reflect the world of our times we live in, its impact on the sensibility of a concerned human being with his exposed susceptibility to the nerve of interior need and the line of external pressure, a brutal conflict he brooded on, and expressed with depth, not literally. His work was an instant failure, one of the worst efforts of art ever attempted by a writer. Why? For one, his characterization of Tessa missed the mark, lacked the real "her," change and all. Distortion wasn't enough. He couldn't capture the rhythm. Better to *con*tort, to train a more accurate focus of mirror, and get the true reflection. *Any* device, for truth. Yet he couldn't handle it; and Morgan Popoff had only thin realization, not the true substance. Morstive put his pen down, and waited for dawn, to sleep again. His feelings were so absolutely low, a dangerous depression was inherent, and an instinct for suicide. Dawn delayed, and the thoughts sank to emotion's bottom, from which recovery must be frantic and quick, if at all. He was quite hysterical. The ego was crushed, the id blew the lid, and the superego whipped and whipped, to no effect, while the flood dam broke loose, and carried his sanity with it, a worse snap than either Merton's or Morgan's, cracking his stubborn bulwark of control and splitting his forces into mass retreat, disorderly. When dawn arrived, he was a nut. But fortunately, he was aware. It was all a stage effect, planned and carried out, sincerely self-deceiving, to exaggerate dramatic tragedy, to melodramatize the poignant pathos sunk in delicious self-pity, a mood he loved to evoke. What corn! But it worked.

As a substitute, it was excellent. For where he couldn't succeed in rendering fictional characters, he was one himself, and lived out the role, instead of on paper. And this, Page couldn't plagiarize. He had his own author's-rights to himself, and conducted himself accordingly. He was a modern non-hero, like Leopold Bloom, created by the Irish punster, James Joyce. "Except that I'm not in a book," he said, "I'm quite convincing. Too bad I'm not in words, and no one can read me. Or read *of* me. I'm not a stock character. Look at me! How I feel! Oh, these feelings! And now, in the light of dawn, God, my author, commands me to sleep. It's well in keeping with my consistency. I'm never out of character. I contribute to plot, and let the form envelop. Yes, I'm a happy stroke! And symbolic of the modern man's dilemma. Thus, if I can't write, myself, then I hope I'm written about; and so, short of God, when I wake up I'll go search for just the proper writer whose skill needs to use me: and I'll create him to create me, and be created. Then my identity will be literary, and not just in life. I'll have *existence*. Which is *immortal-*

ity's sole guarantee, and that's what I *really* want. With that, I'll have it *made.*"

So he shut down the blinds, and feigned sleep; and was so convincing, so credible, in this artistic act, that soon he *was* asleep, breathing in the role he was made for, next on the acts of his performance. His craft was wide-flung, and permitted of many different actions: in all of which, he gave faithful duplication to the notion of himself, and was his own true replica. Here was a character, indeed!

∞11∞∞∞∞

The first thing he did when asleep was dream. "I remember you," the dream said, but Morstive played aloof: not only cool, but cold. This got the dream worked up. It approached him. "What would you like me to portray, illuminate, convey, crystallize, and touch upon, this fine golden day? I can be prophetic, as well, as you know. Have you any scares, fears? Let me symbolize them; my deep and meaningful distortions will garb your anxiety just in harmless playfulness, and we'll have fun. Fun, like a game."

"Let me shirk," Morstive pleaded, for he was scared. Life was so horrible, and dreams made it lurid, ghastly. Then life seemed tame again. But real things hurt, whether depicted in a dream, or represented in stark reality, as part of the world's gear. In or out, it hurt. How sensitive he was to suffering! He wasn't cut out for it. Or yes, was he? It seemed so frequent to him. This was his forte, his true talent. "I know how to suffer," Morstive said, and the dream said, "I can make you suffer, too," not to be outdone. What a competitive universe this is. Everything is being compared, therefore relative. This makes it cruel. Only absolutes are kind, for they don't need anything else, being self-sufficient. Yet, they can be tyrannical, stubborn to a fault, and utterly selfish: they don't give in. So which is worse? Morstive didn't care, so plunged was he in his dream. Where was he?—he'd *become* the dream? Or did it just contain him, deep down?

The dream devoured him, as in a vortex. The essence slipped

out of his identity, and poor him—he was nebulous. He was both sleeping and dreaming, doing two things at once, personifying American efficiency without even half trying.

The dream deepened, about him, shortening space, and arresting time's illusion, so that Morstive, reaching back, could pluck forward all the people he knew for meetings appareled in a nonphysical dimension. But the usual vanity was prepared. So he put on his special face, with social noncommitment posted all over it—indifference casually superior. People would collide with him. He would come out second best, if at all. So he put his bet on finishing, not on winning. He was fit by his place, and too little a man to argue his piddle of mockery back in destiny's sternward face. His adversaries competed from behind sure destiny, the mover of winds, the settler of architectural monuments, casting a stationary spell over objects that don't move. God, it was drafty!

He put the cover on over his backside, an act literally outside his dream, to shelter his image-awakened sleep. Now with the cozy warmth, he felt secure again, and fair anxiety saw fit to attack him. He heard himself saying, "I'm worried," which seemed to express it all.

"Just a worry?" admonished his dream, contemptuously placid.

"But my worry is so big, I can't see what it comes from."

"Could you call yourself neurotic?"

"Oh no: I'm much too worried for that."

"What, precisely, are you?" and with saying this, the dream was wearing glasses, putting on a much more professional appearance.

Morstive hesitated before answering, for he wanted to be fair. Where was all the population? Soon, they would surround him. Or one by one, hound him in. For he was a sitting duck, for their wandering prey.

"Me? I guess I'm me, that's all."

"That's insufficient, as an explanation," said the dream, still courteous.

Morstive was too embarrassed to continue. "Stop pointing at me," he said, quite uncomfortable. It was hell to be on the spot. Down with his identity. It didn't mean that much. Existence, was one thing he was sure of. He told his dream so. For this labor, the dream rewarded him by smiling. "You look so like me," Morstive said, watching the smile.

"It's your smile, that's why," said the dream, for no other feature was visible.

"It's certainly strange down here," Morstive said, and the dream repeated it. "Are you echoing me?" asked the dreamer, feeling on uncertain ground.

"No, you ape," said the dream, just the way Morstive would have said it.

"What's our relationship?" Morstive wanted to know.

"You to me, that's what," the dream answered, pedantically precise, though metaphysically approximate at the same labor, drifting at an accuracy.

"I quite don't know what to make of this," Morstive said, honestly.

"Are you sure about that?" doubted the dream, and there was the smile again, redoubled.

"Are you smiling because something's funny?" Morstive wanted to know, a true child of curiosity.

"No, because you are," the dream said: "And as for *your* motive, that's for you to tell."

"But I don't know I'm smiling," Morstive replied; and to convince his skeptic, he made a frown: yet it still looked like a smile.

"You're an emotional case," the dream said.

"I'm not; I'm an artist," Morstive angrily snapped, and then despaired: for the futility seized him.

The dream continued to plague him, pursuing him in the width of that ambiguous tunnel, that vertical chamber going nowhere. "It's so crowded with me being here alone," Morstive said, and couldn't think of anyone but himself, nor see beyond his own little nose. Was that egotistical? Or only loneliness? Or the dark void of life's negativity? The dream had stopped listening, and was attentive somewhere else. What else could there be? Morstive belonged here. "What do you see?" Morstive asked, with increased awareness.

"I'm entitled to see more than you," the dream answered, "so don't get jealous. I'm not all-seeing, but I'm pretty prophetic. The Greeks used to trust in me, and now Freud does. And other ages between, like the Romantics. I have quite a historical tradition behind me. Now don't you exploit me for that."

"But I'm depending on you," Morstive said, "because I don't dare to have visions, without you. Or visitations, or glimpses, or 'calls.' Please enchant me into a hypnotic trance. I swoon for your

93

spell over me. I submit, as your all-surrendering subject."

Thus flattered, the dream revealed what it saw, while Morstive was avid with listening, and employed the benefit of vicarious sight. It pointed out many characters, all displayed typically, each at the heart of himself, and being nothing else. "You're as lifelike as can be," Morstive told the dream with a gusto of appreciation.

"Thank you," relented the dream, genuinely taken back. It belonged, after all, to Morstive.

Taken out of his own hide and presented with discoveries of others, Morstive strengthened his subjective outlook by developing a rigid objectivity, severe and impersonal as age, or extreme youth. He saw *into* everything, and read out in literal dimension the Soul, whose exponent all these several characters were, as best as their abilities took them, each in his evolution of personality, the emergence of traits. They stained the future, by virtue of the way they acted: both unpredictable and foreseeable.

oo12ooooooo

Morgan was there, different than before, therefore all the more convincing. "I've been given my old job back," he said: "only more than ever. If today is Sunday, Hulda Stock is mine forever. I'm slightly out of breath. I've been running for my social sanity. The mental institution authorities have been pursuing me. They want to forbid my marriage. These very same dignitaries, I'm told, formally acquitted Merton of doubt as to his full mind. Perhaps the mayor helped *him*, to obey a promise to Jessup Clubb; for what reason, I don't know.

"And this same mayor has been declared illegal for his job, though the court cleared him, and washed up the swimming pool business. All these overlapped interweavings of people. But the world starts with me. Otherwise, someone else is being the Morgan that I am.

"Did I drag Tessa to ruin, whom this mayor helped me to divorce? No, Jessup Clubb was primarily responsible: He lured her from the clean way, and she completed this internal damage to her morals. I am exonerated, save for a brief period as her pimp. Which wasn't as bad as it seems: for she cooperated with such permissive yieldingness, as to take over the business herself, and to exercise the rights of control. Therefore the guilt resides with her, and blame's lost its prerogative to skin-leech on me. I did voyeur some of my own ex-wife's commercial leg-spreading when pinched for some hard-up cash. Yet, being Morgan, no apology is necessary. But I grieved at the loss of my prestigious business post.

"*You* reigned in my power for a little while, and kept me down to my manual labors of indolent unemployed laziness and other such odd jobs, refusing in your capacity to hire me: and in addition, fired Tessa, then supporting me. Yet you were invited to dinner anyway, in this recent day or so, responding to your own invitation, overwhelming my bride Hulda, and my own regal self. We have had conflicts, you and I: ours has been up and down, a relationship between nominal friends at least. I advise you to hang your head: you have accumulated much shame.

"And you wanted my Hulda, and perhaps had won her, at the New Year's party. But I, cured with brief psychoanalysis from an affliction of mental unbalance with the usual emotional repercussions, stepped deftly in between, to claim back what was only mine, and withdraw love from its deposited interest. You liked that, didn't you? Can't you ever obtain a girl for yourself? You play the fool, therefore *are* one. And others pay you in coin, to the value of your own estimate. I'm your business superior, as well as in every other way. How pitiful it must be, to be yourself! Emulate me, if you can. But you're too scared to be defiant, and your talent consists in shrinking up, exposing yourself, and collecting punishment from others. As you deserve. You're a self-schooled graduate.

"I'm inclined, due to my great heavenly resources, to be somewhat the libertine, and therefore prone to infidelity. I've been loved by my dearest Hulda, and Tessa, and Emma as well. And who ever loved you? Your mother? Go marry her then, if you can. You're not equipped for anyone newer.

"Jessup, my friend, is now my enemy. You were never that dangerous. You are harmless, not an adversary. I clown, when I'm with you. And now, for attending serious matters, I beg your leave, and take it anyway. Goodbye, sleeping misfit."

"I don't like this dream so far," Morstive whispered outside his dream's range, "since I seem so fit to be insulted, and can't command a retaliatory voice, but only must listen. Morgan said too much. If it's true, then heaven be my only defense, for I'm my own mockery. But the dream has further powers. Who is the next, approaching?"

Attractively sliding into view and well within the light of focus, Hulda Stock unfurled her proud modesty. There was a tone of scorn, of indeed feminine wit, in her firm countenance. Now let her sharpened tongue attack!

"So nice to be in your dream," she said, looking directly at Morstive. "If I'm married already for its being Sunday, you haven't even given us a wedding present. Surely you don't begrudge my being Morgan's?

"My own ex-roommate, the rather plain (if you don't mind) Emma Lavalla, was in love with my dear husband; and later Tessa was my successful competition, so much so as to marry him. Yet in the end I win. Doesn't that speak much of me? Pine for the me you can never have.

"And you, you wolf, when my husband fixed you up with Tessa, in those days when she was but his typist, you tried hard not to seduce her, didn't you? And succeeded, much to your credit. Yet you seem to have tasted her lately, from the response in your eye, as I, on this stage, fill your dream with talking. Well, others have taken her, as well; and many more to come; for her belated career has been drastically speeded ahead to cover up for an indolent beginning restricted to watchful prudery and a modesty ridiculous to her ugliness. I'm glad she's only she, and I'm all of me. Thank God she miscarried, or my husband would have had a child. Now mine will be his, and for the first time. Ours is true wedded bliss.

"But how can *you* comprehend human relationships? Loneliness is your only contact. Your fate continually stalks you, doesn't it? Your rut of restricted emotional routine excludes therapeutic variety, and always you're lost just inside your freedom, where imprisonment confines you at will, and you voluntarily abandon flight into space, by submitting to time's fate, by which you're forced to be yourself, captive to your own character. You can't soar, like my Morgan! His whole active life is that of an artist, minus your ivory tower. For he *lives!* And whatever you do, it isn't living. You think or write, as substitutes. But even as an introvert, you're a failure. But use your nose, and go ahead and breathe. It must be great fun pretending. You can't even escape from life successfully!

You call this a dream? You only *think* it is, or dream it is. There you go, dreaming again!"

Then, wagging her tail in provocative wriggles, Hulda departed in deep perspective, as though exchanging dreams in her interdimensional wandering. She left behind a perfume trace, her light little reminder.

"Ah, but she's sexy," Morstive said, and visualized her in intimate concubinage with the aroused heat of Morgan, at his furious full response. "They'll pulverize the child, before it's born," Morstive predicted, intoxicated by their vigor. What energy they possess! And with love to skillfully guide it. "Love is quite a difference," Morstive said with baleful rue, "between in the having it and the not. I neither have it nor do it, and my life is predicated on abnormalcy, and is drawn out in the inadequacy of incomplete fulfillment, partial desire, an aim not yet achieved. My growth is yet to come. That strongest of all hours—my maturity—when will it crown itself, the juvenescence performed by timeless love, directly vulgar, robustly delicate? Then comes my life to its complete beginning, and pre-life quits stalling, to gloriously tower to an end."

∞13∞∞∞∞

More company would arrive, but Morstive suddenly valued his solitude. He hated not being able to speak to them, while they took pot shots to riddle him through, kill him on the verbal level. "It's my dream," he declared, as though by establishing this he could either forbid or prohibit more "characters" from accusing him, tunneling in from life, lifted right off the past, and pouring through, penetrating this dream. "I want to stop dreaming right now," he said, dreading the assaults to come. "Get me out of this, will you?" he appealed, poking the dream in the rib.

"Shut up, I'm not through," it said. "Keep on sleeping: this is a marathon you're facing: you can't wake up."

"But don't you understand?—it's day, day—I want to go out."

"Not while you're sleeping," insisted that persistent dream, and forced his mouth shut with a nonphysical tape substance.

Next on the list, less devastating and without recourse to Hulda's furious invective, Emma Lavalla came on. "Oh how do you do?" Morstive said, biting through the plastic silence of his dream-woven gag. Thus he had the last word, but to premature effect. It was but a rhetorical sentence, and Emma had all she could do to dismiss it, with careful feminine inattention. The dream had a mile-long stage, and she appeared at one side. The backdrop was inconspicuous, and now all was in readiness: Emma's monologue, spoken before thought, a simply unrehearsed rambling: the minor drippings of an earnestly not-so-interesting personage, afforded some background role, to pad up a scene or two, as a filler-in: not very intense, either, so far as dramatic possibilities go, being summed up by the word "ordinary": which she was, excusably to a fault, pinched in by the commonplace, framed just so-so, for the camera, if it could, to register. No camera recorded her drab semblance, undream-embroidered. In a word, she was but a bore, but seriously meaningful for her own self, as judged to the person by her life. She wouldn't abuse Morstive, nor reproach him. So he shifted his sleeping position, balanced to hear. He even, moved by the removal of fear to a perch approaching objectivity, devoted some of his concentration to the opening and closing of Emma's mouth, where Merton alone could find a plucked kiss valuable. Otherwise, it occupied a seat for dullness.

Morstive thought about himself, too: how, when he woke up, he was sore in need to seek out an author to represent him, to depict him, as reflected by his "friends." Who would that be? Achieving no answer, he heard:

"I don't like Hulda Stock at all. Who does she think she is? Just because she got Morgan, she has to put on an air? The nerve! Merton is every bit as better, if not worse. And what's more, and finally, he's mine. We eloped, as he insisted, and I was too enthralled to refuse. We even experienced rapture, and an ecstasy in transports. I'll have to marry him, though. Dear sweet boy that he is, and so confused there's no word for it. I'll be the influence of his life, and straighten out where he bends wrongly, in his erratic pursuit for the orthodox. Is he a Christian, now? And a member of every known club yet, affiliated with his plurality of membership. What is he hiding from? So much a joiner, that he's rammed and romped past his outside self, and isn't through running yet. I must stop him. It's enough to be with *me*: what else does he need?

"Everyone says Hulda has got me beat in looks. But I must be appealing, if Morgan so much as took me out, unless for revenge, to spite his Hulda with jealousy in the period of their separation. Well, I like being used! I'm quite glad I didn't kiss him, or let him, if *that*'s what he was up to. I'll be nobody's dupe.

"He ducked me for a decoy, and I worked up an image for him, the mind of my fantasy's eye. Well, he's good-looking, isn't he? Hulda has the deed to that dear land. All right, did I come bad off? Merton is a better consolation prize than most, and with his sociability, his always glad-handing people, he could be in public relations, in a nice office job, while I cook for him at home, and shoo his mother off, and my husband will be known as Mr. Newberg, with respect: Plenty of people will admire me, and even shed a tear of envy, and we'll be well off, and buy our own home. This is a good future. I'll vie with Hulda, and when I die I'll be a proud woman. For I will have formed a husband better than I took him, and lead a natural success by the neck, until it's tied to his post. Yes, we'll be a true wedded couple. The two Newbergs, Merton and I. And the neighborhood will know us, wherever we move. And should he go in for politics, I won't stand in his way. The love will ripen in development, and when I die, it will be happy, and all our children to mourn. It's a good life.

"I had plunged to my disgraceful period, sluttish to the end of my born days, with Jessup as devil's envoy, and Hulda co-trammeled. But the spell broke by the climactic party to top off the year, all came about as it did, and nicely was resolved. I think it was God's will, did it. We humans were too passionate to help, too much in the throes, the blind agony, or whatever terms an author will use to dramatize it. Now I'm all afire to forge us out a fine family, that pure Christian unit. It's a crusade, back to normal: The bones in my intuition give me good guidance, and on earth the river of a woman flows up the gentle stream of God, and time's eternal ocean. Oh, I'm all wet. I'll just be concrete, and leave these abstracts alone. I wouldn't conceive for Jessup, because nature wouldn't allow this unnatural concession to an evil supernaturally beyond my ken. But oh with my honey, the darling oh of me, my gracious Merton, I feel the cry of motherhood, and let the willing centuries come. Blessed they will be, with my offspring. Ah, the earth in me aches!"

"Quite moving, especially for a mind seemingly so uncultivated. That I liked," Morstive said, for the speaker had kept him out of it, and not railed with censure, nor denounced the dreamer himself, but mostly her anger hit at Hulda, for daring to be a better rival than she. "Hulda is prouder and more bitter, I would say, comparing those never-to-be-reunited roommates. And now each is to be married, to her original intention. Both became sidetracked, went through devious channels, and now home are returned, each bosom clasped to her man, and the normal race will proceed.

"I've got to get virile too, and move in while the taking's there, for the world is crowded with girls that blossom into women, with such sheer force that all of nature's backing is behind it, being an angel to the long-run play, with many changes of cast. When I wake up, dream permitting, I'll get me an author to do me; and tend to my finances, which shrink daily; and visit my mother and the other parent; and Lord proclaim me a man, but I'll burgeon forth, and have heartihood. The day of Morstive Sternbump is yet to come."

∞14∞∞∞∞∞

"This dream has a silent period, an interval, intermission. However, fast as the sun travels, by standing still and letting the earth move, I'm asleep yet, as my dream's respectful listener, the willing captive to what I'm involuntarily served.

"I fear the next customer. Who does he look like, while the distance moves him closer, and looming up front comes his identity, advancing by arrears with his existence behind, and fully coming to life. He's okay, he's Merton Newberg: not liable to condemn me. What will *he* say, that his adoring Emma hasn't said for him? For women know how to talk, these days. And the more binding words come out, situations change, to conform; for I think words settle things, and create what they mean; or destroy: it's all the same thing.

"With the one-by-one approach, and not surrounding me, I hear out these interlinking people, who have come to condemn, or be condemned, or even, by the negative route, tortuous, to praise. It's open daylight, outside, so my dream is flooded with light. This approximates life, though I still sleep. Until I wake, I get older. Then, by waking, my age is that much gone, towards the next death.

I'm here, yet. And my pulse is moving all the time. Some ticks bleat out, and others cruise in, while there's flow. It's always me, going.

"I don't mind Merton. He takes that platform in a familiar way, with an orator's stride, and wants to make contact. For he needs to communicate. You can see his lips move, and his heart intent. It thumps in its socket, while his eyes are searching out, finding stray clues, and false scents, to solve the existence he doesn't have, by multiplying his identity, and removing the core still at a further distance, till he's lost it entirely, and joins indiscriminately, hell-mell, to forge an artificial disorder external to his inner one, that has now become natural. Well, he's lost. And life may find him, or death will, and he'll still insist he's lost, and want to join the angels, with their diabolical innocence. He'd do anything, while his soul sits out his life, a permanent absentee. Is he a phony? Yes, but the suffering it costs him gives his geniality a genuinity, and he's everyone's friend, and only his own acquaintance, remote, looking in upon the enmity of his truth, and denying it with blinking eyes, smothered by a pack of breeding lies, where all his system's gone to, in its passion for a formula. And what does he ignore? The true instinct within, spirit of man."

"Glad to be with you," Merton began, groping for a sense of home, the familiarity of his belonging. "Whatever you stand for, or put your belief in, that's my creed too, as we join our harmonies together, and merge our joint enterprise: include me, if you will.

"I'm soon to enter the married state, and share my wife's unity with her. Who shall dare stand between? For what are we, but men? As an old pacifist organizer, I believe in fighting for your right. Men are free—to belong to each other.

"I'll take a career, and my goal is the brotherhood of man. Therefore I aim for public relations, an affiliate of the advertising industry, and just as equally noble, serving human communication. It pays to be liberal. I'm a humanist, therefore rather progressive, somewhat of a free-thinker. But first I consult my fellow men, and learn what the consensus is. No sense in being alone. I've already tried that. It didn't work, and with bitter effect.

"The asylum, which was repairing my sanity, gave me a Christmas vacation, and I came to that New Year's party. Jessup Clubb spoke his sermon so convincingly, I converted like the wind. When God instructs, obedience feels nice. And you gain respect, by providing for God, and He, to return the pact, agrees to give you a good credit, prolonging your immortality. Thank God for religion. It puts things in place, and dusts away the webs of confusion, showing me where to go. I laze my will in it, and reserve my scheming for earthier ends. The church is a great thing to belong to. Membership doesn't end, just because you happen to die. No, it lingers on.

"And my bride Emma will be a Christian woman, amend her early ways of fallen chastity, and learn ideally to be a partner, the spirit of cooperation. I'll have her with child, by being legitimate spouse to her, to efface Jessup's awful taint, whose transactions were illegal, on a low basis, nor could she contract his seed and translate it to the joy of offspring, when all wedded bliss was lacking, and only an illicit affair. Something must be said for institutions. Marriage is one.

"But am I a rebel, or not? I've joined queer causes, and had unorthodox convictions, fads in the fashion of time, clutched for just to be different, a stray spark from the ordinary, which I detest as well. I'd like, within the social framework, to be specially unique, on the advanced guard of new enlightened movements, at the fore, touching the future before anyone else, providing someone safely pioneered it, and I get wind, find out what's to be, and precede all the mass, getting there first. Yes, I'm a progressive intellectual, and think left. Then left becomes right, or I abandon it. For ultimately, I want it to be popular. It's a risk, and I dread being alone. Huddled up in the mob, selective and discerning with good taste, enhances my identity, as a social citizen. The world, after all, is bigger than I. I meet it, and join forces with the proper authorities. So let's say that I'm a conforming rebel. That gives me margin to recover, fall back, in the event proven wrong. I want my cause to *win*, if I support it, like an owner of a stock. Otherwise, I give it up, and seek a better winner. There are so many movements. You've got to smell out which will succeed. You place your bet on a faction, so it bears the weight of *you*, and should *it* flounder, then you're lost. So joining is not only passive, it's prophetic for the outcome, and carries the brunt of your fate. Loyalties and allegiances, then, should be studied carefully, based on pragmatic appeal. Like when you back a candidate, you expect patronage, and a plum of political spoilage. What can it do for me? That's why Piper Cole joined Ira Huntworth, for the mayorality, and such benefits conferred downward, as accrued to the office. I got my kicks, from what I joined in the past: but as investments, some lacked soundness, and the dividends turned out lousy, and lowered the rating in my prestige, giving bad publicity to my name. I'll be in public soon. I've got the knack. It's no trick. You find out where the current blows, and predict it. I'll hide my record, and drive a clean bandwagon, from my seat in the back. This requires instinct, and my smell is good, to ferret out what's to come. Why not politics? My body gives no discernible odor, and with Ira swept out of office, I can unleash a mayor campaign. I'll get acquainted with the party boss, and pull a big deal. And my marriage will render me that much more available, showing responsibility. What the public wants, I'll give them. For that's what I want, too.

"Yes, I'm through with small-fry cliques, and unpopular fronts. No more shadowy blocs, shyly embarrassed with showmanship arrogance behind the screen of decency, off from the fringe of repute, rebuked into unacceptability. Now I'll join, for profit! And *lead*, as the best way to follow.

"That ex-mayor pardoned a formal stamp worth of reacquired sanity, putting my mind at ease. Thus all crazy notions are forbidden, in the law's sanctity, and I'm free from asylums forever. Even neurosis is illegal, thanks to that political maneuver. I can't help, now, feeling secure. Anxiety is private, but a well-adjusted personality requires the mayor's approval, and a city's edict, by the representative process, power delegated. Therefore I must be political, to have my insides wiped clean, and personal notions repressed in the interest of a civic sanction; condoned as a citizen, whatever my doubts are as a matter of my individuality, prone to absurd notions from within. I'll be outward in spectacle, and ride a reputation, crushing the protests of the psyche. My emotions will be for the record, not for myself.

"My confidences, if any, should not be revealed beyond the precincts of this dream, if you please, Mr. Sternbump. Concentrate on hushing this up. Or being asleep, you may forget anyway. Dreams are rarely remembered, or shattered into a state of distortion, recollected unclearly. You seem quite alert, and your dream has the paradoxical quality of being awake. This illusion helps you to keep dreaming. I'm touchably real to you, no?

"No doubt its being day contributes to this illusion. Your hours are odd. I rarely appear in a daydream, unless Emma dwells on me, as love quickens the imagination, and holds a form in unseen clarity. It's fun to elope. I cut a romantic figure, by dashing away in a trail of swoons; Emma captivated by my side, oozing surprise and shock, but holding on, bagged by a good husband, to her gain as a possible wife. Most losses are real gains, so we calculate the eventuality of losing, as the only preamble to winning. It's cunning, the machine endeavors of a human race, clinging through bad times and good for the prize of advantage.

"At the party, I slapped her as soon as I came in, for having defected from our moonlit vows. I claimed her, having just been released. But when she saw Morgan, she offered a serious flirt, which he disdainfully rejected. Only then, without recourse, she rebounded on to me. Of course, her memory thinks otherwise. Her self-interested expedience would retrospect a fidelity that never wavered, on grounds current to our love reinvested.

"Yes, we *are* concerned. Thus we lapse, and stray, shaking and trembling at the foot of truth, not daring to face truth directly, looking in its stern implacable eyes, its impersonally detached visage, so cruel with indifference. We'd rather fumble, and be fools, than be sadly wise from the onslaught of unflinching terror, truth unmasked. Therefore I say, it's me, not Morgan, who's Emma's first choice. It makes for a cozier romance, that way.

"Well, I've taken up a good part of your dream. Although silent, you've courteously attended me, through the rambles and bypaths of my oblique and meandering speech. I'll take Emma to task, to help obliterate Morgan even from her past, seeing as source the spite of Hulda's rivalry, competitive emulation, the gregarious adoptation of an adversary's loves and hates, so closely enchained are we, one man's heart in another man's body, a woman's bitchiness residing in another's fancy, as we interlap, link and penetrate our weavings, all in the soul of one, and one person stranded within the minds of the many, a bond of sympathy, a species and many distinct individuals, group man and mob man, an instinct in the common race. Society is the largest aspect of us, and we the smallest integer within. We band to form a unit, but total mankind is our complete framework, men past and men to come, surviving now and here in conflict. As mayor, I propose to introduce harmony. This is my immediate platform. My hat is in the ring, as a candidate for the best interests, you and me and them, all will benefit. I'm the utopian one-man cure-all for anyone's ill. Apply to me, and troubles die. The people thrive, when I'm the city's crown. I campaign to please everybody, with promises too ideal to keep, ideals of illusionary promise, while the city grinds on, like a prehistoric mammal surviving through the zoos of the present day, creeping loudly into the future, rebuilt continually, cosmopolitan even to its new set of false teeth, a metropolis on four legs, six of which are limping simultaneously, and the other eight dormant for the time being, while twelve feed needy relief on crutches, vomiting taxes all the while, and no St. George to slay it. And I'll be its trainer, its mayor. Its keeper, warden. Its caretaker, maybe.

"Its undertaker: Yes, that too. Such is my term, and its.

"But ah, I jump ahead. With most unseemly haste. That's off the record. At that, here's the leavetaking I'll instigate. We both have work to do. You must badly have to go to the bathroom now; while I, though I've enjoyed your dream, must re-enter into the *public* domain, the official world. It's there, among succeeding failures and failing successes, where my name must make a mark, and all Newbergs henceforth prosper. Goodbye, and give me your vote. We'll see each other again, by all that is calm and peaceful, the serenity of a world on hell. Well, my goal is begun."

"This guy is really transformed!" Morstive gasped, discontinuing his dream while making a trip to the bathroom. "I guess life changes us; extremes launch other extremes, leading further to still more complications, from which extremes are the only solution, to alleviate the problem. Well, what exclusive forecast I was host to, by that guest's flattering confidences, a secret now, but later known past knowledge. How illuminating, this dream! It's already maken me wise. And the day's hour has declined, so the light shows, for the speedy twilight, the dusk of the soft winter day, like an old-fashioned lithograph, from the collection of a faded connoisseur, along with other Victorian relics. Now it's back again to my bed's warm cloud where time floats up. High up, with knaves' tricks."

∞15∞∞∞∞∞

"What—no transition! The dream is just as close as life again, the audience has been recalled back, the curtain rises on a lit stage, tolling the doom of another act. What character will now reappraise himself, rehashing the puddle of a past, to confuse a certain future for the crooked line of straight progress, time's creative destruction? No, it can't be Jessup Clubb! And without the robe, and the beard shaven! What will this kidnapper confess? I feel mercy struggling with me, a compassionate tendency to forgive. He's my co-martyr, but on a professional basis, the better to undergo institutional punishment and forgo the private accusation of guilt, burdens of a personal conscience tormenting without recognition, unpublicized, unsung by the free press and the vultures of communication, religious division. He's complex, and uses saintliness for a license, permission for the promotion of unsaintly violence, broadcasting suffering among others, destruction and trouble for all his fellow men. He doesn't sound nice. Is that my thought *of* him, or is *he* my thought? I'm only me, but what's this? I'm dreaming this, but it's so real that it seems like a dream. *What* dream? What's life?

"But I'm wasting my own dream by philosophizing. Jessup is obviously impatient, a fugitive from the law, a suspected convict, with already a crime behind him, redder than blood, blacker than a night from which moon and stars have been removed, to illustrate the dark side of sin, and graphically demonstrate how devoid of light is bitter evil, the devil's spite.

"These are strong words. Let Jessup explain. I'm ready to judge him, and very quick to condemn. Am I biased? No, merely prejudiced. I know my verdict, already."

"I am guiltless, utterly guiltless," began Jessup Clubb, on a ringing note. "I am my own redemption, cleansed with the sweet dirt of Ira Huntworth, who sweats stink like a leper's sores—we atone by kissing. And the ugly becomes well; the barren teeming; the sour honeyed over.

"I cast no first stone, having not sinned myself. *Not*, I insist, you disbeliever. I confess, that my only scandal is in being too good. For I am a victim.

"Persecuted? Yes, I have been. I have suffered.

"And for what? All my ordeals, tribulations, the spiritual consecration of my agony—toward the deliverance of men.

"I hereby declare, all men are forgiven. They have not done wrong. For they knew not what they did.

"I am mankind's supreme 'superego,' if you'll pardon the modern concept. I observe life, and I peer into death. I see that man is vanity, and folly is all the variety we have, until immortality conquers death. What more can I say?—having said all.

"I hear voices, protesting me. The mob is of many tongues, and all incriminate. They want to tear down. I, to build up. And as I strive to build, I stand on a weak edifice, and the foundation crumbles. Thus are we made of flimsy sand, and weakened by the washing waves. What will endure?

"I have many tears to weep. In each glistens an eternal wail; in each, sighs of infinity. All souls still live, in each core.

"Compassion, and you are no longer a brute. Have I kidnapped, and fallen thereby? I am but a man. I prove my divinity. What can requite me? An infinitely great understanding, beloved by the Lord. We are but men. And love is our vehicle.

"Behold that we breathe. A breath passes, and so does a spirit. We are disembodied. Soul, soul, is everywhere.

"Nay, do not be cruel. I beg you, not to judge me. The Lord witnesses. Let Him proclaim, whether I be stricken with guilt, muddied by my foul infamy, or absolved with beatitude, pure as my original innocence.

"The disaster that befell Adam, was it mine? It was everyone's, old and young alike. Then why condemn me? Who the hell am I to be a scapegoat? Leave off, I tell you!

"You bum, I'll kill you. Get the hell out of here. You stupid slop of a dreamer. You have a fine right to accuse! I'll slay you, and if you find heaven in the dark, your blindness has grown eyes. Get the shit out of here. You stupid bum."

Morstive's dream was turning into a disturbance, led along the pricky road of a nightmare, with its accompanying discomfitures. Physically shouting out could provide quick relief. Thus, "I fear him! He's incorrigible! Wake me! I demand to wake up!" Morstive uttered, as directives to the airy captor that held his consciousness helplessly bound to all that glaringly filled it from sources wild and free, not tried, but consented to too easily.

"Shut up, he's harmless," the dream said, and Morstive was obliged.

"By far I'm a higher martyr than he," he said, "for I never inflicted this on him! What crap I have to take, a mingled concoction of false piety and obscene raillery, the vulgarity of oaths and cussing enmity, coupled with pretensions along the sublime, invoking God for a father. It's all pure baloney. It's just trash. But not trifling trash. It's in the ominous stage, to what's wickedly lethal. Where is

107

society's protection? How can *he* be at large, lurking out free, while innocence cowers but has no running room from peril's monstrous venom?"

"That's nice," said Jessup, overhearing this: "That's quite kind of you. I'll return the favor, some day. I have loads of invective to lash at you. You, Morstive Sternbump, I detest more than anyone else. Any power I have, will go to your suffering. My labors shall be unremitting. I shall slay you."

"I'm afraid!" gasped Morstive, gripped in the strenuous grip of a nightmare, a wrestler's lock-hold, as Jessup came forward, intent on mayhem, with a dirty look in his eyes.

"Now I'll give myself something to be guilty for," that coward said, aglow in the sweetness, the kindness even, the intolerable benevolence, of his audacious deed. He was tawny, even more, without his beard. He dressed normally. But somehow, he didn't look sane.

He approached. Morstive screamed, and woke up the neighborhood.

∞16∞∞∞∞

Because by now it was full-fledged night, the sleeping hour of spooks and other creeping things, chilling to the casual fright of blood, making it congeal. "He constituted what I may call a threat," said Morstive. "Thus one's offensive expression of paranoia is transferred to the victim, an equally *defensive* paranoia, suspicion breeding an open mirror between two faces, the hated and the hater, alternately in turns, each suspect and suspecting. This disease is contagious, a product of man's gregarious conflict with himself, hence with others. Expecting harm, we give it first. We're prepared, by assaulting. We protect ourselves from hostile aggression (real because imaginary) by launching the offensive, getting the antagonistic jump. Only a hermit is safe, yet he has imaginary devils to contend with, and bitter angels of accusation, an open war of airy phantoms, striking him almost at will. Fight! That's what man does.

"I'm really awake! This is splendid, I'm free.

"Was that Jessup Clubb, or my image of him? In fact, where is time?

"The stop clocked. Have I been sleeping a whole day, after failing to write last night, following a restaurant orgy of eating and intercourse, starring my own stomach and Tessa Wheaton? Then I'll be damned. I never know when to expect my next surprise.

"Although I was hungry last night, the sleep killed whatever satisfaction I had, and the dream ate it away. Dreams are hungry, they consume us. I must raid the snack for a refrigerator.

"And yet the lights are blinking in apartments, reveals my faithful but dumb window, that discreet aperture through which I may visually relate with what I suppose is an outside world. In winter the darkness is early; what my fright had considered midnight, an eerie tomb and a dancing grave, is now merely the supper hour, and all those folks are home from work. I can see the tables set, there are so many of them. Or was there no work, being Sunday, and Hulda Stock has become Popoff, as both parties to the betrothal whispered down my dream's ear, or shouted with hilarious mockery? And then, is it February, or not? Where have I all this time been? Chasing elephants in a safari? I've been right here, an indiscriminate entertainer, conducting open house with no guest list or doorman to weed crashers out. What have I grossed in knowledge profit? And who's to tell? After all, my own life is intimate to me; but its practical details are so subject to flux, I feel left out. Won't somebody introduce me to that weirdest of specters, the me I've never known?

"That 'me' must carve a dent somewhere. What I've been through is meat for art's gravy. But what's the sauce's formula?

"I have every inspiration and insight, and lack only style. The content is endless, but the words clash, and never concord. If this isn't frustrating, I wonder what frustration means? There's something to laugh about, in my life.

"My parents must be worried over me: but I told them never to phone, and they were intimidated. My duty is due to them, and guilt shall prepare me a visit. They gave me birth. What can I give them?

"And my money, is another problem. I have unemployment benefits, but the stocks are worn out from where I was surprisingly hired as an executive last year, as Morgan fell. Yet my bank account still holds, obviating the necessity to worry. Yet insecurity bothers me, because numerically and quantitatively my money falls short, although the quality is good. American currency is first-rate, if you're an American. I suppose I owe it some patriotism, finding myself included in the nation's overall economy, as a statistic in records and files everywhere, keeping bureaucrats working overtime. In spite of this, I'm anonymous. This guarantees my privacy, except for myself. For I'm visible to me, and my name is evident, wherever I go. Identity is not at all unthrilling. It has its satisfactions.

"Yet I'm mysterious, a stranger to the community. The municipality, in which I exist, has no kind words to say to me, or unkind. I chafe a bit, being ignored. Yet I hide. Who wants publicity?

"I'm the most complex me I ever knew, for who else do I know? Since creating me, my parents, due to humility or inadequacy, have hidden away from my formation, leaving things to chance. Here I am, too late to change. My form is so mobile, it's stagnant. I drift, like a rock. The atmosphere affects me, the world is my undoing, current events ruin me; and the cosmic scheme, history in the process of becoming, leaves me out so *in*, I have no one to consult but myself, who has only blank information to give. I should give God a chance. His reputation has fallen, but in olden times He was considered quite the Thing. I should let Him work on my ignorance, to either purge me through it, or indict, as a helpless case. I'm what they call passive, and play an active role in abetting this passivity, until I've really got myself going: nowhere in both directions, and everywhere in the center. Thus trippingly I comingly go, and the going gets nullified as soon as sent. I scamper up, gather rolling dust, while time collects every second's variation of Morstive Sternbump, and deposits me neatly in the public dump. Should I protest? Yes, it's my compulsory legal right to, in this machine era of regimentation, for everybody is another copy of me, just as inarticulate. And I—duplicate *them*. This entitles me to a part of humanity, as my due. I stayed born, once I got here, until maturity let me slip through, cleansing my adolescent face of the pimples. Shall I greet middle age? In my late twenties, I should wait. Let *it* come, as I observe my passive state, like a king chained to a throne, stuck to his reign, but the throne bit by bit has become, due to hidden wiring, a gradual electric chair. This is my regal fate, and my just doom."

Morstive chewed away, jawing his food down, and with each

bite he crushed a meditation. The thoughts first were masticated, then mashed, and finally dwindled down to assimilation, to remote stretches of his blood cells, districts along outlying suburbs of what he called his greater body, from where centrality radiated to share its core with each democratic particle.

∞17∞∞∞∞∞

Although completely rested, with recently derived food energasticity that should whet his activity lust, he found himself browsing among drowsiness, tired with idle complacency, suffering a saturation of self. Back he went to bed, and begged his dream to stay away this time. However, the latter's circuit was not complete. It needed to expand, like the military elbow room Germany needed to ease Hitler's mind. Just before dropping off, Morstive conditionally requested a truce of armistice with, should he appear again, the vindictive Jessup Clubb, ignited to religious frenzy. "I'll placate you," Morstive suggested, "and follow a policy of appeasement. Do not nightmare me and violate the neutrality of my dream. Submit your griefs to arbitration, and be diplomatic with your woe. I shall cooperate, by sympathizing. Go ahead, now. I shall tune you in."

"Roger," came Jessup's wavelength, subdued and contrite, abashed even, willing to negotiate a confession-type communication, not batter and smash Morstive with fury, but letting the guilt seep out, splash by glob by drop, blood with a taint. "I am calm now," said Jessup, deepening into his dream, glaring with a force of realism; "I am mild, as our Savior was, a holy man. My ways have been wrong ways, my days have rotated into nights, and the dark hours have been the greater, the bright hours the lesser, my innocence must prompt me to say. What is a man, that he sins? Or woman, for being fallen? Where does evil tend? Bless me, please. Morstive Sternbump, I commission you God. This is delegated power, use it carefully. Absolve me, that I be purified. Redeem me. Do not hesitate. But why are you silent? Your dream is as the world, muddied sometimes, now clear. Your weather, it must shine.

"Time ago, it had it, there was a commerce of friendliness

111

between us. I introduced you to Morgan Popoff, a dear buddy of mine, and was even responsible, at my suggestion, for fixing you up with Tessa, as half a double date. It was she, New Year party before last, whom I jinxed (she being virginal then), by prophetically hurdling her into a strumpety future, and predicting the puncture of her last line of defense and the bastion of her reputation, the puffed-up bubble of her prudery, though you yourself failed to crack it. Yet, feeling guilty immediately, I asked her to scratch me, and dig in the modest length of her nails. To me, I'm everybody's martyr, so everybody thinks. I have also been called inhibited, by those whose comprehension is not stout to sufficiently delineate me; I began outside the sphere of most men, and shall end beyond mere mortal barriers, suffused with powers of rare usage, gifts of uncommon magic. My origin was history, fables and lore have supported me, and my forward destiny transcends the cult of scope, as dimensioned to literal materialism of short minds. To comprehend me, invention has yet to come up with conjury's true measure. In me, mystery's end is just beginning.

"And in me resides God's devil, those inseparable companions, absolute evil and ambiguous good. This is our soul's evolution, the spirit's fit survival, in the fighting jungles of our kind. Imbued with that deity, and those demons, I behave with strange purpose, and with wild tragedy. I am the most alone of men, the breed of man's scourge, the divinity of our traditions. My life is part of death, and lives to exalt it. Then see me not as a mystery, but as a myth in breath, manifesting the sadness of the unknown, as I pierce this unquiet earth, and oddly unbalance the even, terrify the complacency out of men, shake their lots and commend a brief courage, as opposed to the sunken failure of their success, the puny triumph of a vegetable's ultimate decay and its attendant pleasure to plight the path to ripeness, and blight the sweet hour in the prime. We fell off delight's forbidden tree. Its processed apple juice, we drink today.

"A serpent divided is a united conquest, and in dear time we plucked independence, and became the colony of our own law. We bear fruit, but we are the seeds that the fruit blows, the pitfalls of abuse, winter's springtime death. Beautiful works of art have been created, and noble things have been destroyed. How much of us endures; which ones of our tribe, what members of this declining race, erected paper monuments to immortality, cardboard plaques daring the wind's teeth and war's criminal onslaught? Patterns of us must survive, the blueprint of the future. Tomarrow is always in our bones. Three tomarrows, and there's crumbled dust.

"When night changes into day, how free is the sun? Patiently, we climb. The horizon is round and endless, the skies bless us with their kiss of light, and we live death into life again, and tear youth out of age. Beauty advances, ugliness recedes, and truth is an enigma in our mind. What should we do? What thoughts do our actions prepare? Where does it lead? How far, yet how near? Oh my son. I am your father. Morstive Sternbump, you have volunteered to be kidnapped. You must die. Why not now, if you have no objection? Whoever sacrifices, gives life and birth to other men. This is the law. Indicate when ready. I always knew you could be a better martyr than I, and today we'll carve out the proof, won't we? Yes, I've already commissioned you God: but of a junior variety, through whose agony, by your atonement, I'm purged, your friends redeemed, mankind absolved. Can you do more for us? Submit. Your love for life is a way of saying you're afraid to die; a fear that reduces your dignity and maligns your noble nature. In your own dream, you're kidnapped, and ransomed out eternally, for you to pay the supreme price. Are you game? This will be your manhood; for affirmation is truest blest when eclipsed by negation; and the personal furies of your force, the private stature of your vanities, will be transformed to other values outside the life of your will, serving higher good to come. Isn't this a wonderful challenge? It's an exclusive opportunity. You'll be worshipped, your birthday celebrated, your name taken in vain; and men will blame you, or praise you, or pray to you, depending on the state of their fortunes, the stakes their harvest plays for, the rise and fall of self in deed and act, to gain the possession of happiness in relative goods of wealth, to acquire means to scare bad days from the doorway, and to barter against the sadness, bargain with destruction, head off life's enemies. You'll have a hand in all this, and be the target of their superstition. Be a Savior. It's your only salvation."

Morstive found a direct voice to oppose this, and said no at once. "Though I be the medicine man to a fertility rite, or be Him Whom bending knees and dancing feet implore for the beneficence of magic spells to subdue common evils in the sessions of merciless nature, I refuse anything not human, and require my own existence. I don't aspire, hung up as you are, to elevated roles beyond my skin's ken: you project your own fantasies on me, and externalize for a scapegoat, which I won't be. I defy you. You bred your misfortunes, inadvertently perhaps, but now go live in them, submit to the penalty of society, the punishment for your abnormality. Don't thrust it on me. You can't escape. Kidnap is a serious offense, and your death is expected in trade. I'm not you; don't intimidate me, and rub on my strange face your own familiar trouble, for which yours can be the only responsibility, the grave you yourself dig. Now that I've established my distance, and refuse to be your god through which your behavior is acquitted; now that you can't depend on me (for I have forsaken death, to keep my mortality going, and live to uphold a limited destiny allotted to my frail powers in my upkeep), and can't foist off on me, palm off, the knots of your doing, I bid you back up, relinquish your intentions, and detach your problems from my possible solution: I can't help you. Is that enough?"

This reply, uncharacteristically firm, a formidable upholding of his integrity, commended Morstive to his dream, and so staggered the latter that its hold was loosened, for Morstive to awake, the defensive victor for the day. "I did myself proud," he said; nor had dawn arrived. "It's well I should sleep again," he said, "to consolidate my victory. I submerged my antagonist, and lost my fear. I'm the king and tyrant of my dreamworld, the monarch of this pictorial fantasy. In *this* arena, my record fares the best. Let me play out all further battles here. I am equal, in the armed fortress of my dream, to all plots and attacks, as my counterweapons annihilate the entrenched enemy, and catch him before his slaughter goes off to beat me in surprise offense. Too bad life isn't *always* a dream, now

I've learned to ward off phantom blows in the vision of an unseen battlefield. All this terrain's unknowability somehow is secure. The land's intangibility serves safe refuge.

"Outside, I physically expose myself, and bring my bruised pain back into a dream here, where I repair and retaliate. This is like my art. This is writing. Life unnerves, dreams restore, and art gushes. Here we recuperate, and the writing healing fountain starts. But these are pictures, not words. I dream I write, but when I write I only dream, which spoils the whole point. I get, then, the worst of two worlds, and am trapped down the middle. To forget, I'll sleep. Jessup is subdued. He'll confess, and not involve me, save as I observe his torment, detached indifferently from his fate. Lull me, Sleep. Jessup is tame. Oblivion's anxiety-free, and will graze with fearless leisure on this random moving meadow, where no fox lurks. I graze, entrenched in grace."

∞19∞∞∞∞∞

"I'll behave, this time," Jessup promised, contrite as ever. Morstive turned on his side, in a posture of easy nocturnal hearing. Jessup resumed his harmlessness, and made of his apology the ruinous tale of his confession.

"A son was my obsession. Why, I don't know. I admired Morgan, whose ability to get one I considered very high; and I cursed Tessa, for miscarrying his son I planned to steal. I needed, always, to interfere. Others had to do my bidding. They were my instruments. I even used me. I tried to get a son myself. Supported by both Hulda and Emma, in their own apartment, I entranced them to be my mistresses, so that either-or may bear a child, and get my business on with. It was my mission, my life's work by dedication, which by crook or proxy or directly may utilize any end to its technique to key the lock and be complete. Hulda and Emma proving barren, or myself sterile, I despaired how bootless and fruitless it all was. But behold: Morgan, then married to Tessa, got his wife in the family way, in an interesting condition. Snooping the scent, I came down to kill. As her lover, I impatiently prodded her interior, to hurry on the eventful birth. I fooled too much, hurt nature to revenge me, and soon after Christmas a miscarriage frustrated my plan, and my newest life was cramped with death. You can imagine my feeling. I was heartbroken.

"New Year's eve, and I was resolved. We met on the way to the party, and took a taxi together. Once there, I sermonized, and was credited with many converts: Merton among them. Those who had children donated them all to me, in return for religious indulgences, free passes past admission to heaven's gate, though they were to continue to sin to wear out life's duration. Such compromise is a deal of double concession. An accomplished hypocrite, I get both ways at once: worldly hell and the hellish world. Paradise would complete my plans.

"Those who hadn't children, among my converts, ran up a bill of credit, on the offspring to come. Thus I dealt in futures, taking stock of the bondage. I was so elated at this coup, how well it had come off, the drunken pleasure of my evening's success . . . guilt struck me. I asked to be crucified, to culminate my triumph. However, they wanted you, instead.

"That struck me as an apt substitution. Yes, you would have done, only you wanted to live. Myself, only death can correct me. Thus we both escaped, on penalty of life.

"But with the year's first few suns and an access to sober reconsideration, those parents reclaimed their sons, and left me childless. All promises were void, and my hope legally blasted. How furious, how cheated, how deliberately spiteful—against myself—turned in my wrath; and from the many city's carriages I kidnapped my first child: a boy, a bouncing baby. How proud a papa I was!—and stole a cigar to celebrate. I smoked it for jointly all mankind, at once.

"The law is pursuing me. To escape detection, and feel free, I shaved my Christian beard, and exchanged my slavish robe for a busy city suit, such as you see me in. Where I fled, and how I'm doing, I dare not to reveal, being a wanted criminal. There is no reward for my capture, so it does you no profit to lead to information that would result in turning me in. I'm a fugitive, and as I run I hide. Is there any more regrettable life? And yet, no one seems to care. My only pity is self-pity; as sympathy and compassion are absent from the scoundrels who run the city and those docile governed, too meek to show mercy. The less mercy, for the worst crime. For the child is dead.

"The child is sacrificed, but I roam free. Yet who worships me? Who, among the many? My occupation is an unpopular one these days, what with the quacks and charlatans who imitate me, debasing the role. A true martyr is rare to find, and is not developed, but is born. I had the talent. Some call it genius. I'm that stamp's archetype.

"My 'son' is dead. What am I living? I get no joy. Sex didn't please me, for I wanted a child. As a professional sufferer, I never permitted myself happiness—it was a forbidden indulgence, and bad for my reputation.

"Now, I am fallen. Or soon to be. Morstive, don't wake up. For if you do, I shall be captured.

"Religion bids me destroy—but *I*'m the one destroyed. Hear me out, asleep.

"I'll go on from here. My oration is incomplete.

"Or it's a dirge. My own pre-funeral.

"Alas, that sadness has mistaken life for death. I grow pious again. Cruelty and viciousness, the bitterness of unrelieved malice, convert me to a holy man. I surrender my guilt to my glory, and of my conscience I make a halo, and wear it for heaven. Having sinned so much, I know all about it.

"Examples flood me of party and people events. The pushing past squeezes me narrowly into now. It comes funneling through the recent, to pressure the present out of shape. Doesn't the past ever end? It doesn't let us breathe. Old deeds *are* the present events.

"A living death is pursuing me out of the past: a child's murder. I did it for eternity, but it winds up a punishable crime, though I claim special exemption, court amnesty, boast an immune right. I did it for divinity, but it plagues me, being mortal. I killed a human child. It wasn't mine. But I killed it anyway. Thus my sin is compounded. Blood demands what blood gave. Society *longs* for my blood. This is true redemption.

"And what must that ex-mayor think? For not only was I, the jury head, to clean up his innocence and acquit his evil of its actuality, erasing the graft from men's eyes and obliterating his simple part in a perfect scandal of the infamous top official level, involving an elected mayor's honor and his party's conscience: but I was to restore him to his job! Can I commit a miracle? After all, I'm human too—in off hours. I'm only divine by profession, but a guy's got to make a living.

"I can't do everything—like molest fate. Page Slickman, and Piper Cole, and you, I was supposed to tamper with: in the conference I had with the mayor (then in jail), visiting his cell. But isn't his jailbreak punishable? And Piper and Page along with him—they all three escaped, and came to tear up our party. The law's lenient, these days. But you can't beat a kidnapping rap. My number's up, decidedly. Inside me are my bones and skull, and they won't have long to emerge. Much as I like them, I hate to see it. I will have lost so much.

"But what did the mayor do for me, that I should hold in heart my unkept promise? He was supposed to get me a son—but I had to kidnap one, and forfeit my life. He reneged; it's not fair. But those other jail items enumerated in our pact—have subsequent eventualities been manipulated, or left to chance? All those people we listed, that you know—what's been happening about them?

"But me—I'm in the worst mess. But they're pathetic, too.

"I'm confused, in my moral crisis. How can I bother about others? What do they mean?

"Yes, it's all a mystery. Don't ask me. My game is up. I won't fake it any longer. They got the bead on me, the goods, I'm caught: it's court, and condemnation. Now no beard can identify me, nor the long robe, though still I have an aquiline nose, and when I'm not fat I'm emaciated—just like my model, so long ago. Different painters painted Him different ways, according to the way *they* were. Does it make sense, or justice? I want to ask one thing: Will I rise again: On my assumption, will I be resurrected? Wait till Easter, and find out. Am I just a perverse adoptation of the Original? Do I represent the more advanced decadence? These are my own graven times. Much of a myth has been made of me. Good Lord, was it deserved?

"I'm confused, between me and the Original. Which is which?

"Morstive Sternbump, goodbye. The dawn has arrived. My number is up. My goose is cooked. I *made* the bed, so I lie on it. In the end, I pay. Even me. Thus is holiness measured, by its degradation. I'm a common criminal, in democratic eyes. How have the mighty fallen, with the leveling off of divinity, the truly mean average. For all that, a man's a man. That's me, too."

The voice's echo, not the seen Jessup, was the shriveled remainder. Was this a dream? Only a dream can handle such a palpable.

"He's gone!" awoke Morstive, as his dim bed returned, and himself, and that blunt clock, the window. "Glad I wasn't sacrificed. I'm sure he's crazy. Maybe they should write a bible about him: I will, and call it 'The Brand-New Testament.' It'll be up to date. Gosh, what a life he had! And his death still in front of him. He has a lot to die for, doesn't he? He'll get there. He's the dying type.

"Well, so much for him. Or will there be more? He's no easy yielder, but a stubborn rascal. Did a demon get in him? For a spell, yes.

"Ah, but I'm back to me. *I*'m here, anyway.

"But what am I? Never mind. I'll just *assume* I'm me. Who else is?

"It was pleasant to yawn. I haven't opened my mouth that wide in many a day. Why do I feel so good? Because *he*'s going, and I'm not? Well, I confess it. It makes me feel just a bit safer, when some *other* culprit gets it, to exhaust the law—and put off death. Justice claims a victim, and so does death. Now they're both surfeited, and won't go looking for me. Not in this bed, anyway. Gosh, I feel comfortable. I like my life. I wouldn't miss it for anything.

"I hope it requites my sentiment. Why should this all be one-sided? I'll be coy, and let life woo *me*. I'll hide what I feel about it. I won't be taken for granted, by such an important matter."

∞20∞∞∞∞

"I'll get up, as only proper, for morning is here."

"But Morstive, I want to keep going," his dream said, refusing to be put off. "I offer you a new visitor, whom you made physical love to not too long ago. For you, that's a rare occurrence. So you ought to welcome her."

"That could only be Tessa. I'm all perked up. I'm honored."

"You're honored? Then she's honorable?"

"Were she not, I'd have no right to be honored. I'm morally aquiver or lascivious for her tight little company. Drag her on, at once."

"But hasn't she been degrading herself?" the dream asked.

119

"Yes, but she's honest about it," slandered Morstive, passing moral judgment: "She's a fallen woman, and therefore lying down. But how else can you get at them? It's convenient."

"You're crass," the dream said.

"Just practical," said Morstive. "I know my meat where I like it. Will you permit me to make love to her?"

"It's out of my jurisdiction," the dream announced, "so violate her at your own risk. I can wake you at any time."

"Well, serve her up, I'm ready," Morstive said, with a knife and fork handy and a plate to drape her over. His appetite was huge. He was going to feed. His carnality was presupposing. His saliva juice was on fire. It would be tempting. She must be gaunt now, sure. As always. But he could close his eyes. In a dream, it was proper for impulse to be fired up, and instinct inflamed. His pajamas were bulging. Good, let her casually appear. Every man's woman, Tessa Wheaton.

"I'm not what I used to be," she said, and blushed with modesty. It was very becoming. So was she: becoming gone, just dripping away. Her moral stature was corrupt. There was just nothing to say. In her defense, she was no longer prudish. But in overdoing it, she had somehow become excessive, and was lacking thoroughly in restraint. Nor did discipline hinder her from falling so actively as she did, the professional playmate of every man's tool. What an incredible comedown. It was scarcely decent. And hardly moral. She blushed, and it became her. "It's against my principles," she said, "to behave badly. Therefore I don't behave at all. That is, not actively. I passively accept. But that's behavior too? It's as much a choice as active behavior? Then I'm responsible. Can I fault me? There's something I may not resist. It's my human nature, sinking below earth level, finding compulsive death in love's abuse, the hysterical sale of my body. Times have changed. Long ago, you tried me. You failed. Now, no one can fail. Isn't it a shame? And all I have is a blush, the most natural cosmetic. I apply it continuously, all day long. And far into the night. I can't tell who my company is. I never wear my glasses at that time. I want to look my best. But they're always feeling me, they want my touch. How coarse, and brutal. For essentially I recoil, being refined. Inherently I'm a maiden. I'm too delicate, by nature. I'm sensitive. I feel everything. Too much, you might say? Too little is bad, too. Society has abjured me. I die in men's underworld arms. In mankind, just what are men? I used

120

to have a husband, Morgan. Jessup became my lover. They must be universal, between them, for now the universe has followed: just variants of them. All men are one man. Or two. Or anyway, three. Or back to one again. One man is all men? And nothing is all that I am. But I'm still desirable, as nothing. Then nothing *must* be something.

"Or is nothing the only thing that does not exist? Then, nothing itself is *not*. There *is* no nothing.

"Then what are my feelings, my me? I've been plundered of my past.

"It's terrible to have fallen. Can't I get up again?

"Don't sleep with me. I'm chaste, you know.

"Yes my whole body is. Except the central hole, where all ends 'meat.' Well, it's my undoing.

"I have a future ahead of me, behind in the past. I must pursue it, and catch up.

"I long to be as I was. It was so exciting, then.

"Don't feel sorry for me. Let me be she who feels sorry. I know what it's all about. Knowing has destroyed my ignorance, betrayed my innocence, and subjected me to original sin. I'm in no position to protest. Therefore I weep. What are my tears worth? Not as much as years. Yet both teach experience.

"And what I learned is my result. I find myself *this* me. Ah, what sorrow! This is like hell. Are you Dante?"

"No, but I'm sad, anyway," Morstive replied, as his bones exuded sympathy, compassion utmost; "I want to weep with you."

"I do it better alone," she sobbed, as the bedroom went into a tremulous echo shake.

"It's unbearable," Morstive said, and all of humanity wept with him. An uncompromising deluge. This couldn't keep up. It should stop, topped off by a totally distracting act. To change the air.

There was Tessa Wheaton. She looked so apathetic. What could revive her? He lifted her dress, and went to work.

"Ouch, it hurts," she said.

"Not for long," he said, and found the rhythm pleasant. "I must be dreaming," he said: "Rarely can I find this in life."

"*Now* you can," she said, her modesty all undone. She was a brazen whore.

They finished with a bang, and she began to whimper. "Life displeases me," she said.

"You must convert it, then," Morstive offered, "more to your desire. Surely I imagine your life was difficult. Come now, my child (though I'm younger than you are): bespeak your sorry heart, divulge the dope, what's the matter, honey? You can talk to your Uncle Morstive. I like you, really. Now don't look so sad. Wipe your eyes. Insert your glasses again. You're homely, you know. And thin, and anemic, and neurotic. I know you have a Protestant origin: Joy means excess, or am I being redundant? Well, I'm here to help you. Can I? Lie down on the couch. I can talk to you, but with other dream characters I wasn't allowed to—I could only listen. I'll talk again, but after I have a lot to listen to. From you. Your lower mouth is shut, so open your upper one. Sex is done, now let ideas spout. Lighten your loaded head. Just talk, without thinking. Later on, you can think about what you say. Now, don't inhibit yourself. What are you thinking of? Come on, now. My ears are quivering with impatience. Talk about Morgan. That should set you going. Do you still like him? Have you any envy for Hulda? Do you accuse Jessup most of all? Being a woman, you ought to speak, without my urging you. This is silly. I can't wait forever. My dream must end, so I can eat again: dream food isn't very nourishing, and not filling either. Enough. Must I command you? Slut!"

"Don't insult me," the indignant Tessa worked herself up: "I hate all men."

"Ah, *that*'s behind it," said Morstive, taking careful note: "Beginning with your father, no doubt?"

"Yes, the fool."

"It becomes interesting," Morstive said. "And I'm sure you have more to tell me."

"What are you—a detective?" Suspicious mistrust in that.

"Not at all," smiled Morstive, like a public relations executive denying his affiliation with a mob union gangster corporation, while betraying what he's denying. Now to proclaim intimacy. "I'm your friend," he said, emphasizing the last syllable—a complete word.

That melted her, chillily. In a reverie of an automatic rote, she spoke like a record scratched to work by the rut-rusted needle of an old crackling machine. It had a familiar ring, or rather groove. "I've been through this before—it's déjà-vu," Morstively silent intoned. He was hearing what he already heard. When? In another now.

"*Are* you my friend after this sex we stooped down to? Only platonic means friendship," she said. "I loved Morgan once, and we were merely friends. He told me his whole life, all his love affairs, confided his ambition, and I was his confidante—and maternal helpmeet as well. He took me out to lunch, where we were working. Always, he paid—the executive, and I a typist. He had been broken up with Hulda. It was such a relationship!—and then we had to spoil it all by getting married. He taught me sex. I never cared for it, though. Too much sweat involved, and much too intimate. How could I feel private? And what he did, I wouldn't tell my own grandmother. Even to her dead corpse in her grave, I wouldn't dream of admitting to such a natural crime; even though I did love him—love him to my own extraction, on the idolatrous side. He was my God. And I was his sunshine, but only when the weather was too hot. But he had economic difficulty, and I was pregnant. Out of work, he declined fast. What could I but take a lover?—who wanted not me, but the child to be. Jessup Clubb this was, who was in the mystic business, at a flat profit. He manufactured haloes, I think, and distributed them through the open black market, at cut-rate mark-me-down, for hilarious consumption. They gave off a yellow effusion, and when eaten lit up the belly, for a translucent glow. It was somewhat holy, in a materialistic age. Religion is an ancient profession—nearly as old as mine—and my lover did well at it, reduced to pauperism and poverty. We were quite an odd pair. Forever was too long for our bond, so it would snap short of that.

"Miscarriage between Christmas and New Year, as my history continues. My lover deserted me, naturally. Morgan wanted to sue divorce, as I prostituted myself. But too late, and he became insane. He watched me at my tricks. And hot things they were, too!

"He escaped from his mental disease, and *I* asked divorce. But no, he pimped me instead, for revenue. We had to eat, didn't we?

"Reduced to that sad state: you were partly at fault. You refused my proxying him a job, and fired me, by offering me a cigar, last July was the date. Then when he came himself, needing you to hire him badly, absolute power had corrupted you, and again you rejected him. What an insidious beast you are! Morstive Sternbump, the unthinkable. You're beyond being repulsive—you're impossible.

(She snarled.) "The mayor divorced Morgan from me at lunch. It was his last public act. It was the gutter for me. Jessup had forecast it, over a year ago, calling me a strumpet, while I scratched him. He loves suffering inflicted by others; I'm the independent type, proudly self-sufficient, and cause all my suffering myself. My life has treated me raw and ugly. It's a disgrace. You can provide your own illustration. Imagine—a back room in a restaurant, you had me in. I can only command an insignificant sum, being unblessed by a ripe body. I'm scrawny. There are more bones to me, than meat. Yet you're not demanding, if you derived pleasure from me. But was *I* pleased? No. The next time, maybe. Maybe some day I'll come. That will snap me out of it, I'll get married, and observe such daily decencies as society minimumly requires. Or am I dreaming? No, you are. But this is all true about me. The truth is a downright lie. I've played it false. Thus, the ruin is mine."

"You poor thing," pitied Morstive, as the broken woman limped away, racked with evil disease. She had stood, not used the couch, in being the party to that confession. "Wasn't that pathetic?" Morstive asked his dream.

"It's afternoon, believe it," said the dream ambiguously, the dream with Morstive in it.

"I should wake up then?"

"If you prefer—it might do you good."

"And I can eat?"

"That's not my business. Eat, but then return. I summon you, though you'd be hardly sleepy. Some finishing courses, on the agenda."

"Some finishing touches, or new courses on the menu?"

"Stop verbally correcting me."

"Who will your introductions be completed by? I have a right to know my own guests."

"You *already* know them."

"To *anticipate* them."

"They're nothing to look forward to. But be flattered by your visitors. They're all crookedly busy, but they take time off to look in on you courteously. To exploit you at a profit?"

"That's an insulting interpretation. I want to be liked, even by them."

"Who?"

"The ones who are due to arrive. *You* tell *me.*"

"I will, but you're angry."

"You're slow. Stop hesitating. Announce them, in their arrivals' advance. I'll be prepared."

"For who?"

"For *them*, dolt!"

"Namely?"

"That's *your* role! Tell me."

"What?"

"Who they are!"

"Who is *anyone?* Identity is a sticky problem."

"Then *nominally*, say who they are."

"By name?"

"That's sufficient. I'll know the rest, by association."

"In memory?"

"Memory is expectation's infallible instrument."

"But the *un*expected occurs, to *confound* memory."

"Let me take *my* chances. Who are my impending guests, my dear whimsical Dream?"

"Page Slickman wants to interview you, and some mysterious unknown person, rumored to be feminine. The unseated mayor, Ira Huntworth, who aspires to higher things to come, would like to present himself to you—a political matter, I believe. Piper Cole is training a fighter for the championship, yet *he* wants in on your company, also. Morstive Sternbump, are you getting popular?"

"Only where *you* are concerned," Morstive said, so widely shunned by so many people in the small part of life where dreams don't interfere. He shattered his dream, and ate from the refrigerator, spilling what remained on his drip-and-dry pajama, to be laundered later. This was real, not dream-food. He was well pleased, having escaped nightmare, particularly from Jessup's little horror drama. Morstive was still safe, and getting filled. True satisfaction, in chunky chews.

Where had the day declined? It must be February already. No telephone ring, no newspaper, a hermit's oblivion indoors. For security, he should look at his bankbook. Meanwhile, where was life going? How would he justify it? That he merely ate, and drank? Not enough. Someone should write a book for him, and in it life would be managed. A semblance of order, for posterity.

"I'm ready to sleep again," he announced, in order to dream. The mechanism was turned on, but the bed had been broken by lovemaking with light Tessa. The dream was on the blink, momentarily. Just some slight disorder. A roar of static was heard. In piercing decibels.

"We're having control trouble," said the mechanical gadget engineer, piloting the station.

"I have three or four important guests," Morstive said, "and I won't be kept waiting." It was annoying. Outside, a winter sunset. Brief, and complete—like life.

Still the dream wasn't ready. Morstive was irate. Why was waiting invariably a boiling issue of untimeliness? That's how it seemed, for when the spirit was set, why *then* the technical difficulty? The static was punctuated by clear intervals now. But Morstive was peevish. One little churlish outcry, a little audible pout. Just to warn the world not to interfere again, with his privacy. Or *to* interfere, when helplessly self-bound.

"I'm irritated," he said, but was told he must sleep, and by so cooperating would help to assure success. Yet he wasn't tired. "I'm too well rested," he said, but it was in his sleep. Only the dream heard him.

In so doing, Page Slickman advanced. "I'm you," he said.

And Morstive heard himself denying him: "Not at all: *I*'m me, I'm afraid."

∞22∞∞∞∞∞

"I have some legal connections," Page began to advocate, "which can prove beyond the letter of the law that your identity is now exclusively mine, by the rights and possession of ownership."

"To whom do *I* belong, then?" Morstive dared to ask, hardly at all now sure of himself.

"To me, as well," he was assured, as Page took over.

"I'm not your *apartment?*" Morstive wondered, his confidence all gone.

"No. You're me entirely."

"That's awful, if my existence isn't dependent on itself. What must I do, then?"

"If you're smart, you'll offer me a price."

"To buy myself back?"

"Precisely. But the expense has gone up. It's very steep, I'm afraid."

"What am I worth?"

"That's up to you."

"But aren't *you* in the driver's seat twirling the steering wheel of bargaining power?"

"Yes, but I'm playing it close to the vest."

"Vested what?"

"Interests."

"But if you're me, or I'm you—I forget which—then the money I pay you for me is paid by you to me as well. It's all our hands, so there's no transaction."

"You're paying me *in order* to get yourself back."

"So that's the deal?"

"I've played my hand. What's yours?"

"The same hand. We're each other."

"Stop confusing us. I mean business."

"Then if you're me, so do I."

"You better draw the line *somewhere.* "

"So we'll stand divided?"

"Only if you pay me."

"But I'm *freely* me."

"Not with me, you're not."

"It'll cost me? But you as well: we're both in the same business."

"You're rocking the boat."

"But we're both in it."

"Look, pay me, and I'll set you free."

"But I *came* free."

"Not any more."

"How can you just *confiscate* me, when I have inalienable liberty?"

"I did it, it's done. But I didn't take away your *life*. You still live, physically."

"But alive, physically, I'm now you?"

"That's my claim, which is uncontestable."

"But if I'm you, what, yourself, are *you?*"

"You're getting personal. Mind your own business."

"But you *are* my business—being me."

"Don't split hairs. I own us both."

"Am I your annex?"

"I colonize you—while also *being* you. You're *me*, but *mine*. I own you."

"It just isn't fair."

"Not for you."

"But I'm you."

"This is entangling. Pay, and I'll cut you loose."

∞23∞∞∞∞∞

The squabble flew circularly. The dream tried to monitor it, or moderate, or arbitrate, but the disputants drowned it out, at every turn. Their convolutions were grim, for the stakes were high.

Variations on their repetitions became inexhaustibly infinite. Apparently identity is a person's life, *plus* the meaning it means for him. But what it means for others affects this. Morstive was clinging, but Page was tugging.

Morstive was worn down to shrillness. He sounded some petty notes: "It's *my* dream."

"But since you're me, it's all mine. *I'm* dreaming this. So behave, or I'll stop dreaming—and where will *you* be?"

"Where you are. You molester!"

"You're calling *yourself* a molester, then."

"But who's who?"

"Let's not get into *that* again. I'm both, and you're me."

"Then *I'm* both, too."

"You're both you and your greed."

"*My* greed! You're extorting me, for money."

"I'll get the best of you, yet. In fact, I *am* it."

"But it's the same, if I'm you."

"You're me, but I'm *more.*"

"More than what?"

"More than whatever's competed against."

"Look, make our minds up. And ourselves, while you're at it. Or is it 'each other'?"

"Don't try equality. It won't work."

It was a stalemate—but somehow, all in Page's advantage. The dream had had enough—it went to sleep!

Thus joining Morstive's sleep. But Page argued on. He lived as himself, on alien mental terrain.

∞24∞∞∞∞∞

All bad things must come to an end. Even here, the topic changed, in installments. The war waged elsewhere, with the quicksand dried up over an issue semi-smoldering, never buried. The dreary dream woke up, to keep audience. Reluctantly, it heard:

"I must insist that we're different," Morstive said, "and furthermore that's obvious. I consider us separate."

"You're a poor mixer," answered Page, "and you ought to join society some time. Doesn't it get lonely where you are?"

"Yes, but I was taught to expect it—realistically, I mean."

"I feel sorry for your education," Page shortly replied, "for having only you to learn from it. What a waste."

"But I'm as good as any man," Morstive opinionated, "and better than myself any day."

"Don't be too sure," Page warned him, a born gambler. Odds were against his underdog opponent. But Page had something to exploit from him. Thus, a contest was on. Even in that dream setting.

"Have you come here for a purpose?" Morstive asked him.

"Yes, are you hiring out your book to anybody? I represent whoever it is, as an agent."

"But the book is not written," Morstive said, "until I find out who the author is."

"Is it a novel?"

"I don't know—I didn't write it."

"Then at least you can be objective about it."

"No—it's mainly about me," Morstive explained, thus plotting no outline, though floating up a theme.

"I want a cut," demanded Page, "a share of advance and royalties, plus the name of whoever it is who's written it—which is my own assumed name; as the creative inspiration was mine. What did you say your book is about?"

"Me, no doubt," Morstive asseverated, "and others as well. Some people will go in, as characters; including, to fill up the sexy angle, women, who are sex incarnate, in *my* book. But non-female portrait types, too. The mayor that was, and our holy mystic, and even you, configure in it, the personality of your ingredients being so admixed, in this relative table of character study."

"Under what name do I go by?" Page Slickman advanced the notion.

"Your own, of course, who else?" Morstive assured him.

"Then I'll sue you," Page said, looking for money.

"I warn you, you have no evidence," Morstive was quick to declare, "as not one word has reached print."

"Then I'll publish it myself," Page helpfully suggested, "and endanger you with a libel suit. Your malicious defamation of me was not one hundred percent nice, in my opinion. Go ahead and write it."

"Though I think lowly of you," Morstive said, "you can't convict me, since the book is entirely nonexistent."

"What has that got to do with it?" Page said, coming at basics: "Its creation is a fixed eventuality, and inevitably there's sure to be a book."

"Why are you so ambitious?" Morstive asked.

And in return was told, "I have what I call a wife to support, though where she resides is out of town. Plus a few debts, and to shore some funds of capital. And for a cash payoff or two. And to dignify a minor bribe, with investment potential. In addition, there's something else."

"I agree with you," Morstive said, though the room was dark, in the shadow of early night. Who was Page Slickman, and by all means why? Morstive yearned to know.

"I can't see you; have you a mustache?" he began, "and are you well-dressed, in the latest fashionable style?" Morstive described him by questioning. Page combined all the answers with "Yes," yet was elusive, hard to pin down. He was shrewd, and quite worldly wise. Morstive continued to attack: "Identity is unmistakable, obviously yours is yours, and mine belongs to me. You're of the world, and calculate to get ahead. I'm from within, contemplating a book, despite all previous failures. I'm much more sensitive than you are, and have the further advantage of being younger. My paunch is more noticeable, true, while you're slim. But you gamble, and I don't. And you're a shady dealer. I find it easy to fail, when success permits. You're handier with the women. And you were in jail. Possibly you're a crook. I belong to the underworld, but the *psychic* one: You're more practical. You kind of got a city contract for a swimming pool, and subsequently it blew up into a scandal, with the mayor proven innocent and therefore run out of office. You're guilty, but free yourself. I wonder where justice is? And if located, can it be prodded to see? It may just have glimpsed you. You're cloaked in mist, obscurely veiled. You crook!"

"If you write that down," threatened Page, glowering now, "I'll persecute you, strip your identity, and make you void of all meaning, cleaned out of social significance, bankrupt in soul and dead in body. And I save my ultimate threat for last."

"Don't tease me. What's your intention, thus violently expressed?"

"I'll kill you, yet," Page promised, despite its obvious antisocial connotations and darkly negative aspect.

"I *hope* not," retorted Morstive, who was sweet on life. He liked it here.

"You've made crime a career?" Morstive hinted, getting sly.

"No, I was selected, crime's chosen appointee. I don't see why all the fuss. Aren't you a criminal yourself?"

"Only in thoughts, not in deed," Morstive said, having cultivated his ethics until they outstripped morality and were even righteous, haughtily pure, the very steeple to the edifice of holiness. The syrup of sanctimony brimmed its jar in spiteful trickles. "*I* don't get myself *arrested*," said the cagey Morstive, secure in the graces of the law, though not of the Lord.

Page recoiled in snakelike slither, sleeked out in that neat, refined cosmopolitan fury. "My mob will eliminate you," he announced, frightening Morstive.

"Spare me," the latter said, having learned humility: his masochism now subjected to an effective test, a wily threat. "I love you," he tried to say, but knew how inappropriate the words were. Page Slickman, from his inside vest, had produced a machine gun. These bullets were apparently real, until further notice. Who would argue with such a hypothesis?

Page trained his finger to hold still, despite the tremoring trigger. It was a sure art of discipline, an astounding feat of restraint. "Thanks for not shooting me," Morstive said, all at once. Or was he really thankful? He slightly wished it, his repressed affection for death and its unknown comforts, its secret dark consolations, its weird triumph in a way. Spared, he had to speak, and only gratitude tumbled out. "I'm forever indebted to you," he said.

And Page seized upon this: "Sign where the dotted contract shows the line," he said; which is how Morstive Sternbump became Page Slickman, in a correspondent alteration of his personality. This would be inconvenient, this strange relationship: being another man. It was almost obscene. And it entailed risks. Would he ever get himself back, and be emancipated from his tyrant? Piper Cole had once pretended being a lawyer, so he should help him. How dependent he was, poor Morstive, on others, and now confiscated, annexed, to the Page Slickman personality, foreignly alien. His dominion was altered, and now he had only colony status, with misrepresentation. This wasn't enough. Should he protest? How could he, being Page Slickman? It was touchy. Uncanny. And also unright. It violated his sacred canons of a man, the right to be himself. Or was he asking for too much, too soon, at the wrong time? Play cool, and see what happens.

"Yoo-hoo—I'm you!" Morstive smiled, disgusting Page: Who promptly disowned him.

The strategy had worked. What next, however? Who was he to be?

∞25∞∞∞∞

A blurred nimbus of light appeared, smoky vapor, cinders from the occult. An emanation, thus introducing the Mysterious Woman. It was she who had kept Page's apartment, and was the absent New Year's Eve hostess, with her existence everywhere nonmanifest. She was just that "something else" which Page referred to in accounting for his ambition. Way back, Morstive, asking for Page, had phoned her. Nor would she offer him, a stranger, a meal. A visit from a detective proved equally futile, who, though resorting to self-torture, failed to arouse her sympathies to get her to squeal, Page being at that time out of town, and his whereabouts a matter for investigation. Her gender was a carefully guarded secret, too delicate to probe. Sex is not clear-cut, as the races are, but hugs to the borderline, preserving a fresh fascination. Identity, when revealed, thus becomes flavored with great interest, and a high degree of what scientists call "appeal," which is at the root of physical curiosity. She had even been a telephone operator, when Morstive had sought Page out to be his agent, on a literary pretension. All that made her real. So many factual unknowns. Memory clustered around her—insubstantially. She even, most amazingly of all, existed. How life surprises one! A regular contradiction to ennui, with its morbid craving for the expected. And the apartment—was she in charge again? Page had "taken over" at the party, due serenely to her most conspicuous absence, which everyone noticed. It had been subject for much comment.

Yet the vacancy of an "at-rent" sign was visible all this year, which had piled up into February. What was what? Morstive couldn't relate, the senses didn't come clear. Yet here was this apparition in front of him, a darkened kind of iridescence. How might he construe this, let what construction play upon it? Analysis must cut through everything, reduce the bewilderness, and simplify this confounded befuddlement. If not, Morstive must write, or select a hired writer, to keep the occasion neat. Problematicals confused him, with his refusal to accord to mathematics its place among quantity's heavens, where figures reign from remote to zero and tabulate the intensity of men. Was Morstive a little baby, not to know the truth?

He questioned Page as to his gambling episode at the party, dicing a skeleton in a closet, and losing bones-down, but winning by bareness. It was eerie.

"Can we disclose anything?" he asked, as his resistance broke down. His customers: Page Slickman with a record at the law longer than crime itself, on either hand; and that "person" beside him, who wasn't even nearly wearing a dress, so little would she divulge herself: How outlandish, not to relieve Morstive of the suspense he acquired at their expense. "What to do about it?" he pondered, and was quick to conclude nothing—which was his hunch at the beginning, though carefully mistrusting it due to lack of evidence. Just such a world was he living in, where coinhabitants were as though dead, though life was therapeutically thumping in their veins, on theory level. How it worked out in practice, he didn't know.

"You're dismissed," he said, and watched their disappearance, seeing therefore nothing. "Wasn't that enchanting?" he said, glad to have his own identity back, which Page Slickman had ordered for himself, at gunpoint. "Well, that was exciting," Morstive mused, suffocating these words in the rotund orifice of a yawn, which indicated he was tired, his spirit jaded, on a plane approaching monotony, a haven in bleary holiday for a heart worn out by spending too much emotion where the world didn't need it, and for return acquiring what cynics smilingly refer to as wisdom, which is a pretty shoddy commodity. "I'll turn the Page on *that* dream episode. But look who's here! Keegan Dexterparks! Why don't you like me? Because I'm white?"

"*Most* people I see are white. I hate being black. I want to get white myself. *You*'re white, I want your whiteness. Let's trade our outside skins, meaning our whole bodies. The names and personalities will be traded too, to keep the original bodies company. I mean a whole, total swap, your package for my package. Is it a deal?"

"But why pick on me? What did you have against me? And why not trade *another* white for his skin?"

Keegan Dexterparks started to answer, but paled off into nothing when the dream abruptly finished him out. The dream was asked, "Why didn't you let him stay?"

"I can be whenever I want the inscrutable enigma of my traditional dark irrationality. *Sometimes* I spray an illumination or revelation; but mostly an impenetrable murkiness defies all interpretative meddling into clusters of pseudo-symbolism. Accept my vagaries. You're *my* guest."

Morstive was about to say, "But you're *mine.*" But the dream went back to business. A new scene was witnessable, and *actual* guests would walk on, putting Morstive in *his* place, the dream in *its.* The world receded. But when had it last advanced?

∞26∞∞∞∞∞

"Who's that group of muscles organized around a man? And they're all black, though at the center of them, focusing identity, isn't Keegan Dexterparks, but a Negro heavyweight of West Indian origin owned by his manager, Piper Cole: who also is plus two hundred pounds, distributed in blocks of fat around a structure of sloppy obesity, the mayor's bodyguard before both were evicted, and a convicted non-lawyer, with a gambling disdain for what the law allows, formerly merely a poor boxer, who owed me an unrepayed favor, but lost any bout with a decent purse, mostly by the technical route. In jail he was handicuffed to what was then his sworn mayor, whose stink he imitated, to consolidate party loyalty, and provide sure followship to his harassed leader, from whom, at the party, he defended a heckler, being a brute and a bully, both, and interested in his own pocketbook. He's assembled some bookies, with the title of heavyweight championship under challenge by his colossally developed athlete, through whom all hunger and former poverty and licking up the mayor's behind will be rectalled, or wiped out. So much for his awful past. Do I need him for a lawyer? Such services are illegal—he's barred from license. How did he fool anyone at all? He's stamped by a cheap counterfeit. And he contains the ethics to thoroughly fix this coming fight, with the champ he's opposing to take a dive. That's not fair. Hello! What do you want?"

"I'm lookin' for the gym," said Piper, with every faculty in command of him. His charge was wearing boxing gloves and

trunks, demonstrating an exceptional physique. "Win, damn you,"
Piper told him, and was greeted by a nod. Both looked sullen,
determined. "We gotta win," Piper repeated, "money's at stake.
You gonna go out and get it, kid?"

"Yeah I sure am, bossman," his disciple answered, the promising contender.

"When's the fight?" asked Morstive.

"Comin' up," said Piper: "Don't you get no paper?"

"No. Is it February?"

"Yeah. We're late for the fight. Let's go."

Watching them vanish, Morstive felt like a real fan. Would it
be on television? He had no set, but he'd go to a bar, and nurse a
beer to the outcome. How great, the sporting life.

∞27∞∞∞∞

Unrehearsed, Ira Huntworth approached. "I'm aimin' for governor," he said, "and Albany's my destination. It's right near the
garbage dump. What convenience! Everybody will like me if I'm
governor: the whole state."

"Should I vote for you?" Morstive asked.

"If you want."

"Okay, then I will," said Morstive. Why not?

"What are your qualifications?" he asked, however.

"Whatever you name, it's on the record. All there, that's me."

"I've never voted," Morstive pledged.

"Citizenship," the ex-mayor reminded him, almost automati-
cally. Politics is a public performance. If you smoke in a back room,
then you're a boss. Otherwise, it's civic to be a civilian, live in a big
city, buy a daily newspaper, and avoid crime with minute circum-
spection. This is a difficult achievement, but quite rewarding, and
character-building. An exemplary moral-lesson-personified edified
the anonymous man-in-the-street, Morstive of no office. A celebrity,
on even terms! Morstive was tied-tongue. Then he shoved his shyness out.

"Have you bathed lately?" he asked his former civic leader,

appropriately personal for the occasion, living the life of a public bathtub.

"Everywhere," the answer came, "wherever I'm included un-der anatomy. Examine a chart, see the ligaments and the structure that glues skin to bones, and water has invaded every part, in the person of me. Which only the best soap could reinforce, from the city's free supply. It's wiped all but freckles away, cleaned off my record, and left me logically bland for the name of governor. I'll colorlessly stand by, unnoticeable. Government by non-interven-tion, is a frequent practical motto. I'll stand aside, with a benevolent twinkle. I'll look discreetly away, at times. Have you seen a clean man? I'm he."

"But don't you protest too vigorously, in your repeated heated assurances, the hazy rhetoric of conviction? My nose is an honest liar. It reports to me, like a quarantined spy, of a permeable odor, which unmistakably appoints your body for source and origin. Such concrete evidence is hard to deny. Surely your intelligence, which as a phenomenon must exist, accords this fact the truth."

The mayor blanched. He wanted to deprive Morstive of the offending nose. But why lose a vote? So words would do, instead. Morstive's nose was impugned, as too semitic. "Take a razor and slice it off," the mayor advised.

"What! To spite my own face?" replied Morstive.

"Then stop smelling me," the mayor officially commanded, from former authority while keeping his "mayor" title.

"Only if *you* stop your stink," Morstive required. Thus, their delicate little subtle little refinement of conditions kept up a whince and dilation, as though from nostrils.

"Funny to argue with *you*," said Huntworth, "for I also dis-puted with your one-time boss, at New Year's party, the night you were framed and fired. He put up his money as solid proof that I stink, which on his part was a commercial gesture."

"Turkel Masongordy? He's been boycotting my dream, it seems. Hadn't he contributed funds to back your mayor campaign? What was the fight about, at the party?"

"He accused me of stinking, as *you* just did."

"First evidence of mutual taste between me and him. *Then* what?"

" 'You *think* I stink,' I qualified, as a dainty rejoinder. 'I *know* it,' he insisted, 'and I have money to back it. That proves it.' Uncouthly, he was saying that money talks. I told him to keep his nose to himself. And for you, I say likewise. I'm lumping you together with him. You're both too coarsely keen. And all other smellers, as well. Contagiously deceived, I can say. Unanimous noses, all with one illusion! The truth is I'm dainty, my fragrance fresh as morning dew, or mother's virgin milk. You're under illusion so long as you keep up your abominable sensitivity. Restrain that blunt factor, if you please!"

"I knows what I nose," said Morstive, puckering his. He accused the ex-dignitary of slighting the sanitation department's essentially garbage-collecting, rubbish-disposal dual roles, from the stench of office. Then Morstive launched further pellets: "Other glaring defects are evident, and smirch the political unassailability of your character, furnishing fond fuel for your fiendish critics. To single out one select feature, recall the New Year's party: you stank in the bathroom, handicuffed to Piper Cole, despite frenetic efforts by Hulda Stock, among others, to use the lavatory for physical hygiene. At last, the hour being late, you emerged, but purely naked! This shortened the gap of horror between smell and sight. And yet!—despite your high position in the stratosphere of public affairs, not a single guest recognized you! What effrontery, you might say? True, but it revealed you to be a do-nothing mayor, as well as a be-nothing. Imagine! And in this age of excessive publicity. Your campaign poster, your frequent newspaper photos, the numerous caricatures, the feature magazine articles, and television itself—failed, pompously failed, to communicate the sketch or outlines of your frazzled identity to the body politic that you governed! And with the swimming pool scandal so recent! Clothes were put on you, proving decency can apply to anyone. You outlow your own least, which is the best I can say for you, by humane forbearance. You're great to practice charity on. I think you're worse than yourself, which is as far as worst can get, by bitter analysis of comparison. How did you get out of jail so easy, and get acquitted so fine? Was the judge bribed? But Jessup Clubb, on whom you depended as effective means to resume your elected job, forged a parody of your innocence and yet here you are unemployed! Collecting the dole, again? And what promises have you ever kept? Jessup had to steal his own son, though you divorced Tessa Popoff from Morgan, and devised Merton Newberg as sane—who'll replace you, some day, in the mayorality. At least you left Keegan black—an accomplishment, though without the boastibility of difficulty. While in office, you thought to investigate who, by all means, was Page's sexless friend: and the result is nil. Emma and Hulda—Jessup instructed vaguely, and you lost the drift anyway. You lost your office, but not your orifice. On the whole, you're a hole. A windy one, at that. You keep all noses clattering. As a comedian, you insult all comedy. The jest would be on you, if only there were wit in you for a jest to be known by. But your stone of wit wears a wooden heart, in the paper wind. The wind issues, from where? From wet air. Air's your sire, you dripped from it, as its sole heir. You're just a drop. But the drop is dry. Then all that you can be, is only one no. The plural of 'no' is the nose, that knows you, that knows your singular 'no.' "

"No, I say," sputtered the mayor.

"Don't 'no' me. I 'know' you. You've been overpublicized, for such an underfigure. At court, where you were acquitted, the television spectacle you made of yourself showed you as a putrid human, so low that even disgrace wouldn't stoop to belt you one. Have you a redeeming virtue? Yes, you'll make a good governor some day: you're innocuous, and your platitudes convince a crooked state that evil is a recommendation for a candidate's eminence, by his being passively servile to it, incorruptibly corruptible. There. My language has been restrained. You've been overlooked, your crimes unpunished. Justice had its eyes wide open, and saw all it blindly could, in the darkness of its light. You're forgiven—by so much!

"You're my fellow human being. As such, I honor you.

"How long can you hide behind fraternity? Forever, in our tight little species. Our threatened race. Our dear and close pack.

"But you stink. Really! You do! Go on, get out. Out, I don't care if you're famous. After you, solitude is bliss. I've been visited. I have one desire left. Dream permitting, I must wake up."

∞28∞∞∞∞∞

"Hasn't this been exciting?" asked the dream, stroking him fondly; "so many extraordinary people! Bet you learned from speaking with them, battling them in bruising opposition, and hearing their words of memory that break on the past like the rockbound smash of waves. Surely, you'll arise wiser!"

"What year is it?" Morstive asked, slipping out of his battered bed, too broken to be used any more.

"*This* year," he was informed, while brightening the toilet with his famished urine.

"I feel better now," he post-biologically reflected. Now to get visual, tactile bearings. The window was black night, nominally dark. "It's not day," he said, and drew a conclusion.

The idea of eating occurred to him, habit having cured him of shyness in that capacity. He devoured the contents of his refrigerator, and drained it down with a whole bottle of milk. Alert energy returned, a lengthy rest having restored his vitality to its original ebb. Yawning, he fell asleep on his toes, having an unemployment insurance check to collect as well as the groceries for shopping, should morning accommodate him by coming. It would.

Then it did. Dawn preceded the day, brighter and lighter, in the middle of a normal business week, or thereabouts, to the end. He would be active now, and be what they say alive, employing his force to that extent. Would his soul consent? Without positive doubt, given the factor that living is a useful occupation, and worth the continuous effort, his wearying application. To do! That's his credo. Being would come later, directly as a result, or in spite of behavior. Roused to life's call, heeding it, Morstive Sternbump arose: the world's strange soldier, peacefully at attention while the wars crash and jump about him, the clash of unending personality. He must explain it. There would be words to tell, thing-manufacturing words, to square off the round edges and make the complex plain, the insipid worth telling, and the usual highly rare. "I'll use my life," Morstive said, "as though I were the material, transformed by the intellect of sense into the emotion of formed art. I'll get someone to do it for me, and I'll advise him. We'll collaborate, but he'll write. Then all this will be settled out, and I'll afford to sleep without dreaming: a priceless luxury. Today is a new day. It changes the people I already know, they move, marry, advance, relapse, and degenerate. I must hurry, to fix the image, while in flight. They'll stand still, to have their portraits taken, and abandon the next transformation. I must freeze them, rendered immobile by still art, between the strides of their pulse. The blood beats faster, while time retreats. Death is more than an outline: it eats the horizon, and worms forward, like ink that destroys a lithograph, obliterating the surface. I evacuate to the depths, that observation may ripen, and truth take minute detail of itself, the mirror to its own reflection, thus indicating a world. Which is where I came in, a junior member, receding dimly to a senior. I choose to know: that's my passion."

He resolved to be active, and was blessed with success: he tripped, and fell; but recovered; and strove forward, on so known a rug that his very path was a regression. "I must make strides," he said, and with swollen determination he inhaled a lungful of each air, right to left. His center was missing, tilting equilibrium on odd fulcrums of imbalance, extremes dynamically counterpoised. How diversified, his wide visionary contradictions! All the more was an order of art imperative. To pattern incompatibles.

The window went outdoors, as his eyes wildly saw. "Life!" he prided himself on, his most common uniqueness, that exclusive secret to his dormant existence, which he vowed to bring forth, ignite the debut, opening out through time into the spaces where art roams, experience littered everywhere, the transconfusion. "I want everything," he proclaimed, while possessing a fistful of nothing in each hand, those symmetrical rations. "I'm rich," he said, and desire spread a silver carpet before him, where he'd go to pot on a crux of gold, down by the dreamy rainbow, in the meadow of his delight. Forward! And with swaggering boldness, he meekly hesitated, torn between himself and himself, on either extreme. "Which?" the question grew, like the pregnant belly of a child full of mother. The answer was a rebirth, and there evolved from Morstive Sternbump another one, similar in character, but poorer in the passing of time. "It's late now," he said, with his casual insight. He would always say it.

∞29∞∞∞∞

Downstairs, the fair constancy of his neighborhood was molested by several construction projects, in the increasing pace of modernity, replacing that which, for consolation, was relegated to history, and ultimately to antiquity itself. It was typical of Morstive's day, what with holidays past and spring getting the old incentive back, that the ancient sun was brought forth in a new setting, and did its shining with Morstive in mind, fighting back the chilly afternoon, and eluding, like a fox at bay, the hunter's braying hounds—a squadron of chasing clouds. The sun rolled free, but lower yet, and half its dominion turned to shade of that peopled complex we call a city. "I'm convinced it's February," Morstive said; and thousands of newspapers, on the very front page, confirmed his creative anticipation. Given time, prophetic outbursts of impatience become mellow and true. "I'm correct and up-to-date," Morstive said, and felt secure. His pride was flirting with new audacity, raping the modest femininity of his humility. "I'm certain," he said, though neglecting to affirm what his certitude had in mind, as his confidence sought to remain vague, or be otherwise threatened, to lose its foothold on the concrete solidity of conviction. He moved from street to street, ambling like a pedestrian, keeping his body neat from collision with passing motor vehicles and their superior, though cruising, strength, being steel-like, and he contained in a soft enclosure of his own flesh, weak and prey to doctors. "I'm doing well," he said: but dusk was gently swift, and the rush hour crushed him. Others brushed him, people coming and going from everywhere. People seemed to be growing out of people. Generationally, this was always true. Like a new springtide of leaves. Like the world, continued. All this pure growth. It was incredible, how birth outnumbered death. "I won't be married myself," he said, "but I'll bargain down my life against a book, and make the book supreme."

Hurtled here and there, chance and waywardness threw him into a stray meeting, and his horizon immediately filled with Duncan Durowetsky whom, somehow, he had always known, yet not acknowledged. It was fate, fortune, and circumstance: nor did he ignore it.

"I have writing talent," Duncan said, "but no theme of my devising worthy of the labors of my style. What do you suggest?"

"Me," Morstive answered, as they were now sitting in a coffee shop, with opportunity serenely singing to him. "My life, my friends, and hates," continued Morstive, taking that certain slant, "comprise ample material, the very stuff that lives to be inspiration. I've been looking for you. You're he."

"Who?"

"You. I want you."

"For what?"

"It's plain. I want you to do my writing, share elements of comedy in the tragic absurdity of my life, and, in effect, *be* me. Sacrifice yourself: I've lived: you can write."

"What do I get for this?" Duncan Durowetsky replied.

And was told, "Gratitude. Fame. And a little money."

"Splendid," the new author declared; "let's begin writing."

"Do you want facts?"

"I'll create them."

"Fine. I approve of your spirit."

"And your idea was hot."

"Let's cool it down, and make it permanent."

The two friends left the coffee shop, guided by their harmony's terrific vigor, for in their aim they were one, though prone to conflict. They walked straight down into the night, pursuing the gradations of evening, the shades of decreasing twilight. What though the night had no moon? They could conjure it, and by imagination's trick illuminate all the sky, give it a ferocious battlefield for unfurling rockets and the death latent in all magic. They had a book to scheme, the brave plan of a book built upon life, the lyric transformation of pain. What dramatic structure to give? Morstive was reinforced: he had help. Duncan Durowetsky had arrived. Who—who was Duncan Durowetsky? Air, water, and land, in a joint tripartite agreement, hurled the delivery of that heavy question, searing February with its burning request. In truth, pray, who was he? He was but he, as Morstive well knew, who kept personalities out of it. "I won't damage your reputation," he told Duncan, "by referring to you."

"No need," Duncan replied, bent on his creative task. It was awesome. It could crack their combined strength. Had they the force to withstand it? How well could they combine? The work— would tell.

As they averted an avenue, choosing a street, grim Duncan Durowetsky gave his work the utmost concentration, by forcing it into the project of thought, of which the brain's fertile apparatus is a delicate progenitor, or the robust forefather.

"Begin writing," Morstive said.

But Duncan said to wait. "When ripeness gives upon us," he said, "surely we'll crush the word, and drink wine from it. We

143

abound in spring. The land oozes it out, a total piece. It swarms. Can we nest it?"

"It's only February," said his sober partner.

And was retorted with, "Springs need February, in their arduous preparation, to make their toilet. We'll use it. All will serve us."

"Is it nature, or artificiality?" Morstive asked, and aggravated his mate.

"Let me contemplate," he was told; "the business is serious and deserves us to be deliberate. I'm working for you. Ours is a business partnership. Can you be impersonal? Then be it."

"But how can I be *me*, then?" Morstive asked, feeling already limited.

"Broaden your scope," he was told, "to include the universe. It exists, you know."

"Yes, but what about me?"

"Don't worry. You're there, just the same."

"I am?"

"Yes. Your identity conceals you, doesn't it?"

"Surely; but I want to be *shown.*"

"Be secretive. Don't be a brash politician. Your privacy is your holy spirit. Observe it. Without it, I wouldn't be with you. Go in, and be silent."

"Now?"

"Yes."

"In February?"

"Any time."

"Why?"

"Don't be a fool. You exasperate me."

"I do?"

"You know you do."

Morstive was hurt. "Are you better than me?" he asked.

"For our purposes, yes: we have a working agreement. Don't upset it." Morstive kept still, except for his huge appetite, which rambled on, and chewed food instead of emitting words. "Your weight is exhausting gravity," he was reminded; which by temperament he astutely ignored, so as in full conscience to stuff his body with fuel, and choke his smothering soul. They were together, in a restaurant. At a late hour. In the month of February.

"I feel a hush," Morstive said.

"Sure," Duncan said: "you made it."

"I did?"

"Emphatically so," he was encouraged: for Duncan was taking notes, industrious already. "Who were your 'friends'?" he asked, while Morstive enlarged upon them, using the contents of his dreams as well as the less convincing digest of his experience, such as it had been. They worked late, and so as not to annoy the management they ordered coffee; for they were hypnotized, into a semi-ordeal, by the burden confronting them: to transplant life into the soil of art, and let it bloom as life, just as fair, though sprinkled with a few teardrops, and spruced up and sprimmed down wherever cutting was needed, and trimmed of graft, and spliced to observe the order of growth, the miracle sequence of decay.

"How's your garden?" Morstive asked, but the other didn't heed him, true in focus to the demands of his industry. "Make it good," Morstive said, but the other merely wrote. Morstive's life gained hope: it would break through.

They traded addresses and telephone exchanges, and departed by their separate ways. Morstive was exhilarated. He walked home slowly, to detain, draw out, relish, the exultation of his soul. "What splendid condition I'm in," he said, but to his annoyance the spell was broken by the advent of his usual loneliness, that steady companion. "Duncan Durowetsky is cold," he said, "and so dedicated to literature, he's not much fun. I suppose he has blood, but the corpuscles don't dance merrily, they merely read books. How droll —I mean dull—an occupation, since life gleams with sparkling intensity, and he subdues it. Or am I wrong? Does he accelerate it? Or reflect it? He's shrewd. But his only joy is in words, which are abstract inventions, the code mankind uses to assure its safety and alleviate the hazards of communication, between among and through men, linking the race. He swears on words, and lives by them. Is that healthy? Shouldn't he be psychoanalyzed, and set straight? But is his sickness his strength? That which he writes on? Or is he strong, converting the sickness to the image of strength, as secondaries are employed to serve the devices of a primary power, to which they are subordinate? How does he earn a living? He's only interested in me, and the motley clan of my acquaintance. Artists are queer. Not fairies, I mean, but just strange. I thought of myself as one, but it was a poor job. I even forgot to paper the typewriter; but mainly, I'm not gifted: that's the excuse.

"As he writes down my memories, those characters are undergoing change right now; how will he arrest them, and in the stead of that uneven motion and hectic rambles, transgressing forth and across, restrain all the relatives and forge from that flux the illusion of an absolute, tested but not destroyed by time? His skill is essential, to produce a natural artifice, a work so integrating the parts that vitality is conducive of the whole. And *I'll* get the credit!

"Or will *he* sign it? Does that greedy bum want blood yet? It's my story, isn't it? Let him be an obscure ghost, while I gain measure and life, the stature of the breathing. He'll quiz me. He asked me the color of Jessup's beard, before shaven; the height of Tessa Wheaton, though scrawny; an aspect of Merton Newberg's facial expression; the clothes Keegan Dexterparks wears, while whitely waiting out his blackness; the speech timbre and pattern of Emma Lavalla; the weight and volume of Morgan's face; the quality of Hulda's eyes; Ira Huntworth's posture; Piper Cole's gait; and the activity rhythm of Page Slickman, at play and work. He's curious, like the innocent publisher of a new-born encyclopedia, whose volumes have been to the bindery, and whose pages were printed, but as yet a wordless emptiness appears, a pregnancy for each subject. And *me*, he wanted to know about. The most subjective intimacies! Nothing is holy, but he must dissect me: what my parents were like, my sexual anxieties, my compulsive eating, my financial setup, the love epochs of my life, and other trivia. Is he a photographer? Why must he violate me? I'm entitled: *I've* got privacy.

"And why I don't vote, and what I think about when in the bathroom, and such rot. What liberties he takes! Merton's ambition to be mayor—how will my fine writer reconcile that tidbit to the same subject's flimsy past, his promiscuous memberships? And Ira Huntworth for governor—this whole ludicrous process takes time. How will the future be apprehended, though the substance of every day builds its structure slowly; or is someone's *history* his essence, or just a slice of time? And what of Hulda's and Morgan's children? Must my writer wait, or can he anticipate them? And will Tessa

146

Wheaton reverse her trend, and some semblance of normality bless her later years' propriety? And the fled Jessup Clubb—religion threads in the balance, and the hasty law comes pursuing, avenging one death for the murderer's. And Keegan Dexterparks, nursing an old wound from me, while plucking black threads from the white vat of dye.

"Piper Cole's on the line: big money, with the heavyweight championship: A bum himself he had been, and now owns a crooked management on so promised a challenger, to lift the crown and take the top, as the bookies relent to murder a killing on the price, the punch that knocks out the honest holder of the title and lets in gangster rule. Then of Page—will the gender of his accomplice be solved, to spot the light on his speculations of rank crime, that thief of all snatchers from the group of individual identity? When are characters people? How does art transform them, and how does mere time? What is just one life?

"What pasts will our futures erase, and what presents will they accommodate? Will Emma breed children to Merton, and he, in his field of public relations, attach raw religion to the refinement of politics, boosting his stock in the local plums to filch, the prize posts? Morgan now, the executive master as of old, shall his promotion evolve to vice-presidency and profits of commercial enterprise organize his tighter business firm in incomes of higher financial expansion? And Hulda, the true bride to mint the promise of former coinage, shall she generously reproduce, for further Popoffs to come? Will Ira Huntworth take cleaner baths, and soapier skin sag and rally around his brutal density of bones, odorless for state party bosses to shift their candidate? Will Keegan grow progressively white on white women conquests? And will his forgiveness one day touch upon me? For what I may never have done, but in his kept invention?

"Shall Tessa enjoy a man, and condemn the many for the one, nor hate her sexual opposites?—and sanctity of regained virtue exalt her participation among the delicacy of social peerage, in this middle class kingdom? Does Page Slickman hold gambling reigns on Piper's campaign on the ring? Shall Jessup suffer, and atone—will he redeem, corralled into fugitive sacrifice, the sins of combined humanity?—or is he evil kin to the hidden devil, the blight on youth and innocence? Will Morgan be faithless, intoxicated by his own power?

"What-comes-before, shall my writer attach in harmony by connective association to the what-about-to-befall-us-later, as destiny is formed on innumerable accidents? What fate will be, to release the past from its term of obligation?

"And what of me?—central to this, shall I remain single, nor crowd my loneliness out with but one girlfriend? Shall economics see me shiftless, the drifting job-shirker? The old bond with my parents—when will I visit them? And tomorrow's groceries for tomorrow's shopping. Who for that am I, in the constant variation of my traits? Is this writer capable, to delineate degrees of such exhaustion, on a canvas of smaller refinement, details that grope for the whole? Still another spring awaits me: holding what, storing what surprise, in the tedious expectation? I don't savor this any more. My life has jilted me, and I'm a compromise, a discarded product of an out-of-work factory whose workers, like me, are beneficiaries of the welfare state's unemployment compensation: our contribution as prominent individuals to society's national world, the dearness and cheapness of goods, material consumption for spiritual dividends.

"But that doesn't answer it—who is Duncan Durowetsky, and out loud Why?, that he should cross my path, and balance constructive destruction. Time is the maker of words, and words reform events, for fiction refines fact, conveying to reality the image of the real. May Duncan Durowetsky survive me, and his affairs prosper, while mine decline. Confusion has bound my sense, the weather of contradiction has pervaded the integrity of my intellect, while my body rages for passion. Hunger typically equips me, and for every heart in Duncan's standard breast, I betray, under my lining, the equivalent of at least another stomach. The world is in a dizzy, and I intake food, and give off the energy of doubt. Thus my loneliness excels, for Duncan cooperates: His, the pure lust for words, and mine, the explosive appetite that craves emotion, are brothers of durable twinship, mutually antagonistic. We have so much in common, separation affords us a contrast by which we develop the seeds of similarity in the soil of duality, a hotbed to choke the bud and wilt the blossom of smothered flowers to be, a garden of pagan wealth, the abundance of nature's fertility. What are we asking for? Only all, in brief notation, to crystallize the broadness and confine in capsule brevity the pageantry of all this endlessness, the multiple parades that crowd the avenues and roads to shrink space. We want to extract the spatial abstract of the temporal, reducing every particle of time to only one series, in which is represented the myriad additions and the layers of enfolding dimension, network of all relatives. Science and art stagger the world. We labor. And play at what we work, turning dead at each result. More is continually produced, a saturation of superfluous excess, extending more indefinitely, infinitely adding to more, so that we shall suffice with less. Less subtracts, and by these repeated diminutions totals finally nothing, ending at the first balance, and justifying the beginning by all the sequences to the last. There went Duncan Durowetsky, and I from the opposite: we converged, crushed the center, merged, and now are one: he, the artist, and I, the man. God knows little more, though quite a deal less.

"Home. But what is home? And for the lateness of the night, the earliness of the morning requites. Then what can I do, or how be, not countered elsewhere, before or behind? Thus I'm covered. This drama I exist has its internal measure, this spark of crucial ego. I join Duncan tomorrow, and needs will drag me to their tasks. I perform out the role, live inside my essential, and these be my acts. I prepair to bed, awake as me. Asleep, or rising, thus I remain. What can Duncan do about this? And those who participate to scrape the edges of my orbit, are being altered now. Duncan Durowetsky, write.

"Unclad between civilian uniform and the night's pajamas, then completed by this transition, and follow the cozy line into womb-like warmth. A tremendous dream glowered and glared on my recent nights, in sparkling fits and the subdued tremors concealed in nightmare, deep rumblings, the earth within. The active thoughts, as the mind collects. Piece-material feelings, all the glows and lights piercing my central sun, or emanating to form concentric spheres. How now a galaxy have I, the cells of the brain, my burning me. So subjective, the call has come for Duncan Durowetsky, to shed and reflect, bare to reveal, inside made outward, chaos and anarchy celebrated by the union of words, a class of art medium not to persuade, nor convince, nor communicate, but to borrow expression from itself, creating what it finds.

"Help me, Duncan. If you're me, I'm but you, and lots of space between, a lifetime length. I'll dictate, you write. I'm not posturing, it's a serious urge, not playful. Who of us does God select, wandering as He does? Or does He discriminate? Or divide? I'm going by. Pass you coming. Tell me when. Till then. Be what I do, and let me read it. Do what I see, and let all read. Reading is what's written, life being passive, showing what activity does. The silent brain, and the understanding emotion. At bottom, the heart.

"The sleep is taking me. Do I wake, while you sleep, Duncan? And do you commit to consciousness, spelling out in outward blocks of letters, what I dream by, as my body fulfills its life, the span of forceful years, gathered in a collection by time, deposited against our name, aging the prime out, the chief prime being death, decay's solution, a way of heaven's return? Who are 'us'? Who were those who visited me, the forms of familiars, the names of those various identities? Speak, if ever. I'm prone to know. This chance is fate, and darkness illuminates, the soul's recognition of a fact. Burden me with perception, and deepen my total concept. I want all answers, or none."

Thus Morstive slept, and nearby within a confining city at a far sufficient distance, Duncan met against his mind those companions of Morstive's fantasy, the occasional familiars to one man's reality: and Duncan rendered them, sketching bare their outline, focused at Morstive's center, from whom these loves and pains and hates radiate, and to whom report, with results. So the world trembled, words raced to overhaul time, and time dwindled with life. The human soul, forced into a box by words, with holes for breathing, and other artificial apparatus. Duncan lived as Morstive, to instill his pen with wonder and confusion at first hand. Duncan took over. Morstive reminisced, and sank his vitality into decline. His experience was being contemplated, transferred to another realm, a further screening, projected by a single writer's imagination; and what he lacked, Duncan gave him, within the temperamental consistency: life as reviewed by art, corrected, and punished with caricature. Satire was Duncan's medium, showing bluntly the foibles and vanities of others revolving through, and including, Morstive's fullest circle, himself gone outward, touching perimeter with equal lives, on decreasing dimension. So Morstive Sternbump lived, to be: and found his own clarity deepened, treated with critical scorn, by that belated creator. And with that, identities, submitted to form and passed through verbal thought in creative transformation, discovered their own existences, with the usual and expected surprise: dismay, and joy.

For that was what they were, the processing of finality, to bypass and survive: keeping them hot, inside.

Morstive woke up, feeling new. His newness was this: it was about to, and becoming; his own future was Duncan's baby, to discreetly control, wean carelessly, and instruct wrongly. What an opening out!

PART 3

ooooooooooooooooooo

oo1oooooo

"I'll go," said Morstive, "and watch television tonight. There's a big fight on. It's for the heavyweight championship. That's real sports for you. Already, I feel athletic.

"It would be fun to bet, but the odds are prohibitive, against the challenger by twelve to one, and the ratio ain't through yet, in the progressively increasing span between. No contest! Is this a joke?

"The papers has columns and columns on it, full of commentary. The editorials are ablaze. So many crooks will attend it that the honest men will have to stand, and get obscured view behind posts. This is utterly sensational. I can't wait.

"The telephone. Yes—Duncan? Hi! No, the champ ain't takin'

a dive. Why'd he do that for, and spoil his title? You mean Piper Cole's bribin' him? Hot news! What dirt, this boxin' racket. It makes morality look sick. What? You mean the bookies is playin' along? And Page's got a piece of this? Where'd you do your sleuthin'? You ain't only a writer, you're a detective hound, your nose flat on the trail. Excitin', ain't it?

"No, who me?—I ain't bettin'. How'd you dope this out? Boy, you could make a killin'. You ain't kiddin'. You'll need to retire for life, after this. What, you ain't bettin'! To keep your writer's-impartiality, as you call it? What a sucker! You mean the law is wise?— and the trap will cave in, expose Piper, and his association of crooks? Wow, what a crazy deal. I'm watchin' it on the big eye tonight. Where?—in a bar. It ain't on here? You mean blacked out? Darn! I'll get it on radio then.

"Yeah, I'm a fan all right. I'll root for whoever wins, after the decision. Safe, that's me.

"Yeah, okay. So long.

"Golly. Duncan's right on it. A smart kid. I hope he can write, now.

"What a scandal this smacks to be: upper bracket, on the cash level. And my own 'friends' in it!—Piper, what owns the challenger; Page, a gambler, ruling a mob; and ain't our ex-mayor in it somewhere? The odor says yes, it's his style of perfume.

"Wow! And I'll listen in tonight. Crooks in public! This is too good. Crime, in intimate familiar surroundings, and the big dough, a killin' we all dream of. How splendid to be in New York, where all this happens. The society of legal robbery, cosmopolitan sophistication. And the police commish? Paid off, no doubt. But the district attorney—there's a bother. Piper, the key manager in charge, faked law himself once, and the fat boy's got contact. Bet all the prosecutors are bought, the law enforcement agents bribed up to their last pair of teeth, and the promise of a pension to come. What thrills democracy holds. I like our way of life.

"Here's a bill in the mail. It's from Morgan: the cheat: It's for assumed cost at prevailing rate of what the wedding present would have been, that I should've sent, for they're a pair in marriage now, the Sunday bride and groom, already arranging matters between them for the stork to have a baby, and once they peg down the bird they'll adopt it, and be famous as a mother and father, to preserve the future for their good sort. I'm billed for a present I didn't sent!

And he's got the job I was fired of, that I had got when they laid him low. Time, I suspect you!—you've been moving.

"Now I gotta visit my mother and father—who're they? They're strangers. They once had a hand in me, but when I got on my two feet I ignored them—and since, they're moaning like blue music. Hell, all they gave me was a name. And even that is too funny-sounding, not dignified or royal, like Hector and Achilles. So I'll visit them, and they better gimme a good meal—those lousy bums."

"We both stayed home for you, though it was a working day, our dear child: to prove how we still love you: we put ourselves out, we still make sacrifices, you still owe us. We earn your gratitude, so where is it? We don't ask for anything else. You're our little boy. Why did you have to grow up, and spoil everything? Is *that* how you thank us?" Mrs. Sternbump said, Morstive's mother, and the wife of his father, whom she represented in that opening speech in her generous use of the editorial "we."

"What's cookin'?" Morstive said, a backhanded way to rebuff them. The same old war.

"Have I got any brothers or sisters?" Morstive asked, assuming it was his right to know.

"You're the only one we can think of," his mother replied. So Morstive was his own exclusive brother, to enjoy in front of the mirror, and also the only sister he would have. Quite a workload.

"The burden's too much," he said.

"Now look, I'm past the age of child-bearing," his mother checked him with.

"You weren't before," Morstive coolly said, "or you wouldn't've had me."

"Darling, tell him to shut up," said the father. So she did. The past, all over again.

"Before I scram, what religion am I?" asked Morstive, another belated attempt. Curiosity never dwindles. It hibernates, then strikes, when the honey's flowing again.

"How do we know?" answered his mother, who had become stout. And the father, with his bald hair, sat by, like military support.

"You mean I ain't got none?" Morstive asked.

"Nonsense—Every child should be religious," said his mother, upholding piety. She should talk.

"But what *specific* one am I?" Morstive asked.

And his mother said, "Stop throwing big words at me! We didn't go to college, like you did—snob!"

"Damn you!" Morstive said, faint praise at that. The son was angry.

"We reared you as best we could," said the mother, "and my conscience is clear."

"What conscience?" Morstive was quick to put in, a misunderstood sarcasm. For she began looking for one, under the kitchen cabinet, and between knobs of the stove. To her, everything existed, and was solid to be felt. Either abstractions were concrete, or they were as nothing. A concept wasn't substantial, unless its example was at hand, for handling, the sure touch.

"I give up," she said, and the conversation continued.

"And why didn't you accept our Christmas invitation?" she remarked, her breath back.

"I was too busy," her son answered. He hated her, and her subordinate spouse as well, to whom she was affiliated. "I gotta get outa here," he told himself, with the meal tucked up under his belt. He would insult them. "You're feeble," he said.

"We are not!" she answered, resentful. And her eyes approximated tears, to retaliate for the offense.

"Ah shut up. I had a crush on you," Morstive admitted, having read about Freud's Oedipus Complex and imitating it to be in fashion, to provide some substance to an otherwise empty sex life.

"I reject you," said his mother, clutching her husband.

"It was *past,*" Morstive assured her: "Come on and kiss me." So she did, but he felt no thrill; the old gal was gettin' old, that's why.

"So long," he said, and left.

"Our boy!" they said, smiling through the window. Secretly, they were proud.

He got home, and there was her same voice on the telephone that he had endured in person. "Don't call me," he yelled, "don't ever phone me."

"Darling, we love you," said his mother.

"Love, what's that?" he asked. "Why did you leave me alone all my life?"

"You told us to," his mother said, and wept.

"Look, let's stop this sorry business," he finally retorted, and his mother gasped painfully, struggling for breath.

156

"Son, I hate you," she said, and hung up.

"The old gal's gettin' honest in her age," he smiled, and hardened his soul. But his eyes were glistening, the soft sob. He was a failure as a son. As a lover. As a businessman. As an artist. As someone engaged in life. As someone disengaged from life. All these negative talents! What a versatile dilettante, he was, his stunning array of multiple failures, the length and stretch and width, the dimension to and from, his worldly set of accomplishments. His soul was private, unstained: it had not been tried.

"Should have asked her what my age was," he said, regretfully. "Should I call her back? Duncan will want to know. He's fussy."

"Hello Mom? Sorry for the fuss I created. Just want to know something: When was I born?"

"It's so long ago, you expect me to remember?" his mother recapitulated.

"Then why didn't you write it down?" Morstive asked.

"Paper! Paper! Does it serve me bread in my mouth?" she observed, materialistically practical, empress of the citadel of common sense, salted all over in the earth of the tried and true, the worn and the paved.

"Mom, I'm different from you," the dutiful son said.

"You have the nerve!" his mother replied. "Ain't I good enough, for an example? What you want, I ain't got? You're spoiled! I spoiled you!" And she shrieked.

"She's crazy," Morstive observed in silence. "My late twenties, I'll tell him," he said, indicating Duncan. Well, a nice to-do. A written invitation from his parents, and a rather embarrassing visit, shedding no light, but much heat, on the unknown mystery of his past. He put down the receiver, and realized he was unattached: no family.

"I love her, just the same," he said. "But she'll have to die to deserve it. She ain't done enough yet."

God, that was bitter. Time for the fight. The big fight would be on.

Blacked out over New York, where it was held, so fans could go to the stadium. But in February? So cold, for an outdoor spectacle? Someone had goofed: the promoter was off his screw. A rainy, damp night, an army of empty seats, and a few recorders and broadcasters. What a net gate! What a cash purse! And Uncle Sam, for tax reasons, would hold up the pay in escrow, starving the principals: In this corner, the undefeated challenger, from Jamaica—and so Morstive's radio blurred, filling in the thrilling details. All the world was waiting for this. Even time, curious to hear the outcome, had stopped, to take in this notable event. It would make sporting history, and brew a feed of arguments for miles to come. The champ took a bow, amid cheers (they were canned). Then the first round rang, with Piper crouching in the corner calling encouragement, while his big dark boxer passed on to the center of the ring, and thrust out a weak jab, followed by an unprotested uppercut. A right hook to the jaw, and all was over. The champion, also a black man, was down, and as the counting grew to ten his crown fell from his slightly woolly head, changing hands on the instant. An uproar, and then an investigation. Crime inspectors came on, a Senate anti-racketeer group, a committee for fair practices, philanthropic charitable organizations, and others concerned. What an obvious fake! The fight had been fixed. Morstive's radio grew scarlet, recounting this. An insult, to the American scene.

Piper Cole was immediately arrested, and sentenced to be charged. The new heavyweight champ was exported, as an undesirable commodity, a contaminating immigrant. It was a stroke of ill fortune, for Harlem had planned to celebrate him in a party that night, and donate to him its reigning beauty queen for a bride in priceless match for a sturdy undertaking, in reward. What liquor would have been consumed! Under cover of identity, Page Slickman slipped out. A notorious bookie ring was uncovered, as a front for still further thugs, a racket that stunk to the skies, and offended God's nostrils, in His perch among the clouds. The city was mayorless, so Ira Huntworth was not held, except as a material witness —though he had been careful not to attend. Law is no respecter of excuses, but creates ground rules as the circumstances afford, giving sensation every scandal. What newspaper copy it would make! The headlines could literally scream, black against white. Morstive was weakened, and considered fainting, to release him from amazement. What a world! For sports lift up the heart, and ennoble the human soul. Boxing is a black man's art, but white men manage them. Piper Cole was in trouble, but literally speaking was only in jail: in many people's opinion, too good a place for him. Hell would have snobbishly rejected him, on principle: He being unworthy of such a privilege, whose audacities on earth inspired no eternal punishment, for so foul were they that men were suitably entertained, and the public agreeable to it: as spiritual fodder, it restored their nourishment.

Morstive gasped. God! Duncan phoned him: "Did you hear that?"

"Sure did, boss," Morstive answered, with humiliation. He too was a human.

"What reaction did you have?" Duncan pressed him.

"Will it go into the novel?"

"Sure."

"Say I was shocked."

"That makes you look superior, doesn't it?"

"But I'm the hero, Duncan," Morstive pleaded.

"Nothing doing." For the writer was fair, in his compassion for pure art, and nothing less. "I want your character," he said, like a dentist asking for a customer's tooth, at the root of which some solid nerves were attached, a riot of profuse pain.

"Paint me as you see me," Morstive finally admitted, a scapegoat for art, the penalty to blame.

Wow! Life had just witnessed a fight, if the radio is to be believed, that was so putrid, and crooked, morality was lost forever, its deepened maidenhead plucked out and experienced blood festering over the lost innocence. Ethics and religion were wounded to the deep. Goodness was whisked away, to a neutral land, where in exile it would wait for the propitious moment to return, covered in timid glory. Such a wait might outlive the liver's life. Pestilence hoped for an interminable stay. It planned the foulest self-perpetuation. "Corruption is rampant," Morstive said, a descriptive phrase

159

which, however, Duncan kept from appearing in the book, due to excess simplicity, which all clichés have. Wow, to be a citizen, in such a city!

The referee was questioned by the proper authorities, including house detectives. He had not been looking, when the blows rained down, having meditated the solution to a crossword puzzle. He had snapped out of it, however, to see the ex-champ falling, with his palms outstretched in Piper's direction off the apron of the ring, requesting his cut for taking a dive. With twelve-to-one odds, Piper was now a wealthy man, and could afford golden faucet taps for his jail cell and a bed of downy feather, foam rubber cushion, with a soft prostitute to match, assembling the furniture. This, the warden had not permitted, so the fat man remained chaste, and asked only to defend his own case, the permission thereof: a grant denied, for foul play was suspected, and the very heart of legality feared for its entire life at stake, or brutish civilization would fall from the contrived artifice of order, and at the coherent center only chaos remain, the vacuum of men at their folly. The announcer on the radio, to Morstive's eternal gratification, interviewed a stand-in proxy for the victorious new victor, whose throne was held in abeyance till the law should untrack the stalling procedure of justice rescuing an outrage perpetrated on the public, that large body of guilty schemers who waddle in the smirch of tabloid obscenity, with the superlative ignorance that Socrates feigned while spilling mud over Athenian youth. "This smells bad," Morstive suspected, becoming righteous, if only for the wrong reason. Oh, what a rot the radio was: Now, the false mother of the alien champ was interviewed by rehearsal, to dupe a willing public. It was a public relations scheme, with Merton Newberg, who newly held this post, the chief offender. The world was not perfectly right; and justice, delayed or derailed, was slow to respond to this emergency: All the gamblers were driven out of town, like a herd of bellowing sheep afraid of a nanny goat that rattled a tin can to the rope it used for a tail, in the city dump. The garbage men wore gas masks, and sanitation refused to move. Page Slickman was largely suspected, as an accomplice, or leader of a rival gang, mobs wielding machine guns, and a polka tie neckerchief, with spotless dots in his sleek and suave attire. Detectives sniffed like an epidemic of asthma. What pollens or germs would they sneeze at, those undercover truth addicts? What fever would they cough to? The civic air was sweet with rot.

Money, the snoopers learned, was in multiple transference, from the hands of victims to the hands of their beguilers. The economy was at sway, and the counterfeit presses had to work overtime to tide over the deficiency with unnatural green, and balance a slackened gap between need and necessity, legal poverty and illegal wealth. This would breed Communism, yet.

Something should be done. But what? Something so drastic, that the public's other cheek will have so been turned, a resounding slap will have echoed the first cheek's one: thus pudgy symmetry being restored, but beet-red.

∞3∞∞∞∞

Boxing was outlawed, as the legislature approved, retroactive for the moment, but only until the next fight: Sport being a thriving business, a net and trap for enterprising thieves who chronically misbehave to cheat the gullibility of a public, with huge expense. It boosted the economy, so that the nation could subsist. Oh! Morstive was glad it happened, for he forgot all about his problems, like overweight, a dwindling bank balance, a lonely impotence against females, anguish at indignity, being a spiritual orphan, and being betrayed by all those he depended on for solace and substinence, the livelihood of the living. A private life is agony, and the only antidote is a public scandal, a notorious rape. Uniformly, then, all may forget, and join in a common woe, a terror or horror that aids the digestion and excites an attack on your wife at bed, for all the glandular juice is up. It refreshes the air, cough-cough, and employs the untidy germs. Surely, Mother would approve: We need an outlet, a cause, to show vigorous distrust of and vent or feign reproaches on, united to our fellow men. Morstive felt better. This was a catharsis, and he enjoyed it. They should have boxing more often, to weed out the yet unsuspected corrupt. Surprising what evidence is lurking. Where is Jessup Clubb? Fleeing the law, on the lam. He bolted. He's hiding. Well, there's an honest man: he had committed something, for which payment is clear and neat, in the form and person of his life. And poor Tessa Wheaton, where's she?

161

God, the awful scarecrow, in hideous psychological shape, a degenerate. What's happening to the human race? Morgan had lost money on the fight, and was angry at Hulda for it, she being only pregnant, and vulnerable in her defense. Merton had a nice promising job, and headed for mayor; his Emma had the seed for a new Newberg, fertilized in the origin of growth, to propel an organism equipped with protoplasm to endure a world. And Keegan Dexterparks? He was becoming white, as a protest. He was undergoing a skin operation: exchange ebony for a new pigment, the miracle powder of surgery. He confessed all his former crimes, on the basis of being black, and now was setting out on a whitewashed life, superior to the human race for his fair blond skin, the pinnacle of Darwin's evolution. The world changed so much, that March was in order, attempting spring with early tardiness and precocious application. Nature was roused, and required April to assist: which it did, with flowers, the blossoms and blooms in old Central Park, New York's private garden. More and more people were entering a larger world. The world gave, and made room. The corners creaked and cramped with people. Nature was booming, these days.

As spring really sank in, lust roared with a heyday, such a holiday as dreamers dream of, and doers do. Morstive continued living, in case he was needed. His services were not in demand, and for neglect grew sharp and rusty, sinking to an appalling state of non-use, flirt as he might. What was wrong? Was he getting too fat? Likely. But this had happened when thin, too. He would seek new popularity, and enjoy conquests with the fair sex. Learning to assert his gender was the problem. Had he any gender to assert? He was a monk in live civilian clothes, observing a holy order. Therefore, he made no profit from the ring scandal, having neglected to bet, neither having won nor lost, keeping austerity's dry and neutral inactivity. Sensuality *is* money. Or money discharges it.

Yet a killing had been made, and behind-the-scenes gambling had seen nonfortunes lost, and money wildly irregulated, padding Piper Cole with a comfortable income, and the defeated boxer would earn his share, while somewhere Page was involved, and Ira remotely suspected. An international incident, for the new champ had been kicked home with a vacant title on his head, while Jamaica, with clipped Oxfordian calypso accents, collectively rejoiced in sweetness of bombast, a delirium of nationalism in topping the world with one man.

162

In the United States of New York, the human race went pro-
foundly lethargic in a glee of shame. Decline was sweeping people
down, in fits of up. There was a somber rejoicing. Was the latest
extinction trapping the species in its own network of woven decadence? Festivity, everywhere. An end was viewed. What was ending? Celebrate it.

The world was laid out flat, prone, and Morstive Sternbump
had a good time, luxury fit for a king, or a king's favorite subject,
in this stronghold fortress of democracy, citadel of the great and
near-great. Culture would never revive, and all museums went in
mourning, concealing valued paintings under black crepe paper, for
the occasion. Planes drooped at half-mast, in the winged sky. Birds
were frightened, and went south, or came up north, colliding occasionally. In the Pacific, whales fought, spitting fountains of blood
with great exhalations, as though to end whaledom. These were
alarming signs. Omens were picked up everywhere. A reform
movement was afoot. Disarmament conferences were held, at
which it was decided to appease for a truce, in neutral arbitration.
Was it time for peace?

No. Morstive fell asleep, only for a knock to grow against the
loud door, Duncan at the threshold. "Shall we include this in your
novel?" Morstive asked, sleepily, art being far from his thoughts. He
had double pneumonia, and a soaring temperature.

"You're sick," Duncan informed him, with his acute vision. He
had brought a pen along, and paper, to take notes. Spring was
everywhere, in and out. Grass peeped between skyscrapers, patiently eluding the shadows.

"What's going on?" Morstive asked.

"You have the pollen of spring fever, and as a young man your
fancy should turn to love," exacted Duncan, his guardian.

"Why?" asked his victim.

"It would be good for the novel, and add plot to it," Duncan
rejoined, "and convince the reader with your motivation."

"When, and whom, shall I love?" obedient Morstive asked,
while Duncan deliberated, wanting to form him in character,
within the bounds of restraint.

"I want it to be a classical case," he said, while Morstive shuddered; "and you should be unrequited."

"But why?" Morstive, unfailing, asked.

"Why not?" the reply was, for Duncan was determined to write a good book, by including love. Which was, of only, elemental, and dearly simple. And an antidote to hate, against an ugly world. "Life is beautiful," Duncan said; "but only love makes you realize this: then you won't protest."

"Okay, I see beauty," Morstive answered, spring rich outside his window, the flowing colors and the deep lovely feeling, craved by poets for their lyre. "I'm romantic," Morstive said, and reduced his belly, with a constricting act of flattening, forcing the muscles down. Heat came out at him, the torment of internal externality, and he vowed, on rising, to look for an object to love. Love, it was wonderful. He believed in it. Would it come true, this dream? But Duncan prophesied rejection, and Morstive was subdued. He was afraid, but undaunted, in a tremble of heroism. Nobility sang, at its height. He was suffused with the love of self. This subjectivity must seek an outward "she." Where was she, somewhere? Out there. Deeply out. For inward, his was the stuff of love. His heart was *packed* with emotion. Now, where's the dear object?

∞4∞∞∞∞∞

Morstive was in his special state, vaguely specific. His behavior would be irrational, by normal standards. There *were* no standards. There was only his pulse, the heart.

Love moved him, terribly. It was a fit; and getting no better, he relapsed. He sprang out of bed, with the ardor of lethargic frenzy. This was all peculiar. He gave totally in.

So in, the need was "out." In the not-him.

He rushed out of doors, it was spring: "I want someone to love," he said, and trembled at the word "love," if it meant he would receive hurt. There was going to be a party, there he'd meet his captor, and submit. Ah, it would be glad; the heart would pop out of him, rich in agony, and flop into another's being, where it was unwelcome. What a fix! But Duncan had ordered it, to stop the book from being negative and looking hopeless. So M was doomed to love, and, in loving, would fail beautifully, and weep at the world, and the world would weep back, out of its million windows it uses for eyes, the eyes that spy and subside; for love sighs behind them, the most serious comedy Morstive could endure, and part in the pattern of life's whole tragedy. Love! Whom? Ah! Sweet she!

First he wept, to make sure; his tears were all right, the proper wet, and the heart was strong. He would weaken it, wound it in battle, and by dying, be revived. The world prompted him to look inward, for his daily nourishment of beauty: This compelled him, in turn, to search for a likely mate, the co-respondent, with whom to connect, at whose delicious breast defeat would brave him, and submerge him. Okay. It was for the party, now. And die, for a more exciting life, and exercise his courageous heart. He'd have fun, too; he hoped; or if not, despair.

"Darling, how are you?" the girl at the party said.

"I'm okay," Morstive answered, and love tugged him, so he fell. Oh, it was arbitrary, being natural.

"Will you escort me home?" she asked.

"Most certainly," he replied: his manners.

"Oh you're perfect," she said.

"I like you," he said.

"Don't you mean 'adore'?" she begged.

"Then 'adore' it shall be," he agreed.

"It's all too sudden," she replied; "and not knowing you, and furthermore not caring to (nor am I interested), I must inform you that you're rejected. It pains me to tell you this, and you for your part must grieve; and wail; and demonstrate the symptoms of your misery: thrash out, grip your hair, knot your teeth, look low, grab your cock, and put it on fire, and put it out, and dream of me, night and day. Like a knight of old. For I scorn you. Go on your crusade: go. Be chivalrous. I hate you. Or I'm merely indifferent, which is worse. Are you in pain?"

"Yes," Morstive said.

"Good," she said, "just like I wanted. You must be made to suffer; Duncan spoke to me before and told me how to act. Now, you're in love, which vindicates my plan, and I can relax, take it easy. And you—how do you feel?"

"Suicidal," Morstive admitted.

"Oh, that's wonderful," she said.

Morstive was done for, and doomed. All night, all day, he wept, thinking of her. Refusing to see him, she hurt him all the more; and he gnashed every limb he had, and lashed himself, in such frenzy

165

that he was a typical lover. "Excellent performance," Duncan admired; but Morstive was in real, an earnest sufferer, earning philosophy every moment.

"I can't bear it," he said.

But Duncan laughed: "What's bad for you is good for the book, so it's good for you too," he carefully explained, to the pained one, that lump of despair, young Morstive Sternbump, just growing old. And at the usual price, the haggard sacrifice, that senile sufferer of youth's excess. Ah, Jessup would envy him his crucifixion, redeeming love everywhere, atoning for happiness with his own unhappiness, as joy pursues its trace down beneath the world and delight exults, rapture is exalted. And supreme orgiastic ecstasy may be protected, when lacked by Morstive, and safeguarded, for the more fortunate to follow, and the deliriously happy gone to their graves in preceding this Prince, this Savior, this Patron Saint whose benevolence guards love for others, increased by his own deep cosmic failure at it, his thriving lack of success.

"When will I be over it?" he asked, remembering her: When will the Lord regain His earthly resurrection, and tolerably continue to exist?

"I'm interested in this," Duncan said, moved by that Job's-lot of Morstive, to whom the opposite of pleasure was a quickening of successive deaths intensely lived, the flower of unreturned love wilting in the blasts of winter, a stone heart killing it.

"This season is my ruin," observed Morstive, whose self-analysis, submitted to extreme subjectivity, was now turning objective: "Why do I live?"

"You were born," Duncan answered, "for this. Now you're being baptized, and your life's official."

"It isn't my first exposure," Morstive retaliated, struggling for wisdom with all his heart-heaved head, where a windy furnace blasted him in cold fire. The out was in, and the in exchanged to out. His innocence was moaning with experience. The world was inside, but his ache covered it.

"Nor your last," Duncan informed him, the writer of his book.

"She was an instrument of your devising," Morstive accused Duncan.

And this was met with an acknowledgment: "She expedited it perfectly," the writer said, "and gave you over to love."

"Damn," resented the victim, "that such be the function of use. My heart quite aches."

"Just so," Duncan complacently approved, an affirmation documented by a creative smile, contrasting almost symmetrically to Morstive's woeful look, ravaged and forlorn, a look that suggested "Alas," were such a term not outmoded, though its meaning has no placement in time, the recurring factor of all love.

"But I resent doing everything to please you," Morstive insisted. "On the contrary, let me live my life, and draw your art from that, not conform my life to your art."

"We'll both give in an inch," Duncan advocated, "so your acts, and my words, may partake of each other, and be mutually enriched."

"Quite well then," yielded Morstive, and they met doubly to a compromise. "As I grow, your book grows," said Morstive, as the model lived, his life sharing its meaning with the canvas that Duncan copied him onto, with mixed colors protracted from the deep surface of its subject, mirroring the average of his mood from the pigment of extreme. Quite a combination, and Duncan all but became Morstive, to expose accuracy to its own life and be the imitation it is. All in time. The book flew on with Morstive, and Morstive fitted the book: form, and the person.

"The Unemployment Insurance people," said Morstive, with his saddest spring smile, "are after me to work. Work? What shall I do? Suppose maybe Morgan can hire me, back where I once had his job? No matter, though I come down: Life has eaten away the pride from me, nor does dignity appeal for reputation to enshroud it, and appearances are valueless. I'm as I am, lowly, a fact the world will be glad to know, having considered itself my enemy for so long that I've been forced to 'hire' this Duncan Durowetsky to spill my misery into strings of art, that wail out when the cello is bowed by the moving elbow. Oh woe. O melodious dirge, to haunt me down. O solo, not duet. Love's become my true *metaphor*. And that girl— what had I *met-her-for?* Already she rankles, and bruises the brain in my bones. That sweet thing! Ah, love is grand. It appeals to spring, as a seasonable item, and one of variety's spices. Oh, I dream. I'm so alone, it hurts. My mother can't love me, nor can anyone. What an outcast; a spurned commodity I am. Where is someone to lavish even the frailest care? Were I to breathe in this spring air, who would know it? I crave to share."

"With me," Duncan interrupted, and stole that monologue for his book, as an accurate presentation of Morstive's interior. Is sadness so much of art, is grief fit for tragedy? What of brightness, and joy? "Become happy," Duncan recommended, to temper the stew.

"With what?" asked Morstive, speaking far down from his life, which art had usurped and for its own ends confiscated. "Is the novel written yet?" the experimental guinea pig asked.

And, "Not nearly," the grand author replied, now engaged in studying, with first-hand observation, the little-known Morstive Sternbump, that thoughtful man mindful of the intensity of his existence through the pained consciousness of identity, a brain inflicted on itself at useless odds with the body. "Be happy, do what you care to do," Duncan relented; and Morstive went questing after the girl who had spurned him, like a quick green plant that decides to come out, urged by prompting in the seed and a stirring flow of the root, to examine the sun and try the latter's expedience in providing warmth and light, growth necessities. That was on a farm, but Morstive was a city boy, the wild open city, known the world over as both large and monstrous, yet not without its fascinations and its apparent, though actual, beauty.

"Where are you?" Morstive asked, and fled to the girl, only she wasn't where he arrived, at the time he did. Then what good is the place? He wanted to occupy her same space. Would she let time permit it?

Maybe not, but he tried. Tried the harder, the more the failure loomed. "I need to live," Morstive demanded, in his fruitless agony. A mating call: yet others would propagate, not he.

In the Popoff household, where Hulda was expecting, Morgan said, "Now the weather is good. *Now* there shoulda been the fight, not on February, which was a ridiculous choice, for an out-of-door spectacle. Whoever promoted it, well 'stupid' isn't the word, only it comes close. Piper Cole is still in jail. The court case is coming up. In some way, politics is connected. Ira Huntworth is changing parties. Merton Newberg is opposing him. Page Slickman is up for trial, on charges well founded, for his part in that fiasco—the one-round knockout by a twelve-to-one underdog, now under the Jamaica sun—that everyone says is crooked, and the investigation is proving so. And the radio account was warped, plus the television failing. Merton Newberg is convicted of publicity, it being now his profession. All the business world is shaken, and Wall Street, with latest stock reports, has holes in it, and crumbling with Humpty Dumpty on it, like that other biblical wall, called Jericho, and Finnegan was in his Wake from falling, and Thisbe looked through the wall and saw a lion, so it looks bad for commerce. I'm a rising business executive, occupied with the process of making money. My boss's wife got killed, by Keegan Dexterparks, at the New Year's party: who now, lately, has become white. Quite a sprinkling of the new. And yesterday what happened? Tessa Wheaton asked for a job. She came in, on her own power, with only a tiny fraction of division hanging her life by her death, as they swoon to merge. She said she could type. But she squinted. She lost her glasses: among other things, including her honor. In fact, I married her once. Well, bygones. No, she can't work in that office. 'Be a housemaid for me and Hulda,' I suggested. Does that meet your approval, dear?"

"I hate her," Hulda replied, "for marrying you first. She should've waited: it was my right."

"But you'll command her, and be her mistress, and watch her do all the dirty work," suggested Morgan, at whose words a glow appeared on Hulda's malicious face, revenge-bent.

"Take her on, offer her a contract," said that wife: "I handle her."

"Of course," Morgan said, and kissed Hulda: which she dully received, on a pale cheek.

"Oh stop it," she said, "don't be romantic." This was over the breakfast table.

"Have you fallen out of love with me?" the horrified Morgan tactfully put.

"You bore me, but I love you the same," Hulda admitted, in her role as a wife. Their reading matter was propped up, beyond coffee cups, and for him it was a financial periodical and investment analyses, while for her it was a baby manual: how, when having a baby, to carry it off with aplomb and retain the modern sophistication essential for every housewife. It was paperback, for they were cheap, and living by all means.

"I must go to the office," he said, rising.

"Good, that's regular of you," she said, wanting to be alone so she could phone Emma and argue with her old rival on their husbands' respective careers and other competitive factors that bring out the bitch in a couple of changing women granted domestic reform by excellent matches contracted. Their lives have entered their mature phase.

Morgan slipped out of the house, with his attaché case, looking every inch what every inch he looked to be: himself, to the life. Uniquely a stereotype. A very tall man of an endangered round world. He would capture the world, and mold it to himself. To Morganize worldly chaos into one firm strutting image, the self garbed in all outer dimension.

∞ 7 ∞∞∞∞

"Hello Emma it's me. Isn't Tessa Wheaton ugly? She'll be my governess now, for my child I mean, and my own personal maid, a slave I call her. Isn't that sweet? Morgan will hire her. Hasn't Merton got you a maid yet? Then his salary should be increased. Expenses are so high today, how costly and dear. But my husband got a raise. He's so smart, quite a successful type, don't you agree? And at home at night, Emma, what love we make! I shouldn't be telling you this: but an old friend like you, what else are you for? Ah, Morgan does it sweetly: so gentle, yet so firm. My breath is taken away, I die: then revive. Such a man! Of course, we know that *Merton* was formerly effeminate. But he's adequate, isn't he, and reformed to suitably satisfy you—though I heard he only has a little one. How? Rumor, my dear. Even still, he's by many infinities the at-least-superior to the ridiculous Morstive, isn't he?—I know you haven't tried him, but you can imagine: his brains all in his head, and a pot belly littering his stomach. Some wife *he*'ll make—I mean get. I saw him the other day: negligent in the clothes he wears, and thoroughly unemployed. He told me he's collaborating on a book, with some fictitious character he invented named Duncan Durowetsky: and I feigned to believe it! Oh, so silly, Morstive Sternbump, a fool. And do you know Keegan? He's many shades whiter, by being bleached in the sun—of a surgical hospital. A reverse process. And Jessup, who ever heard of him, he's still fleeing. How's your husband's publicity career—does he fit it? I wish him success. That prizefight, the radio botched it, and Merton is blamed, isn't he? Politics, you say? His hat in the ring? Oh darling, I'm so proud! Our next mayor! Good. I'm sure Morgan will help him. He'll help *Morgan?* Now don't get bitchy. Shut up. I'll scream, I'll hang up. Bitch! Fool! Rat! I disown you even as my former roommate, now. I deprive you of our past together. But what more *practical* harm can I do you? I'll unleash Morgan, for this job. He'll growl with wicked freedom, you'll see.

"I'll get my husband to ruin you; he's influential, you know—and has powerful contacts. May you die in pregnancy, and give illegitimate birth to your own fat grandmother, you slob. Oh, you beast. I hate you, a female. You slander us, the female race, and deprive us of our honor. Aren't we superior to men? Then let's act it. There's not a moment to lose. Begin now, and start saving for tomorrow. I hate men, don't you? We'll wipe them out, who needs them? They're malicious. Love? It's rot. They overrate it. We can please ourselves, can't we dear? Well nice talking to you. Sure, I enjoyed it. No hard feeling. Good morning. Call you in an hour. Well, she's hung up. Slob! She's becoming a regular housewife, and spilling out all her freedom, while I'm glamorously seductive, and mysterious in my approaching motherhood. Morgan bores me, so

171

a mild affair will be nice, and quite properly harmless—why not Morstive? Yes, for the fun. He's game, he'll charge me, if I let him. I merely have to throw my dress up, and he'll run away, and peep in, and come sliding back, and ask. I'll try him, and tame him, and train his play, and he'll owe *everything* to me! Such a nice boy, and I'll enjoy myself. It's fun, with Morgan always at work. A girl has to live, doesn't she?

"Goodness! A knock. What can that be?

"Jessup! What are you doing here! A ghost! Go!"

∞8∞∞∞∞

"No, I stay," said Jessup, and hit her. She screamed, falling to the floor, but a vacuum cleaner was roaring in a neighboring house, to blot out her howl of "Rape!" "No, my dear, I'm merely desperate, and need to hide, for the law enforcement agents are hunting me as if they consider that I've done wrong. But wrong is really *right*, in my case.

"Where can you conceal me? Among the hangers in your closet? No. I'd smother. Air, I need. No, the roof is too risky with weather, and I'm exposed. The bathroom? No, you must use it some time, and my modesty and sensitive nose would recoil. The bedroom? That's better. Perhaps I can observe you, and Morgan, attempting love: and criticize the erroneous technique responsible for your lack—but you *are* pregnant! My Savior! Joy!

"No, take that knife away, Mrs. Popoff. I'm as serious as death, and intend to stay. Yes, known to your husband. You've a guest room? Good. I'm a fugitive from the law, and dirty and tired, with my beard grown back again, and I desire a rest, a long sleep. Thank you. You were always wonderful. It's a grand day, isn't it? Spring is here. I love spring. A relative was resurrected, one Easter. Quite an occasion. I believe it's *my* fate, too. Not this year, it's past. Then the next. Now, I can afford comfort, and hope to live."

"But Jessup, my husband might not like you here," Hulda begged to opine, in her womanly way.

"He's so absorbed making money, he won't notice," Jessup

172

reassured her, and prepared for a bath. He was a man at least, not only a god disapproved by the proper authorities. He had a child's murder on his hands, an acquired "son." That, at least, was something to repent of. Good, he'd begin. Then he prayed. It was so eloquent, that Hulda kneeled also, and through their window the magic of the sun's power made a nimbus at their heads, barely above the livingroom floor, the fluffy rug. It was no parlor game. "I want to go into business again," Jessup announced; "halo-manufacturing, and angels' devices, tailor-made. There's a good market. The world is unclean. I'll make a fortune, and will it to my heirs, or heir. Your son, I believe. For so it will be. I christen him mine. Don't moan with horror. Be thankful, and flattered. Now, get me a bath towel. I want hot water. How I've been pursued—what scrapes! What indecencies, how low I've come. But I'll always rise again. It's in my stars. I'm Mister Miracle, the Magic Man. Get me down, I bounce up. Let's restore the past—just *our* share. Have faith, I'm deeply occult. I'm good at it, being so bad. When will Morgan return? Oh, tonight. Well, we have plenty of time. We'll be a pleasant household, the trio. No, not the trinity. *I'm* only holy."

"You shock me," Hulda said, "and what you say is a sacrilege. You're a criminal, you'll be cooked. You committed a bad crime, thus running up a debt. Society will see you pay. Bad man!"

"Don't judge me by conventional standards," Jessup replied, and did a silly little jig. This disconcerted Hulda's strong ethical line. An irreverent guest had imposed himself on her. He felt wild, foolish. In a year he would be dead. Why not make a farce of things *now*, to even it: a little destruction won't hurt, heaven-sent equality, some pre-death mischief. "I'm a child again," gaily romped Jessup, and had fun in the bathtub, splashing and giggling all over.

Hulda was scared, yet calm and terrible, and—with now a stiff reward on his head, a sum considerable even in Morgan's terms—wrathful. She'd make Jessup prisoner, and be a heroine. Once a Greek queen killed Agamemnon, her unwelcome husband, in the bathtub with a net and ax, the former to trap. That was a noble age, but bold Hulda shall restore that mold. Such temptation! And in keeping with her nature, it being not soft or gentle, but brassy and cold, unflinching. And to be in the headline papers, arousing Emma's jealousy. But no—Easter was past, and Jessup must wait: she had a whole year, or rather minus one, to fatten her captive, then do him in. The police wouldn't suspect, and Morgan would be respectful, for so resourceful a wife, so accomplished a bitch. She polished her steel, and smiled: Had she been Scotch, she would have been Lady Macbeth: or Greek, the terrible Clytemnestra. As it was, she was an American, and herself: sufficient enough. The Yankees did well those days.

"Are you happy?" she asked, and Jessup agreed. He was through with his bath, and still alive. And ready to commit religion at the most minor impulse of guilt, a pin-drop on the sensitive soul of Conscience, that gladly projects a light thought to its dark deed, as though the thought *were* the deed, and already done.

"Make a confession," he ordered, whereby promptly Hulda told of lusting, in fantasy and perverse self-spite, after lonely Morstive Sternbump, whom nobody wanted. "Some sin must be haunting you," insinuated Jessup, "that your atonement must be so vast, your sacrifice so deliberate. The deliverance of absolution, relatively speaking, is mine to give. Come. Be not afraid, my child."

"Why are you so strange?" Hulda asked, hypnotized by her fascination. Her dress flew up, and Jessup pressed in, throbbing with contact.

"Now give me some food," he said. So it was given him, and he ate thereof. And he pronounced it good. The Lord did.

"That was yummy," he said. "But I didn't enjoy it. I'm forbidden to."

"Was it distasteful?"

"No. But sin made it so."

"To eat is sin?"

"No. But sinning includes eating, hooked and caught on to everything we do. Sin is life. Life is a blot of sin. My name is sin. As I'm aware, I behave as I do. Being ignorant, your name, Hulda Popoff, appears sinless, but nominally. You are sin. We are sin."

"Then why had you just—penetrated me, as you did?"

"To convince you. We are sin."

"Sin? Only sin?"

"The Lord provides, and it is enough."

"Enigmas! Don't bother me," said philosophy-weary Hulda, as evening fell.

"No, women like things plain," Jessup said, "and understood. When someone dies *now*, his whole past seems different. Even when someone *acts* now, that new act has changed all that he remembers. It's as though each act is a death, to alter what was. Have you followed me, you simple lady-brain?"

"You're getting too deep," Hulda dissented, "and you wore me out, with your holy flesh. Tell me once what death is, and forget."

"Death is where there is no sin, the state of sinlessness," Jessup consistently maintained. "In a year, thus, I shall have no sin: sin will not be of me; I shall have been liberated."

"How grand a way you have of speaking," Hulda droned; "but I've lost my interest. I must prepare supper for Morgan."

"Ah, you simple women!" the profound Jessup observed, "you sexy kitchenfolk: go, do what you only can do, in your sinful absence of free will. You curved bodies, in a straight head. Act on reflex, don't reflect—or if you do, you're not you."

"But if life has free will," Hulda surprised him, "and life is sin, isn't free will sin?"

"Yes."

"But you implied the *absence* of free will is a sin."

"Yes too."

"Then something is a sin, and when it's taken away the nothing that remains is a sin?"

"But *something* remains," ominously said Jessup, "though conditions change, so long as life remains. In death, everything is absent: that includes sin. Ah, holy death: It is so beautifully empty. Can't you just see it? Can't you just *not* see it? When you *really can't see* it, then, and then only, are you dead."

"I'm expecting Morgan any minute," Hulda said, busily preparing the supper. Her hands trembled, as an incredible complexity was confronting her. Two men in one household, both adults and unrelated. Was this bigamy, again? Formerly, there had been herself and Emma with this same Jessup. This way it worked better. Morgan would give it her at night, Jessup by day; and her Morstive fantasy vanished, thus confirming *his* luck: all bad.

"Hi honey, what's for supper," her true spouse called, opening the door.

"Me, I'm here for it," Jessup intoned, and the two former friends, alienated of late and bound by a bond of mutual ill will, confronted each other, one with evident surprise, the other in a doomed pose of uncanny poise, his beard sparkling with absence on his chin. He'd just shaved, to newly contradict his photo on the federal "wanted" posters that could be seen in all post offices, our land over. What popularity! He'd worked hard, for it. Beyond any call of duty. And it won him a just and published fame.

∞10∞∞∞

"What is this?" the master of the household formally elocuted. "Have we, in our upstairs flat, my delinquent Hulda, an enemy of society harbored here? Here, where he squatted, in this very apartment, in your trial of ignominy, your past fallen days? Formerly an intimate of your genital area? Out with him, I say! A scoundrel usurper, daring my dominion, uninvited to my hearth? This was your grim permission, Hulda: a word with you, later. You, sir, with your scheming audacity: depart! I, gainfully employed in the community, the leased rentpayer to this abode of my residence, possessed of these temporary premises, bid you, a scurvy gentleman of no fixed address and demeaned morals abased beyond repute, to leave my habitat. And were my command to meet instantly with your hesitation, dastardly droopard, the police, interested in your whereabouts, shall be notified by myself, as I stand. Sir, remove yourself, at the once. Vacate wholly."

"No," Jessup said, "I'll not. And that's final. I stay."

"Why must you?" Morgan pleaded, without logic.

176

"It serves my convenience, and you must hide me. I'm pursued. And you are, too."

"By whom?" stated Morgan alarmed; "my record is clean."

"You escaped, must I remind you, from an institute of the insane, an asylum for those of infirm mental health. Merton Newberg procured *his* release by Ira, then mayor. You, you're wanted: And your marriage may be annulled, and all intercourse with Hulda void, if the gents with the butterfly nets and the plastic straitjackets locate the place where you are: and I can inform them."

"At injury to yourself?" Morgan asked.

"There are anonymous methods to impart a communicative matter," Jessup insisted with redundance; "and so I blackmail you: Keep me here."

"But that same mayor," shouted the exasperated Morgan, "wedded us. Can't he clear me?"

"His power, as well as his inclination, has been shorn," stated Jessup, who gained his point, and was invited to be a guest on a permanent basis.

He accepted, with his cynical urbanity, and heard, again, Morgan complain, "But can't they find me at my office?—I'm well-known."

"Formal procedures, a stiff operative method, the protocol of organizations, must be observed."

"But my *home* address is lodged with my boss: it's public: income tax forms reach me, and other such official mail. Are *they* insane, who insist on me being so?"

"So it would seem," Jessup hissed, at greater peace than his host, whose agitation disturbed what he used for an appetite during such supper engagements.

"Hot and ready," blared Hulda, cook for this evening of fugitives in the same den.

"I'll eat again," Jessup accommodated her.

And Morgan was gloomy. "No thanks," he said.

"Go and sit off by yourself, spoilsport killjoy," screamed his wife, delighted in this new regrouping of forces. Two docile men to subdue, and she was empress of an expanded kingdom, with a future subject rolling in her belly fluid, whom she'll command the better for coping with these current mature grotesques. Now she'd preside in the regal ceremony of talk. "Tell me, for table conversation, Jessup," she requested, "how till now you've avoided the Federal Bureau of Investigation, Scotland Yard, the Foreign Legion, various espionage groups and agents of the overworld, occult spies peeking in, and your other pursuers. What a frightfully hard time you must have had, tough and rough. How you've endured it, I don't know. Had you adventures on the way? What an outdoors life! Indeed, you're most fascinating, I must say. You're too unusual, to say the least. My own husband is humdrum, an ordinary business-man. You, Mr. Clubb, you're exceptional. We admire you, don't we, dear?" But Morgan wasn't heeding, enveloped by a mood. "He's deaf," she tossed off, Hulda did, and attended Jessup once more, her favorite honored guest, the man who had come to supper, and stayed. Man? Or ghost, or god, or the devil's roving ambassador, the hoof-footed one's troubleshooter on levels of the known world, an earth torn apart, dissension within, and an unfriendly belt of glar-ing space without, though a moon seemed all benevolence and the sun visited daily warmth to prod spring loose from the buds that children adore, extending the world into July, by stationing it at May first, a gay month for romping lovers giddy in the scent of forbidden instincts.

Jessup enjoyed his feast, many courses, and a double helping. He was welcome, and finding it fun. How nice, while life still treated him, to find favor, and be assisted. People had their use. "I like the company of people," he said, and Hulda beamed, taking it personally.

"Thank you: I like being discussed," said she, sweetly.

How harmonious: no discordant note, save alone the brooding of Morgan, that large and fatal figure, whom all horizons beckon, the fortunate child of a future prosperity. "When you have a baby," he suddenly said, while Hulda perked, "it had better be a boy."

"I agree with you, sir, your recommendation is excellent, same as what mine would be," assisted Jessup, though his opinion was not asked.

"What business is it of yours?" snapped Morgan, the commer-cial-minded, a mean gesture, stingy, withholding friendship.

"I'm concerned," Jessup simply stated, a smiling rival, on a different plane.

"Ah, you men, you're always fighting," Hulda noticed, squeezed in the center, psychologically, of warring factions.

"Aren't you proud?" Jessup teased her, with his omniscience.

"So what?" Hulda said, who planned his doom. "I hate you

178

both," she inwardly conceded, out of hearing distance; though Jessup was psychic, with rare powers.

"Control your thinking," he said. She jumped, and knew of sin. Or sin's sinister extreme, evil—many sins multiplied. All her life, she had been in this room, such is the eerie spell of this now, and those two men. *They* were always here, too. Was it April or May? Such an event, two months could span it.

∞11∞∞∞∞

"Who'll do the dishes?" Hulda asked.

"Of course, you will," said the two men in unison, their voices centered upon her. She did, no queen. Another item, to revenge. It all stored up. She'd prize with exquisite pleasure their writhing, their dips in a pool of pain.

"When will Tessa come, to be my maid?" she asked Morgan; an article of news which interested, for he could exploit it, Jessup, the opportunist.

"Soon, we've made arrangements," called back Morgan, her husband, a marvelously virile lover who pleased her, though his out-of-bed personality palled with glowing innocence, for he stank of dullness. "I want a promotion soon," he said; "business needs an uplift. I'm going places, in my own office, behind a desk. Soon, such money we'll have, we'll take a better place, a home for our own. Idyllic, no? With shady lawns, and robins cooing, and the messengers of spring. I love a country life. I'll commute, by early morning train, or my own car. I'll be a suburbanite, and in control of finances, making shrewd investments at wisely calculated intervals with the smartest brokers, at a gainful rate of profit. Success will blot out my previous patch as a flop. I want restoration, plus more. I feel grand already, really about to move. A sensation, I truly am. National magazines, having interviewed me and photographed my glorious face, not to mention this athletic body, will have me featured, and the entire populace will greet my roaring story, a triumph of success. Quite a paean. And you, Jessup? Have you prospects?"

"I'll be dead next year," answered that mystical saint, that paragon of all sadists; while inwardly Hulda responded with "And how!"—Such would be the glory in destroying a significant force of destruction, an honor to her, and would gratify what is most primitive and evil in her, an elemental form of happiness: pleasure and gain from another's annihilation; one's own advancement, at the cost of someone's decease. These tactics, or policies, are inherited from evolution's struggle, and soon only greedy species survive: and dead all the gentle.

"Such a fine evening; I feel, if you must know, content," she stretched, while her admirers sulked, from their different angles. Both were opening the future, like a gift package before Christmas, a present marked "present." And they saw a forecast of the past.

"I missed my supper, feed me now," Morgan asked, getting up, and his energy sang out.

"I'm tired, make it yourself," was Hulda's listless insult.

"Is that being a wife?" Morgan admonished, morosely. "You don't act it, at times."

"Yes, these are my failings," she replied, undaunted. She hated men, and used them. Learning to hate her, men were used by her, in guilt: Their own hatred was intolerable.

So morality went, in the Popoff household. "I was dilapidated, fleeing the law," reminisced the new member, Jessup Clubb; "and my suit was baggy; I had a growth of beard, all wrinkled and unshaven it resembled Calvary, I can assure you, when I had to endure the Cross, or as the biographers said, bear it. But I came through. Here I am."

"Yes, there you are," consented the lord and master of the household, Morgan Popoff, who had taken of his meal and found it good. "What are your plans?"

"Lay low, at first," said Jessup.

"And then?" Morgan followed on a rising note.

"*Still* lay low," Jessup persisted, the guest who had come to stay.

"But not forever, surely?" asked Morgan, getting worried.

"How long is forever?" Jessup asked pointedly.

And Hulda came calling "Oh not that again!" No more abstract metaphysics, for her nasty taste. As self-proclaimed moderator, she'd put her dainty foot down, when men wandered off from realism's confirmed limits.

"Doubt assails us," said her nonhusband, "and certitude is out of fashion."

"I wish I could be sure," chimed in Morgan, joining them. Then they played cards, three-handed. While one won, two lost, and so the evening wiled away, to no ostensible purpose, in the very thick of mystery.

"And to bed," hinted Jessup, with a sly look at Hulda, who, however, favored her husband, who was so well endowed, a majestically erect physique.

"Do it to me tonight," she asked him.

And he said, "Might as well; a guy's got to have fun."

"May I have fun too?" she asked.

"Why not? It's for everybody."

"Everybody!" she complained: "Have you been unfaithful to me? Answer honest, my cruel love."

"Not that I know of," he considered, for his memory went blank, as his passion rose, and the blood rushed out, away from his head, where all business had been cleared.

Jessup heard them, and watched, admiring. "Not bad," he said, apt critic: "The modern technique, no doubt, has its points; and advocates." Then he went to bed himself, serenely, like a child.

"How do you feel?" Hulda asked, waking her husband in the middle of the night.

"Tired," he said.

"You should," she agreed, and turned over, seeking her original sleep. Not a word was heard, till morn. Then the city rooster crowed—the clock. That metallic merciless barnyard tyrant.

"Must I go back to work?" Morgan asked, despite his high executive position, his admired role in the community, his influential ascension to power, raw power: naked and brutal. He washed, shaved, dressed, coffeed, and took leave. The other two residents slept. Jessup in the guest room. Each had one dream, unrelated to the other's. In each's soul, loneliness resided: a kind of joy.

"Now I wake up," Jessup said, and did. Soon after, Hulda followed. They breakfasted, at leisure, she in her dressing gown, with her hair fallen asleep.

"You're luscious," Jessup said, and made a grab.

"I can do with a little contrast," consented Hulda, the woman of two men, with the beginnings of a third restlessly rearranging her tissue, inside. The long day had begun. Spring, in New York.

181

Human beings, and their habits: Not a strict subject for morality, nor an enlightened theological one. The human race. Bitterly determined to endure, at all failing cost. With or without God's assistance, with if necessary, but without if possible. Life felt too good, to leave.

∞12∞∞∞∞∞

Elsewhere, Morstive Sternbump was in love, a revolting feeling because its object felt negatively indifferent toward him, which was ungrateful, but permitted under the Constitution, one of the sacred liberties which democracy upholds: to withhold your emotion. "You're overdoing it," Morstive said.

And she said, "You're overdoing what you've been busy overdoing, in your muddled heart. To me you're ridiculous. You want my love. But I, I have none to give. Now stop it, fool. You're barking up a wrong dress," she laughed, overdoing her cruel mockery. She felt light of heart. To Morstive, it felt empty. What wasn't there, he kept looking for. The "not" he looked for anyway, tied up his looking in its own knot. She would not untie it. He was fit only to be tied. She was in fits, at his folly.

Morstive wept, a significant undulation of his heart, though the weather, by contrast, merely promoted sun, in its friendly way. It was May, by official ordination, and celebrated by rites: Civil Rites, it being a metropolis, and more glass and steel and aluminum than grass, but still everybody rejoiced, including office workers. The new Keegan Dexterparks arrived, fair and shining in his white skin: not even pink. "How do you do," he said, gently, fresh from the etiquette book: white folk's manners.

"This is so-so," and Morstive introduced his girl, who curtsied, while the polite Keegan bowed, from the waist on up, a refined choreography of elegance.

"Delighted," he said, in his prissy way: truly a reformed character: one would almost say different.

"And how are *you?*" he asked Morstive, whom he had always opposed without giving out why.

"You won't hurt me?" asked Morstive, and was assured not.

His "girlfriend," hearing this, whispered "Coward!" into his middle ear, the worst practical insult.

"Can't you see he's paranoic, lady?—let him alone," Keegan defended him, now decidedly more effeminate. "When they made me white in the hospital," he told Morstive, "they sort of demasculinized me, at the same time: it was sort of tied in, a package-deal, like. Or you would say a byproduct. Anyway, I prefer men now. What are your sleeping habits? Want to board bed with me?"

"Not really," Morstive defied him: "I'm straight."

"Oh. That's old-fashioned," minced the snow-white new Keegan, altered beyond recognition, a re-created nature, done over twice and the black eaten out, and bleached of male hormones too.

Morstive was hardly able not to notice, nor could he refrain from putting this question to Keegan: "How did you lose your sunburn?" It was discreet, and gentlemanlylike. The "girlfriend" was amused to hear it, for she considered Morstive a parody of delicacy, squeamish down to the ants in his pants and the weak water in his codpiece.

"The sun was at fault for my original color," Keegan self-defensively asserted; "so while it was cold, in winter, I went into the hospital. 'Make black white,' I told the head surgeon.

" 'That's difficult,' he at first answered; for he was a mulatto, you see?"

"Those half-way people disgust me," Morstive asseverated. "And then what happened next?"

"Next," went on Keegan, with his skin changed and dressed white on white, like a painting that was snowed on and then sprayed over by the whitest base for a binding medium by a snow-struck painter of the abstract category, obsessed with purity for a theme, "the doc asks me, 'Any defects?'

" 'I'm dark of skin,' I answered him, a frank admission.

"He took me over to the light, shined the bulb on me, and muttered, 'That's correct.' He's very scientifically exact, you know."

"I know; these doctors must be," Morstive aided him.

And the newest adult member of an artificial white race went on, with his careful enunciation from thin lips, not some bigots' stage Southern drawl or loose and open Harlem vowels. He spoke prissily: "Then he said, 'How are your eyes?' "

"Who said?"

"The doctor, fool."

"Oh. So what did you answer?"

"So I said, 'I don't know, doc, test them.' "

"And did he?"

"Yes."

"And what conclusion did he come to?"

"That—would you believe it?—I'm color blind!"

"Oh no," gulped Morstive, almost fainting. It was too just, and tinged with poetic irony. "Did you see eye to eye with him?" Morstive asked.

"Yeah, and the ayes had it," Keegan lapsed, a pun for a pun. It was a fair exchange, and both were done in.

When they recovered (along with Morstive's "girlfriend," as he kept referring to her, in his bursts of optimism, uncalled for by the prevailing circumstances of her refusal to have truck or traffic with him, whatever, save to complete his scapegrace ordeal by breaking what was left of what had fairly started out to be a spirit), Keegan painfully described his operation, to which he owes his white supremacy. "I was grateful," he said.

"Did the mulatto do it?"

"No, an intern, or resident: a good job, too. Recently out of medical school. Worked from an open textbook, on pigment-coloration. Now I'm liberated. I'm whiter than you are, friend."

"That's mighty white of you," the stung Morstive protested. His imperishable color must not be maligned. It widened at the stomach, but he was proud of it. Now, he must cite precedence. Were they rivals, being alike? "You forget *I*'m white," he reminded Keegan, and added, "Does your color-blindness require a seeing-eye braille dog to feel out *my* whiteness?"

"Don't be so bold," Keegan told him: "I'm whiter than thou."

"Yeah, but I got there first, and more naturally, you artificial bastard," Morstive pointed out.

"But I was born white myself!" Keegan let him know, as the "girlfriend" stood surprised, not to mention him who called her that.

"Then why were you black for so many years?" Morstive asked. "Were you the guinea pig to an experiment?"

"Not the slightest," Keegan cooled him off. "You see, it was the sun, the sun did it."

"Too much exposure?" Morstive asked, feeling like some Wonderland to equip a million Alices.

"Yes, the sun exposed herself to me, and I, sorely seduced, was tempted from my white path."

"What a shame, you poor bird," and Morstive comforted him, soothing him on his white cheeks, gone blushing for red. The "girlfriend," meanwhile, was unbuttoning Keegan's pants fly, either that or unzippering it as an alternative to realism, to ascertain whether something else was white too. It was. But he was a fairy, so she wasn't interested.

"Now I'll have a parasol, or umbrella, to keep the wicked sun out," lisped the delicate Keegan, new-born. "And down South, I can use the white bathrooms."

"But will your *excretion* be white?" asked Morstive, who hated to brown-nose this new audacious friend.

"Yes, I'll bring my oil paint and brush along," said the former Negro, now quite altered. He felt like a new man. And was one, in fact. Which Morstive couldn't deny.

"But all white Americans," said Morstive to his former tormentor, "were European by origin. You are too, I suppose?"

"Yes, I was given an acceptable birth tree, an admirable pedigree, drawn up as part of the rules of the operation, and post-surgically confirmed."

"Most urgently?"

"No, post-surgically."

"Oh." And Morstive was fascinated. What a wealth of detail. And so colorful. It burned his eyes, almost. And he found he had regained his tolerance; and was neither bigot nor biased, nor even prejudiced, so long as his friend's transformation endured in the present state, whitewashed. "Between us, there's no segregation, let me reveal," relented liberal Morstive, as Keegan embraced him. "On the other hand, I'm not homosexual," warned Morstive, so Keegan let him go, while the "girlfriend" blushed. Supertolerance, it was, and America's racial salvation was at hand.

"What European nation are you descended from?" specified Morstive, stickingly.

"Oh, I'm really a pure American Indian," boasted Keegan naively.

"Then your face ought to be red," warned Morstive.

185

And, "It is," the blushing Keegan answered, chastised. Never again. "I'm of *English* origin," he explained, "Anglo-Saxon."

"I'm impressed," both Morstive and the girl declared, though their voices didn't synchronize, she an octave higher, a soprano out of range, while his stooped low and flirted with a cemetery, rasping the ghosts, those hardened souls. A hue and cry went up, but the hue, in Keegan's good honor, was white, as well the tone might be; and the cry, from all concerned, was, "Well done, Keegan: welcome to the White Race."

"Thank you, gentlemen," Keegan answered, blushing profusely, in reddiness. "I consider it an honor." They all applauded, all the ghosts, and the living, represented by Morstive Sternbump and his unrequited love. Why had the former been hated by the new white man? This dark question was kept in the past. Now, congratulations were in order: not recriminations. So bygones were put behind, as not in keeping with this present white unveiled portrait, in an unofficial little ceremony.

"Well, Keegan, you're my friend, now," glad-handed Morstive, while the girl looked on.

"And you're mine too," Keegan returned, hating to be outdone. He exulted, for now he was as white as any United States President, regardless of religion or creed (in such matters he was independent).

"And in what Church do you believe in?" Morstive asked, reverting again to his analytical curiosity, like a social worker dissecting a questionnaire to learn "traits" and ratios of reactions and other vital data, such information being prescribed as "useful," in our advanced decay of realistic democracy.

"The *White* Church, every time," specified Keegan, in answer: and augmented, "Not only Sundays, either, but seven whole days in one goddamn week, and fifty-two years out of the same week."

"That's doing it," Morstive admitted, "but extreme. Are you a white supremacist? Merton wouldn't like it, the minority underdog lover."

"Hell with Mr. Newberg," Keegan dismissed. "To me, only a majority is splendid: the *white* majority. My belonging guarantees that, my privileged membership. God must love the white people, He created so many of them."

"And yourself included," assisted Morstive, who felt kindly toward his white brother, formerly his black enemy.

"God was always white," Keegan said, piously, almost religiously, with adoration: "and means to stay that way, too."

"Amen," affirmed Morstive.

Which the girl echoed, "Ah, men," disparagingly.

"Who the hell is she?" Keegan wanted to know.

"Oh, a girlfriend," Morstive simply explained.

But she said, "I am not." And she was right. For she left, and never came back, never in a year and many days, eternallywise. She slipped out of sight, and Morstive, the bachelor, was again alone—stung.

"You can love *me* if you want to," Keegan offered, and received a polite thank-you, to the negative. Morstive had his dignity to consider.

∞13∞∞∞∞∞

Ira Huntworth used to be mayor. Now, he didn't enjoy stinking: It merely came out of him, like wax from a dead man's ears. But he was accused of being at fault for it. Who else was blamable? Nor were the smellers amused. But they stuck by their guns, and elected him, to prove that a candidate's stinking was only superficial, and not soul-deep. Who can say that voters are shallow? The great American tradition requires that each man do his duty. On the basis of this, Ira was Mayor Huntworth of New York, and plainly his record stunk: he did nothing, and did it dismally, for the worst results. Crime was legal, and lawfulness was illegal. God, what a mayor!

Piper Cole had assisted him, as a loyal party hack. Mediocrity inspires accomplices. (It can't merely stand on its own merit. So it hunts backing and props. It's bolstered by its own empire of numbers.)

Piper was plainly no good. Anyone could see that.

Nor was Ira any better. It was sorry days for New York.

Morstive had known them both, in days gone by. Now, they were famous: *in*famous.

"How rotten the world must be," Morstive said, "to permit of these clowns, these joking top-level idiots, as administrators to its single greatest city! We're in bad shape!"

"Right. We are." This was Duncan speaking, who was writing a book. The book would include it, for it represented Morstive's viewpoint.

Though not a social agitator, Morstive had opinions, based on response. In this, he was the typical citizen. However way *he* saw things, it was a representative sample, and approximated closely the trend. It's inconvenient for the Sanitation Department not to come, on those big rumbling trucks and those loud garbage grinders, to your house every week or so. And the smell is rotten. Or putrid, it may be described, were not description afraid of itself in these appalling instances. Nor did the Fire Department work, nor the Police Corps. Nothing worked. Not even the mayor.

He was taking a bath all day. You call that being a mayor?

Was he trying to rub himself out? For his only noticeable quality, as voters observed, was his discernible odor. Were it not for that, he could best be described as invisible. His recognizability was on a par with anonymity. Nothing remained, to recommend him. Listen, he wasn't cut out to be a city official!

Then why had he become one? Ah, hang your "head," voters!

Ah, what a shame! Oh, an abuse of democracy!

Well, that's over now. Meanwhile, interim deputies "run" the city. Slip an *i* in that verb, and it becomes "ruin."

The city. What is a city?

It is millions of people. And Morstive Sternbump was one.

Or two, if you include his fat belly.

Or three or four, because he's schizoid.

Or five or more, account of he "created" Duncan.

And add two more, because he allows his parents to exist.

Therefore, that's a considerable segment of the population. Yet the census takers, should they consider him at all, count Morstive to be only one.

Is this computing? Or hasn't some editing or deleting been done?

And Morstive Sternbump, what does he stand for?

Himself. He's old enough, isn't he?

His feelings are hurt. Duncan gave him a bad case of love, by setting on him a girl who ran away. Yes, ran. She ran away.

Morstive is in tears. "I want her back," he whines, sniveling.

"You never really did have her," Duncan encourages him, the gentle author, writing a gentleman's book.

"But I want her anyway," sobs Morstive. Want, want. We forget how percentagely few of all wants get fulfilled during the duration of those wants. With unfulfillment, the wants turn away. But first, they mope; those wan, hurt wants.

Morstive is not found wanting, in finding his wants wanting in their gratification. His wants wander off, in a daze.

"Why is love always so sad?" he asks, from his deep store of misinformation.

"I advise you to take it philosophically," Duncan enjoins, "I really do advise it. Or must I send you to a psychiatrist?"

"No, anything but that," and Morstive shut up. Better dumb than insane.

"But it hurts," he says.

"I'm sure," Duncan consoles him, cynically at that. All this is making good book copy, his sufferings, and Duncan is endowed with potent emotional material to match his flawless style. With Morstive the victim, a heady scapegoat.

"Why is the world the way it is?" he asks, and gets no answer.

Or if he does, it sounds like this: "That's life, what else do you want?"

"Plenty," he would reply, but learns, by now, how fruitless it is to complain. The silent sufferer.

"Having a heart," he says, if permitted, "involves liabilities, not only assets."

"You have sound business sense," Duncan might, to alleviate the pain, praise him. Duncan takes care of his "child." "Morstive is the hero of this book," Duncan reminds himself daily; "and too much torment, and not enough joy, stifles his growth and unbalances his equilibrium. He must be kept pleased, at peaceful intervals between growling griefs. 'Have you a particular pleasure you crave at the moment?' I ask him, the sore target.

" 'May I eat?' the vile slave returns, and I direct him to his poor frozen refrigerator, for scrapes of fare. His belly trembles with joy.

"He drivels with gratification, as though in this are contained the gratifications unattainable elsewhere. They all flock stuffing into this one joy. Here their illusions can't outlast the appetite, but die with surfeit. Then they yowl again, all starved.

"My poor, unhappy subject! How happy he could be! That's the measure of how unhappy he is. What capacity, he has!

" 'Ah, I must be kept happy!' he keeps insisting, an hysterical form of raving, reducing desperation to animal cunning, clutching for little or no straw. 'I wish so evidently to live,' he says, or maintains to say, fighting the awkward years of his removal as a pestilent nuisance from time's onward track, which he opposes. 'Oh, anything!' he bargains for, the smallest creature comfort, the sparsest hope. His mind is deranged, his morals are permanently without foundation, and his instincts are crazed, with denial. He would employ his intelligence, should a useful end promise a mansized reward, a human consolation. 'Enough for love,' he concludes; 'it failed to carry expectation to the proposed peak, where actuals reside. Idealism doesn't pay. I'm corrupt, swallowed in a city. On whom shall I prey, removing exploitation to an advantage that bodes well for the first person singular? I, Morstive Sternbump, must, and insistingly will, delve for a solution. A craven existence nullifies me. Salvation, even at the hands of God, for earthly paradise in my lifetime, is my working goal. May I attain it.'

"Well, I admire his enterprise. He has pluck. He'll go a short way, and running backwards, shirking misery promiscuously to no avail. Happiness, twice or three times in his life, proffers that mirage to encourage his fruitless endeavor, nor be disappointed too soon. 'You're hopeful, in spite of what has befallen you?' I stoop beggingly to ask.

" 'I have my inner dream,' he says, 'at the root of my unflinching spirit. Let no man deprive me of it.'

" 'But what about woman?' I remind him. He freezes, and the suggestion paralyzes him.

" 'I admit to being lonely,' he declares, when recovered: 'Yet I tend to correct it.'

" 'You mean *in*tend?'

" 'Yes,' he looks at me; 'you are very reliable with words. My life suffers. Is there a connection?'

" 'The world is not the most convenient place,' I inform him with discreet restraint; 'and words simply do not add up to anything, whether used with poetic genius or journalistic incompetence. Speaking and writing are not articulate to create a difference from what *is*, the prevailing human discomfort, all our dumb pains and our ventures ill-founded, discoveries of eventual disappointment.

190

You shouldn't complain. What you feel, is felt by all, in comparative degrees. Your similarity to other men defies your claim to uniqueness: What is Morstive? Anyone, who cares to be him, with the consequent problems and attendant troubles. You are not rare, but common, close to the grass root average. That is your doom.'

" 'Thank you, I reject it,' he replies, like a king, with choice. What is his range of selection? Narrow, in scope. He barely is what he is, let alone what he can't be. Why does he try? Well, that's his credit. He tries, so as not to die. Himself he has, and can't afford to lose it, though its returns on his investments are negligent: repudiating, as well as dashing, the fond glows of his hope, romantic aspirations. He ineptly goes about, dodging his own destruction, with sleight-of-foot skill, like a St. Vitus dancer performing Degas-like delicacies of pastel ballet, to the tune of music. The world is wonderful to place our dreams in, for they fall right through, as the planks on the warehouse floor or storeroom den are rat-ridden, and objects can't endure. Least of all man; though Morstive does well, defying all the tricks against him, to keep the stars company and the moon occasional companion, before *his* night departs, which the solar system survives to plan other cosmic freaks in his stead, given enough germination. Birth is cheap, and Morstive Sternbumps, like the daisies on the field and the valley-decorating lilies, are abundant, all too weedy. This one likes it here, despite setbacks, and has forestalled his vacation, put off his inevitable postponement of nature's retreating journey, the holiday back to infinity, to spend what remains of his tidy eternity, risking a few solid hours at the bar of immortality, stuck to the public privacy of his flesh. 'Fun, is what I want,' he says, appeasing it.

"And I, his biographer, say, 'One minute please,' letting him wait. Which is what his ancestors did, and produced him, an off oddspring, the latest misappliance. 'In a second,' I warn him, and go off, he following on, drying his tears for new laughter."

"How's the book coming along?" Morstive asked.

"It's underway."

"How do you do it? What's your secret?"

"Stop prying into my profession. You weren't able to do it yourself, so you needed me. So I have the upper hand, you're dependent. So I can balk at answering what I don't want to. My working habits, my trade tricks, are being put to use. Prattling of them is too self-conscious-making. Go on living, and the book will happen."

"Any clue as to the title? I'd like my name in it, please."

"I'll oblige you, if *art* decides to. The title will be devised, as an over-all commentary on the whole text, once the text *becomes* whole, and is done. At the very end, you'll know it."

"Is a title then an afterthought?"

"Yes. But first the thought must be complete, for the full afterthought to be properly informed. So wait. Wait."

"And the characters in it—will you distort their names?"

"Maybe. Living people are in one dimension; fictional characters are in another. Sometimes there are crossings, from one to the other. We'll see what's indigenous to one, and what to the other. Why speculate? Wait, and see what I do."

"May I *suggest* some names?"

"I may not accept them, but what are they?"

"Picturesquely, make 'Ira Huntworth' into 'Mire Dungdirt.' "

"That's too funny, it's not convincing. What else?"

"Make 'Piper Cole' into 'Wiper Hole.' "

"Don't get obscene. What else?"

"Make 'Merton Newberg' into 'Urgent Jewberg.' "

"That's an insult to a certain religion. What's next?"

"Convert 'Jessup Clubb' to 'Jesuck Crust.' "

"That's pure blasphemy, against a premiere notable of all religious myth. Now what?"

"Turn 'Morgan Popoff' into 'Organ Poppoff.' "

"Stop getting descriptive. I'm not a graphic illustrator. Who else?"

"Instead of 'Turkel Masongordy,' how about the name 'Work-will Paymontory'?"

"Too labored. Too unlikely, like the rest. What else?"

"Instead of your going by 'Duncan Durowetsky,' why not give yourself *this* handle: 'Huckle Neurojetsky'?"

"Oh shut up. You're very fanciful."

" 'Page Slickman' is all right, for the last name fits him. But why not change 'Page' to 'Wage'?"

"It's *my* book, not yours. Your suggestions are futile, I won't adopt them."

"And the women: 'Lusta Snock' from 'Hulda Stock'; 'Femla Bravada' from 'Emma Lavalla'; 'Lessa Weacunt' from 'Tessa Wheaton.' "

"You have an obscene imagination, or something. I'm not writing a novel by Charles Dickens, or an allegory by John Bunyan, or a Restoration comedy by some nameword stylist. I'm writing a *realistic* book. If you don't like it, get out."

"How can I get out, if I'm in it to the point where it's mainly about me?—only secondarily about those others. And you're in it, too, but as an alter-ego of mine, in a way. *I* invented *you*, not you me. I *let* you write this."

"Stop pulling rank. *I'm* the writer, not you. You're the original one: but *I*, surely, *originate* you. Were it not for me, you'd have only *life's* existence (which I can't deprive you of—not legally, anyhow); but not a *fictional* life. So scrape your knees, obediently. Or I'll scrap this book, at once!"

"What an ultimatum! You win. I'll obey. But you're *my* inspiration, for I once envisaged you. I fell into a swoony spell, a deep and mystic trance. This was I don't know when—place it as timeless."

"And what did the voice tell you?"

"It came out of the heavens, or somewhere else. It forecast you. It said these prophetic words, listen: 'Perhaps you can *hire* a writer, lacking the technical equipment yourself; so that what you feel and know, plus what he guesses and verbally indites, can sum up to a pretty good novel? Of course, you must change the names—or *he* must. Or why don't you make him you, to avoid complications, and settle the delicate touchy subject of identity? I wish you good luck. This is a voice from on high. Remember me.' "

"What a visitation! Did you *see* the apparition?"

"No, he was cloaked in a deep mist, in the veil of obscurity. His words had effect. They led me to recognize you, when we 'met,' by a chance encounter. But still, you won't change the names?"

"No. Your suggested names were too contrived, too stilted, too much the mark of a frustrated writer. Back off. Leave it to me."

"My *own* name, I was going to suggest to be left as is. 'Morstive Sternbump'—doesn't that just fit me?"

"It's perfect. You're the right one for it."

"I'm the right *person*, for *it*? But I meant *it*'s the right *name*, for *me.*"

"They're both the same, those two distinctions you made."

"Are they? Gosh, you're deep! But that 'voice' had said that maybe I should make you into me. *Are* we one, really?"

"Let's stay apart, for now. We operate better, separate."

"You're unsentimental, and workmanlike. There was one *more* name I was going to suggest, to be changed."

"Who is that?"

" 'Who'? But 'who' is the *person*. You mean what *name.*"

"Oh, don't get technical. *What*, then? What name? Or who does it belong to?—it's the same."

"It's 'Keegan Dexterparks,' formerly black—and *still* black, in self-consciousness of pseudo-white spirit. His name I would change—"

"Yes—into what?"

"How's this: 'Negrace Prejudark.' "

" 'Negrace Prejudark'?"

"Yes. 'Negrace Prejudark.' "

"All is black. The lights are out."

∞15∞∞∞∞

"Duncan, I'm hungry."

"Go coldly into that refrigerator. You needn't cook it."

"But I *like* warmed-up food. It tastes better."

"*Some* food is all right cold."

194

"I was the victim of a woman's cold *heart.*"

"I warmly sympathize with you, then. Are you *still* in love?"

"Sadly, yes."

"Go outdoors. You need some fresh air. While you're gone, I'll work more on this book."

"Ah yes. The book. About me, and others. But first I'll eat. Give me an example of your literary style. Suppose I woke up melancholy? How would you describe it?"

"You're so food-obsessed, I might put it this way: 'Morstive gulped for breakfast air, swallowed a few toasted yawns, baked sighs, and sipped a cup of hot liquid despair.' "

"That sounds like me, all right. While you were reciting that, I finished the cold food—in actual eating. *Real* eating, not in a book. Thanks for recognizing that I'm sadly heartbroken in love. Put *that* into the book. Unrequited love! What an old theme! For what a new book! But lots of other things will be in the book, too, I bet."

"Leave it to me. Who had gotten you into love in the first place? I arranged for its unrequited nature, as well. And you cursed me, you resented me, for meddling with your life and poisoning your very tranquillity—as if you had had any. Anyway, enough of this love business. It's had its point, I've recorded it already. This love has made you stale. 'Self,' 'self,' is all I hear. Enough of that. Go out in the street. That's where the world is. Go and find it. Go, go, sad romantic idiot."

Morstive is in the street. The world *is* there. What a world! *His* world? Or a world *anti*-him? Same thing, in and out.

The world. Morstive. And the book, between them. The book. Their link. Their bridge (abridged version). The worlded Morstive of words.

Just then, Merton came along. "Be a campaign worker," he advised Morstive freely, "and advocate my candidacy, at the ward level or precinct district. A vote for me is a vote for you. Don't let either of us down. My friend. Nice to meet you in the street. I'm out canvassing. Do you live near here?"

"Yes I'm out for air. May looks good. I just had a cold bite, some refrigerated food. I was talking with Duncan. Do you know him? He tried to console me. I lost in love."

"My sympathies. If elected mayor, I can promise you you'll win her. I plan reform. Does that suit you?"

"Yes, Mr. Newberg," said Morstive. "But I don't understand politics. I feel so anonymous, so out of the community. I want a sense of belonging. Haven't you felt this way?"

"Morstive, I have, yes. We're both alike, you know? Of course, I have a wife, Emma. Her maiden name used to be Lavalla, before she kindly consented to be my bride in marriage, forever do we trust, in love or peace. She's pregnant now. If you smoke, I'll give you a cigar, when the boy's time comes. Or girl, for they're democratically our equals. Now let's go over to a park bench, and end our walking, and watch sweet spring, and the melodious birds. Isn't the air pure? Ah, it makes me sigh. Now let me tell you about myself. First of all, I'm Merton Newberg. Right off, right off the bat. Frank, I like to be.

"I subscribe reform. Did you like Mayor Huntworth's reign? Of course not: *any* nose could tell. Well, I advocate scent, fragrance, beautiful springtime, the odors of delight. Doesn't that sound nice? Then I'm your man! I'm for all underdogs, whether low or not, on majority rule. I'm for *you*, whether you like it or not. Do you like it? Are you content now? No, apparently not. Well, I'll remedy that. How does that sound? Will you enlist your support, my friend? Help me out. I'm in need."

"You make me feel important," Morstive said, "which I'm not —at all. Is that clear?"

"Then I'll help you be *un*important," Merton promised, altering his tactic a bit. "Anything you want, I'll promise it to you. Is that fair?"

"Can you *keep* the promises?" Morstive asked skeptically, wanting to milk this cow for all it could, in bucolic serenity on a gorgeous spring day. "Tweet-tweet," went the birds, darting. How cute. They really brazened the air, a firm blue behind them, as their feathers whisked along, gay on light wings. "Would I could fly," Morstive indulged, in the silent recess of his mind.

"What?" Merton said, surprised out loud. "Don't be private, man; are you a fool? Be public!"

"Why?" Morstive put. "For politics? Government? I like myself better. Not group man, but the individual. I value my liberalness, and dust it up to date, improvising on current themes. New, that's me. Modern."

"But I am too!" Merton demanded. "Only, my scale is broader: I include *all* men."

"That's too much," criticized Morstive, "for it slights me. If you favor the many, the few are ignored."

"But I *love* the few!" Merton proclaimed, getting loud: "Love them off their feet, you hear? Love them against their will, if necessary. But love them. Vote for me—is a vote for you. *Please* support me. Friend!"

"I'll see," Morstive said, and went away, leaving Merton, in a depressed state of mind, sulking on a sitting bench, out in the park, the sprightly square, where all the children played oblivious to their civic responsibilities.

"They'll learn," Merton vowed, a punishing retaliation. "They'll rue the day when they slighted duty. Public-minded, I'll make them aware, forcibly. Nor will Morstive escape, whose assistance he spurned in my hour of need. The individual! How corrupt!

"I'll fix his mettle, and get his goat. I aspire to a mayorality, or my name ain't me. Public relations is my job now, a good setup. I'm learning prevailing opinion, which I seize, then imitate, and toss it back at them, the broad public at large, that corporate body, that municipal entity, for which I sweat, and labor, at my gain—and theirs, if they only knew it. Fair imbeciles! Including Morstive Sternbump, the worst, a loafer, a daydreamer, a nightbedder on his lone, not even a wife to marry, in his sodden bachelorhood. Emma keeps me to the grind, at the wheel. Well, lunch hour is enough, and ambition protests, that I must return to the office, get back to the work at hand. A scandal is brooding at me, for the radio coverage, false testimony, a phony interview, concerning the recent big fight, back in February. Page is being tried, for his part, while his mob lurks, unfriendly on the streets. Ira Huntworth is an able witness, but the whole jury must wear gas masks. What are they collectively hinting at? Are they a pressure group? Everybody's lobbying. For this, for that. What else? Piper Cole is in bad trouble, and the boxing commission, what hired me to distort the broadcast, is being paid off, by henchmen and thugs, goons. Decency is a minor quality about this part of town, and my clean-up movement will unleash such sanitation upheaval that the pipes will ring clear again, and plumbing will be up to Twentieth-Century caliber, safeguarding health for young and old alike, including those of any age, people being born unconsecutively, at odd moments, some soon, others later, while the later are preserved, and the earliest ones die first, as a rule. Humanity uplifts me, and I'm a scientist in fair civic virtue. I'm a good man, and an ample Christian, a regular Sunday worshipper. Emma kneels along with me, at the church, and we make a conspicuously devout couple, to the betterment of my 'image,' serving good publicity for my running, if it comes. I'm cultivating the party boss, a man dense in a smoke-filled room, the mayor-maker, an Italian with dark glasses. He dispenses patronage, on orders from the President. The Governor is hostile, opposing our party. I can conciliate, and fairly please everyone, whatever their game is, down to the least, sulking minority, the lowest peon. I'm not alone. God is with me."

"Go back to work, fool!" It was his wife. Emma, at home, had been phoned by the directors and board of Merton's associates, to go seek him out, who had neglected business. Politics is fine, in part time, as a holiday from the heavier requirements of industry, for Communications was a sprawling enterprise ending halfway round the world, and beginning on Madison Avenue, which made ordinary products look wonderful, fine goods appear marvelous, everyday items partake of luxury's inevitable necessity, creating a demand on the part of the general consumer, exaggerating his particular dopiness into a mob common herd rule, for Joneses and their brothers, their nieces and inlaws, to join in handily, and be what the image says you should be. Much marketing research went into this, coding, tabulating, calculating, computing, and lying. It was a big industry, incalculably invaluable as an economic prop, to bolster the sagging standard of what our ancestors used to call living, if life can so demean itself.

"Coming, honey," Merton answered, and followed his pregnant wife to a curb, where they took a cab, fairly flying to a handsomely upholstered office in the upper fifties, soundly furnished in all business essentials, incredibly modern, with chrome pneumonia panels and sheer synthetic plastic that imitated false wood and untrue metal, and gave a masonry effect of painted brick on linoleum veneer that just didn't come off, but on the whole stunning and stylish, making fashion overnight obsolete, deftly understated in slick layout, the corridors reeking with antideodorant and the ladies all on high heels, who manicured the typewriter.

"Phone call from Morgan Popoff," the receptionist said, at the busy switchboard. A typical working day, in fact the most typical by far, as the latest figures reveal. The bookkeeper was at the ledger, copyists and clerks fluttered and cluttered, against the salary check. This was business, and it was life, at its most businesslike attitude.

"Put him on the wire," Merton said, adjusting the dial system, and wiping off his lapel some almost invisible flint, that little breeder of imperfection. Merton took no chance.

"Hello, Newberg," Morgan said, his voice clear.

"Yeah Morgan hello," the answer went, at rapid-fire. On top level, placed for getting fast, competition at dizzy an hour, men pitted.

"I have finances at my disposal," said Morgan, "capital to reinvest, at profit overhead. I want to support your campaign."

"A splendid gesture!" Merton praised, in his most pleased manner. Like manna from heaven, a windfall, an unsuspected source. "I'm indebted," Merton volunteered, clad in a slim gray suit, with gleaming tie-pin.

"That's one of my conditions," Morgan specified, trumping the recipient by giving with qualification, gain after all being his business also. Who is virtuous, or can afford to be?

"Isn't that self-seeking?" Merton asked, his enthusiasm now dampened by the mitigated generosity, with Morgan's strings-attached offer, withholding the outright sweetness. Deals, all deals! Raw deals, ordeals: No ideals. All because why? That infernal ouster from Eden. Banished to the Garden of Plunder. On exile to Monetary Isle. And stranded there.

Bitterness was coming from another source: his wife. No ease there! Was this part of a general gang-up? Conspiracies are imagined, when life leaks its ebb.

"And I'm going to henpeck you when you're through," whispered Emma into her husband's free nontelephone ear, wounding and offending it thereby.

"Ah, my troubles'll be over," he assured himself, on fire from two fronts, "the day I'm inaugurated. I'll be free. The city, it'll slide."

The phone call was consumed, and left at a conclusive state, pending at a further rate. At the other end, Morgan conducted his business, a steady tyrant over his staff, holding as ever the whip hand, with blows cruising down: his brutal profit-pulling ways, procuring power with puffing purpose, pouring himself unmolested into prime position where ripe money could speak. Merton's office door was closed, and Emma sat shrewishly on his desk, prepared to dictate terms unbrooked by bullish opposition on her husband's puny part, who sought to be a city mayor in the deepest depth where privacy was compelled by public ambition and insanity no longer permitted, in the outward turn of his pressing personality, pitted in the politics of strife. "What did Morgan say?" poked Emma into her husband's business.

"He'll help me if I help him," Merton answered. "He wants there to be no depression, I shouldn't even permit a *re*cession, he wants a full cycle of economic stability, for at a previous period a slump plus a crooked frame-up cost him his enterprising job, and he's within sight of vice-presidency, the promotion of his happiest dreams, and as a mayor I've got to protect him: that is, advocate big business, and ruin his competitors. It's a bribe? No. I've always believed in minorities, and certainly executives come under that heading. So few of them, so many the others. My heart turns liberal, at their plight. Their cause is mine, to the truest sentiment.

"It's labor I'm against, the depressed ranks of lower classes. Up with the substantial, long thrive Popoffs. I'll see to it. Yes, politics is a fine example, an uplifting incidence of opportunities. Ira Huntworth, switching to the opposite party, promises the kind of opposition of splendid service to my cause. Now, Emma, what are you doing here? Have you managed to eject my mother yet, who insists on living on her own terms with us, dictating my career advancement, and dominating our domesticity? *You* must argue, not I. As

200

my mother, she has an initial advantage that handicaps my skills of bargaining, complicating my post-birth attempts at independence. Emma, I hate to become sentimental: but I love you."

Emma kept sitting on his desk, complaining that he substitutes her for religion, and the loyal piety of his devotion embarrasses their family relationship, unnerving her. "I'm no saint," she said; "and as proof, I'll be your secretary."

"But I have one already."

"She's fired, or put to work as a file typist. I have your ambition at heart, and a personal commitment to promote it. Hulda has been taunting me, that her Morgan passes you, dear, in what we wives refer to as superiority. *They* have a maid: Tessa Wheaton, who turned tramp when Popoff ceased to be her last name. Can't *we* afford one? Or must politics take your business profits, to perpetuate your 'campaign'?—which has barely flown off the ground. Have you made a survey? What are opinion trends, tied in with your possibilities? Get moving. This morning, at home, I spanked your mother, and reprimanded her with maltreatment. I want power, too. You're my agency. Keep on being religious, the most conspicuous Christian whose lips move to prayer in this city of unmovable stone. Where will it get us? I'd like to live in a mansion, as the mayor's pretty wife, with more servants than Hulda can boast of in all her brash majesty of pomp. You'll improve our state, won't you, dear? I'll be the driving force; and though my brains aren't too bulging and I'm tempted to henpeck you to shreds, I'll cooperate, and we'll prosper. You do approve, don't you? Speak, and say you do."

"You're pushing me," Merton warned her, "and irritating my capacity. Let me be. Bad enough I'm so mothered by my mother, bossed and bullied by those I must persuade in my quest for position and power, without having you to nag me. Why must you emulate Hulda?—a phase it's well to have outgrown, with just your role at home to content you. Don't interfere. Your education stopped before college, but you barge everywhere you don't belong, headstrong, and I the captive to your wild persevering practicality, your relentless drive. It's my career, not yours. Jump on my bandwagon, but don't direct it. I'll go, and you trail along. Don't be my secretary. Go away."

"Look, I'm bearing your baby, ain't I?" Emma screeched, as the afternoon closed down. "You abducted me, and I eloped alongside: I claim bit for bit all the equality you've got, we halfway split it. You

201

dirty sap. I'm having an affair with Morgan, see? I'm betraying Hulda, he's betraying you. You can call me a bitch, but I got you by the balls, because it's a political disaster to be divorced, and you got to strike the right public image. I'm bored of you. Unspeakably. Adultery keeps me busy, and Morgan can really bruise it, a man better than your mother-tormented boyish tricks on our neat polite bed. You inspire no passion, but you whet all my harpy instinct. You're a crazy queer, with your stupid inner life. And you're fatally in love with me; nothing I do can remedy that. You're a punk. Go ahead, be mayor. But quick about it, and buy me a servant, Morgan preferably, my major manservant. You protect minorities, don't you? Well, what are we? Come on, bust out. Husband, bring me home a few results: you rotten Christian convert, you mad lost dreamer of hypocrisy. I'm waiting. Go on. Produce! Wretch; support me good, you hear? I come from a low background, and now I want comfort. And you're forbidden from my bed. How's this, for a split? Go ahead: and I want some pudding for proof. I could expose everything about you, were I so inclined to choose. Wreck! And do what Morgan says! He's right. Just by living, he's right. And you're left, with your public relations self-marketing into politics, to rake up what's dead of you, to artificially create life. You live by unnatural will, but in your guts and groin, you leftover scum, you're so dead there's no room for your coffin; the world's a general tomb, and your corpse kicks. Well, kick it to fame, glamorpuss, and treat my life nice, you hear, unless you want it really rough from me. I won't disturb you, so let me have my affair. Any interference, and Morgan shall ruin you, for I run him now, and Hulda hangs in a dropping fate, while you, I'm afraid, must wrap up your failure, and form a fine success. How popular you'll be! And the few who know you, like me, will see how cheap popularity is, when such as you command and achieve it. Stop weeping, fraud! It'll ruin your rain-and-drain scheme, and it's false economics to waste a sentiment that has no political issue. Your do-gooding nest-feathers your fake image, you exploit the least play at virtue. Nothing for its own sake, but for you. But you're no you, you're flexibly whatever profits the moment. And what private life you have, I hold the key. You're worthy to succeed Ira Huntworth, but you're too offensive to stink; and the city is just as worse. *He*, at least, did nothing: You, I'm sure, with your pure public-spiritedness, will do nothing possibly right, and get a lot done wrong. Congratulations, in advance. As your wife, I'm proud to convert 'your' seed to a future baby better than you: we'll name him Morgan, won't we?"

"Is he *mine?*" Merton desperately asked.

"Why not? Nominally, anyway."

"Then I must kill you."

"That's wrong, and you know it. It would disqualify you as a mayor."

"All right, then get home."

"Goodbye, dear Merton. Thank you, Your Honor."

"No insults."

"No? Then why?"

"I'm above them: I'm too democratically equal to merit offense. I love harmony."

"You do? Then accept my most cordial discord," taunted Emma, and wore a dimple when she smiled: which won Merton, and consumed that which went for a heart, in that highminded citizen.

∞17∞∞∞∞

Time ripped on, summer succeeded spring, at an orderly rate of sequence. Morstive was worried, while Duncan worked on the book. It was a money problem, and he applied to Morgan Popoff, who had forgone a vacation to handle a press of business at his flowery office high up to which an elevator gives access, home life being spotty, Hulda suspicious of his adultery, and Jessup leeched on for good, it seems—that way that temporary things have of threatening to remain permanent, and be for all time. On the way up, Morstive got stuck, as the opulent elevator squeaked. Nor did Morgan treat him more courteously, offering him no position, though Morstive had to sit and be treated to boasting: "We have a maid now, my ex-wife Tessa Wheaton, who tried to regain her typing job here only she looked slatternly; and Hulda, to keep content, needed a soft weak victim at home, she growing bitchy hormones lately, her furious temper giving me impetus to letch and cheat, Emma this time, while Merton, having received the nomination, sludges through his campaign, on a platform designed to give this city democracy, though it least needs it, so crowded with inferior types. Morstive, I advise you to bear close emulation on me, should you want to get ahead. You're not hired, as you know, on fear you'd jinx this firm's prosperity, the accumulation of a wage scale of dollars. Your former boss, and mine now as well as prior to your reign, Turkel Masongordy, is about to step down, disheartened after his wife's murder, and leave the business to me. My rank is at top vice-presidency, and won't stop climbing yet, with the highest executive capacity my humble goal. I've moved my family out of the city, to the suburbs, topped by a shady lawn, as I commute with prestige. Emma's my mistress, and I'm hot on to a file clerk here, a little tot of a thing. Success seems all the rampage, these days. And you, Bud?—where's *your* advancement going to? We're to each other what we first earliest were, me tops and you downs. Thus, we revert to our respective sea-levels. I'll lord it, while you cower, but we'll weakly pretend the equality game, like actors replaying the roles that fooled audience and selves alike. Evolution made me superior. Fall back, and turn extinct. You were ever mateless though hopelessly annoyed by that. You're still without a woman, what? Well hands off Hulda, you scumless brainsect. I can make you an offer, that of a domestic: You marry my maid Tessa, live-in, and watch Jessup, and my faithless wife. In the capacity of gardener, if your thumb summons green roses. No? Well, all that's said is done. You're free to go hungry, and take off weight. Stay here, unemployed by me. While I earn, you sag: our old ratio, come back.

"Wait, don't go, I'll confide. You know I lost money on that fight February? I get it in my head to blame Hulda, to bet on a favorite at twelve-to-one, and get skinned. That's unlike me, if you know: money arrives, it doesn't depart. Only *you*'re that dopey. And though the loony bin still has a warrant for me, I'm safe out in the country, with Jessup to guard the door, in turn for my not pinching him—wanted in every united state for a rap of deliberate kidnap, with death to cream the cake, plus imitating a religious figure, and the manufacture of false haloes. That loads you up, listener. Don't divulge that essential dope, or I'll do you in. I'm done achin' out my tongue. Better I work, and be quiet."

"All the same, sir," Morstive replied, "if you have no further use for me, I'll be bygone by now, if it so please you, as I may not interrupt. Is that all?"

"Get outta here, bum, and don't come back," invited Morgan, and bent down on his papers, jotted out full with sketchy financial reports, representing money in the concrete, through a notation of abstract figures.

Morstive took his cue, and left. "Exhausted hope in *that* department," he added mentally, while envy consumed him, Morgan being go-ahead, and he himself only depending on Duncan, whose book was in the useless scribble stage, a mere random of words.

Back down in the crowded street, Page Slickman came across, bailed out from the trial. "Bohemian!" the latter scorned, reducing him to nothing, and Morstive knew why: he had a beard.

"Up for an important job interview," he chastised himself, "and forlorn for the lack of a shave! How quite idiotic!" He shook-nodded his "head," Morstive did, and found himself lost in hot midday traffic, on the pedestrian side, the huge summer populace. "This is not to my liking," he said, surveying, in brief, the course his life had run, the lack of up and the ascendancy of down, varied only by the degrees in failure.

From another direction, here was Page again, who said, "You're me, remember; or rather, I'm you. I owe your identity— I mean *own*. If the law, nervous about my machine-gun mob and fight racketeer connection, should latch on adversely to my neck and build a special jail for me with no holds barred, you, Morstive, though you're dressed ill and I well, shall stand in, be me, and I, legally, shall be you, a free citizen in the street. This is only fair trade, so don't question why. My neck is worth bothering to save, and for you you're neckless, from the waist down and the head up. So now I'm not afraid of crime, with *you* to do my penance. I'll be reckless, at will: and get *you* hanged.

"No, don't interrupt; you're so impatient. Who wants to listen to you, with all the hot controversy on current news? Our time is sure inventful—I mean eventful. And I'm involved, not just a bywitness. Will boxing in New York be outlawed? It's an election issue, and that droopy Newberg, protecting everyone's minority, is for barring Negroes out of the ring, on the principle of not to have those precious citizens hurt, nor Jews neither, in the democratic tradition, as immigrants shouldn't be abused, nor clubbed by a mighty fist. So that pansy is tryin' fer mayor, eh? We'll put the heat on him, and link his publicity to the championship bribe, deflaming his fair name on election eve, you bet. As a bookie contact man, I had a hand in that fix, and for vindication I'll go blackmail Ira, who turncoated to another party, all wet with the dry swimming pool I sold him, me the head of a gang that's got push on City Hall, to pay off district attorneys and what not, to enlighten the rabble how we mean to cash in, and own this den of political iniquity. I'm wise now. I ain't sellin' no swimmin' pool, just water under the dam that I flew over the fluid being fluent. But *af*fluent I aim to be—it holds more water, in my private pool. Money solves my solvency problem, if enough of it is there. Me, I love dough, and mean to make it, take it off horses or men, it's all the same. So long, pal. Be me when I need you. You're not good enough for your needs to count. So be the me when I'm in hot water, while I cool off in the guise of you, when times are most slippery. Then I'll slide off." And off he went, while Morstive got the splash of his wake of words, the foam of insult, the spray of contempt. While high and dry goes that chilling guy, surfing over all this humidity. Morstive is stuck. His life is penned in, city deep.

"Why is everyone rude to me?" Morstive asked, jostled and hurtled by crowds of anonymous faces pale above the twisting bodies. City summer is full of sweat, and rank odors. The Twentieth Century is the wrong time to be; it's all so local and particular, and stands inside itself, not out. "Signs to save me," Morstive asked for, ready for religion if necessary, to pump up a little meaning in the shallow waste. But God was on holiday, and left the city to fare for itself, misgoverned by the wrong men, and all the right were stung in futile protest. "Wish I could get away," Morstive decided, in his powerless frame, while money ruined him and directed his misactivity, or activated him with misdirection, with its absentee deprivations, a rule from afar, by not being there. "Anxiety I don't want," Morstive understood, which hardly prevented it from ringing a tug of screeching bells in the moist pit where serenity was blasted, and dim tranquillity hid like a hunted hare in the thickets of the distance, warned off from the sorry spot. Bugles blared, horns honked, and the traffic skidded. Overhead, big buildings surrounded his ego, skyscrapers dashed his human psyche in cold elevated efficiency, the haughty perfection of the almost human inanimate. What air was there, Morstive took, and served his lungs. At least, breathing was a delight. Its function, though mechanical, poured a living dance in vitality's wildest design, the tame audacity of being alive. "I feel better," Morstive said, not realizing why. Troubles can be mental or emotional, but relief is physical gaiety, sheer outlet. "I'll be happy next," Morstive warned himself, prepared for any emergency.

Thus it did happen. And as a happy person, he's no longer interesting, sufficed by a mere state of being, with no remedial action required. He smiled, while the sun declined.

∞18∞∞∞∞∞

Tessa Wheaton is not happy. She's a domestic, now, poor thing, and her mistress is tyrannical, ruling their suburban life. Back to her puritan ways, and typically overexaggerated in the monster of another self, she's grotesquely the opposite of her strumpety postmarriage days, the despair of her morals. Her teeth have fallen out, her weight has become ungainly thin, she's prematurely ancient, an infant prodigy of senility, lost in a tired mind. Any attempt on her virtue is instantly repulsed, in her decided reversion to her old trademark, an immaculate affectation of purity, a prudery in which men are stamped as beasts, all ugly takeoffs on her father, the first and most hideous example. Hulda subjugates her, and in her weakened pride Tessa bows her head, and meekly complies. She's sweeping and cleaning in the morning, while Jessup and her mistress are contorted in the drugged pleasure of sleep, Morgan (for "business reasons") having not returned the night before. She does what she's told, and drowses in the sweet sadness her memory still holds, the short pathos of her life, swept by middle age towards the dreary conclusion. Her rebellion is not evident, pent up short in her shriveled thin breast. Resentment of her lowly dependent status is borne by her quiet willingness to suffer, as she nurses her private misery with humble forbearing, the tedium of her relentless discipline.

Hulda knows, now, of Morgan's affair, and has terminated relations with Emma, pending further revenge. Merton, the cuckold, was the surprise nomination, shocking the collective lethargy sunk in the public. He's campaigning vigorously, with the election not far off. He had made his "deal" with Morgan, in return for financial support, to crush labor unions and keep big business prosperous, averting a deadly repression, which Morgan dreads almost superstitiously, now that Turkel Masongordy is to step down and give over the full corporate reigns into Morgan's keen handling, as he forges his empire. There was the wife-murder case, still to be solved: Keegan's New Year's eve trick to frame Morstive, at that rather rowdy party. Morgan is the full vice president, and he looks it. Emma, though pregnant, is now his private secretary. But there's a file clerk, a tot of a lass, whom Morgan keeps peeking at. August is far too hot and dusty, so September steps up. Emma's child by Morgan is due in late November, though publicly it will be announced as Merton's, to celebrate his expected triumph at the polls, if the current trend and latest predictions of his own market research agency are at all reliable, in the hurly-gurly of estimates. Merton is woeful, for he's in doubt, still thinking the boy must be his, who'll be born soon. The court acquitted him of complicity in the broadcast farce of the boxing fight; though the jury, still, is deliberating on Piper's alleged guilt, as the district attorney has been singularly paid off by an organized cult of bookies, to whom benefits must accrue, while Page's rival gang slithers down the streets, and Page has both hands in two pockets, supporting equal factions, dividing his identity into opposing camps, cornering a vicious market with underhand deceit. But if caught, and condemned, he proposes to exchange selves with Morstive, as a resolve of correct innocence. Meanwhile, he bets on horses, while Piper, who'd like to, can't, locked up in his expensive cell. Hulda also expects a baby in late November, Morgan's as well, but Jessup is tampering with it, in his haste, as in Tessa's case, to have it be born. The danger, as with Tessa, is a miscarriage, unless he desists. He needs a child, that's for sure. A Son, for his death has under a year to be, and all his work must be delegated. Keegan is whiter than ever, so white that he won't vote for Merton. He needs a job, having failed to seduce a man to "keep" him. He's to apply to Morgan, whose virility has never ventured into the land of doubt, due to inordinate success with women. Ira Huntworth, the former mayor, is the brains against Merton, trying to stem the rushing quicksand of tide; for publicity, wisely waged, has created the semblance of a landslide, for Merton's rise to office. Page lurks. His "wife," an out-of-town visitor, is looking for him. The "mysterious woman," party-hostess, is hidden by her protective mystery, and Page is practicing magic, to keep his wife and the other "woman" apart. Ira Huntworth is in trouble. His garbage is neglected, day and night, in regular non-pickups. All the neighbors have moved away.

These days Ira wears perfume—it does no good. And he's been vetoed for governor, next year, by the boss of the new party he's joined, despite his role in trying to avert Merton's victory. Anywhere Ira goes, he remains unrecognized—a tribute to his popularity. Apparently noses are very insensitive, these days.

Of course, the present governor is incumbent, and will run again, and, being of Ira's new party, he retains the boss's loyalty, who rejects Ira for this reason. A new scandal has been cooked up. The city is suing Ira for back payment of private bills the city was charged for during his abortive reign in the thankless role of mayor. In addition, he's off the dole, the unemployment insurance paid by the state in compensation for his being evicted from the mayor's-office. And as told before, the reformed Sanitation Department is ignoring him, in front of his front door, which resembles the back yard of an abandoned fertilizer factory, with the goods prominently on display in the rusty appeasement of weather, attracting goats and other manure-conscious citizens of the bland animal system, under evolution's hierarchy. Plus this: a new exposé: His mayor-salary had been on commission basis, to the extent of city taxes, fluctuating in the uneven ups and downs of a speculative economy, an unfair profits take. All these things he's accused of, and Albany forbidden, though so desperately near to a garbage dump would have been the Governor's mansion. Why did his record go bad, while serving in the bathtub of City Hall? He was no good in debates, and though addicted to puns lacked wit. He believed in do-nothing, and did it: a bland recommendation. This passive servant of evil thus outdid vigilance itself. "Nothing" talks, sometimes. His noninterventional policy had concealed his faults to the point of being obvious. Thus, the point was all too made. Whatever he tried to play down, bounced up like the red moon of sin, hotly self-proclaiming. His dirt was barefaced, the more the hush-up by the pompous bath. Sensation pointed its compass-needle in his unobtrusively transparent direction. He played down to minorities, by *keeping* them down. No, he wasn't corrupt: it just *seemed* that way.

With all the court expenses and lawyer fees on his money-scarce hands, he looks to resume doing a TV commercial for perfume and ladies' soap, with Piper his former cohort, and for lack of demand gets turned down. In a bad mood, he's rude to Morstive, whom he dislikes anyway. That's Ira Huntworth, who now bums on a city bench, and is taking to drinking. Is this his dead end? In the square, the pigeons eye this derelict, and coo away. They know a bad thing when they see it.

In another area, Tessa also is a wizzened spoof of what she ever was. Not knowing that Hulda's marriage is floundering on the rocks, she's jealous of her successor to the Morgan stakes. Around him, a woman becomes competitive not only with another woman but with her own old self. Tessa had asked her new master and old object of idolatry, the going-places Morgan, to use her, for nostalgia's sake and the revival of her sweetest past loyalty, as his dependable confidante. "It's no longer necessary," he rebuffed her, in his firm unpleasant way. His ambition, sparkling to ignition, is soon to grow beautiful flames, and for fuel burn his enemies down. Poor Tessa, the nicety of her decorum now, wasted on a clashing household. With whom may she be a platonic friend now? Not Jessup, hating him for ruining her baby before it was born. No, not him. But he had given her religion, the old-fashioned way, and she melted down on the dear black Bible at eventide, repenting all shadows of imaginary sin, plus real ones true enough, which memory furnished and elaborated on. She's still Protestant; for this reason, Merton won't get her vote.

Periodically, she blushes, to give her face exercise. It's good for moral training as well, recalling chastity's neglected spirit. Having been a prostitute, pains and aches remain, bodily infirmity, carnality broken down with occupational disease, anemic, toothless, dry, devoid of female water at the meeting place of her misplaced thighs, those trembling twins of a violent and vacuous lifetime. Her mistress, when sober, calls her ugly; when drunk, worse. Morgan politely ignores her, a tremendous insult. Her modesty is excruciating, she's prim down to the button on her boots, weighed solid to prevent her from kicking highly like a can-can from ancient Offbachian France. Chastity, to her, is all. Morstive, a recent houseguest, is repelled wordlessly; no one can get in; and Morgan doesn't want to. She loves the self-sufficiency of privacy, which sex cannot provide, not in the normal sense. All men whittle down to Morgan and Jessup—the two types. And the latter is certainly ambiguous. "I'm so alone," she moans, "because Jessup deprived my old age of comfort, my own daily son. He's dead, before born."

"I'm glad," Jessup replies, the favorite household pet of a slovenly mistress, whose dignity is as empty as a bottle of whiskey. Tessa contemplates sabotaging Hulda, invoking Jessup's assistance, her religious mentor, who, up to his own plans, kindly refuses, retiring behind an ethical smokescreen where to plot deadly harm, how to do the most damage before death strips that dark capability. He and Tessa are outcasts from the better society. Of civilization's ladder, theirs are the underneath rungs. Jessup is even being formally hounded. He's at bay, in a household of intrigue. A miracle he hadn't been found, but Hulda was espionaging for the outside, and would in due time turn him in: collecting, by thereby, a nice little neat reward, to go in with her husband's astounding salary, with whom she was on the outs, based on mutual infidelity. It wasn't a moral age.

Jessup was occupied with a business: angels' devices, celestial attire, with haloes the speciality of the house. One room was his, where he conducted his correspondence, kept bookkeeping ledger in account with fixed assets and moving liability, did his manufacturing, purchased and received, requisitioned, and distributed; it was his stockroom, where inventory was hanging overhead, and the mail, for orders and receipts, flowed steadily in and out. He used an invented business name, to draw away suspicion by customers and clients as to his true identity, postered up in the "criminals wanted" notice board of all federally systematic post offices circulating to every nook and cranny of this nation's extensive network. For business, Jessup was nominally someone else. Occasionally, Tessa was his assistant, or messenger at times, when housework with the Popoffs, in whose hire she was employed basically, consented to permit. Idle, Morstive Sternbump visited them, who was given to roving, as an impatience scorned his heart. "Don't snitch on me," Jessup warned him, with an active threat implicit there, not rhetorical. With so short a time of life left, his solemnity was menacing, and levity was an unallowed liberty, as Morstive knew from the bowels of survival. No frivolity, but curt plainness here.

"Why should I?" Morstive sulked, looking gloomy, in September. "Fix me something to eat, please," he requested, and as Tessa did so, he inadvertently stepped across Hulda: who immediately put him to bed, with herself close by, and a bottle between them. "At last I'm enjoying Hulda," Morstive told himself, but it didn't sound convincing: she was a fallen person, now;

211

not that desirable, all-too-forbidding, proud woman he had known.

Everyone was sinking, or rising.

Merton, in his secret bosom, was unhappy, though the election, two months off, promised a majority, if not plurality, of votes decisive in his favor, compelling him, on protest, to announce his acceptance as the city's next mayor. It was swell, but what about his home life? His deal-partner, Morgan, had hired his wife for secretary, on a bonus of after-hours intimacy, which, fatally, she couldn't resist. And was it *Morgan's* child, that she bore? Even religion wouldn't help, in this gross upheaval of the world's cherished values. Victorian complacency, he thought, and the optimism of historical progress, could now be accepted as outmoded. He subscribed to the *new* fashion, and became an existentialist—unusual for a mayor-to-be. Times had changed, and changes had altered time. New was replacing old, as any fool could tell. New which, in a day, would fast age, and be as obsolete as a stone implement which has now been accelerated to a precision tool. The people took over; and Merton was one of them. He smiled, and kissed babies, and catered to every minority group. That widely popular Merton, the people's choice. He chose the people, too.

While his speechifying was winning mass approval, the inspector-apprehender of the Institution of Aberrated Mentality, which Morgan had prematurely escaped, finally tracked him down, and arrived at his suburban estate, passing the garden and knocking on the wooden gate. "Is this the Popoff residence?" he asked; Tessa, the maid, saying yes. Hulda asked who was it. When informed of his purpose, she gave him Morgan's office address, and congratulated herself, for this perfect measure of revenge. However, unforeseen by her, Morgan handled this "visitor" well, high up in his office palace, and bribed him to keep away, and settle the case permanently. Thus the file records of Morgan's internment for insanity were obliterated, to close all further accusation. Well paid off, the official left, and Morgan was free, sane, willing, and active. He had to justify his life's endeavor. Emma kissed him, his private secretary, not knowing that he and the file clerk, young though the latter was, were clandestinely involved, in a scorching affair. Emma was entirely devoted to her lover-employer, though she was soon to become the First Lady of the city. Forces wrapped themselves in conflict, and personalities clashed on all levels. That was in September. More, later.

October arrived, and the Yankees won the World Series. This was expected, but Morstive was elated, having ever been a Yankee fan since the day of birth. The Series went seven games; in the seventh and deciding contest, a ninth-inning double-play ball was ruined by an opposing infielder, who had forgotten his field glasses, so cloudy had the day been. Then, a bases-clearing triple, followed by an inside-the-park homer, in between several crucial walks when pitchers were losing their control, climaxed an enormous Yankee rally; then the Yankee relief pitcher mowed them down, and it was all over. Morstive was all too happy. He wept, and sadly became happy again, remembering that spectacular television spectacle in the Popoff country house. He had succeeded Jessup, as Hulda's major lover. A wonderment, this singular and most edifying mutation in the affairs of his destiny. Tessa cooked for them, begrudgingly. Morgan was often away, and Jessup was pulling in profit on his angel enterprise. The city was rioting over the ensuing mayorality. Then, Keegan Dexterparks, thoroughly white now, applied to Morgan for a job: and was turned aside. Piper Cole was still in jail, the case not cleared up yet. Ira Huntworth was now a bum, thus relinquishing his political career, which had smelled. Or stunk, to put it precisely.

Thus, Merton was virtually unopposed, as Ira had controlled his opponent. Down to the wire, Merton began to sail, and coast. It was a cinch.

∞19∘∘∘∘∘∘

Page Slickman, traditionally, as typical to him, was up to evil, if not too expensive. He adored money, and scattered his deposits in numerous banks, for safety. He was a wise guy, and hemmed in by a couple of strange people: his "wife," visiting from out of town; and somebody else. Tough for a man to be alone, when the dough gets easy and smooth, like now. He paid off the district attorney, and is enlisting his forces to thwart Merton at the polls, no sooner than the eve before. Page is political-minded, with his shrewd Broadway affiliates and wise sharpies behind the sporting set, with shoes shined and wearing apparel nice and sleek, gamblers with a delivery so neat that it would polish a billiard ball with flashy grease, and they can drink too. Page is living in a hotel that changes its address in case the cops get close. Even locations can't be stationary, so swift is Page's life, the fast liver. He even fools him*self,* at times.

He has a long record of crime: draft-dodging, income-tax evasion, and other brands of infamy, which time cannot erase. He dresses perfectly, he does, and keeps a pencil mustache, varying it occasionally with a ballpoint pen, to forge someone else's face calligraphy on his own poker puss, trapped between innocence and guilt. He scares himself, not showing who he is, from one counterfeit second of which momentarily he becomes the thief, to a false hour in a phony day, hidden elsewhere. Page hides from himself, and has hired spies to find him in the guise of someone else, while he gives the slip, and is scared off by his own direction. A clever one, he is.

Somehow, his out-of-town wife, if you can call her that and still fit the necessities of description, has "located" him. It wasn't easy, but she did it.

They kiss, as all married couples do. Then she complains. As all married wives do, and unmarried too.

"What do you want?" he asks.

"You," she replies, in that way that women have of being direct.

"I'll consider it," he says, not knowing quite what to do, nor how, if it came to that.

"Come along," she says.

"No," he says. What should he do?

He just doesn't know. Not even he.

The street scene becomes embarrassing. Morstive intervenes, by chance. Already it's the third week of October. They all wear topcoats. Morstive seems to be everywhere. He is. He got tired of Hulda, that's why. Needs a vacation. She could drink him to death, so here he is, back again. "Take her over," Page says, and gives him his out-of-town wife, beating it on the lam. Morstive is left with her.

"Are you Page?" she asks; "if so, where's your mustache?"

"It shaved me," Morstive found an answer, thinking of points-system in a bookie joint.

"Are you really he?" insists the floating wife, whom Page has evacuated, while the ship sinks, and the waves come up.

"*He* seems to think so," replied Morstive, of whose identity even Duncan Durowetsky, writing a big long book, is entertained by a distinguished set of doubts.

"What do *you* think?" the wife asks.

"I don't," Morstive answered, quickly, to his relief. It isn't easy to not think, but sometimes it's important. This is one occasion, when thinking would be beside the point, and miss the game altogether.

"May I *treat* you like Page?" the wife asked.

And Morstive said, "Don't expect support; but in the bed, if you want."

"I heard that!" Page said, concealed behind a building: "She's mine; you're hers; I'm yours."

"What is this, a romance?" Morstive wanted to know, but whose curiosity was shunted, because a rainstorm enveloped, washing away the characters. All were scattered. Then a twilight sun came out, revealing Morstive as Page, Page as his wife, and his wife as Morstive. To complicate matters somewhat, the "mysterious woman" came along; trailing behind her an incertitude as to who or what, or why even, sex really is, if it comes down to that. It didn't. Those four were assembled; or were they one, or three, or what? A shroud, a veil, teased truth. Who wants truth anyway? It's so difficult.

"And impossible!" someone would say. Yes, that also. Impossible, too.

"I gave the party," said the mysterious person, "but not being there, I wasn't there."

"That's true," Morstive-Page said, one person now. The city, it has a multitude. Merton is about to reign.

20

And storm. The election is precariously near. Close almost.

21

Here it comes.

22

Here it is.

23

It's here!

24

But wait!

25

Yes, wait. Here's why: Page, on election eve, did a nasty trick, and hurt Merton's chances. It was underhand of him, but he's Page, that's he, all right. The way some people are recognized, through their characteristic and expected failings, Page had his identity stamped. But the trouble is, many stamps had been made. Where is he, among aliases? He's gone hiding. Let who dares, dare follow him, the wily one. Shrewdly, his disappearance is permanent; while scoured everywhere for, he tricks everyone, and changes into a new life. His own, you bet.

"Explain yourself," Morstive asked, to the person who had been the hostess at the New Year's party.

"I'm quite me," she answered, and this declaration Morstive just couldn't refute, in all his realism.

"Why were you absent, at the party?" he asked, which to him had the liberal virtue of being an obvious question.

"Oh, wasn't I there?" answered the person he addressed, thus circling the questioner back to zero.

"Did you have money, to live in that opulent apartment?" he asked, expecting the answer.

Which was: "What money, what apartment, who?," thoroughly confusing him, as it confirmed every anticipation.

"How enigmatic you are," he managed to shout, the other taking it in good part, smiling throughout. A smile that said less than the recent words from that same orifice. Thus, communicatively devoid.

Oh yes, the election. How would Page prevent Merton from winning? Were real issues at stake? A conflict of interest? The city was alert. A new scandal? Why not. They were always occurring.

Just then, Morstive Sternbump entered the fray as some called it. Of all abruptions, how, most unpredictably?

He was a last-minute entry, despite Duncan's warning to stay out. His ring was in the hat, for voter or worse. It was a one-man party, and he was the man. Thus people who like to vote for the man, voted for the party, attempting to oust the candidature of his possibility. The election results were to prove negative, with Morstive receiving honorable mention, in last place. But it had been gay, hadn't it? Imagine. Morstive, of all things! Running, of all places! What an open city! Such a target, for critics and cynics, alike.

Morstive failed. So did everyone else. Except Merton. Merton, the new mayor.

This promoted Emma, the concubine of Morgan, to First Lady, in our fair city. How she would love it!

And Hulda, she moaned. She lost her husband, and was far behind in rivalry with her bitter opponent. Tessa didn't care. She did the housework.

Jessup was busy, in the angel business, which, however, he couldn't take with him, should he die: an event which the future brought close, to confirm; as vultures circled, buzzing and bruising the sky overhead.

Morstive continued, visiting Hulda, who liked both the bottle and him: for, apparently, different reasons, as things shaped out to be.

Keegan was white, and whiter as the day grew long. But broke, and effeminate; conditions incompatible: which he would resolve.

Ira Huntworth was on a park bench, bumming. He was panhandling, and got a few pennies, to go a short way toward a little muscatel, and a blurry kind of drink. He neglected to shave, or wash. An odor was discerned.

Piper Cole sulked in jail, but was rich. The fix-fight hadn't been resolved, and his boxer was training in Jamaica, to defend his title: where?, as the reason turned out to be.

Turkel Masongordy, head of Morgan's firm, eased business, preparatory to give full control to his industrious assistant, rewarding a term of faithful and uncompromising management, expanding the capital under investment and keeping the product line in fertile novelty, while the public bought, and bought. He wanted to investigate his wife's murder, Turkel did, and accuse, if necessary, that paleface, Keegan: who had disowned all appearances of his old identity, plus the consequences. Thus a squabble was expected, morbid conflict, with Morstive a key witness.

People passing through time, and time through them. Their weavings had a recorder.

Duncan wrote and wrote. All this was interesting him; Morstive informed him, periodically. It was a major collaboration, the writer with the doer, dragging life down to a posed balance, where art could see through it. The nature-based artifice. Artificial—but naturally. And the book kept on being written, with all those lives aboard.

Duncan got telephone reports from Morgan's country estate, which was eventful. Morstive was out of love, and Hulda would suffice, weakening his glands by strengthening them. He ate there, too. Another hanger-on, like Jessup.

Morgan worked hard, the new head man. It was all his.

Autumn, November, was deeply here. Now it is, that two of Morgan's seeds—one in his wife, the other formed in Emma—ripely yell for an outside life, for two full creatures to emerge. Morgan, he's mighty proud.

He beams. He gleams his teeth. Who so virile as he, or prosperous, or wise? Ah, favored life.

∞26∞∞∞∞

He's succeeded. The majestic Morgan. All is fine, again. Truly, he is himself. And all others, whether they will or no, are not. Tessa takes care of his wife, who moans and groans, while Jessup stands by, hoping for a boy. Jessup's proxy possession is spiritually legitimate, soon. Morgan was but the carnal instrument, the secular soul broker. It's Jessup's reaping, the boy about.

And Emma is brought to labor, the city's First Lady. Quite a social event. And Newberg, the cuckold, has his honor, the city's elect. He should be so proud? Because a majority of minorities voted? He wants to join a cause, but now is burdened by the necessity of leading one: an abstract, rat-encumbered city. All these freaks. And he rules.

Not Ira any longer. The bum.

And Page—is scattered. All of him.

Morgan expects big business, and Merton must set it up for him. Must really make it hum.

Piper begs for a new lawyer. He's tired of jail. The defense ought to plead something else, and get him out. There's a fight he must attend, soon. South at least, where it's warm, not like in February up here, when the promoter lost his mind. Scandals aren't exhausted, yet.

But for dear Tessa they are, the chaste. She's subdued, tranquil, devoted, religious. Half-dead, and the other half, while mildly encompassed by life's terrain, reasonably facsimilating it. Dear Tessa, she's gone. Practically. Virtually. And virtuously, she's here, dead as ever.

And dead, her child. Her child that day never saw, nor the night of life. "Beware of Jessup," she tells Hulda, who groans. Jessup is in deep paternal expectation. His life is leaking out. Time will replace him, but hurry.

And while in labor pains, Hulda drinks, and in her wretched alcoholism weeps for Morstive to trouble the pained area with more intrusion. A doctor says "No," but lacks character, and his words go unheeded, endangering his raving patient. Morstive must attend, too, and freely gets fed, loading off on the Popoff household, with the pompously fancy kitchen and good things to eat. Duncan rarely sees him, ever.

Jessup is behaving peculiarly, in the fashion of those who believe themselves to become fathers. He asks Tessa to scratch him, pertaining to some past event. No, she refuses.

Visitors to the house eye Jessup with suspicion, for his poster is billboarded all over, with a "Wanted" harshly printed both above and below his savior-like photo, attached on top by a halo (this generously advertising his business, which he conducts by another name). He remains all this while undetected. The delivery boy, the midwife, Jessup's own clients that he sees more familiarly than by phone, look him over and decide, "No; he's not the one." Why? Jessup is blessed by good luck. Someone is watching over him: himself, probably.

In some way, he's bent on destroying Hulda, as a general policy of hate. Let him decide the way, though. He's ingenious.

Hulda, on her turn, is determined to turn him in, and win national acclaim and reward. This, too, is a secret. As enemies, they do each other credit, being quite expert.

Jessup both wants her son (if that's who it's to be) and wants her done in by his birth. Nice trick, if he can do it. Very. He tries hard, he does.

Merton wants to be a father, too. As a mayor, he could well afford it. But he has as little claim, technically, to paternity, as evil Jessup does. Poor Merton, at the crest of his triumph, about to be forced to buy bogus cigars, of the bastard cuckold variety, and distribute them to his well-wishers and congratulators, on whom he is to confer his patronage, now that the political plum is his, the prize spot in the middle of the city's heap of dirt, where, for certainty, his throne is erected. But more, he must offer *Morgan* a cigar, the very man who has cuckolded him! Quite an ignominy. Merton is, secretly, proud, and spoils to revenge his faithless wife (kill her possibly?) while putting the blame on an accident, to preserve his public career, and commission a day of mourning, providing beforehand for clouds and rain. Emma betrayed him, that is enough. Now as for Morgan: well, Morgan is too powerful now, he's inviolate. That must wait. Meanwhile, Merton must make things easy for his enemy, and give big business a big edge, in the stakes of the economy. Business administrators will be the *favored* minorities. And those others? They may shift for themselves, and underprivileged sweatshops spring up, dungeons of misery, the beds of lice, waiting-in hospital for vermin and other such unkempt, to-be-squinted-at types, spawned by a fruitful city. But publicly, he was *another* figure, and in his zeal to protect the objects of bias from unfair discrimination, he put before the legislature a bill, after inauguration (it being but November now), to bar black men of all description from ring brutality, eliminating them from boxing. This includes Jews too, who are, after all, Negroes turned inside out; the same, only in reverse. It proved an unpopular motion, and was not passed. Oh well. Merton did his duty, and saw by it. Let those who will, oppose. Or beat him, if necessary. Merton was the mayor. It didn't matter.

His mother, kicked out of the house by Emma, applied for reinstatement. What did she want with her son, the sudden celebrity? Her own husband, Merton's father, was then long dead. She gloried after power, and yearned to have top priority, and be elected president of the local chapter of the municipal Busy Bee Sewing Circle. A fine honor, a true praise, for the mother who had borne a mayor! The mayor was still being born, by her, in a later stage. The truly important things in life are perpetual. He's cast to be a famous infant yet. First let him be.

Page Slickman, unlike the elder Mrs. Newberg, didn't wish her son any good, but had actively, on the eve before election, taken active steps to non-elect his adversary. His means have yet to become unearthed. They were underworld, and buried in the ground. But above ground, Merton had become victor, on a stage lit to confirm this. Was Page shrunken out? What had he ever been? And his thug machine—*was* there a mob? Page did exist. But as Page?

Events had come about. Where were they?

History recollects. What had been collected? And where is that collection?

When "when" fails, "where" is pointed at.

All that was, had been. It now only was. That's a dead "is."

Where was "what was"? It went. That uncluttered the stage, for more to be.

Summer was fled, and Keegan was glad. The sun had threatened to undo what surgery did, but the new white man survived it, with a daily parasol. His skin was lily-white, and tenderly delicate, faint like a baby's, not raw. As a Caucasian Albino, equipped with a new pedigree matched to fit, Keegan, though poor, had to carefully preserve this, keeping heavenly rays from his fair membership card entitling him to join the majority: called a face. And his hands always wore gloves: white, coincidentally. What was, was whitewashed. But would the whitewasher get washed out, in the bargain? Keegan had repented, and disowned his broad past. He would change his name, also, in keeping with his more fashionable identity. Autumn, a harbinger of winter, finds him paler, if that's too possible; so he must be careful not to disappear altogether, and thus completely lose himself, by lacking any color whatever, to the inclusion of blood: which, as an interior development, has stamped us all Indians; though on the *outside* we maintain our lighter breeding.

∞27∞∞∞∞

"Why is everybody in a jam?" Morstive asks; "and conflicts of animosity divide theoretically civilized people, in disunity and disharmony? How many sides hatred has! Hostility within the Newberg and Popoff families, though their legions will increase; yes, civil war, and war waged outside the unit, on separate terms against antagonists close and far, in greed for competitive spite. Jessup against Tessa, Hulda, Morgan, anyone. Keegan against those whose shade of skin isn't, accurately, white. Tessa against men, against Hulda, against herself. Merton against majorities, and against his own soul. Emma against Hulda and Merton. Hulda versus Emma, Morgan, Jessup, anyone. Morgan against everyone. Me against— who? Page for himself, Piper for himself, Ira beyond help. Turkel Masongordy against his wife's murderer. Duncan—I don't know. He just tries to write, so his war is on the level of words, a battlefield of broken verbal bones. The whole world is in conflict too—all its particles, in odd sortings-off, swerving into hostile combinations in all divisive likelihood. There's no end, in conjugations of the verve "to against." Copulations couple from them, to compound into harmonious occasionals. Order is periodical, between strife.

"The mind is for figuring things out. But what to make, of the welter and flux of events, their sheer numerousness, dissimilarities, uninterpretableness? I'm glad Duncan is back of me with words. Words classify, anyway.

"Imponderables, galore. These finite characters, with infinite intertwinings, which I can't disentangle. I act darkly, on this shifting stage. Who *are* these co-actors?

"Examples? Oh, they're everywhere.

"Too many 'cases.' Can't they be lumped up?

"No, for each is a character. But what is the individuality of each?

"Oh, so much has happened. Help me, Duncan, to sort all this out.

"Down to particulars. Who have I missed? Where, on this chessboard elaborate with doings? Who next, in this disordered random?

"As for Page's 'wife' and the other supposèd 'woman,' there's too much I don't know. I'm considered Hulda's lover, but she's about to give birth. I've lost weight, incidentally. What kind of mayor will Merton Newberg make? Undoubtedly he *will*, whatever 'will' comes out to be; a style in which the future excels, time that hasn't gripped us yet, like a modest bride blushing behind her virginity, that's here in the brief flash. Rumors have swept the air. I've been filtered to, by them. What are the latest bulletins? But

223

some *old* news is still current. I'm racing time in reverse, to slow it out.

"I heard that Piper is trying to be his own lawyer, bored of his luxurious jail cell, and needing to manage his fighter: whose illegal defense of a disputed championship is soon to be promoted and scheduled, while sports fans everywhere die of a feverish heart attack. Ira Huntworth, so recently a mayor, is now a pauper: creditors come confiscating his estate, and only his smell remains: a broken man. Page is somewhere, I think. His hotel has an address that changes every day, to confuse the cops. Isn't that something? Facts are stranger than fiction, if you ask for my opinion—Duncan permitting. His work is piling up, from all this.

"Tessa just mopes, and acquires servility down to her craven heart. There's no more spunk in her.

"Morgan is adulterous, and acting like a king. A bastard and a legitimate will be born, same day probably. A girl in his office he goes in for, too. He's piling up the money. He's got tremendous influence.

"Hulda is helpless, beyond repair. Her son will have alcohol, not blood, to break the umbilical cord with. Poor little sucker. Born wealthy, though. If he's to be born at all.

"And Emma, about to be delivered. Of Morgan's other son. While Merton stews.

"Sons, not daughters? Sure. The preferred, superior stock.

"The newspapers are bleeding out speculations on Mayor Merton. Will his policies conform to platform promises, as a matter of practice? But privately, he's in trouble. Will the public notice?

"Who else? Oh yes. Page.

"Who?

"Page has divided up into several Pages, each supported by a central salary as a kind of sinecure, for being related to the original. Not to mention his expense account, which is vast.

"Jessup, though he professes to be an angel, is, in reality, not. Reality? What's that?

"Keegan is low in dough, though high in grade and degree of skin excellence, as a virtuoso in the art of being a white man. It's his vocation, I believe, but he can't cash in on it yet, till he gets his citizenship papers.

"He's being suspected, though (and rightfully, as I can confirm), as the murderer of Turkel Masongordy's wife, who leaves a rich widower behind. At the time, he had tried to frame me, but I wiggled out. Now, I'll be called upon to give testimony, as a sacred vehicle of the truth. Truth? There's that word again.

"Myself, I've gotten thin, believe me! A revelation, but sex did it. Try a pregnant woman sometime yourself, and you'll see.

"But me, I'm low on money, though as yet middle height. Morgan is really tall, and athletic. Duncan? He has no features, no definite identity. All he does is write.

"My unemployment insurance ran out, July I think, and now my only resource is to sponge. But I gotta keep away from the Popoff place, due to the screaming acceleration of birth agony. A rich dame she's become, though drunk, and as Hulda has divorce proceedings, can't I step in, barter her for my bride, and be a vicariously rich husband? It's been done. Security relies on money, of course, in our decadent capitalistic society. And money is best if you *have* it, not if you don't. I can poorly say that that's richly clear. Imagined wealth is distinct from owned wealth. Ideas lack material substance. But the latter has no mental life. My *want* for money is real. Desire is real. Its object—to be gambled for by tattered hope —is out of bounds, locked in the future's vault.

"Oh, I'm only one person. But so is everybody else!

"Piper Cole, he's fat. But he wants to be a lawyer, to extricate himself. Such a lot of profit, to be had. What wealth, up for grabs! We all struggle for it, but some have advantage. Others—merely pull along, to rescue the dynamic excess of leftover wastage, in our brave human struggle. Ah, let me in on it! I crave to have, not to not to have. And I appreciate the difference, as a carnal act of supreme recognition, to survive well, and not to fall out of the evolutionary race. Monkeys have endured this long, so can't I stay too, while the going's good? Earth is a bonus, like a permanent holiday. I'd regret the parting, to be left out. I'm greedy for what, in all my life, I never had. And a little more of the same, thank you."

∞28∞∞∞∞∞

Time, lots of it, flew by. You didn't need a calendar to tell: intuition did the job. Even skeptics were convinced, in the seasonal parade of things. Morstive was now slim. Merton was still mayor. Duncan fatigued himself, squeezing his brain into a million semblances of words, which he tried to connect, as a question of form. He kept phoning Morstive, asking for new information. Hulda, her former name Stock, was still married to Morgan: who was now living in a hotel with a little tot of a file clerk, a cute figure of a lass, preferable to the now aging bearers of his two sons. A new generation was appearing. What more obvious evidence than there being children? The *previous* generation is that much older. Emma was living a proper married life, as the mayor's foremost wife, haughty and respectable. Her boy was well taken care of, by nurses. As for Hulda's boy, Jessup had run away with it, making a wild dash: repeating a certain crime, for which he was still wanted; and compounding his already considerable villainy. It was a reversion to form, on his part, not a daring mutation. Crime-detection officials hung their sorry heads, to have been eluded by a lawless, sinful ambassador from hell, to put a religious connotation on it and ascribe to it a moral verdict, an interpretation in the vein of ethics, supported by large donations from philosophy's stingy philanthropy, calling itself a science. But that's merely academic procedure, and life goes on.

Which it did, hurting some, and pleasing others. But most got the dual brunt of it.

Keegan fainted continually, for loss of blood. His white transformation had weakened him, and subtracted from his energy: hence his effeminacy. He's in a charity bed in a city hospital ward, being administered to. He politely refuses to be anything but white; nor may any shadow darken him.

Jessup is still fleeing, with Morgan's only legitimate son. Hulda, being drunk, ignores this theft. She toys with Morstive, instead. It's more fun.

Merton is trying to be fashionable, but instead the city is imitating *him:* as its mayor, he's top dog.

He's never private, nor wants to be: fearing insanity that way. He has two assistants, or deputy mayors: his own mother, and Emma, his regenerated wife, who has mended her tardy ways, and assumed her conventional role. Merton is gloomy, though: that son of "his" is Morgan's, in private fact. Privacy degrades him, whereas publicly he rules, eminent, with dignity, forbearance, and an almost unanimous esteem: he pleases everyone.

A divorce case has opened, on a charge of mutual adultery: Popoff versus Popoff, as the lid threatens to explode.

Hulda, though she formerly teased her new lover, Morstive, for deficiency in the art of virility, and though she extolled her own Morgan for perfection in that category, is now being plowed by the obviously second-best man: But her bottles of firewater sparkle out the difference, and achieve the supreme compensation. She'll be left wealthy, and Morstive has fortune-hunting ideas, to solve his incurable poverty, by being the new Mr. Popoff—or Mr. Stock. The kid is out of the way, too. So Morstive can be her *son*, as well. More benefits, at the same source.

Now Morgan is king, but the queen keeps separate throne. They've thrown in the towel. It's goodbye, for keeps.

Contrast her with Emma: who goes to church, as the mayor's official wife; and presides over, if not conducting, tea ceremony. She's a stuck-up reformed conservative, so righteous as to have forgotten Morgan entirely, in her fascinating new life. She'll go a long way, with such a husband: though Merton remains silent, plotting; perhaps to reveal her infidelity, showing him the injured party. Then, sympathy would be on his side: the underdog, a cuckolded mayor, beloved by everyone, in all ranks of life, top down through middle to bottom: they'd never forget a sufferer; and he'd win a second term. That's shrewd. The party manager would approve. Politics must utilize private life, to some extent: publicity doesn't harm, should the image be a favorable one. "Poor Mayor Underdog," everyone will call him. He's a true leader.

Right now, Mr. Newberg has an extraordinary horror of solitude, and is always surrounded. Being alone is insane, or promotes such; and he avoids it. He's agreeable to anyone's suggestion, and believes what they believe in, in his ultra-harmony policy. He complacently subsides, defers, to anyone else's opinion: yet, being a leader, he's followed: and his echoings are echoed. He goes right to the people, and finds himself imitated: and he follows suit. He's very permissive; and lets murder be. The police are restrained; for criminals are underprivileged, and must be better understood. So he hires social workers, with compassion in their hearts. All the minorities get priority, especially the top business executives, whom liberal tax laws have so pathetically disadvantaged. No one goes unhelped, in this administration. Everyone is celebrated, like a hero, or—what's the same—its reverse. Everyone counts, city-wide. Mayor is doing a good job. Look how many happy citizens! Not His Honor, however: he chafes within; and goes blank, when he sees Emma.

His mother is a matriarch. Look at her. She's fat, too.

Her son, the magnificent swayer, conforms to rebellion, in accepted social forms. He believes in progression, and look at him now: and what he *used* to be, the popular fads and groups, clans, movements. He's the big boy, now. The causes he espouses are his, beforehand—almost.

And religious? You bet! A *pillar* of the religious set. Even the regional Cardinal takes a back seat, by secular comparison.

But the atheists love him. For he doesn't persecute them.

His sanity is strong, too. On the surface, that is. By worshipping God, he prays for complete sanity; and this is not granted. He's insanely angry. He needs to avenge Morgan; and have his wife quietly murdered, under peaceful city skies.

Abandoned is his former atheism, and he seeks new fashions, correct modes: anticipating them; the mayor with a head ahead. And an immensely popular reign is his, too. He's loved, everywhere. But not at home. Emma has reformed, but he won't forgive her. Love is a difficult thing to understand. It involves pride, too. Merton is desperate, obsessed with her death. And her son's. Not his. Whom shall he hire, for this murderous mission? Alack. Stark days approach.

He's indebted to Morgan, for supporting his campaign. Morgan is angry that Jessup kidnapped his son by Hulda, recognized to be his. He and Hulda are apart, with lawyers intervening. She wants a settlement that can support her scale of drinking, and her "keeping" of Morstive, whose lust is riding at high tide. Morgan truly believes that Jessup is morally corrupt. And has offered a reward for the latter's apprehension, and the return of his son. This, added to the federal reward already posted, adds up to a sum above tidy. Hulda missed it. She had planned on it. All her failed desires were forgotten, dissolved in the splash and fizzle of more drink.

Morgan, a former voyeur and pimp, is considered wholesome. He is, too. Women love him. Oh, the brute!

Psychiatry cured him quickly of a minor breakdown once, and, being in good funds, he bribed off an asylum official, who had accosted him with escape charges. But Morgan is a decent fellow, and abhors cynicism. He's self-righteous, and literal. He's pompously arrogant, and suspected of being a private narcissist, employing women as a thrilling technique. His business is astounding, and he's really making it with that file clerk. Ripping her up, and planting new soil. Her "oh"s can be felt a mile away, heaving in an earthquake. He storms her, and she replies, being pregnant now.

With life, there's death also. Morgan's boss's wife is dead, and the boss retired: Turkel Masongordy, with a summons for Keegan: now in hospital. It reaches him at bedside. "I didn't do it," wan Keegan declares, "for I'm not what I was. Some other me did it, long ago. He was dark, then."

A legal defense protects Keegan; and accuses Mr. Masongordy of being shorter than his deceased wife, and of having married her, ostensibly, for her money; and organizing a business that way: of which Morgan is the current head, though Mr. Masongordy still holds stocks, and is a leading chairman. It will be a court trial, soon; and Morstive must testify, if he's not too busy drinking Hulda's alcohol, chewing on her food, and poking himself into her at all hours, deepening the depression. In her moans, she recalls Morgan, and must drink more.

Morstive sometimes visits Keegan at the hospital; they've become good friends. Morstive honors both Keegan's present and former races: "The man, not his outside," being the principle. However, Keegan, who wants his name changed, wishes slavery to return, so that black men may be put in chains. He has released a vicious white-supremacy campaign, and is accusing everyone of having some mulatto blood, in defiled purity of breed. "Seeing sure is disbelieving. Some surprising people are mulattoes, pure and simple. Don't be naive."

"Like who?"

"Why, Morgan is, Merton is (our mayor), their wives are: maybe even *you* are," Keegan insinuates, blanching all the while.

Embarrassed by these demented ravings, and to tilt the subject somewhat, Morstive asked, "Did you convert the Southern niggers to Commies?" referring to Keegan's former life; the latter almost bolted from the bed.

"There was no riot, I didn't incite them," calmly answered Keegan, cursing Morstive between clenched teeth. He couldn't tolerate his past being raked back up, that he had taken such pains to leave, swearing off all evidence, and imitating the perfectly upright white man, in etiquette, culture, upbringing, cast of skin, and cruelty. He dispensed with jazz, and its negroid overtones; didn't take pot anymore, as injurious to accredited health; and even mended his walk, his talk, everything. Of course, he's degenerate now; abjures women. But that's merely a transitional pain, an evolutionary encumbrance. Changes take time, and are complicated. "You can't transform Rome in a day," it was said. But Italians are all half-Negroes, so what's the use? A paranoic conspiracy grew. All the world had hidden darkness, to cloud the sun away.

Morstive argued with the artificial white man that dark is also tainted with light, and mentioned that values are relative, as well as tints, hues, tones, and the visual gamut of appearance. Appearance may reveal depth, but often misleads as to what's inside. Essence *does* have an outside, but often in deceptive form.

While hearing this, Keegan's new skin began to peel; and the operation began to reverse itself. From extreme albino, the color unblanched itself, shading its degrees forward, well on towards ebony. Morstive beheld all this, in fascination, horror, and trembling. He identified with the writhing victim. Poor Keegan. The surgery had been cheap; but skin is only race-deep. What price color? Plenty.

Will Keegan's masculinity return, as well? Is it the same package deal, only in reverse?

But what of Keegan's newly professed principles? His white supremacy would look ridiculous, when mouthed by his black form. Jewish anti-semitism is easier to get away with, if the offender looks gentile. But with Keegan, appearance was at the heart. He could only be his own color.

What could Page only be? He tried to be Morstive. Morstive once tried to be Morgan. What is it, "to be"?

Being is still. Going goes.

Being *is*. But *is* is inactive, unchanging, no motion.

It's different with Jessup. He's run away.

230

And not alone, either.

He has a "son" with him.

From Morgan's loins, and Hulda's womb. And Jessup's cunning.

He had envied Morgan, the spark and ability. But look who came away with it!

The kid is already baptized. Jessup believed in an early religious start. The right education may countenance later aberrations. A firm base, to forgive flimsy sin.

It's really unreasonable of him to do so: To abduct someone. There's a law of possession somewhere. It applies to human chattel, too.

But what does Jessup care? He's a born angel, ain't he? Too bad he had to abandon his business, the uniforms that cherubim must wear, plus proper headpiece attached, really a slick article. He left it to Tessa, but will she handle it? No, maybe. So meanwhile he's fled, and going somewhere. Where, is nobody's business. The kid needs breast milk. Jessup ain't got any. That's a problem. And what with diapers, and formulas? Surprise: Tessa is in on the scheme, and will join Jessup, at some designated spot. She'll administrate to the baby, as an accomplice. Both refugees from the law, both been bitter and out. Submerged, now they join; and tug in a mutual fate.

Sex is out. That's for sure.

She won't abide it. Not in her present state.

She's frail, and wracked. She's been through too much; or rather, too many have been through her. Her one crowded place, but diffused by time.

Now she has Morgan's son: Once she was maternal to Morgan, then married him. Jessup gave her a miscarriage, upsetting Morgan's seed. Now, Jessup gives her Morgan's son. That's grand. Justice has been served.

And justice is too blind to recognize it. It ought to borrow glasses, and stupidly attempt to peer. What it would see! Enough to justify blindness, that's what.

The world is bumbling on. On the wrong track, in the wrong train, carrying the wrong passengers, and the engineer is the wrong man for the job. The conductors are wrong. The tickets are wrong. On wrong schedule, from the wrong terminal, to a wrong destination. And outside the window, the scenery is wrong. As it goes whirring by.

∞29∞∞∞∞∞

Hulda has forgotten, heartlessly, the theft of her own son. She's close enough to delirious tremors. Jessup had encouraged her drinking, as promoting the godly spirit. She's falling apart, and her center cannot hold. Morstive is there all the time, plugging that well-worn gap: a dream come true too late. He's lackadaisical, and weighs himself each new day. A surprise greets the scale, as his slimness registers itself. This is all he cares about, why be any deeper than that? A coarseness spread on his mind, a casual ease of vulgarity. It's so nice to be supported.

So he failed to be mayor? So what? Now his complacency is private, instead of Newberg's public performance. It's a slow difference, and he didn't care.

He has less anxiety than before, and doesn't do all that compulsive eating. He has free security, living off Hulda, who receives weekly checks from her husband-tycoon, now in the divorce stage. It's in the gossip columns, how the magnetic Mr. Popoff, head of a large industry, has abandoned his pregnant file clerk, and enjoys continuous favors from volunteers of various female tribes, congregating in his apartment, a bachelor penthouse flat, cared for by an extra-particular maid. He's got *her* made, too. No cue, he overlooks. Boy, he's busy, between night and day. Any venture turns success. The redoubtable Mr. Popoff.

Hulda, in the suburbs, hardly knows that Tessa's missing: she has domestics enough. She blanks out, and loses days at a time. This is Morstive's domicile, and he bears it off nicely, sleeping regularly, and waking whenever feasible, to ease his bladder. How soft and plushy, the laze and luxury of drifting down the deep sea of easy, unspectacular existing. No complaints, no promptings, save those within imminent gratification. Morstive, in his spoiled phase. Only one interruption, a summons to court: Masongordy versus Dexterparks. Morstive testifies, and poor black Keegan goes to his death: for the New Year's Eve party bungling with the life of Mrs. Masongordy, who, as a result, died. Mayor Newberg appealed the sentence, defending Keegan for being black. No use, and overruled, by the judiciary. Keegan is put on the hot seat, and joins, in some defunct land, a blond girl he had once loved more than he had ever loved before or since. She had prematurely died, and his grief had never ever subsided. It had raged through, to his very last. This, in a way, completes their romance; the ties are reunited: high up, in the heavenly bias of stars.

Morgan was in the witness box, and a well-divided Page Slickman, and the mysterious non-hostess, who had never attended her own party. Even Ira Huntworth figured, reeking with bum-stench. It added sensation, the deplorable comedown of Mr. Newberg's predecessor in the mayor ranks. For human interest, it was simply stunning—the case—and showed corruption in higher circles, as well as demonstrated the harsh race struggle in a brutal city. Morstive was lionized, and became a celebrated hero of the day, the near-missed martyr. Jessup couldn't rival him, having fled.

Another sensation came to pass, in the coming. Tessa Wheaton, collaborating with Jessup in the abduction of Hulda's Popoff boy, squealed, turned traitor, and betrayed the poor forlorn Clubb to the proper law authorities, who apprehended him. Thus came to an end a crime saga, puzzling experts everywhere. "The holy monster," publicity accredited him with being. But the Popoff divorce case became final, and the parents of the stolen child were now officially separated. The child was awarded to charity, since adultery plagued and discredited its progenitors. Tessa was locked up, in ladies' court. And Jessup was widely interviewed, by criminologists, psychiatrists, and sociologists. Even some ministerial clergy came in, curious, the white-collar tribe, God's interpreters to the masses. What an interesting city spectacle, and indeed newspapers were popular, selling into second editions. Television got in on it, too; and every vehicle exploited it, for home consumption. Business boomed, because of it. This proved Mayor Newberg's economic policy to be sound; but he had murder on his own mind.

Revenge on Emma had to be immediate, and was. Emma, and the nurse wheeling in a perambulator her illegitimate son by Morgan, were thrown into the river, and washed undersea by a strong brave current. Private henchmen of the mayor's, under strict vow of secrecy, had attended to this triple murder, for the baby carriage bearing the baby was thrown in along with the two women. The mayor won overwhelming popularity, by this stroke. Sympathy just oozed in. His luck was so bad, people championed this widower for having the courage of having all this happen to him, and he bore his suffering nobly. He should be sainted, on the spot. What endurance, that he should merely survive!

Strangely, he married his mother, to tide him over the crisis, and relieve the civic burden of grief. Public mourning became municipal reveling, a carousing far into the night. Free things were free, to commemorate the occasion; other items had costly price tags, but were snatched up. What matter money? Aren't we all here for only a little while? Only those like Morgan are immortal; and even they can be tainted, ridden with a cancerous impurity. He was a commercial Casanova, and did everyone in. The women seemed not to be unenjoying it. Chaos breeds its own harmony, and discord abides by rules, when remedied by retrospect. Hulda was drinking herself hollow, and enjoyed almost masculine fantasies. "I'll be a lesbian," she decided, and did. "Will you become a girl, for my sake?" she asked Morstive.

"What, and ruin my reputation!" the latter replied, clinging to the little he had of a belated male factor. Keegan, when white, had wanted to pervert him, also. One must watch out. These danger-traps! But too bad, Hulda's fortune would not be his. He's poor, again, and resorts to looking for Duncan. Coincidentally, his weight increases, and his belly. Poor old Morstive, himself again. The low finding its own level, following a drunken abnormal tide, an untypical flood. He's reduced; and those he knows are becoming shattered, overused by an exacting world. Events had taken toll, and handed out penalties: to all. Look at Emma: she's dead. So is Keegan, by law. And at Easter time, Jessup will follow. That will be an event. Hulda has become perverted, Tessa jailed, and Merton widowed. Morgan is leading a confused life, compounded by lecheries. Ira Huntworth is now a bum. Page Slickman is nowhere, at present, even his hotel having moved to an untold address, foreign to the postal precincts and the regularly daily mail. Where are his wife and that "woman"? "Where" is a very accurate question, in their case, beautifully describing what isn't known. Turkel Masongordy is retired, for keeps. Piper Cole, increased in girth, has resumed his counterfeiting of an illegal lawyer status, for he manages a boxer who's defending the heavyweight championship, somewhere in the States soon. Piper is in jail, his fighter in Jamaica. Morstive is in hell, living meanwhile. Which is usual for him.

∞30∞∞∞∞

"Duncan, explain all this to me," he requested, one soft and quiet day. It was near Easter, and the electrifixion of Savior Jessup Clubb was near at hand, a major religious event for the ages. Reporters from other countries would attend, to get the inside dope at the outside odds of objectivity. They would also attend the championship match, to electrify the world of fisticuffs, connected at large in satellite capacity to cosmic sports, athletic endurance contests, and team competition, on both professional and amateur level. But Piper was stuck, cross-examined for a foul scandal on a ring bribe, and only sloppily defended himself. The party boss came to assist, Mayor Newberg being absent then (attending the leading season social event with his mother-bride). Page was a witness also. The prosecuting attorney (the only unbribed one) allied Cole with strong-arm racketeers and insidious mob connections. Although politically loyal to himself, Piper was accused of having lost money on horses, of having been formerly poor, and a rotten faded boxer now given to overweight. Piper wept, but in an impassioned scene called for the Lord to forgive him. Who could resist that appeal? The jury condemned him to slap one hand with the other, and discharged the case altogether. It was a virtual acquittal, and he got off cheap. With all his riches. He who used to be the bully bodyguard of ex-Mayor Huntworth, was now the proud master of himself, and of others. The fight would be held in Miami, and draw a big crowd: challenger to take a dive. Crooked? Why not? Evil is the conventional fashion, the prevailing folklore. No need to be a rebel, with such stakes.

The law caught up to Page Slickman, and is asking him embarrassing questions, and politely clubbing him on the head when his answers don't tally. He's spilling all, making a full confession, and the mob or gang he runs is being rounded up. "Who are you?" he's asked, and he replies, "Morstive." Then he gets a good beating. For telling a lie. Other questions he's cruelly asked include what he used to be doing out of town, and why he left a wife there (recently returned to the city) in a neglected and unfulfilled sick state. These were hard to answer, even had he been an honest man, which was questionable. More loose threads dangled, from his career. Hadn't he also sneaked out from his trial on his part in last year's February boxing debacle, the fiasco of the bribe? He shouldn't treat the law so cursorily, it wasn't fair in reciprocation to their thorough treatment of him, their huge and almost detailed concern for all aspects of his somewhat irregular life. Page surely was grilled, and the heat at too rapid a tempo wilted him. His tongue just wagged.

His mob was rounded up, and inserted, with individual handling, into jail cells, though (let it be known) under protest.

A divorce was arranged between their leader and his "wife," who had suffered from weeping for him at home, the plight of the ignored.

This also was revealed: he had recently attempted to sell a non-existing bathtub to bereaved Mayor Merton Newberg, for incarcerating his wealth of public tears for having a "child" and belovèd wife torn from him. Thus Page's scale of operating was lower, seemingly; when the full swimming pool was considered, in the era of Huntworth.

His punishment, then, had been to be dunked. Thus another bribed judge was unearthed, and disgraced.

As for the mysterious "hostess" woman, the person whose gender under question was never confirmed to enlighten the curious, she, although never detected, *was* seen to be Page's assistant in his war on behalf of crime, against the combined allegiances of the law-abiding element, that reactionary bloc not quite extinct in society as preserved today.

The Missing Persons Bureau was brought in, and Page was forced to grant them an interview. By then, he felt ravaged.

No one knows where she is now, that person of "mystery." It's a disappearance, the files reveal, as inscribed in records. This is officialdom, at work.

And that opulent apartment she had for the party, the array of glittering drinks—the expense went unaccounted for. Was she rich? Or poor? The abode has been rented, to someone inconspicuous, obviously not her. It had, for some time, been vacant. Had it ever been truly occupied by the person in question? Some say she used to be a telephone operator—an incongruous occupation, in terms of other things known. She was guilty, too, if Page was: an accomplice, no doubt. But Page got all the credit, or demerit; and a stiff sentence was passed on him: making him sad. He had set great store by his connections, to cover him up, for his vanishing act and emerging as another. Some actual people were all along his phony aliases. They had been part-time Pages when the pressure was too hot for one spot. Couldn't someone be him, just then—stand in for a steady duration?

But not one "friend" would help him. Especially not Piper, with whom he had been involved in the scandalous ring episode, and then skipped trial, on premature bail, risking further arrest. The career of Page Slickman had come to an end. All his dash, the way he raped up money, has not been justified in the light of permanence. Duncan Durowetsky, finishing up a book, has somehow stolen a press card, a newspaper pass, to such an event as these prison confines for interviewing Page now. Page will answer sharp, should escape outlet be here. Always an *outside* chance, when stuck and stale to the dank *inside* of a flightless jail.

"The book you're doing is mine: where it properly belongs. I own rights to it, since I'm Morstive, or at the least his literary agent, and yours," Page explained, as though to a gifted child mistakenly schooled up with retarded, damaged ones, and with a pent-up hunger for truth, dear truth, any truth.

"No, I'm writing it, and Morstive is supplying me with material: you're merely *in* it," Duncan maintained, on unfailing dignity.

"Then don't depict me in a poor light," warned Page, getting angrier. The world had failed him, and he had lost.

"Or what?" Duncan demanded.

"Or I sue, you bet," threatened the glowering Slickman, cross and blue.

Soon, the fight would be on. From Miami. For the World's Heavyweight Championship. "But first," Duncan thought, "I'll interview poor Jessup next. Before he's a dead man."

Dead? He will be, too.

A big, gigantic trial, of religious proportions, as laid out by the Bible. Jessup is the hero-villain of all time. He speaks well, explaining himself.

He raves, actually. At the press conference, where Duncan has been admitted, in front of flashing photographers, he makes extravagant statements, whipping up a crowd in a circus frenzy of baiting him. "Let him hang *himself*, with his own wild words." That's the tense atmospheric tendency, toward the doomed one. "But his *deeds* were dark: his words trail feebly, in their monstrous wake."

"I'm normal," he announces, and a startling murmur moves through the crowd. Gasps are heard, the livid quest for sensationalism, seekers of the morbid and the bizarre. What will he say next?

"Gentlemen of the press, please speak well of me, and deal with my legend fairly. I am to be known as the Saint of New York City. Celebrate my birthday every December twenty-fifth. I have never permitted joy to enter my life, but have suffered for all. I would have wished a long life, but I see that longevity is not my due. But death takes all my respect, I grow rich with it. Have I not redeemed all? Though accused of acts befitting a devil—eternity shall judge me as an undisputed saint. By destiny's law, I am. I loved man, and woman. Is that a crime?

"I expect to be written up, in the full glory of my adventures, in 'The Brand New Testament,' which no church should be without. Lo, Easter approaches: my agony, then my resurrection. Have faith in me, that I was the perfect martyr. I killed a child because of it, and kidnapped still another. I see his father there, Morgan Popoff, among you. He is pledged by law to grim silence. Let *my* word suffice. I am the world's father. All children are my children; my power is unlimited. I shall die because of it.

"I'm scared, too. Yes, I am.

"Poor me, I'm a masochist. But my greatness was entwined in that. I saw to it that pain was well distributed. None should shun it. I didn't, and dealt it fairly. Pain is our great boon. It atones sin.

Sin is in everything we do. Sin is us, complete. Then pain must be abundant.

"I rejoice in our misfortunes. We deserve it.

"For me, I prophesize a magnificent immortality. I'm not of you, but beyond you. *You* can't have it, just me.

"Divinity gave me a son, and I killed him. Then another, who is now alive. He is of me. I baptized him.

"Now I go. I am to my doom, through heaven, and to become the life of a daily God. I thank you."

There was much applause, ironically, to demonstrate the stupendous interest. He had captured the public, and the ages stood by, pencil in hand. Here was something crucially historic. God visiting man, in the Twentieth Century.

∞32∞∞∞∞∞

"How did it go, Duncan?" Morstive asked, who had not been a witness, but was at home fudgeting with the ends of his odds, even to meet.

"Gruesome," replied the "author"; whose book Morstive was not allowed to see, despite unmitigated curiosity. The manuscript was in the incomplete stage, and for that reason was not quite finished. Morstive was self-absorbed; fascinated, but discouraged.

"When asked at the last minute whether he was Jewish," Duncan continued, "Jessup hid in a web of secrecy, like a spider with flyphilia. He's a Christian convert, I think."

"What did he say about why he needed sons so badly he stole them?" Morstive put in, as relevant to the conversation, and not unseemly, but rather apt.

"He said his life obsessed him to have a son, to dispense divine justice through the agency of 'paternity'; and then he added something metaphysical, too obscure to catch. He went down boasting, but. And in redeeming his crime (or let that be plural), he looked solemn, and the sizzling electric chair burned him at a holy moment, in his otherworldly guise. No, even in the end, he wasn't natural."

"Did he incriminate anyone?"

"He mentioned that in his will the Popoff boy is heir, though Tessa had confiscated his business of angelic halo devices, and won the grand reward for information leading to his arrest. She turned him in. How will she turn out? How will the law paint her? Her canvas is mottled with flux, in running colors. How can art criticism end, with the painting ever unfinished? Complications arise, and disputes will follow. It isn't a dead issue yet."

"Though *he* is," Morstive nicely put, showing respect for the dead. "And that was Friday, you say?"

"Yes."

"And today being Sunday, Easter-bonnet Sunday, has he arisen? Have the Skies received him? With heraldic bugles and a winged flutter in chorus; and he become a Deity?"

"Hard to say," Duncan replied. "Factually, we can't prove it."

"Explore the grave, dig up—"

"Shut up, don't be morbid, lurid, uncanny," the nonsuperstitious author halted him. "It's only a guessing game. Don't leap too far beyond your safe harbor of self-interest, your homey concerns in sure steps, where thoughts keep low ground for deed. You're here yet, things can be done for *you*. But not if you dream, and indulge foggy notions. Stand up, man! Take account. Be yourself."

"Who?"

"Yourself."

"I don't know who that is."

"Then forget it. But back to what happened. Mayor Newberg made the funeral oration, wildly cheered by the multitude. He delivered a rousing speech, combining the unknown with the known, and praising his fair city. He reconciled everything, so tactful is he. Too bad his wife is dead, and son."

"Not his, though," Morstive said.

"So what? Morgan may be the parent, but he can't caress it. Death has limits."

"Did the *mayor* do the harm—kill his family? What do you think? I won't tell, I promise."

"Yes, I suppose so," said Duncan. "He's got it in for Morgan too, now. But imagine marrying his own mother! Isn't that incest?"

"Mildly," replied Morstive, mastering understatement. Yes, it was peculiar. Grown men don't do that. Not in public office, anyway. And yet, no complaint! The mayor was trusted.

"And the mayor's dirge-lecture, how did he apologize for the life of the mourned?" asked Morstive, as he prepared a bottle of tea.

"Jessup was spoken of very honorably," Duncan obliged, "as having been grossly misunderstood: that actually, he was a great man: an artist, in a way; an innovator; someone miles ahead of his time, whom the masses were not qualified to judge; a supreme martyr, who used crime as a medium, the vehicle for self-expression; and the city was proud to have had him."

"That's odd," Morstive said, while Duncan sipped the tea brew, "for such a vicious creep to draw official praise. I gasp what pliable values there are, these days. Still, he's out of our way. I envy your attending the wake. Were drinks served?"

"For a fee."

"Jessup never gave anyone an easy time—even at the end. Or *was* it the end?"

"Not for *him*, maybe. Or not wholly, being too holy—some divine loophole, he found."

"Well, he's probably resurrected now," estimated Morstive, in good faith. "A miracle boiled down to his natural scale. Serves him right. He ain't through remorsin' yet."

"True," agreed Duncan, as he chattered down a few notes. "The mayor had been made officially sane, you recall, through Jessup's intervening on his behalf, persuading the then-Mayor Huntworth to weave this spell on Merton: whose gratitude, then, clearly shone through this performance. Well, but Jessup's dead now, whatever happened or will happen. What conclusion do you have?"

"Me?" asked Morstive, flinching at this challenge. "Opinions come and go; my mind endures."

"That's noble," the rejoinder came. "But if you ask me—"

"Which I didn't," Morstive cut him with. A harsh exchange was exchanged, but they came to friendly terms again, on a perpetual basis of immortal enmity. The discussion weaved in and out of this, varying pace, surviving the combatants. Words settled, and a stifling peace subdued the small war. It was all in fun; but obviously they were competitors; the match was stubborn. Equally each wanted to win. Their roles differed, but merged somewhat. And the book was not yet born.

"If I were to analyze this," persisted Duncan, getting his way, Morstive's opposition subsiding, "Jessup used religion as a destructive weapon, an injurious purpose. He meddled in others' lives, to their damage; and with a paranoic mask of gracious humility conducted the ends of his wrath, serving self with a vengeance. He manipulated humans, and was ultimately harmful. Tessa Wheaton is a stand in point. But she's in good shape now, considering the vantagepoint of money. The reward for Jessup's capture is hers, and the angelic halo business. I have further news. The Children's Court has granted to Tessa all rights over the Popoff baby, the true parents being irresponsible, leading lives of impeccable immorality of conduct. Tessa has been released from prison; and remember, the baby being Jessup's heir, the dough devolves to Tessa, who's now got a little pile snatched up. But what dough did Jessup have? Poverty was his cult. Morgan's dough, Hulda's dough—for infant upkeep—would partially devolve to Tessa, maybe. She's switched fortunes, anyhow. She'd be a profitable match, if you pay her a little suit. But she'd make a repulsive bride. She's all but almost dead. But why be fussy, with money the object?"

"She doesn't like me though," Morstive said, "because I violated, abused, fired once, refused to help, and otherwise helped destroy, her. But we're *all* guilty, for anyone's disaster. Those who suffer have all to blame. Each life is responsible, our fates interweave, and some get snuffed out, others thrive, and some dominate. Our lives are calm little riots of imperfection. I have no wise cure, as I see all this from insecurity's active eye. The frightened eye, caught in fast motion."

"So you philosophize!" Duncan taunted, as they prepared to sleep. For economy, Duncan had abandoned his own apartment, and had moved in to share Morstive's rent. Tomorrow was a terrific day: From Miami: the big fight. On genuine television. Oh boy! They dreamed about it, throughout. Waking, they wondered: who would win?

Or lose, also. Someone had to lose.

Or was the loss complete, when the fight wasn't fought fair? Ah, all these matters to consider!

$\infty 33 \infty\infty\infty$

It sure was a great fight. Piper's Jamaican just simply won in a walk: it wasn't even that close. No knockdown, though, just adroit boxing. Hadn't the challenger been bribed to take a dive? Yeah, but standing up. To avert suspicion, see? A big crowd attended. They cheered, some booed. Well, whaddya want? Unanimity?

It was a good television show, at the neighborhood bar, where Morstive and his friend Duncan each nursed a drink—a beer apiece —through the whole fifteen rounds. The bartender gave them the evil look, the "what is this?" business. But poverty can't be proud, no. It ain't got enough money to be. That clear, Bud? So don't interfere.

Merton Newberg, at present, was mayor: when his mother let him be. For, old as she was, she required him to duplicate his father at the act that gave him birth, at the inception—or *con*ception, as some technical experts would have it, in their gooey conformity to what wants to be truth but just clucks the feeble gong that sounds to brass, not the golden tone. Morgan Popoff is busy at work; accumulating a riot of a lot of money, and brooding: His son is not his, and that by Emma was thrown in the river: a crime still unexplained, or accidental slip of safety. Thus the cross-currents run. But now Tessa has his Hulda brat, to bring up as she chooses. And that file clerk, before she could bring up a paternity suit, was coerced through a slight physical exertion to submit her pelvic swell, dear little doll, to an arduous abortion; and she got paid off. And she ain't squealin'. If she knows what's good for her.

But when will Merton's revenge crash down?—Emma is dead, and Morgan is a proven adulterer. Morgan ruined Merton's life, broke up a family. The mayor has considerable power. How will he use it, to retaliate, with the cruelest of justice? Morgan was scared. Maybe he should leave town?

Hulda is having an affair with a lesbian, being one herself. Is Morstive to blame, having driven her away from all males, through making a puny example of himself? Well, that's for Hulda to tell;

243

who's too drunk to speak clearly: a mother, who never misses her son. Tessa now is the golden mother.

It was transferred to her, to compensate for a former loss. How dearly she holds it, feeds it out to nurse, weaned on the latest scientific principles. Tessa is extremely fussy about morals: especially those related to the mixture of the genders in the copulative act. An idea, or notion, she wants to purge her head from. She's quite religious, really: and worships Jessup, as the vanished God.

Departed, on up high, like Keegan Dexterparks, is Jessup, but *his* soul is strictly a transcendental matter: and theologists will argue the point: fact based against fiction. Ah, what is legend, what is myth, what is true? Or what is only information, not digested by the Spheres? Ah, and what is lasting life?

Morstive amused himself by diving into these weighty problems, and he bruised the soft foreskin of the flabby muscularity of his innocence, or his grotesque ignorance. Knowledge was always one of those things his familiarity never became acquainted with on terms of sensible duration and the touch of casual comfort accorded to itself by the person's own habit. Morstive was steady in going poor, but a drifter in other ways. Eating no longer delighted him —his old standby, gone stale. What could sensually substitute, now that Hulda has defected to the enemy gender for close warmth upon contact?

Poor Morstive, at loose odds, is moping. He's on his end's edge, sapped of desire, through the lost lassitude of the withered. Hoping for a stroke from the flashing pen, the crusading typewriter, of this Duncan Durowetsky, the man who writes. "Is it finished?" he asks. And the writer writes no.

Morstive leaves him alone, and puzzles things out. Poor Hulda. But she lives, which can't be said for Emma. Emma is where money doesn't matter. So are Keegan and Jessup. Hulda has money's consolation. And Tessa too. Piper's in it big. And the mayor ain't gettin' poorer. Page is all locked up. His money is elsewhere. Turkel Masongordy is well salted. He owns what his wife left, and rakes it in from the old firm. Ira Huntworth? Don't mention him. Where are these people's old dreams, their sweet hopes, their deep plans? So many illusions, stripped and flayed by misfortune's odd and various ordeals. But fortunes gained, too. And reversals. The whole this, the whole that, from there to here. *Then* what?

Morstive meditated on. So much sad human material. "What of

Morgan, pressed to narrow fear by the mayor's impact of eventual revenge, at any close time? The economy is good for Morgan, improves his business, booms his profits; thus Merton has made good his promise. But he loved Emma, whom Morgan ruined. She's dead, with the tall adulterer due to follow, in time's pasture of execution. That lonely field, where joys are done. Only 'when' lingers, in the doubtful bliss of this flower-hungry spring, that eats up the earth. But what of me? I'm one who's living *this* life, forced to endure *this* skin. What will my welfare be?

"Merton had Emma killed, but by ethics Morgan is bound murderer. For each murder, or sequence of tears, an analysis of causes reveals that many are to blame, though guilt is obvious in blood-red deduction on a few foul hands. Those who are victims cannot assign to this culprit or that the sinful burden of accusation; we live in a society; each interacts on the other. We're all in a holy mess; undone by the other. As we commit, we are committed against. We are given, as we give. Innocence is awarded to none: we are guilty, for the company we keep, and for the chain of neighbors we don't even know. We are responsible for every stranger. This is a network, a hive. Not isolated, we are part. Parts cooperate to destroy parts, that the whole may hum.

"Ah, this is gloomy thinking. As Duncan still writes, bidding me to disregard him, I must examine my own state of declined finances and spiritual depression. A book is closing in on me. I'm being a tissue of words. Is my future being typed away too? Is that on Duncan's fingers? Is my past literary, or mine? Is this open world a book? Duncan is finishing out my life. I think back. What happened? Where am I, at the moment? The moment that almost was. That I never drew breath, upon.

"Was I ever this real? Or as a character, do I mouth puppet words? Am I being made to do this? Are these words mine? Or his?

"Is Duncan copying what I say? My life is slowly dragged from open space into the verbal delicacies of a book. I turn literary, before my own eyes. Duncan undoes me, by doing me. I vanish, to appear in another form.

"I tried everything, in life. But here I still am, neutral even in stomach. The upshot, the conclusion, loses me. I'm always behind, and paying for it.

"My identity is a personal mystery, and a public nuisance. Who do I dare to be?—or what 'me' will other people, of whom I'm afraid, permit? Duncan, solve me, will you?"

"Shut up," the writer answered. "I'm working on a difficult part."

"What? The conclusion?"

"I've done that, practically. But a title, can you suggest?"

"It's about me, isn't it?"

"Yes, you and others."

"Have you created me?"

"You created yourself."

"What will you call it?"

"Guess."

"How about 'Morstive Posing as Himself'—an ambiguity—"

"No. I don't like it."

"Well, you're the author."

"Have you finished talking?"

"Yes, but—"

"Do you know spring is here?"

"Sure, but—"

"Then shutup."

"Okay. What do you want?"

"A title."

"Should I give it now?"

"Yes."

"How about—"

"Shutup."

"Won't you let me speak?"

"No."

"Are you me, or am I you?" Morstive began again, and Duncan blew up.

"This book ends," said Duncan, "with 'Others, Including Morstive Sternbump.' "

"The title you mean?"

"What else?"

"Oh."

"So what's the title?" Duncan asked.

And Morstive Durowetsky answered, " 'Others, Including Morstive Sternbump.' "

"That's right. But you're only repeating me. You're not necessary, if you do that. Now we've become the same person. You just did it."

"Did what?" Morstive asked himself. But Duncan wasn't there, any more. *What* Duncan? He never was.

But Morstive had written this book. Was it Morstive? Who else? There was this script. All typed out, on Morstive's typewriter. Hadn't there *ever* been a Duncan? Was there ever Morgan? Ever Hulda? Merton, and Emma? Jessup, Tessa? Keegan, Turkel, Ira, Piper, and Page? What had gone on? What is a book? Who is the world? What is one person? Only one person?